W9-CKD-541

02/24
STAND PRICE
$ 5.00

PRAISE FOR
CEMETERY BOYS

"The novel . . . perfectly balances the vibrant, energetic Latinx culture while delving into heavy topics like LGBTQ+ acceptance, deportation, colonization, and racism within authoritative establishments."
—TeenVogue.com

"This stunning debut novel from Thomas is detailed, heart-rending, and immensely romantic. I was bawling by the end of it, but not from sadness: I just felt so incredibly happy that this queer Latinx adventure will get to be read by other kids. *Cemetery Boys* is necessary: for trans kids, for queer kids, for those in the Latinx community who need to see themselves on the page. Don't miss this book."
—Mark Oshiro, author of *Anger is a Gift*

"A story much bigger than the paper that binds it, *Cemetery Boys* is the tender intricacy we have all been waiting for."
—Kayla Ancrum, author of *The Wicker King*

"This book is magical, tender, loving, and so so so important. I love it with all my heart."
—Mason Deaver, author of *I Wish You All The Best*

"*Cemetery Boys* is a celebration of culture and identity that will captivate readers with its richly detailed world, earnest romance, and thrilling supernatural mystery. This delightful debut is a must-read for all paranormal romance fans."
—Isabel Sterling, author of *These Witches Don't Burn*

"*Cemetery Boys* is nothing short of an astonishing work of art. Aiden Thomas masterfully weaves a tale of family, friendships, and love in a heartwarming adventure full of affirmation and being your best self."
—C.B. Lee, author of *Not Your Sidekick*

AIDEN THOMAS

CEMETERY BOYS

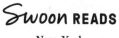
Swoon READS

New York

A Swoon Reads Book

An Imprint of Feiwel and Friends and Macmillan Publishing Group LLC

120 Broadway, New York, NY 10271

Cemetery Boys. Copyright © 2020 by Aiden Thomas. All rights reserved. Printed in the United States of America.

Our books may be purchased in bulk for promotional, educational, or business use. Please contact your local bookseller or the Macmillan Corporate and Premium Sales Department at (800) 221-7945 ext. 5442 or by email at MacmillanSpecialMarkets@ macmillan.com.

Library of Congress Cataloging-in-Publication Data

Names: Thomas, Aiden, author.
Title: Cemetery boys / by Aiden Thomas.
Description: First edition. | New York : Swoon Reads, 2020. | Audience:
Ages 13–18. | Audience: Grades 10–12. | Summary: Yadriel, a trans boy,
summons the angry spirit of his high school's bad boy, and agrees to
help him learn how he died, thereby proving himself a brujo, not a
bruja, to his traditional family.
Identifiers: LCCN 2019036381 | ISBN 9781250250469 (hardcover) |
ISBN 978-1-250-80463-1 (special edition) | ISBN 9781250250513 (ebook)
Subjects: CYAC: Transgender persons—Fiction. | Witches—Fiction. |
Magic—Fiction. | Spirits—Fiction. | Latin Americans—Fiction. |
Family life—Fiction.
Classification: LCC PZ7.1.T4479 Cem 2020 | DDC [Fic]—dc23
LC record available at https://lccn.loc.gov/2019036381

Book design by Liz Dresner

First Edition—2020
10 9 8 7 6 5 4 3 2 1
swoonreads.com

No me llores,
porque si lloras
yo peno,
en cambio si tu cantas
yo siempre vivo,
y nunca muero.

Don't mourn me,
if you cry for me
I grieve your pain,
instead if you sing to me
I'll always live,
and my spirit will never die.

"La Martiniana," a Mexican folk song

ONE

Yadriel wasn't technically trespassing because he'd lived in the cemetery his whole life. But breaking into the church was definitely crossing the moral-ambiguity line.

Still, if he was going to finally prove he was a brujo, he had to perform the rite in front of Lady Death.

And she was waiting for him inside the church.

The black Hydro Flask full of chicken blood thumped against Yadriel's hip as he snuck past his family's small house at the front of the cemetery. The rest of the supplies for the ceremony were tucked away inside his backpack. He and his cousin Maritza ducked under the front windows, careful not to bump their heads on the sills. Silhouettes of the brujx celebrating inside danced across the curtains. Their laughter and the sound of music filtered through the graveyard. Yadriel paused, crouching in the shadows to check the coast was clear before he jumped from the porch and took off. Maritza followed close behind, her footsteps echoing in tandem with Yadriel's as they ran down stone paths and through puddles.

Yadriel's heart fluttered in his chest, fingers brushing along the wet brick of a columbaria wall as he watched for any signs of the brujos on graveyard duty tonight. Patrolling the cemetery to make sure none of the spirits of the dead were causing trouble was part of the men's responsibilities. Spirits turning maligno were few and far between, so the brujos' rounds mostly consisted of making sure outsiders hadn't snuck beyond the walls, keeping the graves clear of weeds, and general maintenance.

Hearing a guitar being played up ahead, Yadriel ducked behind a sarcophagus, dragging Maritza down with him. Peeking around the corner, he saw Felipe Mendez lounging against a tombstone, playing his vihuela and singing along. Felipe was a more recent resident of the brujx cemetery. The day of his death, barely over a week ago, was carved into the headstone beside him.

Brujx didn't need to see a spirit to know one was nearby. The men and women in their community could sense it, like a chill in the air or an itch at the back of their mind. It was one of their inherent powers, given to them by their Lady. The powers of life and death: the ability to sense illness and injury in the living, and to see and communicate with the dead.

Of course, this ability wasn't very useful in a cemetery full of spirits. Instead of a sudden chill, wandering through the brujx cemetery left a constant icy tickle on Yadriel's neck.

In the dark, he could barely spot the transparent quality of Felipe's body. Felipe's fingers moved in a ghostly blur as they plucked at the strings of his vihuela—it was his tether, the material possession most important to him, that kept him anchored to the land of the living. Felipe wasn't ready to be released to the afterlife quite yet.

He spent most of his time in the graveyard playing his music and drawing the attention of the brujas, both of the living and the dead variety. His girlfriend, Claribel, always chased them off, and the two spent hours together in the cemetery, as if death had never parted them to begin with.

Yadriel rolled his eyes. It was all very dramatic, if you asked him. It'd be nice if Felipe could pass on already, then Yadriel could get a good night's rest without being woken up by Felipe and Claribel's bickering or, worse, his terrible renditions of "Wonderwall."

But the brujx didn't like forcing a spirit to cross over. As long as the spirits were peaceful and hadn't turned maligno, the brujos left them alone. But no spirit could stay forever. Eventually, they would become violent, twisted versions of themselves. Being trapped between the land of the living and the land of the dead wore on a spirit, chipping away at their humanity. The parts that made them human eventually faded away until the brujos had no choice but to sever the connection to their tether and release them to the afterlife.

Yadriel motioned for Maritza to follow him down a side path so Felipe wouldn't see them. When the coast was clear, he tugged on the sleeve of Maritza's shirt and gave her a nod. He sprinted forward, weaving between statues of angels and saints, careful to not snag his backpack on their outstretched fingers. There were aboveground sarcophagi and some mausoleums large enough to fit an entire family. He'd walked these paths hundreds of times and could navigate the maze of graves in his sleep.

He had to stop again when they came upon the spirits of two young girls playing tag. They chased each other, dark curls and matching dresses billowing out around them. They giggled madly as they ran straight through the small birdhouse-like tombs that held cremated remains. The tombs were hand-painted in bright colors and stood in crowded rows of golden yellow, sunburst orange, sky blue, and seafoam green. Glass doors revealed clay urns inside.

Yadriel bounced on the balls of his feet as he and Maritza hid. Seeing the spirits of two dead girls running around a cemetery would probably freak most people out, but little Nina and Rosa were nefarious for other reasons. They were both huge tattletales who couldn't be trusted to not rat him out to his dad. If they got dirt on you, they held it over your head and subjected you to torture the likes of which you'd never seen.

Like hours of playing hide-and-go-seek where they always used their non-corporeal bodies to cheat, or purposely leave you waiting to be found behind the smelly dumpster on a hot LA afternoon. It was definitely not worth being indebted to those two.

When the girls finally ran off, Yadriel wasted no time sprinting to their final destination.

They rounded a corner and came face-to-face with the lich-gate to the church. Yadriel's head tipped back. Whitewashed bricks were stacked before him, forming an archway. The words "El Jardín Eterno" were hand-scrawled delicately in black paint. The Eternal Garden. The paint was faded, but Yadriel knew his cousin Miguel had already been tasked with giving it a fresh coat before the Día de Muertos festivities began in a few days. A heavy, bolted lock kept out any trespassers.

As leader of the brujx families, Yadriel's father, Enrique, held the keys and only gave them to the brujos who were on shift to guard the cemetery at night. Yadriel did not have a key, which meant he was only allowed to enter during the day, or for rituals and celebrations.

"¡Vámonos!" Maritza's harsh whisper and her manicured fingernail jabbing into his side made Yadriel jolt. Her short thick hair was windswept. Pastel-pink and -purple curls framed her heart-shaped face, popping against her deep brown skin. "We need to get inside before we're spotted by someone!"

Yadriel batted her hand away. "Ssh!" he hissed.

Despite her words of warning, Maritza didn't seem worried about getting into a heap of trouble. In fact, she looked downright excited. Dark eyes wide, a devilish grin played across her lips that Yadriel knew all too well.

Yadriel crept to the left side of the gate. There was a gap between the last wrought iron bar and the wall, where the bricks slumped. He tossed his backpack over the wall before turning sideways and wiggling his way through. Even through his polyester-and-spandex binder, the bar scraped painfully against his chest. On the other side, he took a moment to adjust the half tank top under his shirt so the clasps didn't dig into his side. It had taken a while to find one that masculinized his chest without being itchy or chokingly tight.

Slinging his backpack over his shoulder, Yadriel turned to find Maritza having a bit more difficulty. Her back was pressed against the bricks, her legs straddling the bar as she tried to drag herself through. Yadriel stuffed his fist against his mouth, stifling a laugh.

Maritza shot him a glare as she tried to wiggle her butt free. *"¡Cá-llate!"* she hissed before finally stumbling through. "We're gonna need another way to get in here soon." She wiped at the dirt smeared across her jeans. "We're getting too big."

"Your *butt's* getting too big," Yadriel teased. "Maybe you should lay off the pastelitos." He grinned.

"And lose these curves?" she asked, smoothing her hands down her waist and hips. Maritza gave him a sarcastic smile. "Thanks, but I'd rather die." She punched his arm before sauntering toward the church.

Yadriel jogged to catch up.

Rows of marigolds—the flores de muerto—lined the stone path. The tall orange and yellow flowers leaned against one another like drunken friends. They had exploded into bloom over the months leading up to Día de Muertos. Fallen petals dusted the ground like confetti.

The church was painted white and had a terra-cotta roof. Starburst windows flanked either side of the large oak doors. Above, a small alcove was set into a semicircular wall, housing another cross. On either side, two cutouts held iron bells.

"Are you ready?" There was no look of trepidation on Maritza's face as she watched him. She beamed, practically dancing on the tips of her toes.

Yadriel's heart pulsed in his veins. Nerves roiled in his stomach.

He and Maritza had been sneaking around the cemetery at night since they were kids. The churchyard was a good place to hide and play when they were little. It was close enough to the house to hear Lita when she called them for dinner. But they'd never actually snuck *into* the church before. If he did this, they'd be breaking about a dozen brujx rules and traditions.

If he did this, there was no turning back.

Yadriel nodded stiffly, his hands clenched into fists at his sides. "Let's do it."

The hairs on the back of his neck prickled at the same time Maritza shivered next to him.

"Do what?"

The bark-like demand made both of them jump. Maritza sprang back, and Yadriel had to catch her arms to keep her from bowling him over.

Just to their left, a man stood next to a small peach-colored tomb.

"Holy crap, Tito." Yadriel exhaled, a hand still clutching the front of his hoodie. "You scared the hell out of us!"

Maritza sniffed indignantly.

Sometimes, even to Yadriel and Maritza, a ghost could go unnoticed.

Tito was a squat man wearing a burgundy Venezuela soccer kit and shorts. A large, worn straw hat sat on his head. He squinted at Yadriel and Maritza from under the brim as he bent over the marigolds. Tito was the longtime gardener of the cemetery.

Or well, he *was*. Tito had been dead for four years.

When he was alive, Tito had been an incredibly talented gardener. He used to supply all the flowers for the brujx celebrations, as well as weddings, holidays, and funerals for the non-magic folks in East LA. What had started as selling flowers from buckets at the local flea market had grown into his own brick-and-mortar shop.

After dying in his sleep and having his body laid to rest, Tito reappeared in the cemetery, determined to take care of the flowers he'd painstakingly tended to for most of his life. He told Yadriel's father he still had a job to do and didn't trust anyone else to take it over.

Enrique said Tito could remain as long as he was Tito. Yadriel wondered if sheer stubbornness would keep his father from being able to release Tito's spirit, even if he tried.

"Do what?" Tito repeated. Under the orange lights of the church, he seemed solid enough, though he was the faintest bit transparent compared to the very corporeal garden shears in his hand. Spirits had blurry edges and were a little less vibrant than the world around them. They looked like a photograph taken out of focus and with the saturation turned down. If Yadriel turned his head a bit, Tito's form smudged and faded into the background.

Yadriel mentally kicked himself. His nerves were getting the better of him, distracting him from sensing Tito sooner.

"Why aren't you two back at the house with everyone else?" Tito pressed.

"Uh, we were just going to go into the church," Yadriel said, voice breaking midsentence. He cleared his throat.

The rise of an unruly eyebrow meant Tito wasn't falling for it.

"Just to check on some supplies, you know." Yadriel shrugged. "Make sure things are . . . set up."

With a *sch*, Tito's shears sliced off a wilted marigold from its stem.

Maritza elbowed Yadriel in the side and tipped her head pointedly.

"Oh!" Yadriel wrestled off his backpack and dug around inside, pulling out a bundled white dishcloth. "I grabbed you something!"

Felipe was too busy with his girlfriend to care about what Yadriel and Maritza got up to, and it was pretty easy to sneak past Nina and Rosa, but Tito was a bit of a wild card. Tito had been good friends with Yadriel's dad, and Tito had very little patience for nonsense.

But offerings of food seemed to make him look the other way.

"Lita just made them—it's still warm!" Yadriel pulled back the layers to reveal a concha. The delicious sweet bread had a crumbly topping and looked like a seashell. "I got you a green one, your favorite!" If Tito wasn't convinced by his terrible lying, maybe pan dulce could sway him.

Tito waved his hand dismissively. "I don't care what you two buscapleitos are up to," he grumbled.

Maritza gasped and pressed her hand to her chest dramatically. "*Us?* We would never—!"

Yadriel shoved Maritza to get her to shut up. He didn't think they were troublemakers, especially compared to some of the other younger brujx, but he also knew laying on the innocent act too thick would not work on Tito.

Luckily, Tito seemed to want to get rid of them. "Pa' fuera," he said dismissively. "But don't touch my cempasúchitl."

Yadriel didn't need to be told twice. He grabbed Maritza's arm and made for the church.

"Leave the concha," Tito added.

Yadriel left it on top of the peach-colored tomb while Tito went back to trimming his marigolds.

He ran up the steps to the church, Maritza right on his heels. With a hard shove, the heavy doors swung open with a groan.

Yadriel and Maritza crept down the aisle. The inside was simple. Unlike a standard church, there weren't many rows of pews and there were no seats at the back. When the brujx gathered for ceremonies and rituals, everyone stood in large circles together in the open space. Three tall windows made up the apse of the church. During the day, the California sunlight streamed through the colorful, intricate stained glass. Dozens of unlit candles crowded the main altar.

On a ledge halfway up the wall stood a statue of their sacred goddess, the diosa who had bestowed the brujx with their powers thousands of years ago, when gods and monsters roamed the lands of Latin America and the Caribbean: the Lady of the Dead.

The skeleton was carved out of white stone. Black paint accented the lines of her bony fingers, toothy smile, and empty eyes. Lady Death wore a traditional white lace-trimmed huipil and layered skirt. A mantle was draped over the crown of her head, flowing to rest on her shoulders. The neck of her dress and hem of the mantle were embroidered with delicate flowers of golden thread. A bouquet of Tito's freshly cut marigolds lay in her skeletal hands.

She had many names and iterations—Santa Muerte, la Huesuda, Lady of Shadows, Mictecacihuatl. It depended on the culture and language, but each representation and image came down to the same thing. To be blessed by Lady Death, to have his own portaje and to serve her, was what Yadriel wanted most in the world. He wanted to be like the other brujos, to find lost spirits and help them pass to the afterlife. He wanted to stay up all night on boring graveyard duty. Hell, he'd even spend hours pulling weeds and painting tombs if it meant being accepted by his people as a brujo.

As Yadriel approached her, propelled forward by his desire to serve her, he thought about all the generations of brujx who had their own quinces ceremonies right here. Men and women who'd emigrated from all over—Mexico and Cuba, Puerto Rico and Colombia, Honduras and Haiti, even the ancient Incas, Aztecs, and Maya—all bestowed with powers by the ancient gods. A mix of beautifully nuanced, vibrant cultures that came together to make their community whole.

When brujx turned fifteen years old, they were presented to Lady Death, who would give them her blessing and tie their magic to their chosen conduit, their portaje. For women, portajes often took the form of a rosary (a symbol that had begun as a ceremonial necklace and was altered with the rise of Catholicism in Latin America). It was a piece of jewelry that could go unnoticed and ended with a charm that could hold a small amount of sacrificial animal blood. While a crucifix was the most common symbol, sometimes a bruja's rosary ended in a sacred heart or a statuette of Lady Death.

Men's portajes were often daggers of some sort, as a blade was required to sever the golden thread that bound a spirit to their earthly tether. By cutting that tie, brujos were able to release spirits to the afterlife.

Being gifted your portaje was an important rite of passage for every brujx.

Every one, except for Yadriel.

His quinces had been postponed indefinitely. He'd turned sixteen the past July, and he was tired of waiting.

In order to show his family what he was, *who* he was, Yadriel needed to go through with his own quinces ceremony—with or without their blessings. His father and the rest of the brujx hadn't left him with a choice.

Sweat trickled down Yadriel's spine, sending a shiver through his body. The air felt charged, like the ground hummed with energy below his feet. It was now or never.

Kneeling before Lady Death, he unpacked the supplies he needed for the ritual. He placed four prayer candles on the ground in a diamond to represent the four winds. A clay bowl went in the center to represent the earth. Yadriel had nicked a mini bottle of Cabrito tequila from one of the boxes that had been gathered for the Día de Muertos ofrendas. He fumbled with the bottle before popping the cap off and pouring it into the bowl. The smell stung his nose. Beside it, he placed a small jar of salt.

He dug out a box of matches from the pocket of his jeans. The flame trembled as he lit the candles. The flickering lights sparked the gold threads in Lady Death's mantle, catching in the folds and crevices.

Air, earth, wind, and fire. North, south, east, and west. All the elements needed to call upon Lady Death.

The last ingredient was blood.

Calling upon Lady Death required an offering of blood. It was the most powerful thing to give, as it held life. Giving your blood to Lady Death was giving her a part of your earthly body and your spirit. It was so powerful that human blood given in sacrifice could not be more than a few drops; otherwise the offering was enough to drain any brujx of their life force, leading to certain death.

There were only two rituals that ever called for brujx to make an offering of their own blood. When they were born, their ears were pierced, releasing a pin-drop amount of blood. This act enabled them to hear the spirits of the dead. Yadriel's ears were gauged with black plastic plugs. He liked paying homage to the ancient practice of brujx stretching their earlobes with increasingly large discs made of sacred stones, like obsidian or jade. Over the years he'd gotten them to about the size of a dime.

The only other time brujx used their own blood as a sacrifice was during the quinces ceremony. The offering was made from their tongues to let them speak to the diosa, to ask Lady Death for her blessing and protection.

And that cut was made with their portaje.

Maritza pulled a bundle of cloth from her own backpack and held it out for him to take.

"It took me weeks to make," she said as Yadriel untied the twine. "Burned myself like eight times and nearly cut off my finger, but I think my dad has pretty much given up trying to keep me out of the forge." Her shrug was casual, but she stood tall, a proud grin pulling the corners of her lips. Yadriel knew this was a big deal for her.

Maritza's family had been forging weapons for the men for decades, a trade her father had brought over from Haiti. She had a keen interest in learning how to craft blades from him. Since blood wasn't used with the blades until a boy's quinces ceremony, it was a way for her to still be a part of the community without compromising her ethics. Her mom didn't think it was a proper career choice for a girl, but when Maritza set her mind on something, it was impossible to dissuade her.

"Nothing gaudy and ridiculous like Diego's," she said with a roll of her eyes, referring to Yadriel's older brother.

Yadriel pulled back the last of the cloth to reveal a dagger nestled inside. "Wow," he breathed.

"It's practical," Maritza explained, hovering over his shoulder.

"It's *badass*," Yadriel corrected, a wide smile pressing into his cheeks. Maritza beamed.

The dagger was the length of his forearm with a straight blade and a cross guard that curved like a sideways *S*. Lady Death had been delicately painted onto the polished wooden grip. Yadriel held the dagger in his hand, solid and reassuring. He traced his thumb along the thin lines of gold paint that radiated from Lady Death, feeling every intricate brushstroke.

This was his dagger. His portaje.

Yadriel had everything he needed. Now all that was left was to finish the ritual.

He was ready for this. He was *determined* to present himself to Lady Death, whether or not anyone else approved. But still, he hesitated. Clutching his portaje as he stared up at Lady Death, he sucked on his bottom lip. Doubt crept its way under his skin.

"Hey."

Yadriel jumped as Maritza placed a steady hand on his shoulder. Her brown eyes were intense as she studied his face.

"It's just—" Yadriel cleared his throat, his eyes sweeping around the room.

Maritza's eyebrows tipped with concern.

A brujx's quinces was the most important day in their life. Yadriel's dad, brother, and abuela should've been standing next to him. As he knelt on the hard stone floor, the emptiness pressed around him. In the silence, he could hear the static of the uneasy candle flames. Under the hollowed eyes of Lady Death, Yadriel felt small and alone.

"What if—what if it doesn't work?" he asked. Even at nearly a whisper, his voice echoed through the empty church. His heart clenched. "What if she rejects me?"

"Escúchame." Maritza gave his shoulders a tight squeeze. "You've got this, okay?"

Yadriel nodded, wetting his dry lips.

"You know who you are, *I* know who you are, and our Lady does, too." She said with fierce conviction. "So screw the rest of them!" Maritza grinned at him. "Remember why we're doing this."

Yadriel steeled himself and spoke with as much courage as he could muster. "So they'll see that I'm a brujo."

"Well, yeah, but other than that."

"Spite?" Yadriel guessed.

"Spite!" Maritza agreed enthusiastically. "They're gonna feel real stupid once you show them. And I want you to savor that moment, Yads! Really"—she took in a deep breath through her nose and clasped her hands to her chest—"savor that taste of sweet, *sweet* vindication!"

A laugh jumped in Yadriel's throat.

Maritza smiled. "Let's do this, brujo."

Yadriel could feel the goofy grin back on his face.

"Just don't screw it up and make the diosa shoot you down with lightning or something, okay?" she said, backing up a few steps. "I can't carry the responsibility of the family black sheep on my own."

Being transgender and gay had earned Yadriel the title of Head Black Sheep among the brujx. Though, in truth, being gay had actually been much easier for them to accept, but only because they saw Yadriel's liking boys as still being heterosexual.

But Maritza had certainly earned the title in her own right as the only vegan brujx in their community. One year younger than Yadriel, she'd gone through her own quinces when she turned fifteen earlier that year, but she refused to heal because it required the use of animal blood. One of Yadriel's earliest memories of Maritza was of her crying inconsolably when her mother had used blood from a pig to heal a child's broken leg. Early on, Maritza decided she wanted no part of healing if it meant harming another living creature.

In the dim light of the church, Yadriel could see her portaje hanging around her neck—a rosary of pink quartz that ended in a silver cross, but the concealed vessel remained empty. Maritza explained that, even though she refused to use her powers, she still respected the diosa and their ancestors.

Yadriel admired her for her convictions, but he was also frustrated by them. All he wanted was to be accepted—he wanted to be given his own portaje, treated like any other brujo, and given the same responsibilities. Maritza, on the other hand, had been offered every right of the brujx, but she chose to reject it.

"Now, prisa!" Maritza said, waving him on impatiently.

Yadriel took a deep, steadying breath.

He tightened his grip on his Hydro Flask, the metal cool against his sweaty palms, as he exhaled through pursed lips.

With a more steadied resolve, Yadriel unscrewed the cap and poured the chicken blood into the bowl. To her credit, Maritza did her best to hide a look of disgust.

As the deep red liquid mixed with the tequila, a gust of wind blew through the church. The candle flames flickered. The air in the room felt thick, as if it were crowded with bodies even though, except for him and Maritza, it was empty.

Adrenaline coursed through Yadriel's veins, and excited chills raced up his arms. When he spoke, he did his best to keep his voice steady and deep.

"Santísima Santa Muerte, te pido tu bendición," Yadriel said, calling upon Lady Death to ask for her blessing.

A rush of air brushed against his face and dragged like fingers through his hair. The flames trembled, and the statue of Lady Death suddenly felt alive. She didn't move or change, but Yadriel could feel something pressing toward him.

He lit a match and dropped it into the bowl. The liquid caught, bursting into flames. "Prometo proteger a los vivos y guiar a los muertos,"

Yadriel said, vowing to uphold the responsibilities of the brujos. His hands trembled and he gripped his portaje tighter.

"Esta es mi sangre, derramada por ti." Holding the dagger, Yadriel opened his mouth and pressed the tip of the blade to his tongue until it bit into him. He winced and held his portaje out in front of him. A thin line of red glistened on the edge of the blade in the warm light of the candles.

He held the dagger over the burning bowl. As soon as the flames licked the steel, the blood sizzled and the candles blazed like torches, their flames tall and strong. Yadriel squinted as a rush of heat hit his face.

He removed his portaje from the fire and spoke the final words.

"Con un beso, te prometo mi devoción," he murmured before brushing his tongue over his lips. Balancing the hilt in his palm, he kissed the image of Lady Death.

Golden light sparked at the tip of the blade and raced down the hilt to his hand. His skin glowed as the light shot down his fingers and up his arm. It traveled down his legs and curled around his toes. Yadriel shuddered, the thrilling sensation robbing him of his breath.

As quickly as it had appeared, the thick thrum of magic in the church dissipated. The candle flames extinguished themselves in the same pulse. The air in the room went still. Yadriel pushed up the sleeve of his hoodie and stared at his arm in awe as the golden light faded, leaving his brown skin unadorned.

He stared up at Lady Death. "Holy crap," Yadriel breathed, pressing his hands to his cheeks.

"Holy crap!" he repeated. "It worked!" He felt his chest, the thunderous beat of his heart pulsing against his palm. He jerked to look at Maritza for confirmation. "Did—did it work?"

The fire in the bowl glinted in her eyes, a huge smile on her face. "There's one way to find out."

Laughter bubbled in Yadriel's throat, relief and adrenaline making him half delirious. "Right."

If Lady Death had blessed him, granting him the powers of the brujx, that meant he could summon a lost spirit. If he could summon a spirit and release it to the afterlife, then he would finally prove himself to everyone—the brujx, his family, and his dad. They would see him as he was. A boy and a brujo.

Yadriel got to his feet, holding his portaje carefully against his chest. He sucked in his lips, tasting the last traces of blood. His tongue stung, but the cut had been small. It hurt about as much as when he burned it trying to drink café de olla fresh off the stove.

As Maritza gathered the candles, pointedly steering clear of the flaming bowl of blood, Yadriel approached the statue of Lady Death. At a little over five feet, he had to crane his neck back to look up at her in her alcove.

He wished he could speak to her. Could she see him for who he really was? What his own family couldn't? Yadriel had spent years feeling misunderstood by everyone except for Maritza. When he had told her he was trans three years ago, she hadn't batted an eye. *Ay, finally!* she'd said, exasperated but smiling. *I figured something was up, I was just waiting for you to spit it out.*

During that time, Maritza had been his reliable secret keeper, smoothly going back and forth between pronouns when they were alone, versus when they were around everyone else, until he was ready.

It took him another year, when he was fourteen, to work up the courage to come out to his family. It hadn't gone nearly as well, and it was still a constant struggle to get them and the other brujx to use the right pronouns and to call him by the right name.

Other than Maritza, his mother, Camila, had been the most supportive. It took time to relearn old habits, but she'd caught on surprisingly fast. Yadriel's mom had even taken on the task of gently correcting people so he didn't have to. It was a heavy burden, small instances piling up, but his mom helped him shoulder some of the weight.

When he felt especially raw, from the constant fight to be who he was—either at school or within their own community—his mom would sit him down on the couch. She'd pull him close, and he'd rest his head on her shoulder. She always smelled of cloves and cinnamon, like she'd just made torta bejarana. As she gently ran her fingers through his hair, she'd murmur, *Mijo, my Yadriel,* slowly coaxing the pain away to a dull ache that never completely vanished.

But she'd been gone for almost a year now.

Yadriel sniffed and dragged his fist across his nose, the back of his throat burning.

This would be the first Día de Muertos since she'd died. Come midnight, November 1, the church bells would ring, welcoming back the spirits of passed brujx to the cemetery. Then, for two days, Yadriel would be able to see her again.

He would show her he was a *true* brujo. A son she could be proud of. He would perform the tasks that his father and his father's father had as the children of Lady Death. Yadriel would prove himself to everyone.

"C'mon, brujo," Maritza called gently, waving him forward. "We need to get out of here before someone finds us."

Yadriel turned and grinned.

Brujo.

He was about to bend down and pick up the bowl from the ground when the hairs on the back of his neck prickled. Yadriel froze and looked to Maritza, who had also stopped mid-step.

Something was wrong.

"Did you feel that?" he asked. Even in a whisper, his voice seemed too loud in the empty church.

Maritza nodded. "What is it?"

Yadriel gave a small shake of his head. It was almost like sensing a nearby spirit but different. Stronger than anything Yadriel had felt before. A sense of unexplained dread swarmed in his stomach.

He saw Maritza shiver just as he felt a tingle shoot down his spine.

There was a beat of nothingness.

Then searing pain stabbed into Yadriel's chest.

He cried out, the force knocking him to his knees.

Maritza fell, a strangled cry lodging in her throat.

The pain was unbearable. Yadriel's breath came in sharp bursts as he clutched at his chest. His eyes watered, blurring the vision of Lady Death standing above him.

Just when he thought he couldn't stand it any longer, that, surely, the pain would kill him, it stopped.

Tension released his muscles, and his arms and legs went limp, heavy with exhaustion. Sweat clung to his skin. His body trembled as he gulped air. Yadriel's hand clutched his chest, right above his heart, where the throbbing pain slowly faded to a dull ache. Maritza knelt on the floor, one hand pressed to the same place. Her skin was ashen and covered in a sheen of sweat.

They stared at each other, trying to catch their breath. They didn't say anything. They knew what it meant. They could feel it in their bones.

Miguel was gone. One of their own had died.

TWO

"hat happened? What the *hell* happened?" Maritza panted at Yadriel's side as they raced through the cemetery. She kept saying it over and over again, like a haunting mantra.

Yadriel had never seen her so shook up before and it made everything so much worse. Usually, he was the one panicking under tense situations while she just shrugged things off with a joke. But this was no laughing matter.

There was no sign of Tito. Yadriel could hear frantic voices across the cemetery. They sprinted past a couple of confused-looking spirits.

"What's going on?" Felipe called to them, anxiously gripping the neck of his vihuela as they ran by.

"I don't know!" was all Yadriel could say.

Because the brujx were tied so closely to life and death, to spirits and the living, when one of their own died, they all felt it.

The first time it had happened to Yadriel, he was only five years old. He woke up in the middle of the night, as if from a nightmare, with only the thought of his abuelito in his mind. When he got out of bed and crept to his grandparents' room, his abuelito lay motionless. His abuelita sat by his side, holding tightly to his hand, whispering prayers into his ear, tears streaming down her wrinkled cheeks.

His father stood on the other side, Diego tucked under his arm. His dad's expression had been stoic and pensive, a deep sadness in his dark eyes. Yadriel's mother folded him into her arms, gently rubbing his back as they said their goodbyes.

His abuelito had died in his sleep. It had been gentle and painless. The only thing that had woken Yadriel was a sudden sense of loss, like cold water dropping into his stomach.

But this was different. Whatever had happened to Miguel was not a gentle passing.

There had to be some sort of mistake. It didn't make sense. Even though he'd felt it, even though he knew exactly what it meant, there was no way Miguel was *dead*.

Miguel was Yadriel's cousin and only twenty-eight years old. Yadriel had just seen him earlier that night when he stopped by the house to snag some of Lita's concha before he started his graveyard shift.

Had there been an accident? Maybe Miguel had left the cemetery and had been hit by a car? There was no way he could've been killed while *in* the cemetery, was there?

They needed to get home and find out what had taken Miguel so violently from this life.

Maritza's legs were longer than Yadriel's, and his binder hugged tight around his ribs, making it difficult for him to keep up. The weight of his portaje tucked into his backpack felt especially heavy.

They rounded the corner and ran into chaos unfolding. Loud voices. People running in and out of the house. Shadows moved back and forth behind the curtains.

Maritza wrenched open the gate in the chain-link fence and bounded up the stairs, Yadriel right on her heels. He nearly got knocked over by someone rushing out the front door, but he managed to wedge his way inside.

Their house was small enough to begin with, and in the weeks leading up to Día de Muertos, "cramped" was putting it lightly. Every surface was used as storage for the impending celebrations. Precariously stacked boxes full of prayer candles, silk monarch butterflies, and hundreds of colorful, meticulously cut papel picado were piled on the worn leather couch. The dining room table had been pushed against the wall and was covered in white sugar skulls waiting to be decorated.

It should have been a scene of preparation for their most important holiday of the year, but instead it was frenzied panic. Maritza clung to the back of Yadriel's hoodie, sticking close as they got jostled around.

Miguel's mother, Claudia, sat at the dining table. Yadriel's abuelita was at her side, flanked by other brujas. They rubbed her arms and spoke gentle words in Spanish, but Claudia was inconsolable.

Grief rolled off her in waves. Yadriel could feel it in his bones. The deep wails of primal mourning made him wince. He knew those cries all too well. He had experienced them himself.

Yadriel could only watch as his abuelita worked her magic.

She continued to speak calmly into Claudia's ear as she pulled her portaje from under the neck of her black blouse embroidered with colorful flowers. It was an old rosary of wooden beads with a pewter sacred heart hanging at the end. With deft fingers, Lita unscrewed the top and smeared chicken blood across the sacred heart. "Usa mis manos," she said in a soft, steady voice, calling to Lady Death. As she murmured, the rosary shimmered with golden light. "Te doy tranquilidad de espíritu."

Lita pressed the end of the rosary to Claudia's forehead. After a moment, the sobs began to subside. Claudia's pained expression ebbed away, smoothing the pinched lines in her face. Yadriel could feel Claudia's pain slowly fade to a dull ache. Her shoulders sloped until she sat back in the chair, limbs heavy. Her hands came to a rest in her lap, and though her face was flushed and tears steadily fell, her suffering was far less severe.

The glowing light of Lita's rosary faded until it was back to pewter and wood.

Yadriel'd once asked his mom why they didn't just take *all* of someone's pain when they were sad. She had explained it was important to let people feel grief and mourn the loss of a loved one.

Yadriel respected his grandmother, and all the brujas, and the incredible powers they possessed. Those powers had just never been his.

Hiccups racked Claudia's chest as Lita removed her rosary, leaving a smudge of red on her puckered brow. One of the brujas handed Claudia a glass of water, another dabbed gently at her cheeks with a tissue.

"Día de Muertos is only a couple days away," Lita reminded Claudia in her heavily accented English. She gave Claudia's hand a squeeze with a small smile. "You will see Miguel again."

She was right, of course, but Yadriel didn't think that would provide Claudia with much comfort right now. Lita had told him the same thing when his mother had died. He understood they were lucky in that way, to be able to see their dead loved ones again, but that didn't make him feel better in the moment. A visit for two days once a year could never make up for the loss of having them around all the time.

And there was another problem: If Miguel hadn't passed to the land of the dead—if he was still tethered to this world—he couldn't return during Día de Muertos.

What had happened to him?

Someone rushing out of the kitchen bumped into Yadriel, and the sound of his father's voice snagged his attention. He tore his eyes away from Claudia and wove through bodies to get to the kitchen, Maritza following close behind him.

Inside the kitchen, a handful of brujos stood in a group, their eyes on Yadriel's father. Enrique Vélez Cabrera was a tall man—genes that Yadriel had decidedly not inherited—with an average build. He had a bit of a gut, which pressed against the red-checkered shirt he wore tucked into his jeans. Enrique had kept the same modest haircut and bushy mustache for as long as Yadriel could remember. The only difference now was the salt-and-pepper hair at his temples.

After Yadriel's grandfather passed away, Enrique had taken up the position as leader of the East LA brujx. Lita was his right hand, serving as the matriarch of the family and spiritual leader. Enrique was well respected and looked up to. All the men in the room gave him their undivided attention, especially Diego, Yadriel's older brother, who stood at Enrique's side, nodding vigorously at every instruction his dad gave.

"We need to find Miguel's portaje. If he hasn't passed on to the land of the dead, he'll be tethered to it," Enrique told the group, gripping the edge of the small wooden table. His voice was low and gravelly, his eyes intense. Yadriel looked around, and every brujo's face held varying degrees of shock.

"People are already searching the cemetery—he was on shift tonight—but I need more to go to Claudia and Benny's house," Enrique told them. Even though Miguel had been in his late twenties, he'd still lived at home to help his disabled father. Miguel was kind and patient, and he'd always been good to Yadriel. A lump lodged in his throat. Yadriel tried to swallow it down.

"Someone get one of Miguel's shirts and go wake up Julio; we might need his dogs," Enrique added, and another brujo ran off.

Julio was a cranky old brujo who raised pit bulls and trained them to track by scent. It was a skill that came in handy for locating bodies and tethers of lost spirits.

"Search everywhere!" Enrique stood upright, his eyes searching the crowded kitchen. "Has anyone seen—"

"Dad!" Yadriel pushed his way to the front.

Enrique's head snapped to him, shocked relief hitting his face. "Yadriel!" He grabbed Yadriel and crushed him to his chest, squeezing his arms around him tight. "¡Ay, Dios mío!" His rough hands cupped Yadriel's face as he pressed a kiss to the top of his head.

Yadriel tensed, automatically resisting the sudden physical contact.

His dad gripped his shoulders, looking down at him with a frown. "I was worried something had happened to you!"

Yadriel stepped back, pulling free of his dad's hold. "I'm fine—"

"Where *were* you two?" Diego demanded, his light brown eyes darting between him and Maritza.

Yadriel hesitated. Maritza gave a useless shrug.

There was a reason they had performed Yadriel's portaje ceremony in secret. A reason that Maritza spent so long making his dagger without her dad knowing. The brujx practices were built on ancient tradition. Going against those traditions was seen as blasphemous. When Yadriel had refused to be presented to Lady Death for his quinces as a bruja, they wouldn't let him go through it as a brujo. It was out of the question. It wouldn't work, they'd told him. Just because he said he was a boy, that didn't change the way Lady Death gave her blessings.

They wouldn't even let him try. It was easier to hide behind their traditions than to challenge their own beliefs and understanding of how things in the world of the brujx worked.

It made Yadriel feel ashamed of who he was. Their blatant rejection felt personal because it *was* personal. It was an outright rejection of who he was—a transgender boy trying to find his place in their community.

But they were wrong. Lady Death had answered him. Now, he just needed to prove it.

Orlando rushed into the kitchen, pulling his dad's attention.

"Did you find him?" Enrique asked.

Orlando shook his head. "We're still sweeping the cemetery, but there's no sign of him yet," he said, taking off his baseball cap and wringing it in his hands. "We haven't been able to sense him or anything—it's like he just vanished!"

"Dad!" Yadriel tried to make himself taller. "How can I help?" Everyone's eyes went right over his head.

"More of you start searching the streets, fan out from the front gate," Enrique said, a heavy hand still resting on Yadriel's shoulder. "He wouldn't have just left his shift for no reason."

Orlando nodded and headed for the door. Yadriel moved to follow, but his dad held tight to his shoulder.

"Not you, Yadriel," he said, calm but firm.

"But I can help!" Yadriel insisted.

Another brujo slipped into the kitchen, and Yadriel felt a pluck of hope in his chest.

Tío Catriz was his father's older brother, though, just looking at them, it was difficult to tell. While Enrique Vélez Cabrera was broad and rounded, Catriz Vélez Cabrera was lanky and angular. He wore his long black hair looped into a knot at the base of his neck. He had high cheekbones and a hooked nose. Traditional, flared plugs made of jade and the size of a quarter adorned his earlobes.

"There you are, Catriz." Enrique sighed.

"Tío," Yadriel said, feeling less outnumbered.

Catriz threw Yadriel a small grin before turning to his brother. "I came as soon as I felt it," he said, a little winded. His fine eyebrows pulled together. "Miguel, is he . . . ?"

Yadriel's dad nodded. Catriz gave a slow, somber shake of his head. Several brujos in the room crossed themselves.

Yadriel couldn't take all the standing around. He wanted to do something. He wanted to help. Miguel was family and a good man—he helped provide for his family and had always been kind to Yadriel. One of Yadriel's favorite childhood memories was of riding around on the back of Miguel's motorcycle. Yadriel's parents had explicitly forbidden him from going anywhere near it, but if he begged enough, Miguel would always give in. Yadriel remembered how his helmet was way too big and heavy as Miguel would give him a ride around the block, barely going ten miles an hour.

Realizing he'd never see him alive again hit Yadriel with a fresh wave of grief.

"What if we can't find him?" Andrés asked, breaking the quiet. He was a skinny, freckle-faced boy, and also Diego's best friend.

The muscles in his dad's jaw tensed. People exchanged looks.

"Keep searching. We need to find his portaje," Enrique told them. "If we can summon his spirit, we can ask him what happened." He rubbed his fist across his brow. Clearly, his dad didn't think Miguel had died and simply passed peacefully to the afterlife. Yadriel agreed, he just couldn't see how that could've happened with how violently his death felt. "Hopefully, it'll be with his body."

Yadriel's stomach clenched at the idea of finding Miguel's lifeless body lying somewhere in their cemetery.

Andrés's face turned an impressive shade of green. Yadriel couldn't believe he used to have a crush on him.

Enrique picked up his portaje from the counter. It was a hunting knife, much larger and more severe than Yadriel's, but still understated compared to the style of the young brujos' portajes.

Like Diego's and Andrés's. Their knives were longer, with a slight curve, too big to be practical or easily concealed. They got their names engraved into the blades and added flashy charms. A small cross hung on a one-inch chain from Andrés's hilt. Diego's had a gold-plated calavera. "Gaudy," Maritza called them. Adornments were impractical and completely unnecessary.

"We need to get going," Enrique said, and everyone started to move.

This was it.

He would help them find Miguel and lay his cousin to rest in the brujx graveyard. This was the duty of the brujos, so he would do it. Now that he had his own portaje, maybe Yadriel could even be the one to release Miguel's spirit to the afterlife.

Yadriel stepped to follow his dad, but Enrique held out his arm to stop him.

"Not you. You stay here," he instructed.

Yadriel's stomach plummeted. "But I can help!" he insisted.

"No, Yadriel." A loud ringing had Enrique digging his cell phone out of his pocket. He swiped his thumb across the screen and lifted it to his ear. "Benny, did you find him?" he asked, expression tense.

Everyone in the group stilled. Yadriel could hear rushed Spanish on the other side.

But his father's shoulders slumped. "No, we haven't, either." He sighed, rubbing his forehead. "We're trying to gather more people to help search—"

Yadriel leaped at the opportunity. "I can help!" he repeated.

His dad turned away from him and continued to speak into the phone. "No, we haven't—"

Yadriel scowled, frustration boiling over. "Dad!" he insisted, stepping in front of him. "Let me help, I—"

"*No*, Yadriel," Enrique hissed, frowning as he tried to hear the voice on the other line.

Normally, Yadriel wasn't prone to arguing with his dad, but this was important. He looked around to the brujos in the room, for someone to listen to him, but they were already filing out. Except for Tío Catriz, who gave Yadriel a puzzled look.

When his dad made for the front door, fierce determination made Yadriel step in his way.

"If you'd *just* listen to me—" Yadriel wrestled his backpack off his shoulder and yanked open the zipper.

"Yadriel—"

He plunged his hand inside, fingers grasping the hilt of his portaje. "Look—"

"*¡Basta!*"

Enrique's shout made Yadriel jump.

His dad was an even-tempered man. It genuinely took a lot to get him rattled or for him to lose his temper. It was part of what made him a good leader. Seeing his dad's face so red, hearing the sharpness of his voice, was jarring. Even Diego, standing just behind Enrique, was startled.

The room fell silent. Yadriel felt every pair of eyes on him.

He snapped his mouth shut. The cut on his tongue stung, sharp and metallic.

Enrique jabbed a finger toward the living room. "You stay here with the rest of the women!"

Yadriel flinched. Hot shame flooded his cheeks. He released the dagger, letting it fall to the bottom of his backpack. He glared up at his dad in an attempt to look fierce and defiant, even though his eyes burned and his hands quaked.

"The rest of the women," he repeated, spitting the words out as if they were poisonous.

Enrique blinked, anger flickering to confusion, as though Yadriel were suddenly coming into focus before him. He removed his cell phone from his ear. His shoulders sank; his expression went slack. "Yadriel," he sighed, reaching out for him.

But Yadriel wasn't going to stick around to listen.

Maritza tried to stop him. "Yads—"

He couldn't take the look of pity on her face. He veered out of her reach. *"Don't."*

Yadriel turned and shoved past the onlookers, escaping through the door that led to the garage. It banged against the wall before slamming shut behind him as he stomped down the small set of stairs. The lights sputtered on, revealing organized chaos. His dad's car was parked off to one side.

Seething, Yadriel paced back and forth over the oil-stained concrete, his breath ragged as his ribs strained against his binder. Anger and embarrassment warred inside him.

He wanted to scream or break something.

Or both.

His dad's face—the look of regret when he realized what he'd said to Yadriel—flashed in his mind. Yadriel was always forgiving people for being callous. For misgendering him and calling him by his deadname. He was always giving them the benefit of the doubt, or writing it off as people not understanding or being stuck in their ways when they hurt him.

Well, Yadriel was tired of it. He was tired of forgiving. He was tired of fighting to just *exist* and be himself. He was tired of being the odd one out.

But belonging meant denying who he was. Living as something he wasn't had nearly torn him apart from the inside out. But he also loved his family, and his community. It was bad enough being an outsider; what would happen if they just couldn't—or wouldn't—accept him for who he was?

Frustration broke in Yadriel's chest. He kicked the tire of the car with his combat boot, which did nothing but make pain explode in his foot.

Yadriel cussed loudly and hobbled over to an old stool. Wincing, he sat down heavily.

Stupid move.

He scowled at the black sedan, and his angry reflection stared back at him from the windshield. All the running had made his hair fall out of place. Short on the sides with a swath of hair on top, Yadriel put a lot of time into styling it. His hair was one of the few things about his appearance he could control. While he couldn't get button-up shirts to fit right—either they were too tight across his chest and hips, or comically huge—he could at least get his hair faded and use what little allowance he got on Suavecito pomade. It was the only stuff that could wrangle his thick mass of wavy black hair. He couldn't thin out his round cheeks, but he could grow his eyebrows in thick and dark. The combat boots were as much practical as they were aesthetic. They gave him an extra inch of height that, while minuscule, helped him feel less self-conscious about how short he was compared to the average sixteen-year-old boy. It was small changes, like mirroring how Diego and his friends dressed or wore their hair, that made him feel more at home in his own skin.

There was a rustling from the corner, followed by a curious, trilling mewl. A small cat ambled out from behind a stack of cardboard boxes. Although, she looked more like a cartoonist's rendition of a cat, with a large notch in one ear and her left eye always squinting. Her spine was bony and a little askew. The tip of her tail was practically bald, and she held her back leg awkwardly.

A heavy sigh released some of the anger in Yadriel's chest. "C'mere, Purrcaso," he cooed, holding his hand out.

With another happy trill, she hobbled over to Yadriel, the bell on her blue collar tinkling as she went. She rubbed up against his leg, leaving tufts of gray fur on his black jeans.

Yadriel managed a small grin, running his fingers down her crooked back before scratching under her chin, just where she liked it. He was rewarded with loud purrs.

Purrcaso had joined the family when Yadriel was thirteen years old. It was around then his mother had tried teaching him how to heal. Brujas usually learned their trade long before their portaje ceremony, the women in the family walking them through the steps.

Yadriel's mom had been trying to dip his toes into the healing waters, but, even at thirteen, he knew it wouldn't work. Yadriel knew he wasn't a bruja. He'd already come out to Maritza, but he still hadn't worked up the courage to tell his mom. The closer it got to his quinces, the more panicked he became.

Everyone figured he was just a late bloomer, or maybe he was just nervous about coming of age. That's why, when he and his mom found a small gray cat on the side of the road walking back from school one day, she decided to use it as a teaching moment.

They could sense the cat was injured, even without seeing the way she limped. Maybe she'd been hit by a car, or lost a fight with a dog or one of the terrifying raccoons that ran the streets at night. Yadriel felt a small pang in the corner of his mind, could feel the pain radiating from her leg. When he was younger, Yadriel hated the brujx ability to sense others' pain. He'd always been terribly empathetic, and being able to sense so much suffering in the world affected him.

Yadriel's mom had set him down on the curb and gathered the cat into her billowy skirt. She unwrapped her portaje from her wrist—a jade rosary ending in a vessel that, at first glance, looked like Our Lady of Guadalupe, but if you looked closely, you'd see the figure was actually a skeleton. His mom unscrewed the top, let the chicken blood drip onto her finger, and then brushed it across the statuette of Lady Death. She spoke the words, and golden light illuminated the rosary.

It was such a small injury to fix, and on such a tiny creature, Yadriel should have been able to heal it easily with his mom's help. With her warm smile and gentle encouragement, he held the rosary to the cat's leg. His hand quaked, scared that something would go wrong, or worse, that it would work, showing that he was supposed to be a bruja. His mom placed her hand over his and gave it a small squeeze.

Yadriel spoke the final words, but it backfired.

He could still picture the drops of scarlet on his mother's white skirt. The terrible yowl. The sudden, sharp pain of the poor cat piercing into his head. The stunned look on his mother's face. It couldn't have lasted more than a couple of seconds before she'd taken the cat and quickly healed it herself.

In a blink, the terrible sound had stopped. The pain vanished. The small cat's eyes closed, a ball of fur in his mom's lap.

Yadriel had been inconsolable, convinced for a long moment that he had killed the poor creature. His mom pulled him to her side and spoke gently into his ear.

Shh, it's all right. She's okay; she's just sleeping, you see?

But all Yadriel could see was his failure; all he could feel was the crushing weight of knowing he couldn't do it. But, more than that, he knew *this* wasn't him. He wasn't a bruja.

His mom brushed her cool fingers along the side of his face, pushing his hair from his eyes. *It's okay*, she'd said, like she knew it, too.

His mother hadn't been able to patch the cat back together completely. The backfire had done damage not even she could repair, but the cat wasn't in pain. They took her home, and Yadriel diligently went to work making sure she was well fed and taken care of. Even now, she slept in his room every night, and Yadriel always snuck her bits of chorizo and chicken after dinner.

Yadriel's mom had affectionately named the cat Purrcaso, after the famous artist's crooked paintings.

Purrcaso was more than a cat, much closer to a companion. When Yadriel missed his mom, it was like Purrcaso knew. When he got that dropping feeling of guilt in his stomach, Purrcaso would curl up in his lap, loudly purring. She was ball of warmth and comfort in which his mother's magic still lived.

Purrcaso curled up against the toe of his shoe. Yadriel rubbed the soft fur behind her ears until her amber eyes slid shut.

His mom never pressured him to try healing again. In a community built on such staunch tradition, the news that Yadriel couldn't heal, to them, meant he didn't have magic. His quinces was postponed indefinitely.

The brujx thought he was just a product of the dilution of magic slowly working its way through their lineage. But Yadriel and his mom knew the truth.

She bought him his first binder online and helped him tell his dad and brother. It was hard explaining himself and his identity not only to his family but to their entire community. They still didn't understand, clearly, but at least with his mom around, they were working through it together.

His mom championed for Yadriel to be given a brujo's quinces, to be welcomed into the community as he was—a boy. She'd taken on the task of trying to explain to his dad that he was a brujo. He was a boy.

He can't just choose to be a brujo, he'd heard Enrique say from the kitchen one night as he and Camila spoke quietly over sweet coffee.

It's not a choice, his mother had said, her voice calm but firm. *It's who he is.*

She told Yadriel the others just needed time to understand. But Yadriel's mom, his advocate, had been taken away from him less than a year ago. Without her, there was no one to stick up for him. Now, he was treated as a magicless brujx. Someone who could see spirits and sense suffering, but who would never be a full member of their community.

"What a mess . . ."

The voice made Yadriel jump. He looked up and found Catriz standing at the door, a cigarillo between his fingers. He looked tired, his expression one of grim understanding.

Yadriel's posture relaxed. "Tío," he sighed. His eyes slid back to the door, wondering if maybe his dad would follow his uncle out here.

"Don't worry," Tío Catriz said, taking a drag from his cigarillo as he descended the steps. "Your father and the other brujos already left." He pulled up a plastic lawn chair and sat next to Yadriel. "It's just you and me." Catriz placed his hand on the crown of Yadriel's head and grinned. "Como siempre."

Yadriel sighed a laugh. A small part of him had hoped his dad would be the one to follow him and apologize. But his uncle was right, it was always the two of them on the outskirts of the brujx. At least they had each other, and Catriz understood Yadriel's yearning, unlike Maritza, who was entirely uninterested in being a part of the brujx and had no qualms about being an outcast. She seemed to enjoy being contrary.

Yadriel stuffed his hands into the pocket of his black hoodie. "I can't believe Miguel . . ." He trailed off, not wanting to speak the words.

Catriz gave a slow shake of his head and took a long drag from his cigarillo. "So young, so sudden," he said, smoke billowing from his nostrils. "I wish I could help, but . . ." He shrugged his angular shoulders. "They don't find me of much use."

Yadriel let out a short laugh. Yeah, he knew that feeling all too well. "What the hell happened to him?" he asked, repeating the same words Maritza had said earlier.

Catriz sighed deeply. Yadriel followed his uncle's gaze to the door, beyond which he could still hear muffled voices. "By the sound of it, your dad has already rallied the troops to find out."

Yadriel nodded stiffly, the earlier exchange with his dad burrowing its way back under his skin. "All the brujos," he grumbled under his breath, toying with Purrcaso's tail.

"Well, not *all* of them," Catriz pointed out casually.

Yadriel winced at his own insensitivity.

Catriz had long since been left out of the brujos and their tasks. It had been thousands of years since Lady Death had gifted the brujx their powers. At the beginning, the brujx powers rivaled that of the diosa. Women could regrow an entire arm or pull someone back from the brink of death with little more concentration than you'd need to do long division. The most powerful of the men could even bring the dead back to life when their spirits were beyond the brujas' reach.

But now, with the dilution of power over the generations, such extravagant use of their powers was impossible. Their magic was not a bottomless well. Drawing on your power to heal the living or guide the dead pulled from that well, and it took time for it to fill up again.

Brujx were getting weaker, and there were those who were born with such shallow wells of power they could barely tap them for simple tasks without risking death.

Like Catriz.

Yadriel felt that his uncle was the only one, other than his mom, who really understood him. The brujos treated Yadriel and Catriz the same. Neither had been given their quinces, nor been presented at the aquelarre during Día de Muertos.

Held on the second night of Día de Muertos, the last night the spirits of past brujx spent each year in the land of the living before returning to the afterlife, the aquelarre was a huge party held in the church. Every young brujx who'd turned fifteen and had their quinces pledged to serve Lady Death and help maintain the balance of life and death, as had all their ancestors who came before them. Then they were officially presented to the community.

Yadriel and Tío Catriz both knew what it was like to see others perform their magic, to sit on the sidelines, powerless to do anything themselves.

But now, Yadriel knew he *could* do the magic.

His tío Catriz had no such luxury. As the eldest son, Catriz should've been the leader of the brujx after Yadriel's abuelito died. But since he wasn't able to perform magic, the title had been passed to his younger brother—Yadriel's dad, Enrique. It was an understanding that had been established long ago, when both boys were small children, but Yadriel would never forget the look on his tío's face when Enrique was presented with the sacred headdress that recognized him as the next leader of the East LA brujx.

Hurt and longing.

Yadriel knew the feeling all too well.

"Sorry, Tío, I just meant—" he rushed to apologize.

His tío's chuckle was warm and his smile forgiving. "It's all right, it's all right." He clapped his hand on Yadriel's shoulder.

"We are alike, you and me," he told Yadriel, scratching his stubble as he nodded with a jutted chin. "They are stuck in their ways, in their traditions, following the ancient rules. Without powers, they see no use for me."

When he said it, Catriz didn't sound bitter, just matter-of-fact. "And you, mi sobrino—"

Warmth bloomed in Yadriel's chest, and a smile dared to pull at his lips.

Catriz hummed a sigh, giving his shoulder a squeeze. "They won't even give you a chance."

Yadriel's smile fell. His heart sank.

The door to the kitchen opened, and Yadriel's abuelita came stomping into the garage.

Yadriel and his tío sighed in unison. Living in a multigenerational Latinx household meant privacy was always fleeting.

"There you are!" Lita Rosamaria announced with a huff, snapping the hem of her apron with a flourish. Her gray hair was tied back in a knot like she always did when she was cooking. Which was, well, always.

Yadriel inwardly groaned. He really didn't feel like getting lectured by his abuelita right now. He scooped up Purrcaso, holding her in the crook of his arm as he got to his feet. Catriz remained sitting, taking another drag from his cigarillo.

Lita propped one hand on her wide hip and shook a long finger at Yadriel. "You don't run off like that!" she chided. Lita was a squat woman, even shorter than him but with a presence that made the cockiest brujo shrink back when she scolded. She always smelled like Royal Violets, which lingered on Yadriel's clothes long after she released him from a back-popping hug. She had a strong, trilling Cuban accent and an even stronger personality.

"Yes, Lita," Yadriel grumbled.

"It's dangerous! What with poor Miguel . . ." She trailed off, crossing herself and muttering a quick prayer to the dios.

Maybe he was being selfish. He wasn't trying to make the situation about him. Didn't he deserve to fight for himself? But maybe now wasn't the time.

Yadriel frowned. Tío Catriz caught his gaze and rolled his eyes—a grand gesture when Lita wasn't looking.

"Make yourselves useful!" Lita said, crossing to the shelves as she dug through the boxes.

"¿Dónde está?" she grumbled to herself, talking so fast in her thick Cuban accent that the *s*'s at the end of her words got left behind.

The garage held a plethora of artifacts and items. Glass display cases and sturdy wooden boxes held ancient weapons and carvings. Sacred regalia and featherwork were kept in the house in fancy containers away from light until they were taken out for special occasions, like Día de Muertos.

Yadriel often got tasked with climbing into the rafters to take down boxes for whatever very specific item Lita was looking for.

She pushed aside a box of chachayotes in her search. The hard shells, sewn onto leather that were worn around the ankles during ceremonial dances, rattled. Purrcaso's ears perked where she sat in the crook of Yadriel's arm. She leaped down to help investigate.

"What are you looking for, Mamá?" Catriz asked, though he didn't move from his seat.

"¡La garra del jaguar!" she snapped, as if it were obvious. Lita turned, consternation pinching her wrinkled face.

Yadriel knew about the claw of the jaguar, mostly because Lita would never let him forget it. It was an ancient set of four ritual daggers and an amulet in the shape of a jaguar's head. The ceremonial blades had been used back when the dark art of human sacrifice was still in practice. When pierced into the hearts of four humans, the daggers used their spirits to feed the amulet, giving the brujx who wore it immense—but dark—power. Lita liked to pull the daggers out on special occasions—including Día de Muertos—to scare younger brujx and lecture them about the treachery of abusing their powers.

"Have you seen them?" Lita asked.

Catriz quirked an eyebrow, his expression placid.

"Aye, yi, yi," Lita said, flapping her hands at him dismissively.

When Lita looked to Yadriel, he simply shrugged his shoulders. He didn't particularly feel like being helpful.

She sighed heavily, clicking her tongue. "Your father is under a lot of stress right now, nena," Lita said solemnly.

Yadriel cringed at the offensive word. Navigating pronouns was a minefield when language was based on gender.

"Ay, poor Claudia and Benny," Lita lamented as she fanned herself with a hand, not even noticing his reaction.

Anger simmered under Yadriel's skin again.

She fixed him with a stern look. "This is a job for the men, and we need to leave them to it. Ven!" Lita waved him toward the door. "I have pozole in the kitchen, come warm up—"

His deadname slipped from her mouth.

Yadriel flinched and took a step back. "¡Soy *Yadriel*, Lita!" he snapped, so suddenly that both Purrcaso and Lita jumped.

Catriz stared at him. Surprise quickly turned to pride.

Lita blinked at him for a moment, a hand pressed to her throat.

Yadriel could feel his face grow hot. The knee-jerk reaction to apologize was on the tip of his tongue, but he bit it back.

She sighed and nodded. "Sí, Yadriel," Lita agreed.

She stepped closer and gently cupped his cheeks in her soft hands. She planted a kiss on his forehead, and hope lifted in his chest. "Pero siempre serás mijita," she told him with a chuckle and a smile.

But you'll always be my little girl.

The hope came crashing down.

Lita turned and went back into the house, leaving Yadriel on the steps.

He scrubbed his hands over his face and clenched his jaw to keep his chin from wobbling. He should've been out with the rest of the brujos, searching for Miguel. He wanted to use his portaje, to show them that he wasn't powerless. He could help them find Miguel. If he could just *show* them—

"I'm so sorry, Yadriel." His tío's hand grasped his shoulder.

Yadriel dropped his hands to his sides and looked up into Tío Catriz's face. His uncle's expression was pained. Even though they were outsiders for different reasons, Catriz was the only one who could understand what Yadriel was going through. He was the only one, aside from Maritza, who put the work in to understand him. The rest of the brujx seemed to ignore him. They were so worried about calling him by the wrong name or gender, they would avoid him altogether.

But not his tío.

"I wish your mom were still here," Catriz confessed.

The crushing ache of missing his mom filled every space in Yadriel's body. Sometimes it was dull, just enough to prickle if his mind wandered too far. Other times it burned.

Without her, Yadriel was floundering.

"What do I do?" he asked, hating how desperate and defeated he sounded.

"I don't know," Catriz said.

"¡Catriz!" Yadriel heard his abuelita call from inside. "I need más frijoles!"

Catriz exhaled through his nose. "I'm just useful for reaching things on the top shelf, apparently," he said dryly. Catriz opened the door, and the smell of chicken and chilies wafted from the kitchen.

Before he went inside, Catriz paused, giving Yadriel another tired smile. "If only there was something we could do to show them how wrong they are."

Yadriel stared at the closed door after Catriz went inside.

His hands tightened into fists.

He went back into the house and cut through the kitchen without looking at anyone and went straight up the stairs.

"Yads!" Maritza called after him, but he didn't stop.

The small lamp on his bedside table was the only source of light in his room. Yadriel tossed his backpack onto the unmade, full-size bed shoved in the corner by the window. On his hands and knees, Yadriel dug his arm under the bed, searching for his plastic flashlight.

He heard Maritza walk in behind him. "Yads?" she asked. "What are you doing?"

"Grabbing supplies," he said. His fingers closed around the flashlight, and he yanked it out.

She frowned at him, her arms crossed. "For what?"

"If I have to prove myself in order to get them to listen, then I will." He clicked on the light to make sure the batteries still worked. "If I can find Miguel's spirit, figure out what happened to him, and release him to the afterlife in time for Día de Muertos, they'll *have* to let me be part of the aquelarre." Yadriel turned the beam on Maritza. "You coming?"

A large grin curled her burgundy-painted lips. "Oh, hell *yes* I am."

Yadriel smiled back. He felt dangerous and electric, adrenaline tingling through his fingers. "Good." He tossed her the flashlight, which she easily caught out of the air. Yadriel stuffed an LED camping lantern and box of matches into his backpack and double-checked that the candles, bowl, and the rest of the tequila were still in there.

He pulled his portaje out and removed it from the leather sheath Maritza had fashioned for it. He turned the blade over in his hands, feeling the even weight, running his thumb along the painting of Lady Death.

In a few short days, his mother would return for Día de Muertos. He would be able to see and speak to her. He would show her his portaje, and she would see he'd done it. All that was left to do was find Miguel.

Yadriel turned to Maritza. "You ready?"

She smirked, tipping her head toward the door. "I've got your back."

THREE

By the time they went back downstairs, all the brujos had dispersed to help search for Miguel. While Lita was back to work in the kitchen, a handful of women remained gathered around Claudia. They were all too happy to look the other way as Maritza and Yadriel bolted out the front door. The brujx cemetery was right in the middle of East Los Angeles, surrounded by a tall wall that concealed it from prying eyes. Yadriel could hear dogs barking in the distance and the thudding bass of reggaeton blaring from a passing car.

They passed by some brujx still looking for Miguel.

"Anything yet?" an older one asked.

"Nothing behind the eastern columbaria," said another.

"No sign of him near his family's mausoleums, either," said the spirit of a young bruja, a worried but determined expression on her faintly transparent face.

"What's the plan?" Maritza asked, her long legs easily keeping stride with Yadriel. She wove between tombstones, careful to step around flower vases and framed pictures.

"Find Miguel's portaje, summon his spirit, find out what happened, and release his spirit before Día de Muertos starts," Yadriel said as they started jogging through rows of brightly painted tombs. "That way, he can come back to celebrate with the rest of the brujx, and I can be in this year's aquelarre."

"Uh, there's a lot of gaps in your plan," Maritza told him.

"I didn't say it was a *good* one."

"Where are we going to look?"

"His parents' house." Clearly the brujx weren't having any luck finding Miguel in the cemetery, so where he lived was the next logical place to look. The quickest way there was over the abandoned back gate in the oldest part of the cemetery.

The closer they got to the original graveyard, the older the tombs and headstones became. By the time they were in sight of the old church, the cemetery was mostly a collection of simple, cross-shaped tombstones. On most of them, you couldn't even read the names.

Yadriel and Maritza slowed to a stop. The old church loomed before them.

When the first brujx immigrated to Los Angeles, they had only built a small church and graveyard. But as the community expanded, so did the cemetery, and eventually, the original church was just too small to hold them all. Finally, a couple of decades ago, the new one had been built, along with Yadriel's home.

In comparison, the old church looked like an ancient ruin. Wild vines had overrun the two brick walls that met behind the church, giving the building a backdrop of dense, shadowy green. There weren't many street lights nearby, but it was East LA, where the sun never seemed to set. Hazy pollution and city lights washed everything in an orange glow, even in the middle of the night.

The church itself was made of a variety of differently shaped and colored stones, all patched together with clay. There was a small bell tower on the roof, directly above the wooden door, that didn't seem to house an actual bell anymore. A small wrought iron fence about waist-high surrounded the church. A few headstones lined the inner graveyard.

"Mira, there." Yadriel nudged Maritza and pointed to the back wall. There was a spot through the veil of ivy where the old entrance to the cemetery was located. Yadriel couldn't help but grin as he jogged around the edge of the fence to the gate.

"See?" Yadriel shoved a fistful of ivy out of the way. The iron bars towered over them. Two handles met at a very sturdy-looking lock meant to keep non-brujx out, and their secrets safe. "Shortcut!"

Maritza let out a low whistle. "Good thing I'm not in a skirt," she grumbled to herself before wedging her foot onto a crossbar and hoisting herself up.

Yadriel tightened the strap on his backpack, ready to climb up after her, when he got the feeling someone was behind him. It wasn't an all-at-once realization, more like a slow creeping on the back of his neck. Yadriel turned, but there was only the old church and graves. The hum of traffic and the far-off sound of a car alarm drifted from the distance.

With a shake of his head, Yadriel turned back to the gate. He needed to focus on the task at hand. He gripped the ornate handle to pull himself up, but as soon as he applied pressure, it turned.

He scrambled out of the way as the gate swung open. Maritza yelped. Yadriel clamped a hand over his mouth, laughter leaping from his throat as Maritza nearly toppled off. When the gate groaned to a stop, she was halfway up and holding on for dear life.

"It was *unlocked*?" she hissed angrily through the ivy, her face pressed between the bars.

"Guess so?" Barely contained chuckles shook Yadriel's chest, but his brow furrowed. He examined the lock, jiggling the handle up and down. "Wait, why is it unlocked?"

The brujx went to great lengths to keep outsiders from getting into their cemetery.

Maritza landed next to Yadriel, a little less than graceful. "Some idiot probably forgot to lock it up," she grumbled, bottom lip jutting into a scowl.

"But why would anyone even *use* this gate?" Yadriel asked. People were supposed to come in or out of the cemetery only at the main gate by his family's house.

Maritza turned to him, arms folded across her chest, an expertly lined eyebrow arching. "Uh, you mean aside from sneaking out in the middle of the night?"

Yadriel threw her a withering look. "But—"

A chill dropping down his spine sucked the breath out of Yadriel's lungs.

He and Maritza spun toward the abandoned church at the same time. Yadriel's eyes skipped across the windows, half expecting to see someone staring out at him, but they were just black, empty cutouts in the wall of stones.

"Did you feel that?" Maritza asked, her voice barely above a whisper.

Yadriel nodded, unable to pull his eyes away from the church, afraid to blink and miss something. The hair on the back of his neck prickled and goose bumps ran down his arms.

Maritza shifted closer to his side. "Is it a spirit?"

"I don't know," he murmured. "It doesn't seem quite right . . ."

It was normal to feel spirits: the cemetery was crawling with them, after all. It became background noise, kind of like the hum of Los Angeles traffic; after being around it long enough, you stopped noticing.

But this feeling was something else. It was an odd tingling, one that felt like the presence of a spirit but also pricked at that certain spot in his head, suggesting pain.

"Is it Miguel?" Yadriel wondered, squinting as he tried to latch on to what he was sensing.

"I'm going to go check it out," he told Maritza, heading for the church. Even if it wasn't Miguel, whoever it was—a spirit or the living—might be in trouble.

"If I'm a brujo, then it's my responsibility to help lost spirits cross over, right?" he said over his shoulder as he hoisted himself over the small fence.

Maritza didn't look so sure, but she followed him anyway.

Yadriel searched the leaning headstones, trying to catch sight of movement, or a clue, or anything as they crept toward the old building. The tingling sensation was now a steady buzzing under his skin, like when he got phantom sensations of his phone going off in his pocket.

"This place kind of gives me the creeps," Maritza whispered at his side, rubbing her arm. "What if it's haunted?"

Yadriel huffed a laugh. "Of course it's haunted, this is literally a cemetery full of spirits," he said, trying to use sarcasm to calm his own nerves.

Maritza punched his arm. "I mean like a *monster* or something."

"There's no such thing as monsters." Yadriel went to one of the tall windows, but, even after wiping at it with his sleeve, he still couldn't see anything but blackness inside.

Maritza stopped and stared at him, wide-eyed. "You didn't just say that—did you really just say that?" she demanded before throwing her arms in the air. "That's *classic* start-of-a-horror-movie dialogue you just threw out into the universe!"

"Oh my God, you are so dramatic," Yadriel told her. "I'm going to check it out," he said, more to himself than anything. "You can wait out here alone or go inside with me," he told Maritza.

He got all the way to the front steps of the church before he heard Maritza cuss under her breath and chase after him.

The wooden door to the church was dark and warped. Yadriel crept up the steps, barely catching himself from stepping on a long, rusty nail. He swept a few more scattered nails to the side with his shoe and noticed some boards in a stack to the left.

He tried the door handle, and it turned easily under his grip. He lifted his eyebrows at Maritza, and she scowled back. With effort, he pulled the door open. The wood groaned as it dragged over stone.

Through the doorway, darkness yawned into the depths of the church. The odors of dust, wet soil, and mildew tickled his nose. Before

Yadriel could dig the lantern out of his backpack, Maritza flicked on her flashlight. Yadriel's fingers brushed against the cool steel of his portaje and he pulled it out. The weight of it in his hand was reassuring. If there was a malevolent spirit haunting the old church, he would need his portaje to release it.

And if it was a criminal on the lam, well, it'd come in handy for that, too.

"After you, fearless brujo," Maritza said with a grand gesture.

Yadriel cleared his throat and, with lifted chin, went inside.

The lantern doused everything in a cool blue light. The beam of Maritza's flashlight swept back and forth between several pews that stretched toward the front of the church. When Yadriel closed the door behind them, it became oddly quiet. The heavy stone muffled the constant thrum of noise that came with living in the city.

Yadriel tried to ignore the strange pressure in his chest, like someone had tied a string to his ribs and was pulling him farther into the church.

A carpet ran down the aisle. At one point, it had probably been red, but time had turned it coppery brown. Lancet windows lined the walls, set in intricate molding. Wooden beams arched high into the apex of the ceiling where the light of the lantern couldn't reach.

"I haven't been here in ages," Maritza said, her voice uncharacteristically soft as they moved between the pews.

"Me either."

Up ahead, several glass prayer candles winked in the blue light from the altar. "Not since your mom caught us playing hide-and-seek and we got grounded for being 'disrespectful,'" he added.

Maritza laughed fondly. "Oh, yeah, I forgot about that," she said, her beam of light now focused on a door to the left of the apse. An identical one stood to the right.

"If Bahlam appears and drags us down to Xibalba, I'm going to be *pissed*," Maritza hissed.

Yadriel rolled his eyes. "Yeah, I'm sure Bahlam, the jaguar god of the underworld, is hanging out in this old church, waiting for a couple of teenagers to—"

The feeling in Yadriel's chest tugged more urgently, cutting off his words.

Something dark stood in the middle of the altar, but Yadriel couldn't quite make it out.

He nudged Maritza. "What's that?"

"What's wh—"

The flashlight's beam swept to the altar. Hollowed eyes stared back at them.

"Santa Muerte," Maritza gritted through her teeth.

A semicircle of dusty candles in ornate golden holders stood at various heights. In the center stood a figure in a dark shroud. The skeleton was covered in a black robe. The linen material was moth-eaten, and gold thread accented the hems and sleeves in lacy patterns.

Yadriel only realized Maritza was gripping his arm when she let go.

Uneasy relief had Yadriel chuckling as he grinned over at her. "You're real jumpy tonight."

That got him two swift punches to the arm.

He leaped out of her reach. "She's just the original Lady Death from when this place was first built," Yadriel said, lifting the lantern to cast the lady in bluish light. It was an older representation, one that incorporated the more ancient symbols. A very real scythe was held in one hand, and a clay orb rested in her upturned palm.

The skeleton itself was smooth and yellowing. Her jaw was open wide, and she was missing a few teeth. Yadriel wondered if they were real bones and she was an actual skeleton.

But he was distracted by the headdress she wore. Layers of spotted-owl feathers made up the smaller inner semicircle. These were sewn together and fastened with small plates of gold in the shape of crescent moons, almost like buttons. The feathers layered under the owl's were the unmistakable plumage of the sacred quetzal bird. They were an iridescent green with hints of blue, like peacock feathers but twice as vibrant.

"Why would they just leave her here?" Maritza asked from somewhere behind him.

"I don't think she was abandoned." Yadriel shrugged, gently brushing cobwebs from Lady Death's shoulder. "I think this church is just her home."

He found himself smiling. He liked this classic version best.

Yadriel moved in closer, and he could feel energy swarming beneath his feet, like standing on a geyser, water rushing just below ground.

"Do you feel that, too?" Maritza asked.

He nodded. "It's stronger in here," he said. Whatever spirit had led them here was close.

Yadriel took a step back, and something crunched under his shoe. Hopping to the side, he found a silver chain with a small pendant lying on the dusty floor.

Maritza moved in. "What's that?"

"I think it's a necklace," Yadriel murmured, setting the lantern on the ground.

Carefully, he picked it up. As soon as his fingers made contact, a shiver rolled through his body. He held it up to the light. A medal hung from the chain, barely larger than his thumbnail. The edge of the medal read SAN JUDAS TADEO across the top, and RUEGA POR NOSOTROS along the bottom. In the center stood a man wearing long robes with a book held against his chest and a staff in his hand.

The medal was in bad need of cleaning. The silver was tarnished, but it certainly wasn't old enough to have been abandoned in the old church all this time. Only the raised form of St. Jude himself was bright silver, as if it had been polished by someone rubbing their thumb against it over and over.

Yadriel reached for the medal, and as soon as his fingers touched the cool silver, electricity flooded through his veins. He sucked in a sharp breath. Something pulsed under his feet in rhythm with the thudding of his heart.

"What's wrong?" Maritza demanded as Yadriel tried to catch his breath.

"It's a tether," he said, and a spike of adrenaline made him feel light-headed.

Once a spirit was attached to a tether, they couldn't venture very far from it, which was why things like haunted houses existed, but there weren't many stories about a single ghost who roamed an entire city. It was only when the spirits were free of their earthly bindings that a brujo could release them and help them pass peacefully to their eternal rest.

Yadriel had never actually held a spirit's tether before. They were incredibly powerful. Some of the brujx claimed mishandling a spirit's tether would get you cursed.

But Yadriel had never heard of anyone ever actually getting possessed, and he had no intention of disrespecting this tether.

"But it's not Miguel's, that's not his portaje," Maritza said, reaching out as if to touch it before thinking better.

"It *could* be Miguel's," Yadriel tried to reason, his hope of finding his cousin fighting against logic. He squeezed the medal in his hand. Warmth spread through his palm and up his arm.

He turned to Maritza with a smile. "There's only one way to find out."

Maritza gave him a skeptical look.

"I have to try—what if Miguel's spirit got tethered to this instead of his portaje?" he said, twisting the chain between his fingers.

"It might be attached to someone who's gone maligno," Maritza said, casting a pointed look around the dilapidated church.

"Then it's a good thing I've got this, isn't it?" Yadriel said, pulling out his portaje.

Maritza eyed the dagger but then grinned. "All right, brujo, work your magic."

The rush of excitement made Yadriel feel giddy as he knelt before

Lady Death. Maybe it was the feel of the dagger in his hand or the magic he now knew flowed through his veins, but for someone who usually erred on the side of caution, Yadriel felt recklessly brave.

He dug into his backpack and pulled out the clay bowl. Quickly, he poured in the rest of the small tequila bottle and some chicken blood, then grabbed a box of matches. He stood and tried to take a deep breath, but he was too excited, practically buzzing. His palms were sweaty, making it difficult to light the match, but it finally caught.

He glanced over at Maritza, and she nodded encouragingly.

Yadriel had seen his father summon a spirit. He knew what to do and how to do it. He just needed to say the words.

The flame inched toward Yadriel's fingers. There was no time left to second-guess.

He held out his arm, the medal hanging from the chain looped around his hand. It glinted in the dim light.

"Te—" Yadriel cleared his throat, trying to breathe around the lump that had formed. "¡Te invoco, espíritu!"

He dropped the match into the bowl. For a second, it sizzled in the blood and alcohol before there was an explosion of heat and golden light. Yadriel sprang back, choking on the smoke.

The fire in the bowl burned calmly, casting orange light over a boy. He was doubled over on his hands and knees before the statue of Lady Death, clutching his chest.

Yadriel could hardly believe his eyes. "It worked!"

The spirit's face was screwed up tight in a grimace, his fingers knotted into the material of his shirt. He wore a hooded black leather jacket over a white tee, faded jeans, and a pair of Converse.

"That's *not* Miguel," Maritza tried to whisper, but she'd never had a very good inside voice.

Yadriel groaned and dragged a hand over his face. On the bright side, he had actually summoned a real-life spirit.

On the not-so-bright side, he had summoned the wrong one.

"Obviously," Yadriel hissed back, unable to look away from the boy as he gasped for breath, the muscles in his neck straining. He had that translucent quality around the edges, like all spirits. The boy's eyes swung to them. He had a handsome but very angry face, his grimace now more of a sneer.

"Well, at least it's not a maligno spirit?" Maritza offered.

The boy staggered to his feet, upright but unsteady. "Who the hell are you?" he snarled, dark eyes blazing, sharp as obsidian.

"Uhhh" was Yadriel's unhelpful reply, suddenly unable to form a coherent sentence.

"Where am I?" the boy barked, head tilting back as he took in their surroundings. "Am I in a *church*?" His attention swung back to Yadriel and Maritza with an accusing glare. "Who let me in a *church*?"

Familiarity prickled at the back of Yadriel's mind, racing to place his strong features and booming voice.

"Uh—well—you see," Yadriel stammered, not really sure how to explain their situation, but he wasn't given the chance to finish.

The boy's eyes snagged on the necklace still dangling from Yadriel's hand. "Hey!"

Yadriel saw the anger swell, hunching his shoulders and propelling him forward. The boy stomped up to him. "That's *mine*—"

He reached out to snatch the necklace, but his hand went right through it. He tried again, and when his hand slid through it a second time, he froze, blinked, and waved it back and forth.

The boy's eyes went wide, and he let out a strangled shout, stumbling back. *"Wh–what—"* he stammered, looking between his hand and Yadriel and Maritza, "the hell is this?"

"Wow, this is really awkward," Yadriel said, scratching at the back of his neck.

Maritza seemed less worried. "Well, there's no denying you're a brujo now," she said, circling the boy with keen interest.

He scowled at her. "Who are you, and what are you doing with my necklace?" he demanded, looking to Yadriel for answers.

"Well, uh, I used it to summon you," Yadriel tried.

The boy arched a thick eyebrow. "Summon me?"

"Yeah, we thought it belonged to Miguel." What was the gentlest way to tell someone they were dead?

"Our cousin," Maritza specified.

The boy didn't seem at all interested in who Miguel was. "It's *mine*," he insisted with a growl. "It's got my name on it, see?" he said, fingers curling in demand.

Yadriel turned the medal over to find that a name had indeed been engraved on the back. He blinked. "Oh." The delicate cursive letters read JULIAN DIAZ. Yadriel's eyes went wide, snapping back to the boy's face. "*Oh*."

Julian Diaz. He knew Julian Diaz, or rather knew *of* him. They went to high school together. It was a large school, with more than twenty-five hundred students, but Julian had a bit of a reputation. He ditched a lot, but when he was roaming the halls it was hard to not notice him. He had the sort of presence that demanded everyone's attention without needing to ask. Julian was loud, rarely took things seriously, and was known for getting into trouble. He was hard to miss, attractive in a severe sort of way with that diamond-shaped face. He had a narrow, stubborn chin and a sharp voice that always seemed to cut through every other one in the quad.

"What do you mean by 'summon'?" Julian asked again. He was staring at his transparent palms, turning them over as if trying to solve a puzzle.

"Do you happen to know how you got here?" Yadriel tried in an attempt at being tactful.

Julian glared. "No!" he snapped. "All I remember was walking down the street with my friends..." He looked around, as if trying to find them in the cold church. "Then something—someone—" He frowned.

"Happened? I dunno, I just remember getting knocked over, maybe I got jumped or something." Julian rubbed absently at the same point on his chest. "Then the next thing I knew, I was in this *church* with you two."

Three beats passed before Julian's eyes suddenly went wide. "I died, didn't I?" The fierceness was gone, leaving his voice small and weak. "Am I dead?"

Yadriel winced and gave a small nod. "Yeah . . ."

Julian stumbled back a step, his body wavering in and out of existence for a moment, like a camera trying to focus. "Oh, Jesus." He pressed both hands against his face. "My brother is gonna *kill me,*" he groaned against his palms.

"Looks like someone already beat him to it," Maritza said, reaching out to poke her finger right through Julian's elbow.

"Quit it!" he snapped, wrenching his arm away. Julian turned his scowl to Yadriel again. "So, what, I'm a ghost now?"

Yadriel didn't know what to make of him. Julian didn't sound angry or dismayed. If anything, he was annoyed, as if this were just an inconvenience.

"Spirit," Yadriel corrected.

"What's the difference?" Julian asked, flapping his hand at Maritza as she hovered like a fly.

"Well, I don't know if there's a *difference,*" Yadriel ventured, fidgeting with the necklace in his hands. "I think maybe 'ghost' is sort of . . . derogatory?"

Julian stared at him, his mouth in a hard line, an eyebrow raised.

"We use the word 'spirit,'" Yadriel supplied.

"Who's 'we'?"

"Oh, right. That's Maritza—" he said, pointing at her.

Maritza wiggled her fingers in a wave.

Julian took another step away from her.

"And I'm Yadriel. And, uh . . ." Yadriel dug around in his brain for the right words. He'd never had to explain who brujx were and what they did, on account of it being a huge, sacred secret they devoted their lives to keeping.

Whoops.

"We're brujx—brujos can see spirits, and uh, help them cross over to the afterlife," Yadriel explained.

"And brujas can heal people," Maritza added.

"So, you're witches," Julian said with a dubious look.

Yadriel shook his head. "No."

"'Cause you're dressed like a witch."

Maritza snorted.

Yadriel looked down at himself. He was wearing black jeans, his favorite combat boots, and an oversize black hoodie. The burning bowl of fire in front of him and discs in his ears probably weren't helping. His cheeks burned red.

"We're brujx," he corrected.

Julian frowned. "That literally means witch—"

"No, 'witch' is—"

"Derogatory?" Julian guessed, an amused smirk tugging the corner of his mouth.

Now it was Yadriel's turn to scowl.

Julian looked over at Maritza. "So, you can heal people?"

"Oh, no, I don't heal," she replied casually. "You gotta use animal blood, and I'm vegan."

"Right." He turned back to Yadriel. "And you can apparently summon ghosts and send them to the afterlife, whatever that means."

"Yes—Well, no—" Yadriel fumbled, trying to explain himself. "I haven't done the releasing part *yet*—"

"Wooow," Julian crooned, head bobbing in a nod as he looked between the two of them. "You guys are really shitty witches."

Annoyance flared in Yadriel. "Look, this is my first time, okay?"

Julian blinked slowly at him, unimpressed.

"Spirits, like you, sometimes get stuck between the land of the living and the land of the dead," he tried to explain.

Julian rolled his eyes. "Uh-huh."

"Spirits get attached to a tether"—Yadriel held up the necklace—"which anchors them to the land of the living, so, to help you cross over to the other side, I just need to destroy the—"

"No, no way!" Julian shook his head and waved his arms. "My pops gave me that necklace!" He tried to snatch it from Yadriel, but, again, he was left with a fistful of empty air.

Maritza chuckled.

"No—just *listen*." Yadriel brought out his portaje.

Julian scoffed, which was not how Yadriel thought any sane person should react to getting a knife pulled on them.

"What are you going to do, *stab me*?" Julian's laugh was sharp as he tapped a finger to his temple. "Already dead, remember?"

"No, I'm not gonna *stab* you!" Though, to be honest, it was more tempting by the minute. "I use it to destroy the tie keeping you here—"

Julian opened his mouth to argue, but Yadriel pressed on.

"I'm not going to destroy the necklace! It'll sever the tie anchoring you *to* the necklace, and you can go to the afterlife and be at peace, okay?" he snapped.

"Yeah, nah." Julian squared his shoulders. "I'm not cool with that."

Yadriel groaned. Of course the first spirit he summoned wouldn't just be released willingly. No, he had to get stuck with one who had an attitude problem.

"Ghosts need to take care of unfinished business before they cross over, right? Well, I've got unfinished business," Julian said, brow furrowed. "I wanna check on my friends. They were with me when I died. I wanna make sure they're okay."

His face twisted between annoyance and something that could've been worry. "And maybe they know who got me," he added as an afterthought.

"I really need to do this, and, like, now," Yadriel said. He didn't feel good about it, but he didn't have much of a choice, either. "We still need to find Miguel, and, besides, if you stay here like this for too long, you'll turn all dark and violent and start hurting people."

He thought that was a perfectly reasonable explanation, but Julian crossed his arms over his chest. "Nope."

Yadriel looked to Maritza for help, but she just shrugged her shoulders.

"Look, I didn't want it to come to this," Yadriel told Julian. Drawing himself up, he gripped his dagger in his hand. "We don't like releasing spirits by force—"

A thick eyebrow quirked. "I thought you said you've never done this before?"

"But you're leaving me no choice." Yadriel held the necklace higher in the air.

Julian remained where he stood, defiant and unmoving, but his wide eyes cut back and forth between his necklace and Yadriel's face.

"¡Muéstrame el enlace!" Yadriel called out. His portaje glowed bright, filling the church with a warm blaze that made all three of them squint. A golden thread sparked to life in the air, starting from the pendant of St. Jude and ending at the center of Julian's chest. He tried to sidestep it, but the line followed.

Yadriel inhaled a deep breath, ready to say the sacred words. "¡Te libero a la otra vida!"

Julian squeezed his eyes shut, bracing for impact.

Yadriel sliced his portaje through the air, aiming directly for the golden thread. But, instead of severing it, the edge of his blade caught on the line. The dagger vibrated in his hand, and small sparks flew from where they met. The thread didn't even so much as bend.

Out of the corner of his eye, Yadriel saw Julian's posture relax. He could sense the obnoxious smirk on his face.

But he wasn't giving up. Yadriel raised his arm and tried slicing through it again. The force of its sudden stop jolted up his arm, into his shoulder. He tried sawing at it, but all it did was send more sparks flying.

The light of his portaje dimmed until it was back to gray steel. Disappointment dropped heavily into Yadriel's stomach. "Shit."

"Man, you really suck at this," Julian said, looking entirely pleased with himself.

Yadriel turned to Maritza. His heart hammered in his ears, and his throat felt like it was closing up on him.

The sudden aching in his chest threatened to swallow him whole.

"¡Mira!" Maritza was immediately at his side, her voice calm and soothing as she gripped his arms. "Don't worry about it, this isn't your fault!" She jerked her head in Julian's direction. "He's probably too bull-headed to force to cross over—"

"Hey!"

Maritza ignored Julian. "Just like Tito, remember?"

"Maybe," Yadriel mumbled, shame hot on his cheeks. Maybe that was the explanation, but what if it wasn't?

"Look," Julian called, taking a step forward. "I'm willing to look past this and cut you a deal."

Yadriel and Maritza turned to him.

He looked much more relaxed now, his attention glued to the golden thread attached to his chest. "If you help me find my friends and make sure they're okay, I will *willingly* let you do your witchy thing and send me on my way to the afterlife or whatever." He plucked curiously at the thread. It was already fading away.

Julian glanced up at Yadriel and splayed his palms out at his sides. "Deal?"

Yadriel looked at Maritza. He was already in way over his head, and something told him this wasn't going to be as easy as Julian made it sound.

"I don't think we've got much of a choice," Maritza told him.

It was either help Julian and do this on his own, or go to his dad and tell him what happened. Yadriel would get into a boatload of trouble for sneaking around, defying the ways of the brujx, and disrespecting their ancient ways.

And, worse, there was no way they'd agree to let Yadriel be part of the aquelarre.

"Fine," Yadriel agreed begrudgingly.

A satisfied grin pressed dimples into Julian's cheeks.

"But you have to do what I say," Yadriel said, shaking his portaje at Julian before stuffing it into his backpack.

"You got it, patrón."

"I'll come back for you in the morning—" Yadriel started, moving to place the medal on the altar with Lady Death.

"Wait, *what?*" Julian's eyes went wide. "You can't just ditch me here!"

"I can't take you home, someone will see you!" Yadriel told him.

"I'm not letting you abandon me in a haunted church—"

"It's not haunted!"

"If I'm in here, and I'm a ghost, then it's haunted!" Julian shot back.

Yadriel growled. "That's not—"

"And it's creepy!" Julian thrust his hands toward Lady Death.

"She's not creepy!" Yadriel argued, feeling defensive. "Maritza, help me out here—"

He turned to her, but Maritza stood off to the side, an amused look on her face. "He's got a point. You *did* raise him from the dead, so he's kinda your responsibility now."

When Yadriel spluttered indignantly, she continued. "I mean, it's probably safer if you can keep an eye on him, don't you think?" she suggested in a tone that was supposed to be nonchalant. But Yadriel knew better.

Yadriel glared at her, his cheeks burning. He squeezed the necklace in his hand, trying to come up with a better reason to leave Julian in the old church than not wanting to hide a hot boy in his room.

A hot *dead* boy.

Yadriel groaned. He couldn't believe he was going to agree to this. "You have to hide from my family, okay?"

Julian's face lit with triumph.

Yadriel fastened the necklace around his neck. In order to take Julian with him, he needed to take his tether along, too. "They can't know I'm sneaking around helping out a spirit." It would be tricky, but as long as he didn't linger around the other brujx long enough for them to sense Julian, they could maybe get away with it. And he didn't much feel like spending quality time with his family anyway.

"Got it." Julian sounded sure enough, but his eyes snagged on his St. Jude medal around Yadriel's neck, a deep crease between his brows. "Wait—" He gave a small shake of his head. "How do I hide from them if they can see ghosts?"

Yadriel blinked. "Uh . . ." He looked to Maritza for an answer.

She threw her arms up in the air. "Don't look at me! I'm just a shitty witch who can't heal nobody, remember?" Maritza turned down the aisle and waltzed toward the door.

Yadriel pressed the heels of his palms against his eyes. Typical.

A cold chill suddenly ran up Yadriel's right side, making him shiver. He opened his eyes to find Julian right next to him. If the spirit were alive, their shoulders would've been touching. Julian was taller than him, enough to have to angle his chin down when they were standing so close. He had a very serious look on his face.

Yadriel took a step back, pushing down the fluttering in his stomach. "What?"

"Can ghosts eat?" Julian pressed his hand to his stomach. "'Cause I'm, like, staaarving, man."

"Oh my God." Yadriel slung his backpack over his shoulder and stomped after Maritza.

"Hey, I'm seriouuus!" Julian whined.

Julian went on ahead, and Yadriel moved to close the door behind them, but something made him hesitate.

He still had a strange feeling in his gut. A nagging sensation, like he'd forgotten something. The ground below his feet still felt charged. He stared down the aisle to where Lady Death was little more than a black smudge in the dark church once again. Yadriel stood there, listening and searching the shadows, but all he could hear was Julian complaining about wanting a cheeseburger while Maritza pretended to gag.

Yadriel waited a moment longer, but when nothing happened, he closed the door behind himself and jogged through the tombstones back to Julian and Maritza.

FOUR

W here the hell are we?" Julian turned in slow circles, taking in their surroundings as Yadriel and Maritza led the way back to the main church and Yadriel's house.

"Cemetery," Yadriel and Maritza said in unison.

Julian rolled his eyes. "I know, but *where*?"

"East LA," Yadriel supplied.

He watched Julian, whose hands were tucked into the pockets of his bomber jacket as he casually strolled between the headstones. The taller boy's eyes roved, drinking everything in. If it weren't for the fact that he was a spirit, Julian would've tripped over three different grave markers by now. But, instead, he walked right through them with no problem.

"Really?" Julian's head canted to the side, sparing Yadriel a confused squint. "I ain't never seen this place before, and I know the streets of LA like the back of my head," he explained.

"Back of your *hand*," Maritza corrected.

Julian waved her off. "Whatever."

"It's secret," Yadriel supplied, feeling a bit dumbstruck as he trailed behind the other two.

"Right, right, right," Julian nodded, his head bobbing over and over. "The secret society of *witches*."

Yadriel felt like he was in the middle of a very weird dream. How could they be so calm? Julian had barely batted an eye upon finding out he was dead. Maritza effortlessly weaved between sarcophagi and urns as she stared at her phone, her long lavender fingernails typing away.

Yadriel couldn't understand it—this was a huge, ginormous big deal! He'd summoned a *spirit,* and now they had to placate Julian before he'd let Yadriel release him to the afterlife. Día de Muertos was only a few days away. Yadriel was on a deadline. How was he supposed to help the brujos find Miguel if he was babysitting Julian Diaz?

If he wanted to prove himself in time to be presented at the aquelarre, they needed to get down to solving this mystery, and fast.

"What's the last thing you remember?" Yadriel asked, quickening his pace to catch up to Julian. "Before you, you know"—he gestured vaguely—"died?"

Julian didn't seem affected by his lack of tact.

His shoulder lifted in a shrug. "I was just with my friends, walkin' through Belvedere Park—"

"When?"

"Tuesday night."

"Well, it's still Tuesday." Yadriel checked his phone. It was past midnight. "Or Wednesday morning, technically."

Julian frowned. "How did my necklace make it to your spooky old church if the last place I remember being was Belvedere Park?" he asked, as if it was somehow Yadriel's fault.

"How am I supposed to know?" It was a fair question, but one he didn't have an answer to. "Maybe you were here and just don't remember."

Julian hummed, unconvinced. "I'd remember this place." He shook his head and continued on. "Besides, I'm pretty sure someone jumped me. It was, like, right after sunset, and we were taking a shortcut to King Taco—"

Maritza glanced up long enough from her phone to offer, "That place is the *best.*"

A grin split Julian's face, white teeth flashing. "Right?" He pressed his palm to his flat stomach. "Their chicken sopes are—"

"Then what happened?" Yadriel cut in, continuously glancing around for anyone else in the cemetery.

Raised voices alerted him that someone was up ahead. Julian opened his mouth but Yadriel cut him off.

"Shh, wait!"

Yadriel steered them clear of the pair—a brujo arguing with the spirit of a feisty old woman.

"You couldn't even get the flores I asked for?" the woman demanded, gesturing to a bouquet of what Yadriel thought were very pretty roses in a vase at the foot of an ornate angel statue. "I hate roses!"

"Ay, Mamá! It was the best I could do!" the brujo exclaimed. "I can't fight with you about this right now—Miguel is missing; people could be in danger—"

"Oh, so they're more important than your own *mamá*?" the woman demanded, her chest puffing up indignantly.

Yadriel heard the man groan as they crept out of earshot.

The closer they got to Yadriel's house, the more on edge he felt. He kept an eye out for flashlight beams announcing the presence of people still looking for Miguel, but there were fewer than earlier. That probably meant they were starting to concentrate their efforts outside of the cemetery.

Yadriel should've been with them.

"Okay." He gestured for Julian to continue his story. "Go ahead."

"Like I was *saying*—we took the walkway over the freeway," Julian went right back to explaining. "Luca ran up ahead because he likes taking the ramp down real quick—" Julian stopped in his tracks, black eyes going wide. *"Fuck."*

Maritza started and Yadriel ducked, thinking he'd spotted someone. "What— What's—?"

"What happened to my skateboard?" Julian threw his head back and groaned, scrubbing his hands over his face. "I just put new axles on that thing!"

Yadriel arched an eyebrow at Maritza, who returned it with an amused look.

Julian spun to him, his eyebrows pinched. "We gotta find it!"

Yadriel blinked back at him.

Was this guy serious?

"I really don't think you're gonna need it now," Maritza pointed out, but he plowed on.

"Man, if that guy took it!" Julian's mouth pressed into a surly line, the muscles in his sharp jaw jumping. "I swear, I'll—"

"What guy?" Yadriel interrupted before Julian went off on another tangent.

"The guy who jumped Luca!" Julian fumed. He started talking a mile a minute, gesturing wildly as he walked backward. "Luca yelled, and when we caught up, there was some dude that had him backed up against a wall. Probably tryna mug him or something, which is dumb 'cause he's never got any money." He snorted. "So, I just ran up on him from behind and shoved him. I thought I knocked him over, but he turned and before I could take off . . ." Julian walked right into a stone sarcophagus up to his waist without noticing. He stopped, suddenly deflated. His shoulders slumped and his eyebrows tipped. For a moment, he looked watery, his edges smudged. "Everything went black." He rubbed absently at his chest. "Next thing I knew, I was with you two."

Yadriel felt sorry for him. He didn't know what to say to someone who'd just found out they were dead. Trial and error had shown he was no good at soothing people or bringing them comfort. It had never been his forte. He wasn't his mom.

He looked to Maritza for backup. She pressed her lips between her teeth and gave a small lift of her shoulder.

"It's not a lot to go on," Yadriel admitted. Where would they even start?

Julian was ready to supply an answer. "We need to go find my friends," he insisted, eyes locked onto Yadriel with a fierceness that made him shift back. "I gotta make sure they're okay. If something happened to them and it's my fault—" Julian cut himself off, his face lighting up. "I can text them!" He looked down, patting his pockets.

A strangled shout caught in his throat as he noticed where he was standing. He scrambled back, frantically swatting at his clothes.

"What do you think, Yads?" Maritza asked, watching Julian freak out with an amused expression.

"Really? You couldn't tell me I was standing in a coffin!" Julian barked, chest heaving.

"*Sssh!*" Yadriel hissed.

"Probably got dead-people dust all over me now—"

"You're going to get us caught," Yadriel warned.

Julian shook out his arms, scowling. He hissed a *tch* through his teeth before grumbling. "Messed up, man . . ." He plunged his hands into his pockets. "Where's my phone?"

"Probably with your body," Yadriel told him, not really knowing how to put it delicately, but Julian seemed more annoyed than distraught at the mention of his corpse.

"We can try finding them at school tomorrow," Yadriel added, answering Maritza's question.

"Tomorrow?" Julian shook his head. "No way, we gotta go find them tonight—"

"We can't go tonight," Yadriel told him.

Julian began to object. "But—"

"It's already well past midnight," Yadriel said. "And if my dad finds out I'm running through the streets this late with a spirit I summoned against the rules?" He shook his head. "I'm gonna get grounded—"

"Grounded?" Julian repeated, face screwed up as if he'd never heard of it before.

"They won't let me participate in the aquelarre—"

"I have no idea what that even means—"

"And then we won't be able to do *any* looking tomorrow," Yadriel insisted. He could see his house now. All they had to do was get Julian inside unnoticed. "Not to mention, it's a school night, and I gotta be up in a few hours—"

"*School?*" Julian looked downright offended. "Are you seriously worried about *school* right now?"

Julian let out an indignant groan but somehow refrained from arguing further. Instead, he stuffed his hands into the pockets of his bomber jacket and scowled at Yadriel from under his furrowed brow. "I don't get a ghost version of my phone or nothing?" he murmured to himself.

"Maritza? Yadriel?"

Yadriel jumped and spun to find Diego and Andrés walking toward them. They each held a flashlight in one hand and their curved daggers in the other.

"What are you doing out here?" Diego asked, frowning at Yadriel and Maritza. He spared Julian only a quick glance. Spirits in the cemetery were nothing special. If Yadriel could play it off, maybe they wouldn't get suspicious.

"Uh," he said, staring blankly at his brother.

"We were trying to help look for Miguel," Maritza supplied easily. When she and Yadriel got caught doing something they weren't supposed to, she was the one who could talk their way out of it. "Enlisted one of the spirits to help us check out the old church," she said, nodding her head in Julian's direction.

Diego looked at him properly this time.

Julian didn't respond for a moment. His attention flickered to Diego's and Andrés's portajes before he eyed the brujos, an unimpressed look on his face. Finally, he jerked his chin up in that nod guys always did to greet each other.

There was a long pause where Yadriel was sure his brother could see the guilt written across his face, or at least hear his treacherous heart pounding in his chest.

But then Diego nodded. "Cool, I'll let my dad know you guys checked it out for us." His attention swung back to Yadriel. "You need to get home before Lita gets pissed."

Yadriel just nodded, heat flooding his cheeks.

With that, Diego and Andrés turned and took off.

Yadriel let out a heavy breath.

"Who are those fools?" Julian asked, crinkling his nose.

"My brother and his friend," Yadriel said, wiping the back of his hand across his forehead. "At least he and my dad aren't home, all we have to do is get you past Lita." Yadriel turned to Maritza. "You should probably head home."

Maritza laughed, sending her pink-and-purple curls bouncing. "Oh, hell no!" she said, propping her fist on her hip. "I wanna see how this plays out!"

"Won't your mom get pissed?" Yadriel asked, annoyed and trying to not be offended that his crisis was a source of amusement for her.

"I already texted her—said you needed some moral support after getting into a fight with your pops."

Yadriel frowned. "Oh, thanks."

"No problem," she said, smiling at his sarcasm. "Besides, you suck at this sneaking-and-lying thing. If anyone is going to get Casper into your room without getting caught—"

"I'm standing right here!" Julian chimed in.

"—it's me."

"How *are* we supposed to get him inside without Lita seeing?" Yadriel asked, anxiety lighting his already frayed nerves on fire.

Maritza wiggled her fingers. "Sneakily." When Yadriel glared at her, she dropped her hands to her sides. "It's late, your Lita is probably passed out in front of the TV watching Telemundo," Maritza pointed out.

Julian, apparently having gotten bored with the conversation, had wandered over to a headstone and was trying to pick up a marigold laid across it with no success.

Maritza had a point, but there were still other factors to consider. "Okay, yeah, they're out looking for Miguel right *now,* but eventually they're going to come home, and *then* what are we going to do?"

"Whoa, one step at a time, Yads!" Maritza told him. "Let's just get him upstairs first. We'll deal with tomorrow, tomorrow."

Julian wandered back, looking equally doubtful. "So I'm staying with her?" he asked, hooking his thumb toward Yadriel.

"Him," Yadriel and Maritza corrected in unison.

Julian's brow furrowed. "Him?" He blinked at Yadriel, as if clearing his vision.

Yadriel's skin grew hot under the scrutiny. He stood straighter, taller. His sweaty palms clenched into fists at his sides. The muscles in his body went taut as he lifted his chin in what he hoped was a look of stubborn determination.

Maritza crossed her arms over her chest, eyebrow arching. "Is that gonna be a problem?"

When Julian didn't respond fast enough, Maritza snapped her fingers.

Julian's attention swung back to her. "No," he said, face screwed up in a way that suggested both confusion and offense.

"Perfect." Maritza turned to Yadriel with a cheery smile. "Let's go!" she said before heading for the house.

Yadriel scrubbed his hands over his face. How had he gotten himself into such a huge mess in such a short amount of time? Exhaustion plowed into him like a truck.

Next to him, Julian cleared his throat. "So, uh . . ." Julian rocked back and forth on the balls of his feet, glancing around. "Where's your house?"

Yadriel sighed and followed Maritza down the path flanked by squat mausoleums. "There," he said, nodding to the church looming in the distance. "We live in the little house next to the church." Smoke still billowed from the crooked chimney.

"Yo, you live in a *graveyard*?" Julian asked in bewilderment.

Yadriel shifted the weight of his backpack. He was used to the strange looks and laughs that came when people at school found out he was the weird kid who lived in a cemetery. Throw in being openly trans, and he was *very* used to stares and jokes. "Yeah," he said, anticipating a similar reaction.

Instead, a wicked grin curled Julian's lips. "Sick," he said, nodding his approval.

A surprised laugh jumped in Yadriel's chest. He gave Julian a curious look, studying his profile as he stared ahead at the church. He had a heavy brow and a sloping nose that ran in a straight line from his forehead. Classically handsome. He looked just like the stone statues that adorned the alcoves of the church. An Aztec warrior reincarnated.

When Julian caught him watching, Yadriel quickly looked away.

"Oh!" Julian said, as if suddenly remembering something. "You've got food, right?" he asked. "'Cause I wasn't joking about being hungry."

Yadriel huffed an irritated sigh. "Gotta get you past my abuelita first." He gestured for Julian to follow. "But she's been cooking all day."

"*Homemade* food by your grandma?" Julian burst out, unable to contain himself.

"*Sssh!*"

"Oh—" He dropped his voice. "Sorry."

He moved closer to Yadriel. A chill tickled the back of his neck.

"Wait, can ghosts eat food?" Julian asked in his ear, very concerned.

Santa Muerte, help me.

FIVE

Yadriel crept up the steps, Maritza and Julian following close behind. Blue light flickered against the lace drapes of the front window.

At least Yadriel knew his dad was still out, which was a relief, and not just because Yadriel was about to sneak a spirit into the house right under his nose. After their blowup earlier, Yadriel still wasn't ready to face him. His stomach twisted thinking about his dad's inevitable attempt at an awkward apology.

Julian was actually a welcome distraction, and an excuse to avoid his family altogether.

Said dead boy was currently wandering the front porch and getting way too close to the windows, apparently without a care in the world. Julian reached for the wind chime hanging from the awning, his fingers going right through the pieces of polished glass.

"Hey! Get over here!" Yadriel hissed, waving him back.

On her tiptoes, Maritza was able to see through the small window cut into the top of the front door. "She's sleeping," she said with a smug look. "Told you."

Slowly, Yadriel pushed the front door open, and it let out a low creak. He waited for a moment, but when he heard deep, rattling snores, he knew they were in the clear. Yadriel slid through the door, closely followed by Maritza, and Julian trailed behind.

Lita sat in her armchair in front of the TV, head leaned back and mouth wide open. Yadriel closed the door behind them as quietly as possible.

Meanwhile, Julian just strolled right inside. "Whoa, when's the party?" he chuckled, looking around at all the stacks of decorations.

A sharp snore from Lita made Yadriel and Maritza jump. Yadriel froze, heart pounding in his chest, but she only stirred a little before falling back into the sawing rhythm. A telenovela played on the TV.

"Santa Muerte," Maritza whispered, pressing her palm to her forehead.

"Julian, shut up!" Yadriel glared at him, cutting his hand through the air.

He ducked, holding his hands up in concession.

Yadriel led the way to the kitchen, motioning for the other two to follow.

The small kitchen was still warm with the smell of cinnamon, sweet bread, and pozole. A huge Crock-Pot simmered near the sink. Trays of pan de muerto and colorful concha took up all the counter space. A large clay pot sat on the stove from an earlier batch of café de olla.

Julian's eyes went wide and he sucked in a breath, but before he could make another outburst, Yadriel shot him a glare, holding his finger up to his lips. Julian nodded, his eyes roving over all the treats.

"Seriously, what's all of this for?" he asked in a whisper. Or in what was apparently a whisper by Julian standards, which wasn't much of a whisper at all.

"Día de Muertos," Yadriel said as he started to load up on food. "It's kind of a big deal for us."

"Oooh, right, right, right," he nodded.

Maritza crept to the stove and peeked under the Crock-Pot lid. "Is any of this vegan-friendly?" she asked, giving the pozole a sniff.

"I think it's all got chicken in it."

Maritza wrinkled her nose. "I'll keep a lookout," she said, returning to the living room.

Julian hovered over the pan de muerto, practically drooling over the round sweet bread. Each bun was adorned with bone-shaped details. Some were covered in cinnamon sugar, while others were dusted with pink sprinkles. Yadriel figured it was the only food Julian could actually eat. He left the pozole alone. He doubted trying to feed a spirit soup would go well.

"Does your family celebrate?" Yadriel asked as he picked out some pan. They were still warm. His stomach growled.

"Nah, not really religious," Julian said with a shrug, wandering over to some bound stalks of sugarcane in the corner.

Yadriel took a detour to the fridge and put some ice cubes in an empty glass. The cut on his tongue was puffy and starting to throb.

With an armful of food, he led the way back to the living room. He poked Maritza's side to get her attention and nodded toward the stairs. He motioned for Julian to follow her. "That way," Yadriel told him. "My room is the last door on the left—"

The creaking of Lita's armchair made Yadriel stop short, but this time, she didn't settle back into sleep. She let out a tired groan and sat up in her chair.

Maritza stared at him, wide-eyed, and Yadriel frantically shooed the two of them toward the stairs. In a panic, Yadriel moved to shove Julian, but his arm sunk right through the spirit's back.

It was like being plunged into cold water, ripping a gasp from his lungs as one of the conchas fell to the floor.

"¿Quique?" Lita called, the nickname she used for Yadriel's dad. Her voice was thick with sleep.

"It's just me, Lita!" Yadriel called back, breathless as ice pulsed through his veins.

Lita yawned and pushed herself up out of her chair.

He flapped his hand frantically at Julian, who raced up the flight of stairs. Maritza took off after him.

Lita limped over to where Yadriel stood, conchas balanced in one arm. Maritza and Julian froze, trying not to draw her attention.

Lita frowned at Yadriel. "I was worried."

He did his best not to look guilty, urging his heart to stop beating so fast. "Sorry." He bent to scoop the fallen concha off the floor. "I just needed to . . ." He trailed off, waving the bread in the air, not knowing how to finish.

Lita nodded, bracing her hands on her hips. "I know, I know," she told him.

He seriously doubted that.

Lita opened her mouth to say something, but then stopped short and shivered.

Yadriel's heart leaped.

Brow furrowed, Lita rubbed at her arm.

Yadriel held his breath and forced himself to not look at Maritza and Julian on the stairs. If Lita saw Julian in the house, sneaking up the stairs with Maritza, he was screwed.

In a flash of movement, Julian raced up the final steps.

Yadriel sucked in a sharp breath.

Lita turned her head a split second after Julian ducked around the corner.

Leaving Maritza crouched awkwardly on the stairs.

"Maritza?" Lita asked, squinting up at her through the dark.

She jumped to her feet and smiled. "¡Hola, Lita!" she said with a cheerful wave.

Yadriel exhaled.

Lita gave Maritza a stern look. "Ah, ah! Es muy tarde," Lita said, disapprovingly wagging her finger between her and Yadriel. "You have school in the morning. Time to go home!"

Maritza's bottom lip jutted out, and she glanced up the stairs, but Yadriel shot her a pointed look. They'd nearly gotten caught already. He wasn't about to push their luck.

"But—" she started to whine.

Lita cut her off. "Come," she said, motioning for Maritza to come down. "We'll call tu papá and have him pick you up."

Maritza stomped back down the stairs.

"I'll see you in the morning," Yadriel reassured her as she headed for the front door.

"You better text me," Maritza threatened.

Yadriel wanted to tell her if she didn't want to miss out so badly, she should've taken Julian home herself, but it was a bit late for that.

Lita looked at the contraband in his arm and smiled. "Ah! Finally eating!" She chuckled. "Bueno, bueno." Lita arched her back in a stretch. "You eat and go right to bed. You need rest," she told him.

Yadriel forced a small laugh. Being sleep-deprived at school tomorrow was the least of his worries. "Sí, Lita."

"I need you to look in the rafters for la garra del jaguar mañana," she went on with a huff.

"Yes, Lita."

"Don't know where they went—"

When Yadriel turned to go up the stairs, she called after him.

"Ah, ah!" Lita tapped her cheek. "Un besito, por favor."

Yadriel bit back a groan and planted a quick kiss on her soft, warm cheek.

Maritza smirked from the front door, and he could've sworn he heard a muffled chuckle from upstairs.

"Buenas noches, mi amor." Lita smiled. "¡Pa' fuera!" she said to Maritza, ushering her out.

As soon as the door closed behind them, Yadriel tore up the stairs. At the top, he looked down the hall toward his room, but there was no sign of Julian. He frowned. "Julian?" he whispered, moving down the hall.

"What?"

Yadriel spun around.

Julian stood at the opposite end of the hallway. He pointed at a slatted door. "This is a closet," he said, giving Yadriel a critical look.

"I said *left*, not right." Yadriel jerked his head, and Julian followed him into his bedroom.

Once they were both inside, he closed the door, wishing it had a lock.

Julian stood in the middle of his room, looking around. It occurred to Yadriel how messy it was, with clothes tossed here and there, drawers half-closed, and the bed a tangled mass of blue sheets.

He felt embarrassed and awkward, not knowing what to do with himself or the spirit in his room.

Julian didn't seem bothered, or even to notice. All of his attention was locked on the food Yadriel was holding. "Can I eat?" he asked, dark eyes glancing up.

"Uh, yeah." Quickly, Yadriel pushed a heap of clean clothes off the old office chair. "Here." He cleared a spot on the desk, moving textbooks, an incense burner, and his bus pass out of the way so he could set down the pan. "Have at it," he said, dusting the bits of sugar off his sleeves before plucking an ice cube and popping it into his mouth. The cold provided instant relief as he pressed his tongue against it.

Julian didn't need to be told twice. He threw himself into the chair and rubbed his palms together, a smile lighting up his face. But his hands hovered over the buns. "Wait, how am I supposed to eat this if I can't touch stuff?"

"It's pan de muerto," Yadriel told him around the ice cube, but all Julian replied with was a frown. "It means—"

"I know what it means," Julian interrupted with a roll of his eyes. "I *can* speak Spanish; I just choose *not* to."

That was a weird thing to say.

Yadriel wanted to ask what he meant by that, but the irritable look Julian shot him said not to. "We make this food *for* spirits," Yadriel explained, biting back his curiosity. "I mean, we can eat it, too, obviously, but we use it for ofrendas to welcome spirits back for Día de Muertos." He shrugged. "It's spirit food."

Julian didn't need to be told twice.

He snatched up a bun and took a huge bite. Yadriel found himself grinning as Julian threw his head back, letting out a triumphant laugh.

"Oh, man." Julian hummed appreciatively, shoving two more bites into his mouth. His knees bounced under the desk, and he swallowed with effort before stuffing more into his mouth. "*So* good," Julian mumbled, eyes rolling in ecstasy. In a matter of moments, he had chomped down three pieces of pan.

Yadriel's mom always used to say Lita's pan de muerto was so good it'd wake a dead man just so he could get a taste. Apparently she was right. Maybe he should've grabbed more.

Cold water slid down Yadriel's throat as the ice cube he sucked on melted. He did his best to appear aloof, but that turned into him rocking on the balls of his feet and watching Julian. Yadriel shook his head at himself. Staring at Julian while he ate was weird. He couldn't remember how to act normal.

Sitting down seemed like a nonchalant thing to do, so Yadriel plopped himself onto the edge of his bed.

A chirruped mewl made him jump, his heart lurching into his throat. Julian spun in the chair. The mass of blankets rustled, and Purrcaso crawled out, shaking herself off.

"Jesus, you scared the hell out of me," Yadriel said, gingerly picking up the small cat and placing her in his lap. He teased his fingers down her pointy spine and she purred in appreciation, her forgiveness immediate. Her tiny presence let the tension in his shoulders ebb.

"Holy shit," Julian laughed, the deep kind that came from his belly. "That's one messed-up looking cat!"

"Shut up!" Yadriel snapped, pulling Purrcaso close. "Don't make fun of her." Her enthused purrs reverberated against his chest.

Julian held up his palms in defense. "Hey, hey, hey, didn't mean any disrespect! But, c'mon—" The chuckles started again, and he did a very bad job of holding them back. "She *is* pretty funny looking."

Yadriel glared, but Purrcaso was unfazed. She wiggled out of Yadriel's grasp and clumsily leaped to the floor. With a trilling meow, she hobbled over to Julian.

He sucked the sugar off his fingers. "What's up, little one?" he asked before looking up at Yadriel. "She can see me?"

"Cats are like little spirit guardians," he said with a shrug. "They hang out in the cemetery all the time. My mom said they were good luck. Cats can see spirits and sense them nearby, just like us."

Julian reached down, and when his fingers brushed against her fur, a wide smile split his face. "I can pet her!" He scratched her behind the ears, and Purrcaso's eyes slid shut, leaning into the touch.

Yadriel was surprised at how quickly she took to him. Usually, Purrcaso was uninterested in anyone other than him and his mom, but here she was, drool gathering at the corner of her mouth as Julian scratched her furry chin.

"Never had any pets growing up, but I always liked cats," Julian told him.

A thought occurred to Yadriel. "What about your family?"

Julian's shoulders tensed. He didn't look up. "What about 'em?"

"Don't you want me to talk to them, too?" Yadriel asked. As uncomfortable as that sounded, it was weird that Julian was so worried about his friends but hadn't mentioned his family at all. "You're not worried about your parents?"

"Don't got parents," Julian said, his words curt. Gruff. Purrcaso batted at the unraveled end of Julian's shoelace.

Yadriel blinked. "Oh . . ." Growing up in a multigenerational household and being part of a huge Latinx community, the concept of not having any family was both foreign and distressing. "But you mentioned your brother. Isn't he going to be worried?"

Julian let out a sharp, bark-like laugh. "Trust me, me being dead is a *good* thing for him. Probably a weight off his shoulders. Best thing that could've happened." He spat the words out like they were bitter.

Yadriel frowned. That sounded . . . awful. His own family was far from perfect, but would he be better off without them? Or vice versa?

"When can I start moving stuff?" Julian asked, finally looking up. The discussion about family was clearly over.

Purrcaso limped over to one of Yadriel's hoodies on the floor and curled up, settling in for another nap.

"Moving stuff?"

"Yeah, you know—" Julian stood and paced the room. He couldn't sit still, and he couldn't stop himself from trying to touch things. He thumbed a stack of books on the desk and rapped his fingers against the closet door. "Like slamming doors, stacking chairs, stuff like that," he explained, coming to a stop before the altar on Yadriel's dresser.

The altar was three steps tall, covered in an orange, magenta, and royal-blue shawl that had once been his mother's. It was adorned with half-burned candles of different colors and sizes. The bottom step had black-and-white photos of his relatives—his maternal grandparents standing outside their yellow-painted home back in Mexico, his paternal grandfather squinting through his glasses at the new cell phone they had gotten him for his birthday.

Julian bent down to sniff the unlit incense.

Yadriel snorted. "You're really taking this 'ghost' stuff literally."

Julian tilted his chin and grinned in a way he could only describe as preening. "I'm very committed to my new lifestyle."

A surprised laugh bucked in Yadriel's chest.

Who was this guy?

"Practice," Yadriel answered with a shrug. He thought of the large metal shears Tito used to tend to his precious marigolds. "You've got to concentrate and focus."

"Mm," Julian hummed, pressing his lips together. "Not exactly my strong suits."

"I've gathered."

Julian looked up. "What?"

Yadriel cleared his throat. "Lucky for you, the closer it gets to Día de Muertos, the more powerful the dead become," Yadriel said. "It's only a couple days away, so you'll be moving stuff around in no time. *Don't touch that*," he added when Julian reached for his statue of Lady Death.

Julian snatched his hand back. "I know her," he said, pointing. "Santa Muerte, right?" he asked, turning to Yadriel.

Yadriel blinked, surprised. "Uh, yeah." He stood and came to a stop next to Julian.

On the top step stood a small painted statue of Lady Death he'd gotten during a trip to Tepito, Mexico. She was made out of white clay and wore a white huipil with rainbow-colored flowers along the neck. Her skirts were layers of red and white. A gold sash was tied around her waist, her oily-black hair braided over one shoulder and accented with tiny painted marigolds.

"We call her Lady Death; she's our patron," Yadriel explained, affectionately straightening the skeleton dressed in her huipil and skirts. "She's the one who gave us our powers. She looks after us, and we help her maintain the balance of life and death."

"So, she's your patron *and* your patrón." Julian grinned, quite pleased with his own cleverness and ignoring Yadriel's groan entirely. "She's one of our saints, too," he told Yadriel, head bobbing in a nod. "Bunch of folks have little altars for her. Someone's always pouring out mezcal for her at parties. One of my friends got a big tattoo of her across his chest. My brother's got one on his arm." He tapped at his own bicep. "I've always been more partial to St. Jude, myself . . ." Julian's eyes slid to Yadriel's neck, his brow puckering.

St. Jude. Yadriel had nearly forgotten. He pressed his fingers to the medal at his throat—Julian's medal. Yadriel remembered how possessive he'd been of it back in the church. It clearly meant a lot to him.

"Who's that?" Julian suddenly asked, pointing to the picture of Yadriel's mom. It had been taken the Christmas before she died. She was mid-laugh, wearing a red dress with the Christmas tree lights behind her. Delicate earrings made of multicolored hummingbird feathers dangled from her ears. She had a heart-shaped face and brown hair that she'd always worn down in natural waves.

Yadriel took a large step back. "My mom." The words were clipped, making it, hopefully, clear that it wasn't a topic for Julian to play another round of twenty questions.

Julian quickly withdrew his hand and stuffed them both into his pockets. "Oh."

Yadriel steered the conversation back to Julian's original question. "Well, you won't have long to try it out—going all *Paranormal Activity,* I mean. Hopefully we'll get everything sorted out—make sure you're friends are okay, figure out what happened—soon." He crossed his arms and leaned against the desk. "Like, before Friday."

"Halloween?" Julian smirked and nodded his approval. "Awesome. Very on theme."

"Día de Muertos kicks off at midnight, the night of October thirty-first," Yadriel explained. "We clean up the graves in the cemetery to prepare for the spirits to arrive, like cleaning up the house before family comes to visit. Everyone takes special care of their portajes—"

Julian nodded along as if he understood perfectly. "Right, right, right."

"We set up ofrendas for the spirits of the returning brujx. We put out pictures of them, their favorite foods or toys, little mementos, stuff like that. They lead the spirits back to the world of the living, that's why we use candles and bright colors, like the marigolds. And the smell of the food, of course."

Julian rubbed his stomach, as if remembering the taste of the pan de muerto.

"Then at midnight, the bell tolls, officially starting the celebration and signaling the arrival of the spirits. They get to stay until it ends at sunset on November second. It's like a two-day-long party and you get to see everybody."

"Like your mom?" Julian asked, his gaze shifting back over to the picture.

Yadriel's stomach twisted. "Yeah." He was both excited and anxious to see his mom again in just a matter of days. There was a lot he needed to accomplish before then.

Julian studied the altar with an intense expression. "Is it like . . . for anybody?" He didn't look at Yadriel when he spoke.

"How do you mean?" Yadriel asked, not understanding the question. It was hard to keep up with Julian's constantly shifting train of thought.

Julian's hand went to his neck, his fingers searching at the dip of his throat. "Like do normal people come back, too?" A frown pressed deep lines into his forehead. "Non-brujx?"

"Oh—no." Yadriel shifted uneasily. "It's just brujx." Was there someone he wanted to see?

Julian nodded. "When you raised me from the dead—"

"Summoned your spirit, you're not a zombie—"

Julian rolled his eyes. "Right, that. You thought I was someone else. Miguel?"

Yadriel's heart clenched. "Yeah, my cousin," he said.

"How'd he die?" Julian asked.

"We don't know," Yadriel confessed, lifting his shoulders in a shrug.

"Wait," Julian shook his head. "Then how do you know he's even dead?"

"It's a brujx thing. If one of us dies, we can all feel it."

Julian still looked confused. "But you don't know what happened?"

Yadriel shook his head. "Only that it was . . . bad." He remembered the sharp pain he'd felt. How it'd ripped through his chest. Goose bumps skittered down his arms at the thought. Yadriel frowned at himself. He felt helpless and frustrated. He was supposed to be helping the brujx find Miguel. "Hopefully they find him. We *need* to find him," he corrected himself. "He could be anywhere, for all we know. If we're wrong and his spirit *didn't* get tethered, and he managed to cross over to the afterlife, at least his spirit will return during Día de Muertos, so he'll be able to just tell us himself," Yadriel said. "But still, the sooner we find him, the better. It's not good for a spirit to be wandering around alone."

Julian sat up straighter. "Why not?"

"Spirits can go maligno—turn dark and evil—if they stay in the land of the living for too long." The thought of that happening to Miguel made him feel queasy all over again.

"How long?" Julian asked with an edge to his voice.

"It varies," he said, knowing it wasn't very helpful. He'd never seen it happen up close. The brujos kept on top of it, and it wasn't like Yadriel was allowed to perform the releasing ritual, anyway. "Sometimes it happens quick—the spirit loses themselves and they turn violent," he said with a shrug.

Julian had a strange look on his face, and, at first, Yadriel couldn't place it. His jaw was flexed and his body rigid; his mouth in a hard line, nostrils flared as he stared at Yadriel.

Then it hit him—Julian was scared.

"But that won't happen to you!" he said quickly, trying to back-pedal. "I mean, sometimes it takes years and years for that to happen!"

Julian didn't look reassured.

"That's why we've got to find your friends tomorrow," Yadriel rushed. "The sooner we do, the sooner I can release your spirit before anything goes sideways."

Julian's expression was doubtful. "Yeah, well, you be sure to use that knife of yours on me before I go full *Exorcist*," he said gruffly, cocking an eyebrow. "Deal?"

Yadriel exhaled a laugh, but he agreed. "Deal."

Julian's shoulders relaxed a little. For a long moment, he didn't say anything and Yadriel felt like a real asshole for being so insensitive.

Yadriel cleared his throat. "Nothing more we can do tonight, though. Everyone else is out looking for Miguel." Hell, maybe they've even already found him and by morning the mystery would be all cleared up. "I'll get you something to sleep on." Yadriel went to his closet and dug around for his old sleeping bag.

"Why aren't you out looking with them? With the other brujos?" Julian asked. He was back in the chair, knees bouncing.

"Well, they won't let me," Yadriel said, pushing a box of old clothes out of his way.

Julian spun himself in a circle. "Why?"

"Because they don't think I'm a real brujo."

He spun himself faster. "Why?"

Yadriel was glad Julian couldn't see his face. His cheeks burned hot. "Because I'm trans."

Julian planted his feet and came to an abrupt stop, swaying slightly in the chair. "Oh." He paused. Blinked. *"Ohhh."*

Yadriel's hand finally closed around the slick material of his sleeping bag and he yanked it out. He hugged it to his chest and faced Julian, waiting for some kind of judgment. Maybe laughter.

Instead, Julian frowned at Yadriel, his lip curled in an annoyed sort of way. "That sucks, dude."

The words were matter-of-fact. Straight to the point. Holding no pretense.

Yadriel hadn't expected it. He exhaled, shoulders slumping. "It does," he agreed. "It sucks a *lot*." He spent so much time holding his tongue and only having Maritza to vent to, it felt nice to just say it out loud to someone else. "Since they don't think I'm a real boy, they wouldn't give me my own portaje or let me have the brujo's quinces—"

Julian scowled. "The fuck?"

"Right?" Yadriel huffed. "They're so stuck in their ways and *traditions*, they wouldn't even let me try." He undid the sleeping bag and shook it out with a snap. "So, Maritza made me a portaje and I did the binding ceremony *myself*."

Julian grinned approvingly. "Badass."

Yadriel found himself smiling back. He hadn't really had the time to process everything that had happened, what with Miguel dying as soon as he'd completed the ritual. It *was* badass, even if he was going against his dad and the other brujx.

"So I'm gonna help *you* find your friends," Yadriel went on, laying the sleeping bag out on the floor. "And you're gonna help *me* by letting me release you to the afterlife, then they'll *have* to accept that I'm a brujo." He sat down on the edge of the bed and leaned his elbows on his knees. "On the second night of Día de Muertos, we have an aquelarre where the brujx who had their quinces that year are presented. This year, they're going to *have* to let me be part of it," Yadriel said with fierce determination.

Julian's expression was suddenly pinched. "Back up a sec—are you trying to prove to them that you're a brujo, or that you're a boy?"

The bluntness of the question caught Yadriel off guard. It took some of the wind out of his self-satisfied sails. "It's the same thing," he said, prickling with annoyance.

"'Cause, if it's to prove you're a brujo, didn't summoning me already do that?" Julian asked.

Yadriel huffed a laugh. "You just don't get how it works," he said, crossing his arms. "That's not enough."

"Not enough for who, though?" Julian questioned. He wasn't being pushy about it, not on purpose, anyway. He just seemed curious, which only irritated Yadriel further. "Not enough for *them*, or not enough for *you*?"

Yadriel froze. The question stuck in his chest. "It's the same thing," he repeated, but was it? Yadriel shook his head. He was tired, and Julian's incessant questions were just confusing him.

"You just don't get it because you're not one of us," he insisted. "Here." He tossed Julian a pillow from his bed.

Julian easily caught it out of the air. "Hey!" He flashed his teeth in a triumphant smile, giving the pillow a shake. "I caught it!"

Yadriel threw himself onto his bed. "Good job. Now go to sleep. I have to get up for school in"—he checked his phone and groaned—"three hours."

SIX

Yadriel went into the bathroom to change out of his clothes and binder and into an oversize sleep shirt and pajama pants. When he got back to his room, he awkwardly dove under the covers of his bed. He didn't like being seen without his binder on, and that was especially true with Julian.

Luckily, Julian seemed unfazed, or, at the very least, uninterested.

"Do ghosts even sleep?" he asked, lounging comfortably on the floor with his hands tucked behind his head.

"I have no idea," Yadriel said, pulling his blankets up to his chin.

Julian refused to settle down. As Yadriel stared up at his ceiling in the pitch-black room, Julian's sighs and huffs floated from the floor. They were quickly followed up by the most asinine questions Yadriel ever had to endure at three in the morning.

"If you turned into a ghost, where would you wanna haunt?"

"I don't know."

"I'm pretty sure the Jack in the Box on Whittier is haunted."

"Mm."

"One time, we were chillin' in the parking lot, and there was definitely some haunted-ghosts stuff happening in the dumpster."

"Mhmm."

"But it turned out to just be a raccoon."

"Cool."

"It almost bit me."

"Wow."

"Damn, when's the last time you cleaned under your bed?"

And on and on it went. When Yadriel refused to respond, Julian just went on talking to himself. Yadriel didn't know it was possible for someone to have so little filter between their brain and their mouth. When Julian spoke, it was a constant stream of consciousness.

Even in the wee hours of the morning, Yadriel knew sleep wouldn't come easy. His relationship with it was always tenuous at best. The events of the night buzzed through him restlessly.

In the span of a few hours, he'd gotten his own portaje and been blessed by Lady Death with the powers of the brujo. And he was still worried about Miguel. The grief of losing his cousin didn't feel real yet. On top of all that, he'd summoned a spirit and was now harboring a dead boy in his room.

Yadriel didn't manage to fall asleep until he put a pillow over his head with Julian's muffled voice wondering whether ghosts got wet when it rained. A couple of times, rummaging sounds nearly pulled Yadriel back to consciousness, but then he always slipped back under.

When his alarm went off in the morning, Yadriel groaned into his arm. He felt even more exhausted than before he'd fallen asleep. He rolled over, hand blindly reaching to hit snooze on his phone. With effort, he forced his bleary eyes open.

To find a black pair staring back at him.

Yadriel thrashed and scrambled back, hitting the back of his head on the edge of the window. In his panic, he'd accidentally kicked Purrcaso off the foot of the bed. As his alarm continued to blare, Purrcaso cried from the floor.

"*FINALLY!*" Julian burst out, annoyed but smiling as he leaped to his feet. "I've been—dude, stop screaming—I've been waiting for *FOREVER!*"

Yadriel's heartbeat hammered painfully in his chest, unable to comprehend anything Julian was saying. He snatched his phone and killed the alarm. Purrcaso stopped her indignant meowing and sat on the dresser, cleaning her paw. Yadriel squeezed his eyes shut, willing the throbbing in his head to stop.

He strained to listen for any signs from his family, wondering if someone had heard his shout, but there was only the distant bumping of his abuelita's Tejano music from the kitchen.

"Are you even listening to me?" Julian demanded.

"No." Yadriel squinted an eye open to look up at him. In his sleepy daze, it took a moment for Yadriel to remember he was a spirit. Standing there in the middle of his room, arms crossed and frowning, Julian looked very *real* and alive. But then Yadriel blinked, refocusing his vision enough to spot the telltale signs: blurry edges and the cool draft in the air around him.

"I *said*, I've been practicing!" Julian huffed. The amount of energy he had this early in the morning was obscene.

Yadriel sat upright, pushing back the mass of dark hair that had flopped into his eyes. "Practicing?" he croaked.

Julian's scowl was quickly replaced with a sharp smile.

He swung back and forth between his emotions so quickly, Yadriel was bound to get whiplash.

"Look!" Falling into the chair, Julian hunched over the desk and pinched his fingers around a crumpled-up ball of paper. It was one of Yadriel's failed attempts at math homework from the day before.

"Look, look, look!" Face screwed up in concentration, slowly, he lifted the ball of paper. Julian turned to Yadriel, a triumphant grin splitting his face. *"See?"*

Julian's eyes burned with wild energy. Yadriel was starting to think it was less up-all-night delirium and more just, well, Julian.

"Good job," Yadriel grumbled, sitting up and rubbing at his temples, warding off a headache.

The ball of paper dropped back to the desk. Julian scowled. "I worked on that *all night*, man!"

"What? I said, 'good job,'" Yadriel replied, thumbing through the notifications on his phone to make sure he hadn't gotten any important messages. Nothing about Miguel. Worry dug into his headache. Had they really not found him yet?

"*Tch*," Julian hissed between his teeth. He slumped moodily in the chair, propping his shoes up on the mattress. The white rubber of his Converse were dirty and cracked, and there was a large hole torn in the bottom of one.

When Yadriel moved to the edge of his bed and put his feet on the floor, he stepped on something sharp. "*Ouch*—what the—?" Yadriel's eyes bulged when he finally took in the state of his room.

Well, now he was awake.

It looked like a bomb had gone off. Or maybe just a human hurricane named Julian Diaz.

"What the hell happened in here?" Yadriel demanded, picking up the unfolded paper clip stuck to the bottom of his foot. It was just one of maybe two dozen that lay scattered across the carpet.

"Got bored," Julian said simply.

Yadriel shifted through the debris. Had he really been tired enough to sleep through all this? "Right." His room was a little messy, sure, but it was organized chaos. The mess Julian had made was just . . . chaos.

"You got shitty taste in music, by the way," Julian told him, his tone matter-of-fact as he nodded to Yadriel's ancient iPhone that lay on the rumpled sleeping bag. The earbuds were dirty, and they crackled if he turned the volume up too loud. It had been a hand-me-down from his brother, and Yadriel used it to store his music, since there wasn't enough space on his newer phone.

"No I don't!" he said, feeling oddly defensive as he picked it up and stuffed it back into a drawer. His yearbook and old notebooks were on his unmade bed next to a Sharpie and more balls of paper.

Yadriel held up the tattered notebooks and glared at Julian. "Did you go through my stuff?"

Julian blinked. "Uh . . . what?" His ears burned red.

It was the guiltiest face Yadriel had ever seen.

"Don't go through my stuff!"

"I didn't!" Julian spluttered.

"You're a terrible liar," Yadriel growled and stuffed the notebooks back in their place on the shelf.

"It's not like I had anything else to do," Julian groused, kicking his feet up onto the bed.

"Don't put your shoes on my bed!" Yadriel snapped.

"They're *ghost shoes*, they can't get your bed dirty!" Julian pointed out.

If Yadriel could've shoved Julian's legs, he would've. But he had to settle on a death glare instead.

"So, what's the plan, patrón?" Julian asked, unbothered.

Yadriel stood and went to the closet. "The *plan* is for me to go to school," he said, digging around for a clean shirt. "And for you to stay here."

"Wait, wait, wait—*what*?" Julian demanded, waving his hands. "*Are you serious?* Why are you going to school? We need to go find my friends!"

"I'll look for them at school," Yadriel said.

Julian gave him a withering look. "They're not gonna be at school!"

Yadriel ignored him and tried to straighten up the mess. He grabbed his jeans off the floor and gave them a shake. There was some cemetery dust on them, but other than that, they were clean enough.

"Hey, are you listening to me?" Julian stood up. "I will *lose* it if you try to keep me here all day!" He held up a finger. "You wanna be haunted? 'Cause, swear to God, you ditch me here I'll haunt you for the rest of forever!"

"You are being so dramatic right now," Yadriel told him, shaking his head.

Julian groaned and smacked his palm against his forehead. "Look at me! *Begging* to go to *school*!" He collapsed onto the bed, his arm thrown over his face.

"You know," Yadriel said, kicking some shoes into the closet, "if you'd just let me *release* you, we could end this here and now."

Julian snorted.

"I know you want to check on your friends, but we also can't let you turn maligno, okay?" Yadriel warned, peering down at Julian, who pointedly ignored him. Yadriel frowned. "You won't be you anymore, you'll turn into a—a monster."

Julian peeked up at him from under his arm. "Bold of you to assume I'm not one already."

Yadriel stared at him, trying to gauge if he was being serious or not.

Julian met his gaze, unblinking.

Knock, knock.

Both their heads snapped to the door.

Yadriel's eyes went wide. That had to be Lita. She knew. She could sense he had a spirit in his room. He was totally screwed. If Lita found Julian, she'd tell his dad, and Yadriel would get in deep trouble for disobeying him and going behind his back and—Oh God, would they kick him out for disrespecting the ways of the brujx?

Yadriel panicked. "Hold on!" he called, grabbing the sleeping bag and tossing it over Julian, but it fell right through him, landing in a heap on the chair.

Julian arched an eyebrow and pointed at himself. "Ghost, remember?" he whispered.

"Shh!" Yadriel hissed, flapping his hands at Julian uselessly. *"Hide in the—"*

The bedroom door swung open.

Maritza leaned against the doorjamb.

Yadriel let out a breath and clutched his chest. "*Jesus*, Maritza!"

"Good morning!" she greeted cheerily. Her eyes swept back and forth between the two of them—Julian lying on the bed, Yadriel clutching his jeans. Her dusty-rose-painted lips curled into a smirk. "How was the sleepover?"

Yadriel dragged her into the room and slammed the door closed behind her. "You're going to get us caught!"

"Chill, Yads!" She laughed, crossing the room to sit on the dresser.

Julian was on his feet. "Going to school is a waste of time!" he repeated, as if Yadriel had forgotten.

"No, it's not," Yadriel said as he snatched a clean pair of underwear and a fresh binder from the dresser. "I've got a math test—"

Julian scoffed.

"And unlike you and your friends, I actually care about my grades." Yadriel closed the drawer with a snap and spun to face Julian.

"Then you gotta take me with you!"

"No way, we are *not* taking you to school with us."

"You can't just ditch me here!" Julian whined.

Yadriel clenched his jaw, his patience wearing thin. "Look—" he said, rounding on Maritza for some backup. There was a highly amused look on her face. "We'll take a vote!"

"That's not fair!" Julian scowled.

Yadriel ignored him. "Maritza."

She arched an eyebrow in response.

"Do you think that Julian should stay here while we go to school?" he asked, sounding perfectly logical and even-tempered.

"Of course she's gonna side with you!" Julian objected, gesturing wildly. "No voting!"

"Actually." Maritza thoughtfully twisted a pink curl around her finger. "I think he should come with us."

Julian blinked, arms still aloft. A satisfied smile broke across his face. "Well, you heard the bruja!" He sat down in the desk chair and locked his hands behind his head. "I'm going!"

It was Yadriel's turn to splutter. *"What?!"* He shook his head at

Maritza. He must not have understood her correctly. "You're not serious."

She shrugged. "I mean, it makes the most sense, Yads—"

"*Traitor,*" he hissed.

Maritza looked like she was trying not to laugh. "Mira! We've got to take him with us."

Julian grinned.

"If we leave him here, he's going to get caught," Maritza reasoned. "He's too loud and can't be trusted not to get in trouble while we're gone."

Julian's grin quickly vanished.

Yadriel groaned and scrubbed a hand over his face. "We *can't*—"

"If he stays here, he's one hundred percent getting caught by Lita," Maritza pointed out. "She's a Cuban abuelita who's got nothing better to do than hang around the house and pick up after a house full of boys."

Yadriel didn't want to admit it, but she had a point. By the time he got home from school almost every day, his room was straightened up, or his laundry cleaned and folded on his bed.

Well, at least today Lita would have plenty to keep her busy.

He looked over at Julian, who appeared hopeful, though mostly desperate. Logically, Yadriel knew Maritza had a point. He knew it was dangerous to leave Julian at home unsupervised, but still.

"Maybe we could just leave him in the cemetery," Yadriel tried, which was met with another series of groans from Julian.

"Yads," Maritza said firmly, standing upright and frowning at him. "What's the deal?"

Heat clawed up Yadriel's throat. "I don't want to take him to school."

"But *why*?"

"Because of what happened with Lisa!" he lashed out.

Maritza's shoulders sank. "Yads . . ." Her expression softened to a look of pity. It made his skin crawl.

Meanwhile, Julian was looking around, annoyed. "Uh, should I know who Lisa is?" he asked, voice edged with impatience.

"She was a dead girl who haunted my elementary school," Yadriel snapped at him.

Julian's thick eyebrows shot up toward his buzzed hair.

"Except I didn't *know* she was dead," he went on, words spilling from his mouth. "So I was just the weird kid who was talking to himself, who *also* lived in a cemetery *and* had no friends!" Yadriel clenched his hands into fists at his sides, turning to Julian. "There, is that a good enough reason?" he demanded.

Julian leaned back. "Oh," he said, his voice awkward and small, cheeks turning red.

"Yads," Maritza said gently, moving to touch his arm, but Yadriel quickly twisted out of her reach.

"I'm going to get dressed," he said. He went into the bathroom with the clothes clutched in his arms. When he closed the door behind him, he let out a long breath, trying to exhale all the tension from his shoulders. Yadriel closed his eyes and leaned his forehead against the mirror, letting the cool glass soothe the throbbing in his head. It'd been a long time since he'd thought about Lisa.

When he was only seven and just starting to understand what the brujx were and how they were different from everyone else, he was friends with a little girl named Lisa. They would play together during recess in the field and hang out during free time in class. Lisa loved to play with the stuffed animals. Her absolute favorite was the floppy-eared spotted dog. Yadriel told his parents about her and always drew pictures of them during art. When other kids in class started teasing Yadriel, he didn't understand why.

A couple of weeks later, his teacher had a meeting with his mom and dad. When they got home, they asked him about Lisa.

Even now, sometimes Yadriel could be looking at someone and not realize they were a spirit. If he wasn't paying attention, it could be easy to overlook. When he was little, it was even harder to spot.

Lisa had passed away the year before from an extreme case of the flu over the course of just a couple of days. It had been sudden and unexpected. The floppy-eared dog had become the tether to her spirit.

Yadriel remembered being inconsolable in his grief, crying and clutching his mom and refusing the comfort of his father, thinking he was going to kill Lisa. As Camila rocked him in her lap, rubbing his back in slow circles, Enrique tried his best to explain.

His dad told him that Lisa was already dead, but that was okay. They didn't force peaceful spirits to cross over. He told Yadriel he had actually helped Lisa—now that Enrique knew about her, he could check in on her and make sure she was okay. If she started to get "sick"—the word he used when Yadriel was little to describe spirits who turned maligno—then he could help her cross over to the other side. It would be painless, and she would be happy.

But when Yadriel went back to school the next day, there was no unknowing that Lisa was a spirit. His classmates were making fun of him because, to their eyes, he was talking to himself and playing with an imaginary friend. Yadriel decided to ignore Lisa. She followed him around; sometimes she would get angry, but mostly she would just cry.

Eventually, Yadriel stopped seeing her. Even now, he didn't know if she'd crossed over on her own, or if his dad released her spirit. He never went near the floppy-eared dog again.

The idea of bringing Julian to school stirred up all the bad memories of Lisa. What if he slipped up? What if someone caught him talking to Julian? The last thing he ever wanted was to draw more attention to himself.

Yadriel let the mundane tasks of getting dressed, washing his face, and styling his hair calm his frayed nerves.

When Yadriel opened the door, Maritza was standing with her hands on her hips, staring down at Julian. He sat with his hands in his lap and his chin tucked to his chest. They both looked up when Yadriel walked in.

He crossed his arms. He was calmer, if a bit embarrassed.

"We talked it over and came to a compromise," Maritza said.

"She threatened to put a curse on me," Julian supplied.

Maritza shook out her curls and continued on, as if Julian hadn't said anything. "Julian says he'll behave himself and not cause any trouble."

Yadriel's skepticism must've showed, because she added, "Or he'll suffer the consequences."

Julian squinted up at Maritza. "I don't know if I believe she can do that." Then, to Yadriel. "Can she do that?"

"Probably best not to push your luck and find out," Yadriel said.

The corner of Julian's lips pulled into a smirk.

"Deal?" Maritza interrupted.

"Yeah, yeah, yeah." Julian stood, waving her off. "I'll keep my hands to myself, no ghost stuff, no being a nuisance, blah, blah, blah. Now can we *please* go? I've been trapped in this room long enough!" Yadriel could practically feel Julian's pent-up energy come off him in waves.

Yeah, leaving him here alone would definitely end in disaster.

"All right," Yadriel sighed in concession. Julian's face lit with a bright smile. "Just one second." He grabbed his backpack and pulled out the mezcal and his portaje. "Last thing I need is to get caught by campus security with alcohol and a knife in my backpack." Yadriel wrapped his portaje in a T-shirt and stuffed it into the bottom of the drawer in his bedside table. It was the only place he knew Lita'd steer clear of.

"Okay, let's go." Yadriel opened the door, but before Julian could step through, he held up a finger. "You two sneak out the front door while I distract Lita, okay?"

Maritza nodded. "Let's go, dead boy," she said to Julian.

He pretended to look offended, but he held his tongue for once and silently followed her down the stairs. Maybe he *was* a little worried about getting cursed.

SEVEN

ownstairs, Lita's Tejano music blared from the kitchen. "I'll meet you outside," Yadriel whispered.

Julian gave a salute, and Maritza ushered him toward the door while Yadriel went into the kitchen.

He was met with the smell of rice and beans cooking on the stove. A metal espresso maker perched on a burner, filling the air with the smell of brown sugar and coffee. Loud music poured from a boom box propped on a chair, the old speakers giving it a tinny edge. Every morning, Lita woke up, brewed café cubano, and made food while she listened to the same CD over and over again.

The normal routine felt strange in comparison to the very abnormal events of the last twelve hours.

Lita stood at the sink, washing dishes. Her operatic bellowing along with the song made Yadriel flinch. *"¡Como la flor!"*

The song echoed back.

"¡Con tanto amor!"

"Morning, Lita!" he called over the noise.

"Vas a estar tarde a la escuela," she sang. For as old as she was, Lita's feet were still quick enough to keep step with the music, her hips swaying in time.

"I know, I know," Yadriel said. He made to grab some food, but

Lita caught his wrist and pulled him to her with surprising strength. Holding him tight, she danced and continued to croon loudly. Yadriel cringed but let her drag him around the kitchen table for the length of the chorus. At least there were no witnesses this time.

Singing and dancing around the kitchen used to be a group activity led by his mom. It always involved laughter and, of course, whiny resistance from him and Diego. Though Yadriel secretly enjoyed it and had just put on a show so his brother didn't think he was a dork.

But now, the close proximity and Lita's tight embrace felt suffocating. He squirmed until Lita finally released him.

Yadriel grabbed the wooden spoon and scooped up some rice and beans. He took a large bite, but as soon as it touched his tongue, sharp pain lit up the cut. Eyes watering, he forced himself to quickly swallow it down. He was starving, but he also needed to hurry and get to Maritza and Julian, so he dug through the Tupperware drawer. He could eat on the way to school.

On the counter sat a small, ancient TV showing the local Spanish news station. Yadriel paused, staring intently at the screen and reading the marquee and list of upcoming topics. The box next to the news anchor showed a live car chase through downtown. For Los Angeles, live car chases were about as reliable as the hourly weather update.

There was no mention of Julian or park muggers.

Okay, maybe the latter happened a bit too often to make it into the top new stories, but shouldn't a missing teenager raise some kind of alarms? He hadn't even gotten an AMBER Alert on his phone. Hadn't someone reported Julian missing by now? His friends? His brother?

And what about Miguel?

"Ay!" The sharp snap of a dish towel against his butt made Yadriel jump. "Get some food and hurry up!"

"Where's Dad and Diego? Still out looking for Miguel?" Yadriel asked, yanking out a small, orange-stained Tupperware.

Lita sighed heavily, bobbing her head. "Sí, been looking all night." She tutted, waving a hand through the air. "Todavía nada."

Still nothing?

Yadriel frowned as he scooped some food into the Tupperware. How was that possible? Had the search dogs not picked up anything, either? How could Miguel die in their own neighborhood without anyone seeing or knowing at least *something*? Yadriel had so many questions he wanted to ask, but Julian and Maritza were waiting for him, and Lita was shooing him again.

Lita handed him a spoon and smiled a tired smile. "Here, now, go to school, and be careful, ¿claro?"

Yadriel forced a smile. "Yes, Lita." He gave her a kiss on the cheek and headed out, the sound of Lita's singing followed him down the path. He didn't see any brujx. Maybe they'd moved their search to beyond the walls of the cemetery.

Maritza and Julian waited for him by the main gate. Maritza scrolled through her phone, leaning against a weatherworn statue of Our Lady of Guadalupe as Julian paced back and forth.

When he saw Yadriel, Julian's bright smile cut dimples into his cheeks.

Yadriel's stomach did a little flip that he did *not* appreciate.

"We good?" Julian asked, dragging Maritza's attention away from her phone.

"Yeah, let's get out of here before someone sees us," Yadriel said, casting another furtive glance back toward the cemetery.

"Yes!" Julian agreed. "Let's go, let's go, let's go!"

Maritza opened the gate, and Julian rushed out as if he were being released from custody on good behavior.

"Don't wander off!" Yadriel called after him.

"Yeah, yeah, yeah!" he said, leading the way down the street.

Yadriel scrubbed at his eyes, and Maritza fell into step beside him.

"Wow, you look like shit," she said with a small laugh. "What happened?"

"Julian happened," he grumbled, watching Julian's back as he led the way, hands tucked into his pockets and whistling to himself, seemingly without a care in the world.

"So the sleepover went well, I take it?" Maritza smirked.

"There was very little sleep involved," Yadriel murmured. When Maritza giggled, he shot her a glare. "Because he wouldn't *shut up*." He got a spoonful of rice and beans and blew on it before taking a large bite. It stung the cut on his tongue, but only a little.

A beat-up Honda full of teenagers drove by, music blaring from the crappy speakers so loud that each beat of the bass sent the license plate rattling. Across the street, a woman dug through recycling bins, pulling out cans and plastic bottles.

"Pretty sure spirits don't sleep."

"I'm gathering that." He just had to summon the most difficult spirit possible, didn't he? He was tired and frustrated, and the closer they got to school, the more tension worked its way into his shoulders.

"And he doesn't seem to be the 'sit there and be quiet' type," Maritza added, eyeing Julian up ahead.

"Definitely not."

Julian wandered along, his head swinging this way and that, turning whenever something on the street caught his eye. When he came upon a beer bottle lying on the sidewalk, Julian ran up to it and swung his leg like a soccer player looking to score a goal. But his foot went right through it, knocking him off-balance and sending him tumbling through a lamppost. He landed on his back, a surprised look on his face before he broke out into laughter.

A laugh bucked in Yadriel's chest. Did Julian just have zero impulse control? It was almost endearing. But only almost.

He gave a small shake of his head as Julian stood up and continued down the street. Yadriel toyed with the St. Jude pendant around his neck, considering the reckless boy ahead of him. He really seemed to not have a care in the world, didn't he? Especially for someone who had just found out he was dead less than a day ago. As someone who was filled with anxiety nearly every waking moment, Yadriel didn't understand it at all.

Julian was certainly a conundrum.

"I bet he's a Scorpio," Maritza said.

"Jeez, Itza, not that zodiac stuff again," Yadriel groaned.

"Left!" he told Julian when he got to the end of the block.

Julian veered right.

"Your *other* left!"

Julian turned on his heel. "Got it!"

"It's *astrology*, and it totally makes sense!" Maritza continued. "His big, obnoxious Scorpio energy is invading your cozy Cancer safe space!"

Yadriel didn't know about all that. What he really wanted was to find out what happened to Miguel, satisfy Julian's demands so he'd let Yadriel release him, and get a good night's rest. His heartbeat felt like a ticking clock, counting down the seconds as Día de Muertos neared.

"Have you heard anything about Miguel?" Yadriel asked, steering the topic toward something useful. Maybe she'd heard news Lita hadn't yet, though that was doubtful. Abuelitas somehow got word out even faster than teenagers with cell phones.

Unfortunately, there was no news to tell. "Mom said my dad went with Julio and his dogs to try to track down his body, but they just kept wandering around the cemetery."

"I guess that makes sense?" he mused. "I mean, if he was last seen starting his graveyard shift, then he should've been there, right?" Yadriel offered Maritza the spoon.

"Vegan?" she asked.

He nodded, and she took a bite.

"But we can't find any sign of him," Maritza said as she chewed.

Yadriel's stomach churned. "Where the hell is he?"

Maritza tugged on the gold hoop through her ear. "No spirit. No tether. No trace," she murmured, staring off into the distance.

"Doesn't make sense," Yadriel said.

"Do you think Julian is somehow involved?"

At first, the question seemed completely out of the blue, but then again . . .

"Maybe." Yadriel frowned. "They did die on the same night, maybe just a couple hours apart."

"There could be some connection, but what?"

Miguel was a grown adult. He was a good man who helped take care of his elderly parents. Yadriel didn't think he'd even gotten a ticket for speeding on his motorcycle before.

Then there was Julian, who—well, Yadriel didn't really know much about him other than he got into trouble a lot at school. He was pretty sure Julian had been suspended at least once for getting into fights, and there were rumors that he was affiliated with one of the local gangs.

How could Julian's and Miguel's deaths be related?

With an aggravated groan, Yadriel scrubbed a hand over his face. "I don't know, but the sooner we get through today, the sooner we can take Julian to his friends."

"Maybe they'll have some answers," Maritza added, but she didn't sound very convinced.

The closer they got to school, the more crowded the sidewalks got. Julian veered toward a boy and girl leaning against a wall, chatting. He waved his hand between their faces. They continued to talk to each other, not even so much as blinking. Julian laughed.

Yadriel hitched his backpack higher on his shoulder and quickened his pace. *"Julian,"* he hissed.

Maritza snickered behind his shoulder.

"Hey!"

Julian finally turned. "What?"

Yadriel cut his hand through the air, motioning for him to come close. "Would you knock it off? Get back here," he snapped, trying to not draw the couple's attention.

Reluctantly, Julian retreated.

Maritza laughed.

"You're not helpful." Yadriel glared at her, and Julian wound his way back to them.

"Hey, he's your ghost."

"I ain't never been this excited to go to school." Julian beamed as he fell back into step next to them.

"You need to stay close," Yadriel told him sternly. "I don't want people thinking I'm talking to myself."

"Gotcha." Julian hovered right behind Yadriel's shoulder.

Cold pressed from Yadriel's neck down to the small of his back. He shivered. "You don't have to stand *that* close."

Julian took a step back. "Got it, got it, got it," he said, bobbing his head along in a nod as they melded in with the sea of people heading through the front doors of the school. It was a large cement building that was two stories tall and a dull shade of beige.

Maritza bumped her shoulder into Yadriel's. "We'll figure it out; don't worry so much," she told him.

"It's like you don't even know me."

She laughed and gave him a shove.

Walking through the halls, it was impossible not to be jostled every few feet by other people. There were too many students, and the school was too small.

"This is really weird," Julian said as a girl walked right through him. She shivered and wrapped her arms around herself. The good thing was that, this time of year, someone running into Julian would just think it was the late October chill. Even though it was only in the high sixties, it was cold enough for students in Los Angeles to be walking around in puffy coats and fur-lined boots.

They reached the turnoff for Maritza's class. "All right, you two behave," she said, heading down the hall. She grinned over her shoulder and waved. "Be good and learn something!"

Julian moved closer to Yadriel's side. "I don't actually have to pay attention in class, do I?"

"No," he murmured quietly, trying to move his mouth as little as possible to not attract attention, but everyone seemed quite content to ignore him, just like any other day.

"Good," Julian said. "'Cause I can't sit still for that long."

"I'm *shocked*."

Yadriel ducked into his first class, and Julian chased after him.

Turned out, sitting still for "that long" meant all of five minutes before Julian was up and roaming the classroom. While Yadriel did his best to take notes on the judicial branches of the United States government, Julian passed the time staring out the window and moving people's pens when they weren't paying attention.

At one point, Julian crouched in front of a boy and shouted in his face as loud as he could.

Of course, the boy didn't move. Unlike Yadriel, who jumped so hard he knocked his textbook to the floor, then everyone turned to look at him. Yadriel face burned crimson. "S-sorry." He scrambled to pick up the book and shot Julian a glare.

Julian clamped his hands over his mouth, dark eyes wide. "I'm *so* sorry," he said, but Yadriel could see his smile peeking around the edge of his hands. Saw the way the corner of his eyes crinkled, not to mention his shoulders shaking with suppressed laughter.

When the lunch bell rang, Maritza met them behind the science hall. There was an open-air hallway that was always deserted, since half the students went off campus for lunch, and the rest of them hung out in the quad. It was a good place for some privacy.

And for Yadriel to lecture Julian.

"You're going to get me in trouble!" Yadriel told him.

Maritza sat against the wall, eating a bag of Doritos Blaze, her eyes pinging back and forth between the two.

"I wasn't trying to!" Julian said, holding his hands up defensively and clearly trying very hard to keep a straight face.

Yadriel glared. "It's not funny!"

Julian pressed his lips between his teeth, but laughter escaped through his nose.

Yadriel turned to Maritza. "Will you do something?" he demanded.

Maritza licked the Doritos dust off her fingers and rubbed her palms together. "Should I curse him now?" she asked, wiggling her fingers at Julian.

Julian scrambled back "Whoa, whoa, whoa!"

The sudden panic on his face *was* satisfying, Yadriel had to admit.

When Maritza laughed, Julian scowled. "Y'all play too much; that's not funny."

"Oh, *we* play too much?" Yadriel threw his head back. "Hah!"

"Wait." Julian squinted at Maritza and tipped his head to the side. "I thought you said you couldn't do magic?"

"I said I *wouldn't* do magic, not that I couldn't," she clarified.

"Because of the vegan thing?"

"Yup, because of the vegan thing." She nodded.

"It's at least locally sourced—the Lopez family runs the local butchery, and they supply the community with animal blood," Yadriel pointed out.

"That doesn't make it better." Maritza scowled.

"Why don't you use your own blood?" Julian asked.

"It's forbidden."

Julian looked to Yadriel. "Why?"

"It's too powerful," he said, leaning his back against the wall as he let out a heavy sigh.

Julian arched an eyebrow. "And that's a problem?"

"It'd be like trying to light birthday candles with kerosene," Yadriel tried to explain. "It'd be overkill. The candles would catch on fire, and then the cake would burst into flames," he listed off. "But then the kerosene is tied to your life force, so you end up using all your energy and magic reserves just to light some dumb birthday candles, and then you're *dead*."

"That seems like a bad metaphor."

"It's an analogy."

Julian waved him off. "Can we just go find my friends now?" he asked. "I told you they wouldn't be at school."

"I still have to take my math test," Yadriel told him for the hundredth time.

Julian opened his mouth to complain, but a voice cut him off.

"Hey!"

Yadriel jumped and turned.

Patrice stood at the end of the hall, giving him and Maritza a curious look. "What are you guys doing?" She was one of their friends, or, well, she was mostly Maritza's friend. During lunch, Yadriel sat with Maritza and her group of friends, which was always some level of awkward. Maritza had way more friends than him, most of them fellow members of the girls' soccer team. Yadriel used to play soccer, too, but not anymore.

"Oh, you know, just plotting," Maritza said casually.

Yadriel glanced from her to Patrice, once again wondering how she could remain so calm and lie so easily under pressure when he always broke out into a cold sweat.

Patrice just laughed and shook her head. "Okay, weirdo." She smiled before waving at them to follow. "Come on, we grabbed one of the picnic tables in the quad."

"Coming!" Maritza scooped up her backpack and slung it over her shoulder. She gave Yadriel a shrug.

He sighed but followed her lead. There was no reason not to, and, besides, ignoring Julian for the next twenty-five minutes sounded like a good idea.

Julian groaned his protest but trudged after them anyway.

The girls piled up on a picnic bench in the quad, laughing and talking together while Yadriel sat on the edge, forcing himself to eat the sandwich he'd bought from one of the snack stands on break.

Julian leaned against the tree that provided the table with shade, arms crossed and expression surly, but his dark eyes continuously searched the crowds of students as they walked by.

"Is *everyone* going to the Halloween bonfire at the beach?" Alexa asked the group, and it exploded into excited chatter.

Yadriel rolled his eyes, which caught Julian's attention.

"What, you don't like bonfires?" he asked with an amused grin.

Yadriel gave a small shake of his head as he took another large bite of turkey and white bread.

"Or do you not like parties?"

The flat look Yadriel discreetly cut to Julian said, *Both.*

The Halloween bonfire was a tradition. Students from all the local high schools ended up there. It was a game of cat and mouse with the cops, on account of the loud music, huge crowd, and, of course, illegal substances. A secluded part of the beach was chosen last minute and sent out via a wildfire of text messages.

Maritza was always trying to talk him into going, but Yadriel avoided it like the plague. The last thing he wanted to do was hang out with a bunch of drunk and high idiots running around near fire *and* riptides.

Not to mention, Día de Muertos started at midnight on Halloween, so he had his own tasks and responsibilities with his family back at the cemetery.

Julian chuckled and wandered over to Yadriel's side. "Why am I not surprised?"

"Do any of you know Julian Diaz?" Maritza suddenly asked, interrupting the conversation about Halloween costumes.

Yadriel sat up straighter but tried to not look *too* interested in the topic.

Meanwhile, Julian appeared all too eager to listen to what a group of girls thought about him.

Alexa, who always wore high-end hair extensions and a permanently sour expression, made a disgusted sound at the back of her throat. "Ugh, yes," she said, rolling her eyes. "He's got a hot face—"

Julian's smug grin was unbearable.

"But he's *so* obnoxious," she added.

Yadriel's sharp laugh made him choke on his sandwich.

Julian scowled. "*Tch*, whatever," he huffed indignantly. "The important part is I'm hot."

"He used to play on the boys' team with that other guy, Omar, right?" said Letti as she juggled a soccer ball between the toe of her shoe and her knee. "They're like best friends or something."

Omar? Yadriel tried to conjure up the face that matched the name in his head, but failed. He could remember seeing Julian around school, but he couldn't remember what his friends looked like.

"Ooh, that was *him*?" Maritza said, looping her rose-quartz rosary around her finger idly.

"Yeah, he was really annoying," Patrice agreed as she braided a chunk of Maritza's pink-and-purple hair. "Always messing around and kicking balls over to our side of the field."

"That doesn't sound like me," Julian grumbled petulantly.

"He beamed me right in the back of the head once and then *laughed* about it," Alexa said.

"Okay, that *does* sound like me."

Yadriel did his best to turn his laugh into a cough, but Alexa noticed and sniffed indignantly, sticking her pointy nose in the air.

"Why do you care about Julian Diaz?" Patrice asked.

Maritza shrugged. "Yadriel was curious about him."

All four sets of eyes swung to him.

Heat flooded his cheeks. "Uhhh." He looked to Maritza for help, but the amused flash in her eyes said she was enjoying watching him squirm. "We, uh, we got assigned a group project together," he finally managed to lie. "And I haven't heard from him."

"Good luck with that." Alexa snorted.

Julian scowled. "I don't like this one," he said.

"He, like, never shows up to class," she explained.

"That's only half true," Julian tried to defend himself.

"Hasn't he flunked out by now?"

"I heard he got sent to juvie."

"Hey!" Julian tried to interrupt. "I've only been arrested once, and that guy totally dropped the charges after my brother offered to fix his car!"

"I was going to try to get his number from one of his friends," Yadriel cut in, trying to steer the conversation toward something useful.

Letti caught the ball and shook her head. "Nooo, you don't want to go messing with them," she warned. Unlike Alexa, she actually sounded sincerely worried.

Yadriel frowned. "Why not?"

"They're, like, in a gang."

Julian balked. *"What?"*

Yadriel looked to Maritza, who frowned back. Yadriel remembered hearing rumors about Julian and his group of friends. He shifted uncomfortably in his seat, hearing them all listed off. Julian was clearly getting worked up, but was that because the rumors were true?

"He and his family are from *Colombia*," Alexa went on, in a way that suggested a double meaning, but when everyone just stared at her, she added, "You know what they export from Colombia, don't you?"

"Coffee?" Maritza guessed in a bored tone.

"Crack," Alexa answered.

Julian let out a string of colorful curses.

"Don't you mean cocaine?" Patrice asked, giving Alexa a dubious look.

"What's the difference?"

"I'm half Colombian on my mom's side, and none of us are drug dealers," Letti pointed out.

Alexa waved a hand dismissively. "You don't count. They're *street* kids."

Julian seethed and Yadriel tensed.

"His older brother took over the family drug trade," Alexa went on. "He runs it out of his mechanic shop."

"Rio is *not* a drug dealer!" Julian barked, but, of course, they couldn't hear him.

"Yeah, I don't remember his name, but he was really hot, too."

"Too bad he's a drug dealer preying on high schoolers."

Julian stepped forward. "No, he isn't!"

"Yeah, you really shouldn't mess with those guys," Letti said to Yadriel, her delicate eyebrows drawn together in concern.

Julian turned to face him. "This is complete bullshit!" he said, throwing his hands up.

Yadriel sent him a furtive glance. This was escalating too quickly, but he couldn't find his voice to put a stop to it. Julian was losing his temper, which Yadriel couldn't really blame him for, but he also didn't want him to do something stupid.

With everyone around, he couldn't exactly say something *to* Julian to calm him down.

"I think his parents are in jail," Patrice added, thoughtfully tapping a finger against her cheek.

"No, his *mom* is in jail, pendeja."

"I thought his mom ran off when he was, like, a baby?"

Julian visibly paled.

Oh no. That was a step too far. "Uh—" Yadriel tried to come up with something to derail the conversation, but they were off and running.

"He turned into a real asshole, like, a year ago, right around when he stopped playing soccer," Letti went on, setting the soccer ball down by her feet. "Always getting into fights and starting trouble in class. Remember when he broke Pancho's nose in biology?"

Julian snapped out of his daze. His face went from white to bright red in a matter of seconds. A cool gust of wind kicked up the fallen leaves that littered the ground.

"Oh yeah." Patrice nodded. "I almost forgot about that!"

"That's because—" Julian started, seething between his bared teeth.

"The violent gene must run in the family," Alexa told them, flicking her hair back over her shoulder. "Apparently his dad was a sicario. He ran away to Los Angeles, but they found him anyways and killed him in the middle of the—"

Julian's shout drowned out the rest of her words. "SHUT UP!"

Yadriel and Maritza both jumped. The other three didn't seem to notice, but then Julian moved, and a gasp caught in Yadriel's throat. There was a sharp gust of wind as Julian swung his leg. His foot connected with the soccer ball, and it went flying across the quad. Yadriel couldn't see where it landed in the sea of students, but he did hear the disgruntled shouts in the distance.

Alexa, Letti, and Patrice all gasped, looking around wildly for an explanation of what had just happened.

Julian stormed off toward the field, leaving a rush of cold wind in his wake.

"What the hell was that?" Alexa demanded, trying to comb out her wind-tangled hair with her fingers.

Yadriel leaped up from his seat. Maritza looked at him, eyes wide with surprise.

"I gotta go," he said.

As he rushed after Julian, he heard Maritza say behind him, "Must be those Santa Ana winds! It is that time of year."

"They're so crazy!" came Letti's voice. "One time, they blew through and knocked my tío right off the roof when he was cleaning the gutters!"

Yadriel chased Julian out to where the blacktop met the field. He slowed to a stop where Julian crouched by the bleachers, his arms folded over his knees and shoulders hunched up to his ears. He pressed his mouth into the crook of his elbow, obsidian eyes staring out over the football field. Tiny gusts of wind swirled around him, sending leaves and cigarette butts rustling.

"Are you okay?" Yadriel asked gently after making sure there was no one around to overhear him.

"Yes," Julian snapped, his voice muffled against his arm.

It was entirely unconvincing.

Yadriel shifted his weight between his feet. "Do you ... want to talk about it?"

"*No.*"

Yadriel wanted to reach out and touch his shoulder, but Julian was a spirit, and his hand would just pass right through. Instead, he sank down and sat, at least offering Julian his company, even if he didn't have any words. He fiddled with blades of grass, stealing glances at Julian from the corner of his eye.

His heavy brow was bunched, deep lines pressed into his forehead as he continued to stare off into the distance. This close, Yadriel could see the frayed edges around the neck of his white tee. Julian's buzzed haircut was uneven and a bit sloppy, like maybe he'd done it himself. He had a scar that curved through his dark hair behind his ear, down to the nape of his neck.

Everything the girls said about Julian, his friends, and his family bounced around in Yadriel's head. He wasn't sure he bought it—that Julian was part of some gang and dealing drugs, one step away from ending up in jail. He thought about Julian's reaction. That look on his face, and his burst of anger. Sure, Yadriel barely knew him, but the guy in front of him just didn't fit their description. Julian told him he didn't have any parents, but that didn't mean they were in jail or killed by a rival drug cartel. If it was just rumors, well, Yadriel knew plenty well what that was like.

And even if the rumors were true, did that matter? Would Yadriel change his mind about wanting to help him because he was a gang member or drug dealer? It *did* make him a little anxious, but still.

Right now, Yadriel could see him as he was; just a dead boy who was worried about his friends. He wanted to make sure they were okay, and probably wanted nothing more than to go home.

Yadriel could at least help him with one of those.

In the distance, the bell rang, signaling the end of lunch.

"Hey," Yadriel said.

Julian's eyes finally flickered to his face.

"Let's get the rest of school over with so we can go find your friends," Yadriel told him. "Okay?"

Julian stared at him, and for a moment, Yadriel was convinced he wasn't going to budge or even reply. But then he dragged the back of his hand against his mouth and stood up. "Yeah."

Yadriel stood up, too, and jerked his head back toward the school. "Come on, math class is this way."

Julian followed without protest.

EIGHT

The rest of the day went without incident. Julian was unnaturally quiet, so much so that Yadriel found himself wishing he'd go back to his mischief making. Ms. Costanzo, the math teacher, had to remind Yadriel twice to keep his eyes on his own test. He kept glancing to where Julian sat at the back of the classroom, knees bouncing as he silently stared out the window.

When school finally let out, they met up with Maritza and started the walk back home.

Julian wandered up ahead. Yadriel exchanged worried looks with Maritza. He really couldn't take Julian's silence anymore.

"So, uh . . ." Yadriel jogged a couple of steps to catch up to him. "Your friends weren't at school, huh?" he said, trying to nudge him into conversation.

"They're fine," Julian said, and his pinched expression told Yadriel that this was *not* the way to lighten his spirits. "They just ditch a lot, y'know?" Julian nodded, as if trying to encourage himself. "They're fine."

Yadriel looked back to Maritza for some guidance, but all she did was lift her shoulders in an exaggerated shrug.

"It was pretty cool that you were able to kick that soccer ball," he tried.

Julian blinked, as if he'd forgotten.

"Soon you should be slamming doors and moving furniture around," Yadriel told him with an awkward laugh. "What with Día de Muertos a couple days out, you'll be full ghost mode in no time. Though," he added as an afterthought, "maybe no more outbursts in front of the non-brujx?"

Julian's grin was back, albeit sheepish. "Yeah, my bad."

He wasn't back to 100 percent, but he was getting there, and Yadriel would take what he could get. "Maybe work on the impulse control while you're at it."

Julian let out a short laugh. "Noted."

"Great, now that the pity party is over—" Maritza slipped between them. Julian rolled his eyes at Yadriel over the top of her head, and he couldn't help but grin back. "We need to stop by my place so I can drop off my crap. Can't go running the streets of East LA like hoodlums if I'm weighed down by my chemistry textbook," she said, hitching her backpack higher on her shoulder for emphasis.

Luckily, Maritza's family lived one block over from the cemetery, so it was a quick stop on the way. It was a squat yellow house with a chain-link fence wrapped around it. The gate had a BEWARE OF DOGS sign, and both her parents' cars were parked in the driveway.

"You stay here," Maritza told Julian, pointing to her mom's silver minivan.

Julian made a disgruntled noise. "How long is this gonna take?"

"We'll be in and out."

He didn't look convinced.

"Stay out of sight," Yadriel told him. "And if anyone looks at you, then they're probably a brujx, so just act like a spirit—"

Julian squinted. "But I am a spirit—"

"Just don't look suspicious, okay?"

Julian looked around, clearly not sure what to do with himself.

"Never mind, just"—Yadriel flapped his hands at him—"just hide behind the van and we'll be right back!"

Julian rolled his eyes, but he did what he was told and crouched down behind the dusty van. "I don't see how *this* isn't suspicious, but okay," he muttered.

"We'll be right back!" Yadriel repeated as he shoved Maritza toward the house.

"I'm home!" she shouted once they got inside, chucking her backpack onto the couch.

"In here!" Maritza's mother called.

Yadriel followed Maritza into the kitchen. Tía Sofía stood at the stove over a pot of brown syrup that smelled sticky and sweet. Another large metal pot sat covered next to it, spilling steam from its sides.

Maritza's older sister, Paola, sat at the kitchen table. She had two huge textbooks opened up, along with a notebook. Paola was a med student at the nearby university. No matter how much of a rush she was in, Paola's hair was always styled into a flawless wash-and-go. Black curls fell across her face as she bent over a notebook. She furiously took notes in between highlighting and placing color-coded Post-its.

The other half of the table was filled with portajes Tío Isaac was either repairing or building for various brujos. There were simple daggers scattered among the more elaborate choices of the younger brujos. Loud, rhythmic clanging cut through the air. The open door to the backyard revealed Tío Isaac, standing at his workbench as he hammered out a blade.

"How was school?" Tía Sofía asked, sparing them a glance as she grated piloncillo into the syrup. On tin foil next to her sat orange cubes of calabaza en tacha—candied pumpkin.

"Lame, as usual," Maritza said, making a beeline for the tray. She snatched up a piece of pumpkin and tossed it into her mouth.

"¡Ay, ten cuidado!" Tía Sofía warned, but it was too late.

Maritza danced in place, waving at her mouth. *"Ah, hot!"* She spat the scalding pumpkin out, and it fell, with a wet *plop*, onto one of Paola's textbooks.

Paola gasped, her pretty face twisting into a snarl. *"Seriously, Maritza?!"* She smacked Maritza on the butt before scooping off the offending pumpkin and throwing it in the sink.

"*Ow!* I didn't mean to!" Maritza scowled.

"Yeah, *sure* you didn't!" Paola brushed the glob of syrup off the page.

"You are taking this way too seriously."

"You don't take school seriously *enough*!" Paola shot back. "What exactly do you plan on doing after you graduate if you can't even heal?"

"Take up forging portajes, like Dad," Maritza replied, as if it were obvious.

Paola rolled her eyes. "Of course."

"What's that supposed to mean?!"

"Would you like a piece, Yadriel?" Tía Sofia asked, turning to Yadriel with a smile, holding up a piece of candied pumpkin on her slotted spoon. Her daughters bickered ferociously behind her.

"No, gracias," Yadriel said with a small smile. His tongue had been bugging him all day and the pain was only now starting to fade. He didn't want to aggravate it again.

"Of course you do!" She laughed warmly. "Here!"

Yadriel knew better than to decline an offer of food from a Latinx mom more than once. Carefully, he took a bite, shifting it to his cheek to avoid the cut.

Tía Sofia waited expectantly. "Good?"

Yadriel nodded and smiled, because of course it was. The pumpkin was tender, and the syrup had just the right amount of brown sugar and the faint zest of orange.

"Good!" Tía Sofia give him a pat on the cheek before going back to her cooking. "Are you excited for Día de Muertos? Ay, of course you are! Tu mamá will be there!"

Yadriel tried to return her bright smile, but it was difficult to muster her level of enthusiasm.

"Yes, it'll be a good year, indeed—"

"No fighting by the portajes!" Tío Isaac called, pausing for a moment on his work. He'd learned the trade from his own father back in Haiti. Tío Isaac scratched at his bushy beard, sweat glistening on his earth-rich brown skin. He huffed a big sigh, his broad chest heaving.

"One of these times their bickering is going to turn into a knife fight, I tell you," Tío Isaac told Yadriel in conspiratorial exasperation. In a house full of hardheaded boricuas, he was vastly outnumbered but never complained about it. Even when all three Santima women broke into a fight, Tío Isaac would just sigh and shake his head. He was a kind man with a deep well of patience.

"You're probably right," Yadriel agreed, eyeing the portajes carefully laid out. He used to watch Tío Isaac work all the time, staring at the portajes with longing, wishing he had one of his own.

Now, he didn't have to wish anymore.

"Are you staying for dinner, Yads?" Tío Isaac asked. The blade he was hammering sizzled as he dropped it into a bucket of water.

"I'm making ta-ma-leees!" Tía Sofia sang, gesturing to the steaming pot.

"No, actually—"

"I made you some rajas con queso ones, Itza," her mom said, lifting the lid off the large pot. The smell of sweet masa filled the room. "Hopefully that vegan cheese melts this time," she added, poking at the wrapped corn husks with a doubtful expression.

Tamales were a staple for Día de Muertos and prepared in obscenely large batches. In ancient times, they were soaked in blood and presented as offerings to Bahlam, the jaguar god of Xibalba. Luckily for Maritza— and everyone else, really—there was no longer a blood sacrifice involved.

"Save them for me to zap in the microwave when I get home!" Maritza told her.

"I make you tamales from *scratch* and you're just going to *microwave them* later?" Tía Sofia demanded, clutching her heart. "And last night you missed out on your papa's diri ak djon djon! He even made it without shrimp!"

"We got *stuff* to do, we're not staying for dinner," Maritza explained.

Tía Sofia huffed before waving her hand dismissively at her daughter.

"Oh yeah, what *kind* of stuff?" Paola asked.

Yadriel could tell by the looks the sisters exchanged that this wasn't going to go well.

"Just to go hang out, nosy! Mom, where's my rain jacket?"

"Esta allí," she said, waving toward the living room.

"That's not helpful!"

"I don't think you two should be going off on your own after school," Tío Isaac said, his large form filling up the doorframe as he wiped off his hands on a rag.

"Your papá is right," Tía Sofia agreed. "It's too dangerous, especially after Miguel—" Unable to finish her sentence, she crossed herself.

Yadriel's stomach twisted into knots. "We still haven't found anything?" he asked.

Tío Isaac shook his head solemnly. "Not yet."

Yadriel just didn't get it. How was that possible?

"Not to mention"—Tía Sofia propped her fist on one hip and shook her spoon at her youngest daughter—"you still haven't tried on the dress I got you for your aquelarre, and you said you'd take those colors out of your hair before Día de Muertos, too!"

Yadriel shot Maritza a hard stare. They needed to find Julian's friends, get answers that would satisfy the stubborn spirit, and wrap this whole thing up before Día de Muertos.

Maritza nodded, reading his look loud and clear. "Ugh, you guys!" she whined. "I'll try on the dress later, and I *definitely* never said I'd re-dye my hair—"

Tía Sofia opened her mouth to argue, but Maritza cut her off.

"I said I'd *think* about it, and I thought about it, and I decided not to."

Yadriel pinched the bridge of his nose. Arguing with her mom about dresses and hair was definitely not going to put Maritza's mom in a lenient mood. *"Maritza,"* he hissed.

Maritza looked at him like she'd completely forgotten that he was there and what the real matter at hand was. "And the sun's still up until like six!" she argued, getting back on track. She paused for a second and then walked her fingers toward one of the blades on the kitchen table. "I guess if we had a couple of these to defend ourselves—"

"No!" her parents answered in unison.

"They *could* take the boys?" Tío Isaac suggested, looking to his wife.

Maritza's eyes went wide. "Dad, no—"

Tía Sofía nodded in agreement. "Yes, mi amor!"

Yadriel always liked how a Puerto Rican accent turned soft *r's* into *l's*, so it sounded like *mi amol*.

"I like that idea!"

"Mom!"

Paola snorted a laugh.

Maritza growled and spun to Yadriel. "You go home and grab— uh—your stuff. I'll meet you there." With that, she turned back to her parents, fists firmly planted on her hips. "I'M NOT TAKING THEM WITH US! THEY ONLY GET IN THE WAY! AND THEY SMELL!"

Yadriel slipped out of the kitchen before it was too late.

Outside, Julian was right where he'd left him, leaning against the van and looking bored.

"Where's Maritza?" he asked, glancing back toward the house where Yadriel could still hear arguing.

"Uh, she got a little tied up," Yadriel told him. Julian looked amused. "Come on, she'll meet us back at the house."

Worry dug under Yadriel's skin. If Maritza's parents were any indicator, they were going to have a hell of a time sneaking out after school. As a whole, Yadriel's dad didn't like him out on the streets after the streetlights came on, but now? The adults were bound to instate a curfew after what had happened to Miguel, especially because they still didn't know *what* happened. It seemed like just a matter of time.

Not to mention, it was the end of October, which meant the sun was setting earlier. They had only a handful of hours to work with.

He led the way around the corner and across the street to the cemetery. He checked to make sure the coast was clear before they slipped through the gate. There weren't any brujx between the front gate and his house, though he could see a couple of figures off in the distance tending to the graves.

"Let's go," Yadriel said to Julian, keeping an eye on the brujx as he waved him forward and picked up the pace. "Before someone—"

"Wait, Yads!" Julian's hand shot out, in an attempt to grab him, but, of course, it went right through his shoulder, hitting him with a shock of cold.

The next second, Yadriel ran into something. The crash sent him stumbling, and he landed on his back, knocking the wind out of him. Around him, things clattered. Yadriel groaned.

He looked up, and Julian was standing over him, his hand clamped over his mouth as he laughed.

"Dude, are you okay?"

Yadriel glared up at him.

"I'd offer you a hand, but . . ." Julian let out another chuckle.

"Glad to see my pain puts you in such a good mood," Yadriel griped as he pushed himself back onto his feet.

"Did you hurt anything?"

"Just my dignity." He dusted off his pants and turned to see what he had tripped over. A stack of milk crates had been knocked over and large bunches of marigolds lay scattered across the ground. Tiny orange petals were everywhere.

"Uh-oh," Julian said, stepping behind Yadriel.

"My cempasúchitl!" Tito fumed as he stomped over. The air around his translucent body rippled like heat waves. He looked down at his beloved flowers and got on his knees, gingerly gathering the bouquets into his arms.

"I'm so sorry, Tito!" Yadriel apologized. "Here, let me help!" He bent down to pick up one of the crates, but Tito shooed him away.

"No! Don't touch!" His round, tanned face pinched into a glower, his eyes cutting back and forth between Yadriel and Julian. "Trouble-makers!" he barked, wagging a finger at them.

"I'm sorry, Tito." Yadriel cringed. He knew how hard Tito worked on his marigolds all year round to make sure they were perfect for Día de Muertos. "We were just, uh—"

Tito's attention swung to Julian who shrank back a step, shoulders hunching up to his ears, a painfully guilty smile on his face.

"Uh, this is . . ." Yadriel trailed off, not knowing what to say. Certainly not the *truth*. What if Tito told Yadriel's dad that he and a spirit boy had ruined some of his marigolds? He did not need his dad getting suspicious or asking questions. He could just lie and say Julian was a new spirit in the cemetery, right? That wouldn't need much explanation, would it? "This is— He's just," Yadriel blabbered, trying to put a coherent sentence together. Tito's eyes narrowed. "He's—"

Tito held up his hand, cutting him off. "I don't want to know! Take your trouble and go!" he snapped before going back to picking up his marigolds, murmuring words of comfort to them in Spanish.

Yadriel certainly wasn't going to argue with him, so he raced to the house, Julian right on his heels.

"Do you think he's gonna tell on us?" Julian asked as they got to the door.

"I hope not," Yadriel said, jumping to get a peek through the window in the door. He didn't hear anyone inside or see any movement behind the curtains. "Tito tends to mind his own business."

"You *did* mess up his flowers, though," Julian pointed out, giving Yadriel a disapproving shake of his head.

"It's not like I did it on purpose!" he hissed back. He didn't smell any food cooking, either, which was a good sign. Yadriel pushed the front door open and poked his head in.

"Hello?" he called. "Anyone home?" he strained his ears, listening for a response or a creak of floorboards, but the house was silent.

At least one thing was going right today.

Yadriel led the way up the stairs and to his room, shutting the door behind them. Immediately, he went to his bedside table. He yanked open the drawer, dug out the wadded-up T-shirt, and took out his portaje. It was still there, undiscovered and untouched. He sat heavily on the edge of the mattress and clutched the dagger to his chest and let out a sigh of relief.

His secret was still safe.

"How long we gotta wait for Maritza?" Julian asked, arms crossed, looking impatient.

"As soon as she's done talking her parents into letting her out," Yadriel told him as he slipped his portaje into the sheath at his hip. "Don't worry, she can talk her way out of pretty much everything."

Julian let out a frustrated grunt and flopped back onto the bed next to him.

For a moment, Yadriel considered Julian as he scowled up at the ceiling, expecting to see the ebb and flow of emotions that seemed to pass so fluidly across his face almost constantly, but, right now, he just seemed so . . . tired. There were shadows darkening the delicate brown skin under his eyes. Yadriel wasn't sure if it was a trick of the light, but he almost looked paler. No, "pale" wasn't the right word, just less solid? Untouchable.

"I just want to find my friends," Julian finally said.

Yadriel felt a little guilty. For the most part, Julian had done everything asked of him so far, but Yadriel still hadn't held up his part of the bargain. Julian was upset, and Yadriel wanted to make him feel better, but in the moment, he didn't know how.

Maybe a distraction was his best bet.

"Why don't you show me what they look like," Yadriel said, picking up his yearbook where it had been left on the floor.

Usually, his family couldn't afford a yearbook. His sophomore year was the first time his dad had bought him one, even though they were hard up for cash without the income from his mom's nursing job. On top of being the leader of the brujx, his dad also worked as an independent contractor to make ends meet. Most of his employees were other brujos, but projects were sometimes few and far between. It was the brujas, working as doctors, doulas, nurses, and psychologists, who were the financial heads of the households.

Even so, his dad had somehow scrounged up the fifty dollars it cost to buy a yearbook. Yadriel brushed his fingers over the glossy pages.

He looked expectantly at Julian, who laid there stubbornly for a few beats before giving up and moving to sit next to him.

"So who am I looking up?" Yadriel asked, thumbing through the pages.

"Flaca won't be in it," Julian said. "Dropped out the end of last year. Rocky should be, though."

"Last name?"

"Ramos."

"Our grade?"

"Yup."

Yadriel flipped to the *R*'s, eyes scanning the pages for "Ramos," but he didn't see a boy named Rocky.

"There," Julian pressed his finger to the page, but not before Yadriel was already flipping to the next one. The page fell right through Julian's hand. Yadriel went back to see where he was pointing.

"That's Rocky," Julian said.

Rocky, or, rather, Raquel Ramos, was a pretty girl with a high, sleek ponytail and striking features. She had a septum piercing and a bored expression. He vaguely recognized her but couldn't say for certain, which wasn't a rarity when you went to a high school with thousands of students.

Julian's mouth quirked into a lopsided grin.

Yadriel glanced between him and the photo. "She's pretty," he said, without really knowing why. He shifted. "She your girlfriend or something?" he asked in his best casual tone.

Julian snorted. "No." He leaned back, propping himself up on his elbows. "I don't *do* girlfriends."

Yadriel rolled his eyes and scoffed. "What? Because you're some kind of mujeriego, or something? Too many ladies to pick just one?" he asked with a flare of annoyance.

"No." Julian's tone was cross, eyes still on the page. "Because I'm *gay*, asshole."

Yadriel blinked. He . . . hadn't expected that. He stared at Julian. "Oh." His mind raced to place this new information with the boy sitting next to him.

Julian glanced up. "That a problem?" he asked with a hard stare and a cocked eyebrow.

"Uh—no, no, that's not a problem." Heat bloomed in Yadriel's cheeks.

"And so is Rocky," Julian went on nonchalantly. "So we cancel each other out."

"Really?"

He nodded. "Queer folks are like wolves," Julian told him. "We travel in packs."

"I—I am, too. I mean—" Yadriel cleared his throat. "I'm into guys." His chest tightened as he waited for Julian's response.

But Julian only blinked slowly at him, as if waiting for Yadriel to reveal something more interesting. "Cool," he said, after Yadriel didn't offer anything else.

Julian nodded to the yearbook. "Luca Garcia."

Yadriel wasn't sure if he was relieved or annoyed by Julian's nonchalance.

He cleared his throat again and flipped through the pages, trying to ignore the fluttering in his chest. He stole a couple of glances over at Julian. He'd said it so . . . "casually" wasn't the right word, but maybe "easily" was. Whenever Yadriel came out to anyone, it was always an ordeal that he overthought and dragged out. It was nerve-racking, waiting to see someone's reaction, whether they would reject him, or even understand what it meant when a trans boy said he was gay.

But not for Julian. He'd said it as almost a challenge. In a way that said he didn't care what you thought.

It was both intimidating and impressive.

Yadriel found Luca Garcia, but instead of a photograph, it was just a black box with the words "NO PHOTO AVAILABLE" across in white.

"Oh." Julian frowned at the blank picture. "He wasn't there that day, I forgot. He was, uh, home sick." He said it quickly and avoided making eye contact.

Yadriel raised an eyebrow at him, and red tinged Julian's cheeks. He was clearly lying, but Yadriel didn't get why. Seemed like an insignificant thing to lie about.

"Go to Omar's," Julian said, waving his hand at Yadriel to turn the page. "He was there. Omar Deye."

Yadriel was tempted to push him for answers, but instead he shook his head and turned to the beginning of the *D*'s.

"He seems . . ." Yadriel trailed off.

"Like a jerk?" Julian chuckled. "Yeah, I know," he said, with a tone of fondness and a smile back on his face.

Omar Deye sat rigid in his photo, back straight and chin jutted, looking down at the camera with contempt. He had dark skin, a tight fade, and a brooding expression. The muscles in his jaw were flexed, like he was clenching his teeth.

"He's all bite and no bark," Julian added, shaking his head.

"You mean 'all bark and no bite,'" Yadriel corrected. A familiar face caught his attention. "And there you are," he said, pressing his finger to the words "Julian Diaz."

Julian wore the same old leather bomber jacket with the hood. There was a huge smile on his face, cutting dimples into his cheeks and crinkling his nose and the corner of his eyes. He was looking past the camera and, judging by his blurry edges, mid-laugh.

It was the kind of face you couldn't help but smile back at.

"Hey, you makin' fun of me?" Julian accused, but he was grinning, too.

"No!" Laughter bucked in Yadriel's chest. "You just look—"

"Yeah, yeah, yeah! Let's look and see if yours is any better!" Julian demanded, gesturing for him to turn the page.

The laughter died in Yadriel's throat immediately. He snapped the yearbook shut. "Let's not." He crossed the room and shoved the book back into its place on the shelf.

Julian remained where he sat, his brow pinched and his laughter uneasy, confused by Yadriel's abrupt departure.

The truth was Yadriel didn't want to show Julian his yearbook picture because it did not read *Yadriel Vélez Flores*. Without legally changing his name—which took time and money—the school refused to use his real name, forever embossing his deadname under his painfully awkward photograph.

As if on cue, his phone buzzed in his pocket.

We're outside.

Julian perked up. "Now?"

"Yup." Yadriel grinned. "Come on, let's—" When he opened the door, voices and the smell of food cooking wafted from downstairs. "Dammit," he hissed. "Lita's back." He could hear her voice loudest among the rest, as usual.

Julian made a disgruntled groan.

"Just hold on a second," Yadriel told him before slipping out the door. Carefully, he crept down the first few steps to get a view of what was going on downstairs. Lita was bossing around three other brujas as they carried boxes of supplies into the kitchen.

Annoyed, Yadriel pulled out his phone and texted Maritza, asking her to come help sneak Julian out.

Can't. The boys aren't allowed inside, remember?

"*Dammit.*" He was going to have to figure it out himself, then. Create a distraction so Julian could sneak out the front door unnoticed. Yadriel slipped back into his room. "Okay, we're going to—"

Julian jumped. The yearbook was in his lap and he shut it quickly with a snap.

"What are you doing?" Yadriel demanded.

Julian blinked. "What?"

"What are you—?"

"Nothing!" The wide-eyed look on his face, accompanied by rosy cheeks, was so guilty that it was almost comical. "Look!" Julian said, jumping to change the subject as he haphazardly opened and closed the cover.

Yadriel's face screwed up in confusion.

"I can pick it up and move it!" Julian told him, flashing a smile.

"Ooookay." Yadriel stepped closer. "Why are you—?"

Julian quickly stood up from the bed, tossing the yearbook to the side. A Sharpie fell through his lap. "Maritza's waiting for us, right? Come on," he said, making for the door. "Time to sneak out and go find my friends," Julian told him as he walked out into the hall.

Yadriel shook his head and picked up the yearbook. Before putting it away, he flipped it open to his picture. His own face looked up at him, smiling in a way that made him look like he was in physical pain. He wore the same black hoodie, his hair carefully styled.

He was about to snap it shut when he noticed.

Beneath his photo, his deadname had been scribbled out with black marker. Under, written in lopsided letters, it read, YADRIEL.

NINE

I can just jump out the window," Julian suggested as they stood at the top of the stairs, trying to come up with a plan.

Yadriel spun to face him. "What?" he said, giving Julian a bewildered look as he toyed with the St. Jude pendant.

Julian stared at it, his fingers brushing the same spot on himself.

"You're not serious," Yadriel said.

Julian rolled his eyes before locking them onto Yadriel's. "What's it gonna do, kill me?"

"I think a bigger problem would be people seeing a body falling out the window."

"Then you come up with something!"

"*Shh!*" Yadriel paused to listen, but the chatter continued downstairs, undisturbed. "As tempting as it is to throw you out the window—"

Julian's mouth flew open, but Yadriel cut him off. "I think the best option is to just walk out the front door."

"You just said we can't let anyone see me—"

"Right, so we've got to be sneaky about it." Yadriel huffed a breath in an attempt to steady his nerves. "I'll go into the kitchen and distract them, and you sneak out the door, okay?"

Julian looked doubtful, but he bobbed his head in a nod.

"Stay close," he said as they slowly moved down the stairs. A shiver rolled through Yadriel, like icy fingers trailing up his spine.

Julian's voice said in his ear, a cool breeze ghosting against his neck, "You got it, patrón."

Maybe that was too close.

They went down the stairs, and Julian pressed himself against the wall next to the entryway to the kitchen. Yadriel cut him a glance before walking into the kitchen.

"Hi, Lita," he said, and he was greeted by a cacophony of hellos. Every set of eyes swung to Yadriel, and he shrank at the sudden attention.

Lita ushered him forward, and Yadriel moved to the other side of the room, angling himself so Lita and the brujas turned their backs on the living room.

"Are you hungry?" Lita asked. "We're making tamales!"

The brujas lined the counter, making an assembly line of tamales. One of them spread the masa into the corn husk, the next laid the filling, the third wrapped the husk and then handed it to Lita, who placed it in a large pot to be steamed.

"Uh," Yadriel hesitated. Julian peeked at him around the corner, waiting for his instructions. He needed to get their attention.

He knew what'd do that trick.

"Save me a tamal for later? I'm not hungry." All four women looked up at him. "I'm not feeling so good."

The whole room broke into chatter as they converged on him. As they asked him what was wrong, everyone touching his cheeks and checking his forehead for a temperature, Yadriel forced himself not to squirm away.

"I have vivaporú in my bag!"

"I'll brew some manzanilla!"

He gave Julian a subtle jerk of his head, and Julian crept toward the door.

"Take off your shirt," Lita ordered him. "I'll get an egg!" She made to turn toward the fridge, but Julian was only halfway across the room, in clear sight.

"No!" Yadriel shouted, and everyone jumped, including Julian.

Lita clutched her rosary and stared at Yadriel. *"No?"* she repeated, clearly offended.

"I'm—I'm okay, really," Yadriel stammered.

Taking the hint, Julian ran for the door and slipped out.

A cold wave of relief crashed over Yadriel.

"But—" Lita began to argue.

"Really, I'm fine," he told her, conjuring up a smile. "And I'm in a rush, I have to go meet Maritza."

Lita frowned.

"We have important school stuff to do," he added, knowing school was a fail-safe excuse. "Big project."

The brujas turned to Lita, and she thought for a moment, lips pursed. But, eventually, she nodded. "Fine—"

Yadriel bolted for the door.

"No staying out after dark!" Lita called after him.

"We won't!"

"And we're putting vivaporú on you when you get back!" her voice followed as Yadriel ran outside and down the steps.

Julian waited for him by a seafoam-green mausoleum. "All good?" he asked, falling into step alongside him.

"Yeah, though I think I just doomed myself to getting slathered in Vaporub tonight," Yadriel said.

"Ah." Julian smirked. "The Latinx cure-all."

"Seriously," he agreed with a laugh. Voices caught Yadriel's attention, and he craned his head to the right. Immediately, he recognized the back of his dad's head.

"My dad used to—"

"Stop!" Yadriel hissed.

Julian's head whipped side to side, looking around. *"What?"*

"Duck!" Yadriel dropped down behind a stone sarcophagus.

For once, Julian obeyed. "What?" he asked again in a whisper. "What is it?"

Carefully, Yadriel peeked over the large slab of stone for a better look. "It's my dad and my brother," he murmured.

Julian scooted closer, pressing cold against Yadriel's side, and stole a look, too.

Up ahead, Yadriel's dad and Diego stood next to each other. Enrique had his arm on Diego's shoulder, and they stood facing two women. Yadriel recognized the older woman as Beatriz Cisneros. She had short white hair, wore a heavy shawl, and was clearly a spirit. At her side stood Sandra Cisneros, her daughter.

"Are you sure you're ready?" asked Yadriel's dad.

"What are they doing?" Julian asked, his voice soft in Yadriel's ear.

"I think Diego is going to release her spirit." Yadriel felt a pang of envy. After a brujo turned fifteen, it usually took another few years of shadowing the older brujos and learning their ways before you were allowed to release your own spirit. This would be Diego's first time.

"Yes, I'm sure," Beatriz said with a warm chuckle. "I was so worried about leaving Sandra alone, but we talked it through." She smiled at her daughter, who tried to smile back, but her chin wobbled. "I've felt the cold creeping in the past couple of days," she said, gathering her shawl tighter around her shoulders. "We need to do this now, before it's too late."

"Too late?" Julian's voice was small.

"Before she goes maligno," Yadriel told him. He nodded to Beatriz. "See how faded she looks?"

Her colors were all washed out, as if she were just a black-and-white photograph. Seeing her was like looking through a fogged window. The details were blurred and undulating ever so slightly.

"Most of the time, when spirits begin to lose themselves, they start to fade like that before they go maligno. Others skip that stage and just turn without warning." Yadriel had never actually seen that happen before, but he overheard the older brujos talking about it every now and again.

He stole a glance at Julian. His face paled, and Yadriel saw his throat dip as he swallowed.

"Time for us both to move on," Beatriz said.

Enrique nodded.

Sandra and Beatriz exchanged quiet words, and Diego fidgeted with his portaje. Beatriz reached forward, her ghostly hand cupping her daughter's cheek. "So silly! I'll be back for Día de Muertos! Now, let's go, my husband is waiting for me."

Sandra walked up to Diego and handed him a red beaded rosary. It must've been Beatriz's portaje, her tether to the land of the living.

Yadriel's dad gave Diego's shoulders an encouraging squeeze and said something into his ear. Diego stepped forward. In one hand, he held the rosary, and in the other, his long, curved blade. The gold calavera charm swung from the hilt, but his hand was steady.

"Muéstrame el enlace," Diego said, his voice strong and firm. Yadriel remembered how shaky and unsure the words had been coming from his own mouth during his failed attempt to release Julian.

The golden thread sparked to life, running from the rosary to the center of Beatriz's chest.

She smiled, several decades' worth of dimples showing in her cheeks.

"¡Te libero a la otra vida!"

Diego cut his dagger through the air.

As it sliced through the thread, Beatriz closed her eyes. There was a flash of golden light. Beatriz disappeared in an explosion of glittering marigold petals.

"Whoa," Julian breathed, dark eyes transfixed and lips parted as the glowing flowers cascaded to the ground.

The light faded until they were just orange petals dusting Beatriz's grave.

Sandra sighed. Enrique smiled at Diego, and Diego beamed back.

"Well done, mijo," Enrique said, tugging Diego into a tight embrace.

Yadriel's throat closed up and his eyes stung. "Come on," he said, standing up and turning toward the gate.

Julian gave him a confused look from where he remained crouched behind the sarcophagus.

"Let's get out of here—"

"Yadriel?"

He jerked to a stop and spun around. His father stared at him, brow furrowed. Diego was handing Beatriz's rosary back to Sandra, falling deep into conversation.

"Uh—" His eyes flickered to Julian, who ducked lower, trying to stay out of sight. "Dad. Hey."

Enrique approached, and Yadriel panicked, not knowing what to do.

Julian mouthed something, and Yadriel didn't need to read lips to recognize the curse. It was like he was arguing with himself. Julian's face screwed up in disgust, and Yadriel had no idea what he was doing, until he rolled forward and disappeared right into the sarcophagus.

Yadriel sucked in a breath, staring at the spot where Julian had vanished.

His dad came to a stop next to the sarcophagus. "Are you leaving?" he asked, eyeing Yadriel's backpack.

"Uh, yeah," Yadriel tried to gather his thoughts and focus. "Me and Maritza are just going to hang out for a little while."

The frown deepened. "I don't think that's a good idea, it's not safe—"

Yadriel tensed. "We'll be fine. She's bringing the boys. We have an assignment for school to work on," he quickly added.

"Oh." That seemed to placate him, but only a little. Yadriel noted he was wearing the same clothes as the previous night. His checkered shirt was rumpled and half untucked. Had he gotten any sleep since Miguel died?

"I should probably get going . . ." Yadriel waited for his dad to turn around and leave already. He shifted, but his dad didn't move.

"I wanted to check on you . . ." Enrique trailed off awkwardly, scratching at his mussed hair. "And apologize." His eyelids drooped with exhaustion. "Anoche—"

"It's fine," Yadriel cut in. He didn't want to talk about this right now. Especially with Julian in earshot.

Or, well, he wasn't sure what the acoustical setup of being inside a stone coffin was like.

"I didn't mean to say . . ." His father squinted, looking for the right words.

Yadriel swallowed hard. It didn't seem fair for his dad to look so conflicted, and for Yadriel to feel bad about it. He wanted to hang on to his anger. He deserved to be angry, didn't he? But that still didn't keep him from feeling guilty. Even if his dad said and did stupid, hurtful things, he was still his dad, and there was something particularly unsettling about seeing him upset.

But right now, he just needed to rush through this conversation so his dad would leave. "Look, Dad, seriously, it's fine—"

"I'm still learning." He exhaled a short laugh. "Your mamá was better at this. And without her here—" He paused, his brow suddenly furrowing as he looked past Yadriel. "Without her . . . ," he tried again but trailed off, eyes wandering to the sarcophagus.

Yadriel tensed. *"Dad,"* he said, trying to regain his attention.

Enrique started, his gaze going back to Yadriel.

"Can we not do this right now?" Yadriel edged around the stone slab so he was standing between his dad and where Julian was hidden. "I'm in a hurry."

His dad frowned, deep creases tugging down his mouth below his mustache. "But—"

"Maritza's waiting for me—"

"No quise lastimarte, Yadriel." Enrique's voice was quiet when he spoke, giving Yadriel pause.

His fingers tightened into fists. A sour mix of guilt, anger, and embarrassment tumbled in his stomach. Red-hot shame burned in his cheeks as he stared down at his shoes.

Yadriel bit back his knee-jerk reaction to say "It's okay," because it wasn't. It didn't change what his dad had said. If it had been a mistake, his slip of the tongue was more telling than his apologies.

Why did Yadriel always have to absolve people of their guilt? He didn't want to be understanding. He didn't have it in him to be forgiving this time.

His dad's words went unanswered as Diego's and Sandra's voices floated to them between the headstones.

Yadriel heard his dad exhale a sigh.

"We're having dinner tonight," he said. "Home before it gets dark, okay?"

"Okay." There was a long moment before, finally, his dad forced a weak smile, turned, and went back to Diego and Sandra.

Yadriel waited, feeling his heart beat out the seconds in his chest, before the three finally headed back toward the house.

Quickly, Yadriel turned and knocked his knuckles against the lid of the sarcophagus. "Julian!" he said in a harsh whisper. "You can stop hiding—"

Julian fell through the stone, landing hard on his back. He scrambled away, letting out a strangled yelp as he batted at his arms and legs. *"Is it on me?"* he demanded. He looked ridiculous, twisting his neck this way and that to check himself, for cobwebs or bone dust, Yadriel wasn't sure what.

"There's nothing on you," Yadriel told him, trying not to laugh.

Julian's chest heaved up and down, pulling against his white T-shirt. He had a horrified look on his face as he stared up at Yadriel, dark eyes wild. "Holy shit," he breathed. "That was *disgusting*—"

"Get up, we gotta get out of here before someone sees us," Yadriel told him, heading for the gate.

Julian rushed to his feet and chased after him, brushing off his arms as he ran. "It was *dark* and it *smelled* and I touched something *slimy*—" Julian broke off with a violent shudder. "Holy shit, I don't know how long that body's been in there, but clearly not long enough!" His face contorted in disgust. "Why couldn't it have just been a *skeleton*?"

"It takes like eight to twelve years for that to happen," Yadriel told him as they rounded a columbaria.

Julian shuddered again, letting out a shaky breath. When he caught up, Yadriel could feel him staring.

"What?" he snapped between clenched teeth, feeling raw, his nerves exposed.

"That was awkward," Julian stated plainly.

A surprised laugh bucked in Yadriel's chest at Julian's complete lack of filter. His unabashed honesty was blunt, but it was also refreshing to not deal with pretense.

"Yeah, it was," Yadriel agreed. The towering gate groaned as he opened it and slipped through.

Julian opened his mouth, and Yadriel fully expected a slew of questions to come pouring out, but Maritza saved the day.

"The hell took so long?" She stood by the stone wall, a hand on her hip and scowling. The boys flanked her.

Julian backpedaled several steps, his palms held up. "Whoa, whoa, whoa!"

The "boys" were two seventy-five-pound pit bulls. They sat on either side of Maritza, their large, square heads coming up to the middle of her thighs. With cropped ears and silvery-blue coats, they sat still, looking more like stone gargoyles than dogs. They wore wide leather collars around their necks and harnesses that attached to a belt around Maritza's waist.

"We got hung up," Yadriel answered before addressing Julian. "What, are you afraid of dogs?"

"Those are *not* dogs!" Julian declared, pointing.

Yadriel rolled his eyes and turned. "Donatello, Michelangelo!" he called. Immediately, their jowls dropped, tongues happily lolling.

"Like the Ninja Turtles?" Julian asked, still hovering at a safe distance.

"*No*," Maritza snapped, shooting him a glare. "Like the Italian Renaissance artists, pendejo." She stumbled as they both surged for Yadriel.

Julian held up his palms. "Yikes, my bad."

"Like I'd name my beautiful dogs after some dumb cartoon turtles," Maritza groused.

Donatello and Michelangelo jostled Yadriel, getting globs of drool on his jeans as they clamored for scratches. When he and Maritza wanted to go hang out around the city after school, Maritza's parents usually made them take the boys. Even if they were gentle giants, they were terrifying to look at. People gave them a wide berth, always opting to cross the street than pass them on the sidewalk.

"You're nothing but big softies, aren't you?" Yadriel cooed. "Julian's just a big *baby*, isn't he?" He shot Julian a pointed look.

Julian scowled in response but still didn't budge.

Maritza snickered.

"It's not like they can bite you," Yadriel pointed out. "Anyways, they can't even see you." He straightened before they could knock him over in their excitement.

"They can't?" Cautiously, Julian moved closer. As if to check, he waved his hand in front of Donatello's face. For a moment, the large dog sniffed at the air, but he went back to licking Yadriel's knee. "How come your cat can, but they can't?" he asked.

Yadriel looked down at them.

Michelangelo's whole body wiggled when he was excited, so much so that his own tail kept smacking him in the face. Donatello, the bigger of the two, sat back on his haunches, eyes half-lidded, panting and drooling happily up at Yadriel.

"*That's* why." Yadriel grinned.

Julian laughed, his shoulders relaxing back into his usual air of careless ease.

"I resent your implication." Maritza sniffed indignantly, bumping

Michelangelo out of the way with her hip. "My dad rescued them from some sketchy guy outside of a grocery store trying to sell them out of a cardboard box. See their ears?" She rubbed her thumb against the short nub of what was left of Donatello's right ear. "That's called a battle crop. People do that when they're breeding pit bulls for dog fighting," she explained. "So there's nothing for their opponent to rip off in a fight."

"Same reason I keep my hair short," Julian said casually as he ran his palm over his dark, buzzed hair.

Yadriel stared at him. Was he being serious? He eyed that curved scar behind his ear again.

"They were supposed to be trained as search dogs, the kind we use to track down tethers," Yadriel told him. "But they didn't pass the test."

"That doesn't mean I love them any less," Maritza cooed, planting a kiss on top of their large, square heads.

"We're just one redhead in go-go boots short of our own Scooby gang," Julian said, looking pleased with himself.

"Are you implying I'm a *Velma*?" Maritza demanded. "I'm a Fred!"

"Obviously, I'm Fred," Julian went on, as if he hadn't heard her.

Maritza scoffed, and they dove headfirst into bickering about who was more of a Fred.

Yadriel shook his head. "Hey!" He had to snap his fingers before they'd shut up long enough to look at him. "So where are we going? Where do your friends hang out?"

"Bunch of places." Julian thought for a moment. "But if they're trying to lay low . . ." He trailed off, as if he didn't like the answer. He gave his head a small shake. "There's an underpass by the train tracks we hang out at; let's try that first."

"Is it walkable?" Yadriel asked. "We can't exactly get on the bus with these two."

"Yeah, we don't have fancy bus passes."

"Fancy" was the last word Yadriel would use to describe the flimsy card his parents purchased with his student discount.

"We walk everywhere, or ride." As if remembering, Julian added, "Man, I hope they found my skateboard."

Maritza shot Yadriel a criticizing look. He only shrugged in response.

"Hey, is your birthday next month?" she asked Julian.

He blinked. "Yeah, the thirteenth— Wait, how did you—?"

Maritza's face was a picture of smugness. "See?" she said to Yadriel. "Told you." With that, she turned and began walking in the direction of the train tracks. Donatello and Michelangelo led the way as her barrel-chested bodyguards.

"But how did you—?" He turned to Yadriel. "How did she know that?"

"Call it witchy intuition!" Maritza said over her shoulder.

Yadriel couldn't keep himself from laughing as he jogged to catch up. Julian chased after them, demanding answers.

TEN

The farther they got from home, the more unsure Yadriel was about this plan. Afternoon LA traffic kept the streets packed, and the air filled with the sounds of honking, sirens, and bumping subwoofers battling for dominance. But as they followed the train tracks, the main roads started to clear until the sounds of traffic were just a droning in the distance. Empty tracks stretched out before them.

The path was littered with broken brown bottles, fast-food wrappers, and cigarette butts. Donatello and Michelangelo enjoyed snuffling through the debris as Maritza tried, in vain, to stop them.

A man in a large black jacket with his hands stuffed deep into the pockets walked toward them. When he spotted Donatello and Michelangelo, he crossed to the other side of the street, staring intensely as they passed.

"If we get mugged or kidnapped, I'm going to be pissed," Maritza told Yadriel.

He laughed, but it did little to ease the tension knotting his shoulders. "Noted."

The warm afternoon seemed to pass right through Julian. The burning gold light that streaked across the sky and splashed against the walls of buildings didn't touch him. Instead, he was washed in dull blue, the color of dusk.

Julian's pace quickened until Maritza and Yadriel had to half jog to keep up with him. Donatello and Michelangelo trotted along, their massive paws shuffling over the pavement.

"Are we close?" Yadriel asked.

"It's right up ahead!"

Yadriel tucked Julian's necklace under his shirt. He didn't want to have to come up with an explanation if Julian's friends noticed it.

"Here, here, here!" Julian waved at them frantically as he raced toward a set of stairs that led down from the train tracks.

"Wait!" Yadriel called after him, panic finally getting the better of him as he chased after Julian.

Luckily, he stopped at the top of the stairs, but was poised to take off, one hand already on the railing. "What?" he demanded.

"What's the plan here?" Yadriel asked, fidgeting with his hands.

"The plan?" Julian repeated, his face screwed up in confusion.

"Yeah, like, what are we going to say to them?"

Julian waved a hand dismissively. "Nothing, I just need to make sure they're okay!"

"Uh." Maritza came up to Yadriel's side. "We can't just walk into your friends' hideout, be like, 'Hey, just checking in,' and then be on our merry way," she told him.

Yadriel nodded enthusiastically in agreement. He was very glad to have another voice of reason.

Julian let out a groan, like coming up with a game plan was a very large inconvenience. "I'll just tell you what to say in the moment!"

"What, like Cyrano de Bergerac?" Yadriel asked with a sarcastic laugh.

Julian blinked. "Uh . . . yeah."

"Do you even know who that is?" Maritza said.

Julian scowled. "Yes!"

He was definitely lying.

"That didn't exactly work out for him, so I really don't think it'll go well for us, either," Yadriel tried to reason, but he'd already lost Julian's attention again.

"Blah, blah, blah! It'll be fine!" he insisted, turning back to the stairs, bouncing on the balls of his feet. "Come on, they're right over here!"

"*Julian*," Yadriel hissed, but it was too late.

Julian was already halfway down the stairs when Yadriel got to them. He went as fast as he could, only tripping once when his heel caught on an uneven step. At the bottom of the stairs, Yadriel rounded the corner to find him in the concrete tunnel under the tracks. Grass grew between the crooked pavers, and small rivulets ran down wide pillars. Pavement sloped up on either side until it ran against the wall of the arch.

"Thank *God*," Julian exhaled, a smile lighting up his face.

A small group of people sat among an assembly of items. A shabby tent that looked like it could barely fit two people was patched together with bits of duct tape. There were some half-filled jugs of water, what looked like a tarp, and a few other items.

The entire section of wall was covered in spray paint. It wasn't a mural, and certainly nothing done by Banksy, but there were some colorful doodles and a slew of words, some in English, some in Spanish, and others complete gibberish. A large skull was spray-painted off to the side in shades of neon purple, pink, and blue. Most of its teeth were missing, but the ones that remained were crooked and gold. Below in lopsided black letters was HAY NIÑAS CON PENE, NIÑOS CON VULVA Y TRANSFÓBICOS SIN DIENTES. In the lower corner, it read, ST. J.

Yadriel recognized the handwriting. A smile tugged at the corner of his lips.

A beaten-up floral couch was pushed against the wall. A girl sat on the back of the couch with her feet planted on the cushions. Yadriel recognized her high ponytail and pierced nose as Rocky. With a skateboard laid across her thighs, she had an intense look on her face as she stared across at a boy sitting on a lowrider bicycle, gripping the high handlebars. His hair was faded on the sides with small dreads on top. Omar's chin was jutted in the same manner Yadriel had seen in his yearbook photo.

Next to Rocky, a thin girl sat tucked into the corner of the couch, her arms crossed tightly over her chest. She had thick dark hair, cheekbones like a supermodel, and a hooked nose. Her eyebrows were drawn with experienced precision, and her fingernails were painted a deep plum. Recognition shot through Yadriel. He knew her; he just hadn't known her as Flaca.

"Hey, pendejos!" Julian called, grinning ear to ear.

The three didn't so much as flinch.

"HEY!"

"They can't hear you, remember?" Yadriel whispered, trying to keep quiet. He could hear Maritza trying to navigate down the narrow stairs with Donatello and Michelangelo.

"Oh." Julian frowned. "Wait, where's Luca?" he said to himself, and then, again, to Yadriel with more urgency, "Where's Luca?"

Yadriel could barely shrug before Julian stomped toward his friends.

"LUCA!" he shouted, an edge of panic in his voice so sharp it gave Yadriel a surge of adrenaline.

"I told you," Yadriel hissed, lurching forward, but his hand went right through Julian's back, spilling ice water up the veins of his arm. "They can't—" But he was too loud.

All three sets of eyes swung to Yadriel. He froze, perched on the balls of his feet.

Flaca sat up straighter and blinked at him. The look she gave him flicked from surprise to recognition to curiosity. Meanwhile Rocky looked unimpressed, and Omar just seemed straight-up irritated.

"Spot's already taken," Omar called.

"Ask him where Luca is," Julian demanded.

"Uhhh," was Yadriel's intelligent response.

It was then a fourth person peeked around the edge of the pillar where they were all gathered. A pair of large eyes looked out from under a swath of golden-brown hair.

"Luca!" Julian's shoulders dropped. A delirious sort of laugh fell from his lips.

Luca moved out from behind the pillar and eyed Yadriel over Omar's shoulder. He was short and wore a faded olive sweater that was far too big for him. The sleeves practically swallowed up his hands. His wavy hair framed his face and curled around his ears. There was a black smudge across the bridge of his nose, and a skateboard covered in stickers tucked under his arm. "Who's that?" Luca asked.

"You deaf or somethin'?" Omar stood from his bike, expression severe. "I *said*—"

"Jesus!" A disgruntled Maritza rounded the corner, pulled along by Donatello and Michelangelo as they panted sloppily. "I nearly *broke my ass* on those stairs!" she announced, rubbing her butt. "Thanks a lot." She glared down at the two dogs.

Donatello happily smacked himself in the face with his own tail while Michelangelo stared up at her, his tongue dripping with drool.

All four of Julian's friends moved at once. Flaca pressed herself further into the couch as Rocky leaped to her feet, standing her ground even though restrained panic glinted in her eyes as they darted back and forth between them and Omar.

Maritza pushed her pink-and-purple hair out of her face and looked up, finally noticing they weren't alone. "Oh, hey," she said, lifting a hand in greeting.

Omar backed up a step, and Luca disappeared behind him completely.

"What do you want?" Omar demanded, shoulders back and chest puffed.

They were getting off on the entirely wrong foot.

Of course, Julian was no help. "My skateboard!" He went over to a very worn-out-looking skateboard leaning against the arm of the couch. It had cracks and raw edges. On the bottom, Julian's name was written in large neon green letters. It was covered in several stickers, most of which had been nearly scraped off, but Yadriel recognized one of St. Jude.

Julian eyed the couch and tent. "Are they sleeping out here again?" he said to himself before scowling at his friends.

"We don't want anything," Maritza said, putting on her best look of nonchalance. "We were just passing through." She glanced at Julian. "Everyone seems present and accounted for, so we'll be off—"

Yadriel inwardly groaned.

"What are you talking about?" Flaca asked. Her attention shifted to Yadriel. Her lips parted. "I know you from school," she said.

Yadriel's face burned under her gaze. "Uh, yeah, I think so," he said, even though he *definitely* knew her.

"You know each other?" Julian asked.

Flaca was the first openly trans person Yadriel had ever met. They'd had a couple of the same classes and had even worked on a history project together. He remembered the first time Flaca wore a skirt to school, and how he'd stared. Yadriel thought it was both incredibly brave and terrifying, all at once.

Flaca was unapologetically herself. They'd been sitting next to each other when she got pulled out of class by the teacher and sent to the principal's office. While other students had oohed and jeered as the teacher ushered her out of the room, Flaca stood from her desk and walked out calmly, not sparing anyone a single glance.

That's where he recognized Rocky from, too. He'd seen her standing guard outside the stall when Flaca used the girls' restroom, throwing seething glares at anyone who so much as looked at Flaca the wrong way. More than once, he'd watched Rocky follow teachers down the hall, yelling at them as they escorted Flaca to the main office. Every time, Flaca held her chin high, statuesque in her confident walk.

It was seeing Flaca, her fearlessness, that encouraged Yadriel to wear a binder to school for the first time. No one else had seemed to notice, but when he sat down next to Flaca, she looked him up and down, smiled, and said, "Looks good."

Yadriel's face had burst into a white-hot flush, but Flaca had left it at that.

When she stopped showing up to school halfway through last year, Yadriel had noticed.

Now, Flaca gave him a once-over again. "What's your name?" she asked.

It was a simple question, but it made Yadriel's chest tight, like his binder was squeezing all the air from his lungs.

"Your *real* name," Flaca corrected.

The tension popped like a balloon. "Yadriel," he said, like a sigh of relief.

Flaca smiled. "Much better."

Yadriel smiled back.

"Who are you?" Omar demanded, bringing Yadriel's attention back to the matter at hand. There were still three other people giving him suspicious looks.

Yadriel hesitated, not sure how to respond. He flicked a look to Julian.

"Oh," he said, as if he just remembered his job. "Just tell them you're my friend."

Yadriel tried to answer as quickly as possible, but the pause while he waited for Julian's instructions was long and awkward. "We're Julian's friends," Yadriel repeated.

"No, you're not," Rocky snapped. She shifted her skateboard in her grip. She wasn't exactly brandishing it, but Yadriel fully believed she'd used it as a weapon before and wouldn't hesitate to do so again.

Maritza looked to Yadriel.

"This isn't going well," Julian observed from the sidelines.

Not helpful.

"You're right, we're really more like acquaintances," Yadriel tried. No one looked very convinced. It was better to get out now before something bad happened. Even if they were Julian's friends, Yadriel knew nothing about them.

"Sorry, we didn't mean to bother you, we just thought he'd be here." He backed toward the stairs.

Flaca watched him carefully, calculatingly.

"But obviously he isn't, so we'll just—"

"Wait!" Luca stepped out from behind Omar. "Have you seen Jules?" His voice was hopeful. Luca spoke with his chin tucked down, glancing up at them through the fringe of his hair. The wide neck of his sweater slid down his collarbone.

"Luca," Omar warned, catching the smaller boy's arm.

Yadriel glanced to Julian for some direction.

"No, you haven't," he said with a vigorous shake of his head.

"No, we haven't," Yadriel echoed.

Luca's shoulders fell. "Neither have we. Not—not since last night—"

Omar gave him a tug. "We don't know them—" he hissed, but Luca twisted out of his grasp with such expertise, his sudden absence made Omar stumble.

"We've been looking for him."

Julian stiffened. "Jesus, Luca." He moved to his friend, reaching as if to grab his chin, but he stopped, probably remembering he couldn't touch him.

Yadriel gave the boy a closer look, not knowing what Julian saw that was making him so upset. But then he realized.

The smudge across the bridge of his nose wasn't dirt but a bruise. There was also a red cut in the corner of his mouth. And was his bottom lip swollen?

"He's missing," Flaca finally said.

Luca nodded while Rocky shifted her weight between her feet, her gaze dropping to the ground.

"¡Cállate, Flaca!" Omar warned.

Flaca brushed him off with an irritated wave of her hand.

For a moment, the pretense and defenses slipped. They were just four kids worried about their best friend. Yadriel released some of the tension he was holding. There was no drug paraphernalia, no guns or weapons that he could see. *He* was the one with a dagger tucked into the waist of his jeans.

If they only thought Julian was missing . . . "What happened?"

Flaca spoke first. "He got jumped by the park."

"We don't even know them!" Omar was still trying to keep their secrets, but it was obvious he'd lost control over the situation. Their concerns for Julian outweighed anything else.

"I got jumped," Luca corrected. His shoulders hunching up to his ears. "Jules tried to stop them. It was dark, he told us to run, so we scattered." He twisted his sleeves between his fingers. "We can't find him."

This wasn't good. There were no leads for them to go off of. If they thought Julian was missing, that meant they hadn't found his body. And it also meant—

"They don't know I'm dead."

Julian stood there, his arms limp at his sides. He stared down at Luca, and his expression—the upturned brows and painful grimace of his lips—made Yadriel's heart ache.

"When we regrouped, he wasn't there, so we went looking for him, but he'd disappeared without a trace," Luca explained.

Disappeared without a trace.

Yadriel's mind raced, fitting the pieces together. Julian had died last night. He got jumped in the park, and when his friends tried looking for him, he was gone. There was no sign of his body.

Just like Miguel.

"Have you guys talked to Rodrigo?" Luca asked, a hopeful lift in his voice.

Julian tensed, but Yadriel tried not to look at him, still under Omar's careful watch.

"My brother," Julian said tersely.

"No, we haven't," Yadriel replied.

Flaca sighed. "Rio probably thinks Jules ran away, too. They got into a *huge* fight a few days ago, and Jules hadn't gone home yet."

"*That's none of their business,*" Omar hissed.

The thundering approach of a train filled Yadriel's ears. As it passed overhead, the wheels clacked loudly, buffeting the air and reeking of diesel. Rocky, Flaca, and Omar seemed to be arguing, their voices impossible to hear with the passing of the train. Luca stood there cringing, plugging his ears with his fingers.

Donatello and Michelangelo tugged nervously against their leashes, and Maritza dropped to her knee, giving them scratches and offering comfort.

In all the commotion, Yadriel stole a look at Julian. He was staring at the ground, his hands balled into fists at his sides. The wind whipped his jacket and tugged at his white tee.

By the time the train passed, Omar looked just as disgruntled, but his mouth was clamped shut.

"Someone needs to tell Rio what happened," Luca said. "But..." He trailed off.

They all looked ashamed, even Omar.

"Their place is right by Belvedere," Flaca stepped in to explain. "And we're too freaked out to go back..."

Yadriel inwardly sighed. He couldn't really blame them for being afraid, could he? But at the same time, he was frustrated. Knowing Julian, there was probably nothing frightening enough to keep him from making sure his friends were okay. But still. Not everyone was as fearlessly reckless as Julian Diaz. Even his best friends.

He almost asked why they didn't just call or text Rio, but he caught himself. Obviously, if they hadn't done that yet, it was because they didn't *have* cell phones to call or text him on.

"Have you told the police?" Maritza asked.

Omar's laugh was sharp as knives and dark as coal.

"They wouldn't listen to us," Flaca said. "We made a police report this morning when he never showed up, but we couldn't even give a description of the guy who jumped him. It was too dark to see anything."

"I don't remember, either," Julian confirmed in a gruff voice.

What was it about his brother that set Julian off like that?

When Yadriel glanced at Julian, Omar's eyes narrowed, trying to track what he was looking at.

"They wouldn't even put out a missing-person alert for Jules," Flaca continued.

"What?" Yadriel shook his head. "Why not?"

"Because he's a Latino boy living in East Los Angeles with no parents," Omar said, seething.

"They decided he was a runaway," Rocky explained. "When a kid goes missing, they assume they're at risk, so you get AMBER Alerts, calls in the media, and police searching and asking around. But if you're a runaway?" She shook her head. "Nothing."

"We can try talking to him—" Yadriel ventured.

Julian spun toward him. "No!" he barked.

Yadriel looked toward Julian on instinct. Quickly, he tried to turn away, but Omar's eyes narrowed. "Maybe he's heard something."

"I said *NO!*" Julian shouted, so loud that Yadriel and Maritza both jumped, hit in the face with a wall of cold. Both their attention snapped to Julian. The muscles in his jaw jumped, nostrils flared and body rigid as he glared at them. His edges flickered.

Flaca, Luca, and Rocky glanced around to see what they were staring at and exchanged confused looks.

But Omar was zeroed in on Yadriel. "What?" he asked.

Yadriel blinked. "What?"

"What are you looking at?"

"Nothing," Yadriel said, way too quickly. He was starting to sweat.

"We just want to find him and make sure he's okay," Rocky said, hugging her skateboard tight to her chest. "We don't want him to end up missing for good."

"Just like the rest of them," Luca added miserably.

Yadriel frowned. "Rest of them? What does that mean?"

"Bunch of street kids have been going missing—that's three now, right?" Rocky looked to Flaca for confirmation, who nodded.

"*Three* missing kids?" Maritza repeated.

Luca pressed his palms against his eyes. Yadriel caught a glimpse of his dimpled chin before Omar stepped in front of him, blocking Luca from view.

"That's nothing new," Omar insisted. "Kids go missing all the time, just no one notices 'cause they're already living on the streets, or their parents threw them out."

Flaca flinched.

"Yeah, but they all went missing in the same area—around Belvedere—and all been labeled runaways," Flaca said. Her fingernails dug into the crook of her elbow. "Whoever took them probably took Jules, too."

"They're worrying too much about me and need to be worrying about themselves," Julian spoke up, walking closer to the group. "They need to go somewhere more safe than *this*," he said, thrusting his arms out.

"Is there somewhere safe you guys can ride this out?" Yadriel asked.

"Usually, when stuff goes down, Rio takes us in," Flaca said in a small, crestfallen tone.

"There's gotta be somewhere else!" Julian fumed, his patience, once again, wearing thin.

"There's nowhere else you can stay?" Yadriel prompted.

"Not everybody's got places they can run off to when they're in trouble," Omar sneered in a way that made it seem like he thought Yadriel was gloating.

It caught him off guard. "There's got to be someone," Yadriel said with a shake of his head. "What about your parents? Your families?"

"*We're it,*" Omar snapped, gesturing between himself and his friends. "We take care of *each other.*" He stood tall, his chin jutting out stubbornly.

"Blood of the covenant," Omar told Yadriel, holding his hands out as his sides.

Julian sighed and said in a defeated tone, "Is thicker than the water of the wound."

"Is thicker than the water of the wound," Yadriel repeated automatically. His eyebrows furrowed, and he glanced to Julian, barely able to keep himself from correcting him for yet another malapropism. Yadriel was so distracted, he hadn't noticed that Luca, Flaca, Rocky, and Omar were all staring.

"What?" Omar hissed.

Yadriel jumped, turning his attention back to them. Their expressions were all varying degrees of shock and confusion. "What?"

"What did you just say?" Flaca asked, staring at him like she'd seen a ghost.

"Uh—" Yadriel rushed for a coherent reply. "The blood of the covenant is thicker than the water of the womb," he said.

"No, you said *wound*," Rocky insisted.

"Did I?" A nervous laugh bubbled in his throat.

"*Shit*, you weren't supposed to say that!" Julian barked.

Yadriel scowled at him. It wasn't like he did it on purpose.

"What do you keep looking at?" Omar demanded.

Yadriel backed up. "I—uh—"

"That's what Jules always says," Luca said, confused.

"How did you know to say that?" Omar pressed.

"Don't tell them!" Julian shouted, his whole body flickering like lightning behind storm clouds.

Yadriel couldn't help but look in his direction when Julian's voice cut through his ears so sharply. He wanted to tell him of course he wasn't going to tell them. Yadriel wasn't going to out Julian as being dead if he didn't want him to, and he sure as hell wasn't going to out himself as being able to see spirits—

"HEY!"

Yadriel's eyes snapped right back to Omar.

"Look at me when I'm talking to you!" Omar took another step forward.

Donatello and Michelangelo immediately lowered their heads, deep growls rumbling in their chests. Their jowls pulled back, baring their teeth in warning.

"*Yads,*" Maritza said, eyes wide with alarm as she gripped their leashes.

"Don't tell them!" Julian repeated angrily.

Too many people were talking at once. It was overwhelming. Panic clawed up Yadriel's throat.

Flaca and Rocky backed up. Omar dragged Luca behind him.

Yadriel burned under each set of eyes.

He didn't mean to freak them out; he was just trying to help, and the dogs were only trying to protect him and Maritza. This was quickly spiraling out of his control.

"*How did you know to say that?*" Omar shouted.

Maritza tried to pull the dogs back.

Flaca tugged on Omar's arm.

Yadriel fumbled, willing himself to just say *something* to cover up his mistake. "I— He—"

"LISTEN TO ME!" Julian bellowed. He grabbed his skateboard from the couch and heaved it over his head with both hands before slamming it down. The wood cracked like lightning against the pavement, echoing through the underpass and straight through Yadriel's bones.

Everyone jolted. Donatello and Michelangelo whimpered, cowering as Maritza tried to regain control and not get knocked over.

The skateboard landed upside down, the wheels spinning.

Julian stormed through the group and tore off up the stairs, a blast of cold following in his wake. It kicked up dirt and bit Yadriel's cheeks.

He stood there for a moment, dumbfounded. Omar, Flaca, Rocky, and Luca had all converged, huddled together as they gaped at him.

Heat flooded Yadriel's face. How had he screwed things up so badly?

"I—I'm sorry, I—"

Omar cut him off, pointing in the direction of the road. "Leave. Now." His voice was a low growl.

"*Yads,*" Maritza warned, already backing up to the stairs, the dogs glued to her hips.

He saw their looks of shock and fear. Rocky squeezed a quaking Flaca, doing her best to look fierce, but it was a crumbling facade. Luca was barely visible around Omar, his eyes still stuck on the skateboard. "I—"

"NOW!" Omar shouted.

Yadriel flinched but quickly obeyed.

Maritza was already heading up the stairs, Donatello and Michelangelo pulling her along. As Yadriel hurried to catch up with her, all he could think about was Julian and his friends. Their faces. He wasn't cut out for this. He'd only made things worse for everyone.

ELEVEN

W ell, that could've gone better," Maritza said as she and Yadriel hurried to keep up with Julian. Donatello and Michelangelo trotted along happily on either side of her, as if nothing had happened.

"Not funny." Humiliation and guilt warred in Yadriel, but he was also pissed at Julian. His emotional outburst didn't sit right with Yadriel. Yelling and getting mad was one thing, but acting out violently was a whole other beast.

Julian refused to slow down or wait, causing Yadriel and Maritza to chase after him through the streets. A line of sweat trickled down Yadriel's spine under his hoodie. October in Los Angeles was not cool enough, and his binder wouldn't let him breathe deep enough for this.

They crossed the street to the iron gate of the cemetery. He didn't need Julian storming in and attracting the attention of the brujx and the other spirits.

Yadriel jogged forward, catching up to Julian's pace. "Hey!" he called ahead. "What kind of machismo bullshit was that?"

He was angry, and Julian's outburst had scared him, which only made him *more* angry.

Julian turned so abruptly, Yadriel reeled back a step.

"You were going to tell them I'm dead!" he fumed, teeth bared. Cold wind whipped around him, sending his jacket flapping against his sides.

Yadriel stood his ground under Julian's lethal stare. Even though instinct told him to back away. "No, I wasn't!" he shot back, trying to channel as much fierceness as he could.

Julian's laugh was sharp, his grin sarcastic and untrusting.

It got under Yadriel's skin, which was probably the point. It took every bit of patience he had left to not lash out in return. "You told me not to tell them, so I didn't."

He met Julian's glare defiantly. "I *wouldn't*," he emphasized.

Julian's snarl wavered for a moment. His stare was intense, questioning, and calculating.

Yadriel met it unflinchingly. "I don't out people," he told him.

Slowly, the harsh lines of Julian's expression began to melt. The wind calmed. The chill in the air ebbed. It was Julian who looked away first.

The tension in Yadriel's shoulders relaxed.

For a long moment, Julian stared out at where the sun had set behind the rolling hills.

In the back of his mind, Yadriel knew it would be dark soon. If they didn't get moving, he'd be in trouble with Lita and his dad. But, right now, there were more important matters at hand than missing curfew.

"I just wanted to give them a clean break," Julian said quietly.

Yadriel didn't think that was possible. He didn't see how anyone could get a clean break from Julian once they entered his orbit.

Himself included.

Yadriel studied Julian's profile. The worry in his brow, his strong nose, and the stubborn curve of his chin. His cheeks were flushed, the muscles of his jaw working. The waning light washed everything in cool pastels. It was like Julian had been painted against the city in shades of silvery blue. A watery reflection.

He was a bit of an ass. Headstrong, impulsive, and definitely obnoxious. But Yadriel could see how ferociously he cared about the people who were important to him. He believed Julian would die for his friends.

He probably had.

"I know you don't want to hurt your friends," Yadriel said, in a gentler tone this time. "Or your brother." Julian glanced at him from the corner of his eyes. "But this isn't *just* about you anymore."

Julian looked ready to argue, so Yadriel hurried on before he got the chance.

"You were attacked last night, and whoever did it killed you; we know that much. But then you—your body—completely vanished, without a trace," he explained. "A couple of hours after that, Miguel died, and now we can't find him, either."

At first, he hadn't put the pieces together. Not until they talked to Julian's friends and they told him what Julian couldn't remember, or didn't know. They filled in the gaps, and the picture being painted was frightening.

"Miguel was supposed to be patrolling the cemetery, and we found *your* necklace in the cemetery," Yadriel stressed, pulling out the St. Jude pendant from under the neck of his hoodie.

Julian's attention went right to it, eyebrows tipping. His fingers went to his own neck, as if yearning to have it back.

"That can't be just a coincidence. Whatever happened to you probably happened to Miguel, too." Yadriel sighed, his hand falling back to his side. "There's something bigger going on here, but I don't know what."

He hesitated, anticipating Julian's reaction before he could even get the words out. "If we could just go to your place—"

"I don't want to go see my brother," Julian snapped.

Fatigue and frustration flared. "I know, but—"

Maritza stepped forward. "If we could get one of your shirts or something, we could try tracking your body down," she suggested with a small lift of her shoulder. "I mean, Donatello and Michelangelo didn't pass the tracker test, but it's all we've got to work with."

Julian looked between her and the dogs, not seeming the least bit convinced.

Yadriel, on the other hand, had hope. "We could give it to them and go back to where you got jumped," he said. "They could pick up the scent and lead us to your body, and maybe Miguel's, too." It wasn't much of a plan, but it was at least somewhere to start. And it was better than standing around doing nothing.

He tried again. "If we could just talk to Rio for a second—"

Julian growled, looking just as irritated as Yadriel felt. *"I don't—"*

"We could ask if he's heard anything. Maybe the police did find your body and contacted him," Yadriel continued. "While we're there distracting him, you could grab something of yours for the dogs to get your scent. I mean, you've been practicing your haunting skills, right?" he pointed out, thinking back to the mess Julian had created in his room.

Julian leaned his head back and made a noise of frustration up at the cobalt-tinted clouds.

Yadriel took him not immediately arguing as a good sign. Maybe he could be reasoned with. "Look, I know all you cared about was making sure your friends were okay," he told him. "But they could be in danger, too."

Julian tensed.

"Whatever happened to you probably happened to Miguel *and* those missing kids." All these connections couldn't possibly be sheer coincidence. "And if we don't figure out who did it, they might go after your friends next."

That got his attention.

Yadriel could see the panic rising. How Julian's hands tightened into fists at his sides. How his eyes flitted around like he was trying to think of an alternative plan.

Yadriel didn't know what to do if Julian said no. This was more than just proving he was a brujo. It was much bigger than that. He wanted to find Miguel and help him. He wanted to help the others. He didn't want Julian to be complacent about the fact that he'd been murdered. Whoever did this to Julian and Miguel, Yadriel refused to let them get away with it.

"We need your help," Yadriel said. "*I* need your help." He leaned in, trying to catch Julian's eyes.

Julian turned. His brow wrinkled as he pressed his lips between his teeth.

"Please, Jules."

Julian flinched, but then his shoulders slumped in defeat. Hope leaped in Yadriel's heart when Julian's lips parted. "I—"

"I'll help you," someone called.

Yadriel, Julian, and Maritza all jerked to turn toward the voice.

A boy in a large olive green sweater stood across the street, a skateboard tucked under his arm.

"Uh-oh," Maritza murmured.

Yeah. This was a big "uh-oh."

Julian's shoulders slumped. "Luca, you idiot," he said as the boy crossed the road and perched on the edge of the curb.

"Hey . . ." Yadriel trailed off awkwardly. How much had he heard?

"I'll help you guys," Luca repeated. He didn't look freaked out, or even upset. He looked more curious than anything.

Maritza and Yadriel exchanged looks.

"What is he doing here?" Julian scowled, pacing back and forth in front of Luca. "He shouldn't have come all this way on his own."

"Look, whatever happened back there was kinda . . . weird," Luca said, a nervous laugh bubbling past his lips.

"We really didn't mean to cause any trouble," Yadriel said, because it was true and he felt like he owed an explanation.

"I want to help," Luca offered again, shifting his grip on his stateboard as his eyes kept dashing back to Donatello and Michelangelo.

Jules groaned and dragged his hand over his face.

Maritza gave Yadriel a surprised look.

"You . . . do?" Yadriel was going to keep his word to Julian, so he wasn't going to offer up any information without knowing what exactly Luca meant, or how much he knew. Or guessed.

Luca bobbed his head yes, a ghost of a smile playing across his lips as he watched Donatello wiggle at the attention.

"See? This! This is your problem, Luca!" Julian barked, throwing his hands up.

"Is Jules dead?"

He asked it so suddenly, and so casually, it left Yadriel speechless and staring.

"I'm not sure I believe in ghosts," Luca admitted.

"Christ," Julian groaned.

"But the skateboard." Luca scratched the back of his head. "Jules has kind of a quick temper."

"No kidding," Maritza grumbled under her breath.

Julian huffed and tugged his hood over his head.

Luca gave them an apologetic smile. "He doesn't mean nothin' by it."

Julian glowered, heavy brow pulled down over his dark eyes, but Luca seemed to be thawing his anger.

"But when he gets mad, he'll throw it like that, y'know? It was really freaky." He lifted his bony shoulders in a shrug. "Plus, you guys were talking to like, nothing." Luca gestured vaguely. "So either you're both crazy, or Julian's dead," he guessed. "And you guys can see him?"

Maritza looked to Yadriel, but he kept his mouth shut. Instead, he looked to Julian. He wasn't going to say anything without his permission.

Luca followed his gaze, searching the air and tilting his head, as if he just needed the right light to see Julian standing there.

Julian's eyes were hidden under the hood of his jacket. Yadriel couldn't read his expression, but he could see his jaw was clenched. After a moment, he gave a curt nod. "Okay," he said. "Tell him."

Yadriel swallowed, trying to find his voice through the tightness of his throat. "Yes," he said.

He regretted it immediately.

Luca's expression wavered between surprise and sadness. "I thought so," he said, sniffing as his large eyes started to glisten in the waning twilight. Luca tried to smile, but his chin wobbled. "Julian wouldn't have just left us without a reason, he wouldn't—" He cut himself off, rubbing at his forehead.

Yadriel felt Luca's grief, rolling off him and hitting him in the stomach.

Julian stood there, body rigid and expression still hidden.

Yadriel tried to come up with something to say that would offer the smaller boy comfort. What would his mom say if she were here?

"Luca—" he started gently, but Luca didn't let him finish.

"Yeah, see, there's no way Rio will see you on your own." Luca rubbed his nose on his sleeve, drawing Yadriel's attention back to the bruise. "He doesn't like strangers, doesn't trust people—kind of like Omar, but worse."

Yadriel wasn't sure that was possible.

"But if I'm with you, he'll at least let you in the door," Luca explained.

Julian crossed his arms over his chest and shook his head. "You little traitor . . . ," he said, but it lacked heat.

"I don't know . . ." Yadriel trailed off, waiting for Julian's guidance.

"I owe him." Luca's expression pinched, his delicate eyebrows bunching together. He tugged anxiously on the frayed hem of his sweater. "Julian, I mean. If he is dead, it's because of me. He was trying to protect me, and then I ran off, and . . ." He swallowed hard.

Yadriel stole a glance at Julian.

He pushed his hood back, expression somber as he looked down at his friend. "Luca . . ."

"I want to find out what happened," Luca went on. "We were too scared to go to Rio, but if he does know something . . ." When he spoke, his voice was firmer, more sure of himself. "I want to help, if I can." He was staring down at the dogs again, as if they were part of the conversation. "I owe it to Jules, and Rio."

Julian winced. "You don't owe me shit," he said in a quiet sigh. He tipped his head to the side, watching Luca as the smaller boy waited for an answer.

Yadriel didn't say anything. This was Julian's choice, not his, no matter how much he wanted Julian to agree to it.

Luca, meanwhile, was distracted. "Can I pet your dogs?" he asked Maritza with a hopeful lift of his eyebrows.

Maritza laughed. "Yeah, sure," she said moving closer. "They're friendly."

Luca immediately put down his skateboard and dropped into a squat, small arms in long sleeves held out to his sides. Donatello and Michelangelo bowled Luca right over, knocking him off his feet. He was practically swallowed up by the large dogs as they nudged and licked at him happily.

As he laughed, hands giving them both a good scratch, Donatello's lolling tongue gave him a particularly good swipe. It slicked back Luca's mass of light brown hair, revealing a large scar running down the side of his face. It was a patch of marbled skin.

Yadriel's heart made a hard thump in his chest. He'd seen scars like it on Maritza's dad's arm. Burns.

She noticed, too, the grin on her face slipping to a look of shock.

Julian didn't say anything.

There was a lot about Julian and his friends that Yadriel still didn't know.

When Julian remained silent, Yadriel said, "I don't think he wants us to see Rio."

Luca stared up at Yadriel with his large deep amber eyes while Michelangelo lapped at his ear. "So you can hear him? And see him?"

Yadriel nodded. "Yes."

Luca looked around, twisting his fingers together. "Where is he?"

Both Yadriel and Maritza looked at Julian.

Julian stood there, motionless as he watched Luca. Even his silence was loud. His stillness was unsettling. Yadriel didn't like it. He almost preferred Julian yelling to this.

Luca searched the empty air, squinting, even venturing to take a step closer. "Can he hear me?"

"Yes, he can hear you," Yadriel said softly.

Hesitantly, Luca held out his hand. "Can he touch me?"

Julian's expression was slack, his spine bowed and eyes dull as they studied Luca. He stepped forward and reached out. His hand hovered just above Luca's. Yadriel held a breath as Julian's face pinched in concentration.

Julian lowered his hand, and his fingers slipped right through Luca's palm.

Luca shivered, his arm quaking inside the large sleeve, but otherwise didn't react.

"It doesn't really work like that . . . ," Yadriel said as Julian stepped back and turned his head away.

Pink bloomed in Luca's cheeks. He dropped his hand to his side and rubbed his arm. He gave that apologetic little smile again.

"Fine."

Julian's voice was so small, at first Yadriel wasn't sure he'd heard right.

"Really?" Yadriel asked, trying to get a look at his face, but Julian kept it turned away. Instead, he gave a jerky nod.

"What?" Luca asked, looking around again. "What'd he say?"

"He said yes," Yadriel said. The relief crashing over him felt so good, he smiled.

Luca smiled back. "I could meet you guys tomorrow morning, give you the night to think it over?"

"It would need to be the afternoon, we've got school." Yadriel nodded toward Maritza.

"Oh, right. Afternoon, then." Luca nodded. "Where should I meet you? Do you live nearby?"

"Yeah, I live there," Yadriel said, motioning through the large gate. The lights were on in his house. The church loomed on the other side.

Luca's eyes went wide. "You live in there? Whoa, no wonder you can see ghosts."

Maritza laughed.

Yadriel grinned and bit back the urge to correct him.

"I'm Maritza, by the way," she cut in. "And that guy is Yadriel."

"Oh." Luca's eyes did that quick little dart to Yadriel's chest.

On instinct, Yadriel curled in on himself, tightly crossing his arms as heat crawled up his neck. He hated that glance, and he hated the mix of embarrassment and shame that came with it.

"I'm Luca." His lips tugged in a lopsided smile. "But I guess Jules told you that already?" He laughed. "Okay, well I'll meet you guys here, then, tomorrow afternoon."

Julian straightened as Luca hopped onto his skateboard. "He can't walk back on his own, it's dark out—"

"Do you need somewhere to stay the night?" Yadriel asked quickly. He was already housing *one* boy in secret, he didn't think he could handle another, but Julian was right—it *was* dark out, and if someone was going around picking off kids from the street—

"You could stay at my place," Maritza offered, toying with her rosary. "I bet if I talked to my parents—"

"Oh, no, that's okay!" Luca waved her off, rubbing at the back of his neck. "My parents live a few streets over—"

Yadriel saw Julian tense.

"I'll just stay there tonight."

Before Yadriel could think of something convincing to say, Luca was already rolling down the sidewalk and around the corner.

For a moment, all three of them stood there, not saying anything.

All the ferocity Julian had shown earlier seemed to have drained out of him. And, to be honest, Yadriel felt too exhausted to be combative, either. "Julian—"

He spun on his heel and glided right through the iron bars of the gate.

Yadriel sighed.

Maritza shooed him. "Go on after him. I have to go home before my mom kills me." She gave a short wave before Donatello and Michelangelo pulled her down the street.

Yadriel raced through the headstones to catch up to Julian. Voices came from the church, and he could see through the windows that the brujx had gathered inside. Warm light spilled from the open doors of the church, washing over the steps and path lined with marigolds. A couple of stragglers made their way into the church.

He remembered what his dad had said that morning, that they were having family dinner. Had he meant a meeting? Or was this an impromptu gathering?

Either way, he needed to get Julian safely into his room before he could figure it out. At first, he thought Julian was just going to barge into the house, but he stopped at the door and waited for Yadriel to catch up.

Tentatively, he opened the door a crack and listened. No music, no voices. Everyone must've been at the church already. He waved Julian in and ushered him up the stairs. "I need to go to the church," Yadriel told him as he pulled his phone out of his pocket to check his messages. "Lita is going to kill me if I . . ." He trailed off.

Julian hadn't acknowledged him at all. He went right up the stairs.

"Hey," Yadriel said, watching him from the foot of the steps.

Julian looked back over his shoulder.

Yadriel frowned at him. "Are you okay?"

Julian gave him a withering look.

It was a dumb question. He was dead—he'd been murdered—and he was worried about his friends; of course he wasn't okay.

"Yadriel?" said a voice from the kitchen.

He froze. The floor creaked. His eyes widened in alarm, but he didn't have to warn Julian. He disappeared up the stairs and around the corner before Catriz stepped into the living room.

"There you are," Tío Catriz said with a sigh. "Your dad sent me looking for you." He frowned and glanced around the empty room. "Who were you talking to?"

"Uh." Yadriel held up his phone. "Just Maritza."

Tío Catriz watched him for a moment, for three heartbeats longer than was comfortable, but then his mouth curled into a smile. "You two really are attached at the hip," he said with a chuckle and a shake of his head.

Yadriel laughed along with him, maybe a little too loud.

"Come on," he said, waving for Yadriel to follow him. "Your dad called a meeting with everyone. Even the outcasts," Tío Catriz added with an amused grin.

"Yeah." His attention was pulled back to Julian. "Let me just ditch my backpack real quick?" Yadriel asked, already inching toward the stairs.

Tío Catriz nodded. "The black sheep might as well show up fashionably late," he said, smoothing down the front of his dark button-up shirt.

Yadriel hurried to his room.

Julian sat on the edge of his bed, elbows on his knees and hands fidgeting.

Yadriel tossed his backpack onto his desk. "Are you okay?" he asked again, a bit tersely.

"I'm fine," Julian replied, not even bothering to look at him.

Crossing his arms over his chest, Yadriel considered him for a long moment. He was annoyed with Julian, but he also felt bad for him. The two emotions were at war with each other, making it difficult for Yadriel to sort through. He just wanted to help. Not only Miguel, but everyone, including Julian and his friends, but things were just getting more complicated and difficult. He wished Julian would cut him some slack.

Then again, he probably needed to cut Julian some slack, as well.

Yadriel tried putting himself in his shoes. How would he be handling this, if he was suddenly killed and woke up as a spirit? If he couldn't speak to his friends and family? If he thought they were in danger?

Yeah, he definitely wouldn't be handling it well. Probably about as well as Julian. Maybe worse.

Yadriel sighed. "I have to go to church. There's some big meeting going on."

When Julian didn't respond, he headed for the door but then paused with his hand on the knob.

"One thing, though."

Julian glanced up.

"If you ever throw a tantrum like that again, and I have any reason to think you're going to hurt someone, especially Maritza . . . ?" Yadriel pulled Julian's necklace out from under his hoodie, letting the St. Jude medal dangle from his thumb. "I'll throw this and you down the sewer. Got it?"

Julian's ears burned bright red. He nodded, shoulders hunching.

"Great." Yadriel left the room and closed the door with a snap.

TWELVE

All the brujx were gathered in the open-air courtyard behind the church. Receptions were held there, from weddings to birthdays. Archways were cut into the stone, painted the same color as the church. It was filled with long tables covered in serape runners and centerpieces made of tissue-paper carnations in clay vases. Dozens of colorful papel picado were strung up overhead along with paper lanterns.

Tables laden with food were set on the outer edges between the pillars. There was pan de muerto, rice, beans, and large aluminum platters filled with ropa vieja. The shredded beef cooked in spices and red peppers was one of Lita's specialties.

Lita had ushered all the young brujx to a designated table and put them to work. Eight brujx from ages six to fourteen worked on crafts for Día de Muertos. Molded sugar skulls were waiting to be decorated. Crates full of freshly picked marigolds, chrysanthemums, and deep purple magenta were stacked neatly to the side, making the air smell like sweet apples.

Yadriel followed his tío and grabbed a plate of food before moving toward the crowd surrounding his dad. Everyone's expressions were tense, their voices lowered as they spoke. He saw Tío Isaac, but he was easy to spot. Tall and broad, he stood at least a head higher than everyone else. But there was no sign of Tía Sofia or Paola.

Balancing his plate with one hand, Yadriel pulled out his phone with the other and thumbed out a message to Maritza.

Everybody's at the church. Where are you?

Maritza's response was almost immediate.

Being held hostage. They're making me try on dresses. Send help.

Yadriel snorted.

Sending thoughts and prayers.

Yadriel's dad stood in the center, mustache ruffled and head swinging back and forth as he was bombarded with questions.

"Enrique," Tío Catriz called. He pointed down at Yadriel, and his father had to get on his toes to see him.

Yadriel shrank as everyone turned to look at him.

His dad let out a relieved sigh, and Yadriel gave him a guilty smile. He squeezed through the sea of brujx to get closer.

"Where have you two been?" his dad asked, voice edged with frustration, though he mostly just sounded tired.

Yadriel felt another pang of guilt. His dad looked exhausted, his eyes bloodshot and ringed with dark circles. How many hours of sleep had his dad gotten over the last twenty-four hours? It couldn't have been much.

"Sorry, Dad," Yadriel said, because he was. He hadn't meant to worry his dad. He had enough on his plate without Yadriel causing him more stress.

"You keep running off and coming home late," Enrique said, like it was a question.

Yadriel tried to think of an excuse. What would Maritza say? "I just—"

"He was with me, hermano," Tío Catriz said, his smile apologetic as he placed a hand on Yadriel's shoulder. "We were having a heart-to-heart, lost track of time. We didn't mean to worry you," he explained with gentle sincerity.

Yadriel stared up at him, surprised.

Enrique frowned, deep creases wrinkling his brow. There was something churning behind his eyes, but Yadriel couldn't quite place it. He got the feeling his dad didn't like that answer, but then he gave a short nod.

Luckily, Yadriel wasn't going to get lectured, at least not at the moment. His dad had bigger matters to tend to.

"How could there be no sign of Miguel?" a younger bruja asked, and the group devolved into more arguing and questions. They converged around his dad again, pushing Yadriel and his tío to the outskirts.

"Thanks for that," Yadriel said to Tío Catriz. "You really didn't have to cover for me." The last thing he wanted to do was drag anyone else into this mess he'd gotten himself into, especially his tío.

Catriz chuckled. "I won't tell if you don't," he said with a wink.

Yadriel smiled back. He wished the brujx treated his tío better. He was a good man and always looked out for Yadriel. Even if it sucked to be a brujx reject, at least he had his tío Catriz to go through it with. Yadriel wondered if things would change once they saw he was a brujo. Would it put a wall between them? Would Tío Catriz be upset? He didn't think he would be.

At least, he hoped not.

"Eat, sobrino," Tío Catriz told him, nudging Yadriel with his shoulder. "And try to stay out of trouble."

Yadriel didn't need to be told twice. He was starving and immediately began shoveling food into his mouth. He slowly wandered around the group of brujx deep in conversation, trying to listen in and gather any information that might be useful.

"Did Claudia and Benny go to the police?" Tío Isaac asked, his deep voice easily cutting through the chatter. "Has Miguel been reported as missing?"

Yadriel's dad nodded, raking his fingers through his mustache. "They did this morning, but it didn't go well." The corners of his lips tugged down.

"How do you mean?" Diego asked. He and Andrés had squirmed their way into the middle of the group, as if they were very important and needed to be at the center of the discussion.

Yadriel rolled his eyes and took another large bite of ropa vieja.

"Claudia and Benny don't speak English very well," Enrique explained. "They kept asking for an interpreter, not wanting to miss anything important and so they could give the police as much information as they could. Of course, that was complicated on its own, since they couldn't say they knew Miguel was dead without explaining how they knew it," he told the group.

Murmurs rose.

Yes, Yadriel could see how that would make things difficult.

"But the officers didn't bring in an interpreter and just kept asking them questions." His dad shook his head. "I'm not sure what happened, but by the time I got there to help, the police were completely brushing them off and started asking if Miguel was a legal US citizen—if they were."

The murmuring turned angry, and so did Yadriel. Over the last few years, more and more people in their community—brujx and otherwise— had been deported. Families were split apart and good people were torn away from their homes. People were fearful of the police and scared to seek out help when they needed it.

The brujx tried to band together and close their ranks. As a community that was already so close-knit and stuck to their own, it only exacerbated their fear of outsiders.

"They got scared the police would find a reason to deport them, so they left. I'm not even sure a police report was actually filled out, but they're too frightened to go back."

Catriz shook his head slowly, the corner of his lip curling in distaste. "Awful."

"Santa Muerte, los ayude," an older brujo muttered, crossing himself.

"Miguel will return on Día de Muertos," a young woman insisted. "Then he will tell us what happened."

"But what if he doesn't?" asked another, and they all broke out into more questions until it was just an unintelligible cacophony of voices.

Yadriel gripped his empty plate, suddenly feeling sick to his stomach. The only new information they had was the police hadn't found Miguel's body, which wasn't much to go on. He was still missing. They still needed to find him.

Even if Día de Muertos was only two days away, there was no way Yadriel was just going to sit around, twiddling his thumbs until Miguel showed up. And if he didn't come back, then his spirit was somewhere, tethered and trapped. He hated the idea of Miguel being stuck somewhere, unable to contact them. Where had he ended up that no one could find him? It wasn't like there were wells to fall down in East LA. There were no cliffs to be tossed off. If a building or something had collapsed, they would've heard about it on the news.

Gone without a trace. Just like Julian.

Yadriel was certain that wherever one was, the other was, too. He and Maritza did have a leg up on the rest of the brujx. They at least knew where Julian had gone missing, and tomorrow they would see if Donatello and Michelangelo could track him from there.

"Oh, good, you're finished eating!"

Lita's voice pulled Yadriel from his thoughts.

Before he could even respond, she'd taken the paper plate from his hands and pulled him toward the table of younger brujx. "You let them worry about Miguel," Lita said sternly.

"Lita," Yadriel said sharply. He didn't want to get lumped in with the kids doing arts and crafts. He belonged with the adults. "I'm not a kid—"

"I know that!" Lita huffed, coming to a stop next to the crates.

Yadriel scowled, not believing her for a moment.

"But you're the best at decorating the calaveras!" she argued, snapping her skirt.

Yadriel looked down at the boxes of blank sugar skulls and the mess of neon icing tubes that littered the table. The older kids sat around, looking bored out of their minds, maybe five completed calaveras between them that were lackluster at best.

Meanwhile, Leo and Lena, the six-year-old twins, sat on the end, squeezing neon blue and green icing into each other's mouths. They laughed uncontrollably, their eyes wild, completely jacked up on sugar.

Decorating the small skulls made of white sugar was Yadriel's favorite part of Día de Muertos, but right now, he had more important things to worry about.

"Lita, do I have to?" he said, trying really hard not to sound like a whiny child.

"Only two days to Día de Muertos!" Lita lamented, sitting heavily in the chair at the head of the table. "Still so much to cook and bake!" she continued.

The teen brujx kept talking among themselves. Leo and Lena were now chasing each other around, smearing icing on their arms.

Yadriel wanted to get out of there and go back to the house, where he could talk to Julian. He was probably still pissed off, but Yadriel hoped he'd had enough time to cool off and listen to reason.

When no one responded, Lita scowled. "Ay, yi, yi, how my back aches!" she announced, louder this time and with a big sigh. She looked around expectantly.

Alejandro, a thirteen-year-old brujo with a big ego and even bigger attitude problem, rolled his eyes. "Aye, Lita," he said dismissively, taking a large bite out of a sugar skull.

With surprising swiftness, Lita had her chancla in her hand. "¡Cállate!" she snapped, whacking Alejandro in the back of the head.

"*Ow!*"

The others laughed.

Yadriel inwardly sighed. He wasn't going to get out of there until he satisfied Lita's demands. So he sucked it up and gave her a smile. "We appreciate all your hard work, Lita," he told her, doing his best to sound as sincere as possible without being sarcastic.

"The supplies for the ofrendas this year are even more beautiful than last. You work so hard," he repeated, sitting down and bringing forward a box of sugar skulls.

Satisfied, Lita smiled and waved a hand through the air. "¡Oh, gracias, mi amor! But I would never complain, I am happy to do it."

Alejandro snorted, but it quickly turned into a cough when Lita's eyes narrowed on him.

Yadriel picked out an assortment of neon-colored icing in tiny piping bags and got to work. The sooner he got some calaveras done, the sooner he could sneak out of there. With painstaking precision, Yadriel traced yellow flowers, purple eyelashes, and green spiderwebs onto a sugar skull for his mom.

There was one for each ancestor they would be welcoming back on Día de Muertos, their names written across the forehead of their calavera.

"You still need to help me look in the rafters," Lita said to Yadriel, drawing his attention. "Still can't find la garra del jaguar."

"The what?" asked Ximena, a short bruja whose quinces would be happening next summer.

"¡La garra del jaguar!"

The younger brujx exchanged confused looks.

Yadriel shook his head but continued to work. He always knew when a Lita lecture was coming. He piped swirls of yellow and light blue onto the calavera's bony cheeks.

Lita huffed, fully offended now. "Four sacred blades! They are ancient artifacts, used to perform the forbidden sacrifices."

Alejandro gaped. "The what?"

Lita preened under the sudden undivided attention.

Yadriel carefully wrote his mother's name in loopy handwriting over the calavera's forehead in red icing.

Camila.

Gently, Yadriel put it in the box with the other completed calaveras. He picked out his next sugar skull to decorate, cradling it in his lap as Lita dove into her story in Spanish, not having the patience to stumble through the nuances of English for such an important retelling.

Lita had been telling the legend of Bahlam, the jaguar god, ever since he was little. He knew the story practically by heart.

Bahlam, the jaguar god, was the ruler of Xibalba. When you died, you had to travel through Xibalba to reach the peaceful world of the afterlife, where Lady Death ruled. Some people were granted safe and direct passage to the afterlife by Lady Death—like those who died in battle, at a young age, or during childbirth—but most had to endure the challenges of Xibalba.

In order to make it through Xibalba, you had to be clever and brave. Also known as the Place of Fright, Xibalba was filled with monsters and death gods you had to outsmart and defeat.

Bahlam ruled over Xibalba. He ate the spirits of all those who failed in their journey. Part man, part beast, he was fearsome and cruel and insatiable. Unsatisfied with the spirits of those he caught in Xibalba, Bahlam tricked humans into helping him cross to the realm of the living so he could feed.

He used fear and manipulation to bend humans to his will. Bahlam told them that, in order to escape his wrath, they must bring him human sacrifices. Without human sacrifices to satiate his hunger, he threatened to unmake the land of the living. To bring death and destruction to the human race and ensure none of their loved ones made it to the afterlife.

To appeal to more selfish people, Bahlam also offered immense power in exchange for human sacrifices.

Under the threat of death and the promise of power, Bahlam's following grew. He gave his worshippers la garra del jaguar. The four blades had to be pierced into the hearts of four human sacrifices while the worshipper wore a jaguar head amulet around their neck. The rituals were performed at a cenote. The sinkholes and underground pools were the gateway between the land of the living and Xibalba. The blood of the human sacrifices would flow into the cenote, and once the last drop fell into the pool, Bahlam would be summoned.

He would emerge from the cenote in his monstrous jaguar form and drag the human sacrifices down to Xibalba. There, he would feast on their spirits. In exchange for their sacrifices, Bahlam gifted them powers channeled through the amulet. The wearer would become powerful enough to snuff out life with the snap of their fingers and bring people back from the dead with a wave of their hand. But power obtained with human life corrupted the mind and poisoned the body.

The followers of Bahlam killed ruthlessly. Wars broke out across the realm, led by the corrupt worshippers.

The balance between life and death was thrown off by so many spirits being trapped in Xibalba instead of passing to the land of the dead, where Lady Death ruled. Seeing the pain and torture caused to appease the jaguar god, Lady Death left her throne to confront Bahlam.

Lady Death fought Bahlam in a war that lasted three days and three nights. Bahlam was strong, but Lady Death was clever. She trapped Bahlam in Xibalba and destroyed all of la garra del jaguar so no one could summon him again.

"Except for one," Lita said, holding up a finger with a knowing look. "This last set Lady Death bequeathed to the very first family of brujos and brujas. These humans wanted to help Lady Death bring balance back to the world of the living and the dead. She blessed us with the ability to heal the injured living, and safely shepherd the spirits of the dead to the afterlife so no one would have to suffer the trials of Xibalba again.

"She trusted us with the last la garra del jaguar as a reminder of what greed and corruption were capable of. Our bloodline carries on this tradition, serving Lady Death. In exchange for our help, Lady Death gifted us with Día de Muertos, the one time a year our people can return to the land of the living. For two days, we get to see our loved ones who've passed."

Lita paused, probably waiting for oohs and aahs, or at least some applause.

But . . .

Yadriel looked around. Leo and Lena looked on the verge of tears. Even Alejandro appeared deeply upset.

"Do you think that's what happened to Miguel?" Ximena asked, eyes wide and chin wobbling. "Bahlam got him?"

Oh no. Yadriel sat up, giving Lita a worried look. Maybe this wasn't the best time to tell the story of Bahlam.

"No, no, no, of course not!" Lita said, trying to laugh it off. "Aye, nena."

She went to Ximena and wrapped her arm around the girl's shoulder. "Bahlam has been locked up in Xibalba. He can't escape; Lady Death made sure of that," she said. "We make sure of that."

Yadriel took the opportunity to sneak away. He tucked the calavera he'd just completed into the pocket of his hoodie so he could hide it in his room for later.

While Lita was distracted, he backed away and followed the outer wall, slinking through the shadows to make an escape. He stopped short, however, when he came upon familiar voices.

His dad and his tío stood next to one of the archways. Tío Catriz stood facing his younger brother, his expression calm save for a small crease in his heavy brow. His father's back was to him, but Yadriel could see the tense set of his shoulders.

Yadriel crept closer, stopping behind a pillar so he could hear what they were saying.

"Times are changing, hermano," his tío said, earnest and almost pleading. "We need to make changes in order to survive. Our lineage is faced with ever weakening magic."

Yadriel strained his ears. What were they talking about? He shifted a bit closer, and the movement caught Catriz's attention. His dark eyes flicked to Yadriel. He moved to shrink back, embarrassed at being caught eavesdropping, but something in Tío Catriz's expression shifted.

He focused back on his brother. "We should be embracing differences, even if it scares us," Catriz implored. "Not rejecting them and pushing them aside."

Pride and gratitude swelled in Yadriel's chest. Was Cartiz talking about him? The concept of having a transgender brujx in their community was still baffling to most, and his dad clearly didn't know what to do with him.

Yadriel smiled. Finally, someone was fighting for him. Of course, of all people, his uncle would stick up for him. Catriz knew what it was like to be cast aside because you didn't fit into the traditional expectations of the brujx.

Anticipation and excitement thrummed in his veins. He rounded the pillar and took an uneasy step closer. Should he just tell them? Was now the right moment? With his tío on his side, would his dad listen? He could tell them how he and Maritza had performed his own quinces. How Lady Death had accepted him as a brujo and blessed him and bound him to his portaje.

Determination propelled him forward another step, and he reached for his dagger.

"Catriz."

Yadriel stopped, fingers pressed to the hilt.

His father's tone was firm, verging on angry. Enrique said his brother's name like a warning, his expression stony. "I don't want to hear it anymore."

Yadriel's stomach plummeted to his feet.

Catriz pressed his palms together. "I implore you to be more open-minded, hermano," he continued. "If we close ourselves off to the possibilities that lie outside of what tradition has dictated—"

"Catriz—"

"We are destined for extinction."

The words hung in the air for a moment. Catriz's and Enrique's eyes remained locked.

When his father spoke, he didn't raise his voice, but his words were unyielding. "I already told you my decision. I will not change my mind."

As Tío Catriz's expression fell to one of defeat, Yadriel's hope fell with it.

Catriz held his hands up in submission, conceding with a slight bow of his head.

Shame simmered under Yadriel's skin and pricked his eyes.

His tío looked at him, an apology in his eyes.

When Enrique turned to follow his gaze, Yadriel didn't stick around to see his reaction. He did his best to hold his head up high and walk confidently away, even though he could feel his heart breaking. He braced himself, expecting to hear his father call for him to stop, for him to offer some sort of excuse or another forced apology.

But no one called after him. Not when he wove through the sea of brujx. Not when he left the church. Only the dead watched as he ran through the tombstones and back to the house, and they stayed silent as well.

THIRTEEN

When Yadriel slipped back into his room, he found Julian lying on his bed. He was stretched out lazily like a jungle cat, one hand tucked behind his head. Purrcaso was curled up on the windowsill, her tail slowly swaying like the pendulum of a clock. Julian stared out the glass. Lights blinked from the hills in the distance, beyond the cemetery walls. They were the closest thing they had to stars in the city. The garden of tombstones and mausoleums stretched out into the dark. Yadriel's old iPhone lay on the pillow next to Julian, the earbud right next to his ear. He tossed a balled-up piece of paper into the air and caught it over and over.

When the door closed behind Yadriel with a click, Julian turned.

His skin was bathed in a silvery glow. Yadriel wasn't sure if it was the moon sharing some of her light, or the effects of being a spirit. Julian watched him with silent regard, the ball of paper held in his hand.

For the first time, Yadriel couldn't immediately tell what he was thinking by the look on his usually expressive face.

"Listening to my shitty music?" Yadriel asked as he tugged off his hoodie and tossed it into the closet.

"Mmm," Julian hummed in reply.

Yadriel removed his portaje and tucked the dagger into his backpack before sitting down on the edge of the bed. Looking down at Julian, he raised an eyebrow. "How is it?"

"Still shitty," Julian said, but a small grin tugged the corner of his lips, teasing a dimple.

Yadriel exhaled a short laugh. When Julian shifted closer to the window, he lay down and tucked the other earbud into his own ear. A breathy voice sang softly through dreamy chords. Julian went back to tossing the paper ball in the air.

Goose bumps trailed up Yadriel's arm where it rested closest to Julian. He sighed and closed his eyes, letting the music wind through his mind and ease the stress knotted in his body. The gentle sound of Julian catching the ball out of the air fell into time with the steady beat.

"It's *sad*," Julian said.

"It's not sad," Yadriel murmured. "Just . . . quiet." Though, he supposed that was why Julian didn't like it. It didn't appeal to his nature.

The tossing stopped and, for a long moment, they lay there listening. Yadriel's body felt heavy, like he was sinking into the bed as exhaustion coaxed him toward sleep. The blanket was soft under his fingers. Yadriel floated somewhere between the real world and a dream when Julian's voice called him back.

"I'm sorry."

"Hm?"

"Earlier. For being an asshole."

Yadriel opened his eyes with effort and turned his head.

Julian stared up at the ceiling, his brow furrowed as he turned the ball of paper over in his hands. "I could lie and say it's because I'm a ghost, but I was never any good at controlling my temper when I was alive, either," he admitted, not looking at Yadriel when he spoke. Julian shifted awkwardly, waiting for his reply.

"Wow," Yadriel said. "You don't do this often, do you?"

Julian finally turned to him with a frown. "Do what?"

Yadriel grinned. "Apologize."

"*Tch,*" he hissed between his teeth. "Man, screw you!" He threw the ball of paper at Yadriel, and it bounced off his forehead and landed on the bed between them.

"*I'm kidding,* I'm kidding!" Yadriel insisted, laughter shaking his words. Julian huffed, and Yadriel forced himself to swallow down the chuckles.

A quiet moment stretched out, accompanied by the gentle flow of music.

"Why do you have to prove that you're a brujo—a guy—to them?" Julian suddenly asked, scowling up at the ceiling.

The question took Yadriel by surprise. Julian was probably still thinking about what he'd heard during the sarcophagus incident.

"Why do you have to prove anything to *anyone*?"

Yadriel shifted uncomfortably. "It's just how it is, how it's always been. In order for them to let me be a brujo—"

"You don't need anyone's permission to be *you*, Yads," he cut in, frustration starting to edge his voice again.

And Yadriel was getting irritated himself. "Because—"

"I mean, you summoned me, so you *have* the brujo powers, right?" he went on. He picked up the balled-up paper again and fiddled with it absentmindedly. "Like, is this Lady deciding who counts as a man and who counts as a woman? What about nonbinary people? Or intersex? Or agender?"

Yadriel was surprised Julian even knew what those words meant. "I'm the first trans brujx—" he tried to explain, but Julian interrupted him with a sarcastic laugh.

"No, you're not."

"Yes, I am!"

Julian shook his head and rolled onto his side so he could properly look at Yadriel. "Nah, there's no way."

When Yadriel tried to argue, Julian cut him off.

"There's no way y'all have been around for thousands of years without there being *one* person not fitting into the 'men are this, women are that' bullshit." Julian sounded so convinced, so *sure*. His obsidian eyes locked onto Yadriel's. "Maybe they hid it, or ran away, or I dunno, something else, but there's no way you're the first, Yads."

All Yadriel could do was stare at him.

He didn't know what to say. He spent so much time feeling isolated—convinced that he was a one-off, an outlier no one knew what to do with—he'd never considered that, somewhere along the line, there had been other brujx like him.

When he didn't respond, Julian flopped onto his back, pressing the paper ball between his palms. "Seems like the magic knows, right?" Julian thought out loud. "Or Lady Death does—whatever makes those decisions. You did the ceremony, and you were able to summon me, right?"

"Yeah," Yadriel said, still hung up on the previous revelation.

Julian nodded. "So, she gets it." The corner of his lips pulled into a grin. "That's pretty cool."

Yadriel looked across at his statue of Lady Death on his altar. Of course she knew—she saw who Yadriel really was. She'd made that clear when she blessed him with his portaje. But he hadn't considered that there was an entirely lost history of brujx like him. Julian was right; it seemed obvious now. There was no way he was the first, and he wouldn't be the last.

"So," Julian prompted again. "Why isn't that enough?"

"It won't be enough for the rest of the brujx," Yadriel pushed back. "They'll need more proof."

"Not good enough for them, or not good enough for *you*?" Julian asked, finally looking over at him.

The question struck him in the chest. "It's complicated—"

"Because—and I'm not trying to back out of our deal, here—but if this is just to prove yourself to *them*—"

"They're my *family*—"

"Well, screw them, if they're making you go through all this crap!" Julian snapped.

Yadriel was caught between wanting to defend his family and appreciating what Julian was trying to say. Mostly, he was tired and frustrated. He was tired of fighting, on all fronts. "It's not that simple—"

"I mean, Flaca isn't any less of a girl just because other people look at her and don't see her as one," Julian went on. "Just because she's not on hormones or whatever, or 'cause she's not 'passing,' doesn't mean other people get to decide who she is. And the same goes for you."

Heat bloomed in Yadriel's cheeks.

"You don't owe anybody shit," Julian told him, stormy anger brewing behind dark eyes.

He was kind of an asshole. Julian was abrasive, sometimes rude, and didn't seem to have much tact. But, for some reason, Yadriel's heart still fluttered in his chest.

He blinked at Julian, not knowing what to say. It seemed way too easy, way too idyllic. Things didn't just work like that in the real world.

It wasn't enough to have summoned Julian, to have been bound to his portaje, or for Lady Death's blessing to flow through him with its golden light. He needed to do *everything* the men could do before asking the brujx to accept him into the community. He couldn't leave any gaps for them to question.

He loved his family, and the worst possible thing would be for them to shun him entirely. He saw how they treated him, and Tío Catriz. If they found out what Yadriel was up to, before he was able to successfully release a spirit, he was worried they—including his dad—would cast him out for good.

But how could he explain that to Julian?

"I kind of wish I could trade my family for yours," Yadriel said with a weak laugh. They weren't even blood, but in the short time he'd interacted with them, he could see how fiercely they cared for one another. Especially Julian.

"I wouldn't trade them for the world," Julian said solidly.

Yadriel smiled. He envied whoever Julian gave his fiery devotion to. It was a warm and unyielding force to be shielded by.

"They seem nice."

Julian gave him a withering look.

Okay, so maybe he hadn't seen much "friendliness," except from Luca.

"Well, Omar seems kinda intense," Yadriel conceded.

"He is." Julian grinned affectionately, toying with the end of Purrcaso's flicking tail.

Yadriel thought about all the rumors Maritza's friends had said at school and Julian's intense reaction. "Is he . . . you know, in a gang?"

His eyes snapped to Yadriel. *"What?"*

Clearly a misstep. Yadriel tried to backpedal. "Uh, former gang member?"

Julian's laugh was sharp. "No." He traced shapes onto the windowpane with his finger. Casually, he added, "But Luca was."

It was Yadriel's turn to balk. "What? *Luca?*" His mind spun. The sweet boy with the shy smile? It didn't add up. "But—but he's so— He doesn't fit—"

"'Course he does," Julian said impatiently. "They steer clear of Omar. Wouldn't be able to pull him in without an all-out fight. Too much work. But Luca?" Julian shook his head in that frustrated way parents did when their kids did something stupid. "You saw him. He's like a puppy—just wants to fit in and for people to like him. He'd do anything to feel like part of a family. He's easy prey for gangs."

Julian sounded annoyed, angry, even, but Yadriel wasn't sure if it was with Luca or the ones who had taken advantage of him.

Probably both.

"His parents don't give a shit about him," Julian continued, his lip curling in distaste. "Most of the time, they don't even notice if he's home, and when they do, they treat him like garbage. They make him sleep outside for any damn thing, like leaving a dirty dish in the sink. His piece-of-shit dad used to use his arm like an ashtray." Julian's anger was palpable, like an electric storm in the air around him. "He didn't show up for picture day because he had a black eye."

Yadriel's stomach gave a sickened lurch. "Jesus . . ." He understood Julian's anger. He'd only met Luca a few hours ago, and the thought of someone causing him harm made his blood boil.

"He got sucked into one as soon as he started high school," Julian continued. "We didn't see him for weeks, and his parents didn't care. One less thing for them to worry about, I guess. By the time we tracked him down, he was living in a drug den and had gotten branded with tattoos." Julian ran a finger along the side of his face.

Yadriel remembered Luca's scar. "What happened?" he asked, knowing the answer would be ugly.

"My brother, Rio." Julian's expression softened just a touch. "He'd been in the same gang when he was our age. He went and got Luca, which is *not* easy." Julian shrugged. "I never asked how he managed it. Maybe they owed him or something? I dunno. But you don't get to just *leave*. When Rio brought Luca home, they'd burned all his tattoos off."

Yadriel sucked in a breath, and Julian must've heard it because he added, "Usually, it's blood in, blood out, so it was a better alternative."

Yadriel involuntarily cringed. That was a sort of pain he couldn't even begin to imagine. Even just getting a burn from the oven was nearly unbearable.

"Rio's got the same kind of scars on his arm. Luca was laid up on our couch for *weeks*. It was like if he wasn't sleeping, he was just moaning in pain," Julian said, wincing as if he could still hear it in his head.

"Why didn't you take him to a hospital?"

"No health insurance. Luca got real sick, we did everything we could, but it still got infected. He got a fever. My brother heard about this lady who did, like, natural healing stuff? Y'know, weird herbs that smell terrible, made him drink stuff that looked like dishwater. After a few days he felt better. His scar looks way better than Rio's now. Whatever she did worked."

"I wonder if it was a bruja," Yadriel said.

Julian looked over at him. "You think?"

Yadriel shrugged. "Kind of sounds like it, doesn't it? If he was in that bad of shape, and she healed him that quickly . . ." It definitely seemed in the realm of possibility.

"So there's witches out there who can heal people like *that*." He snapped his fingers. "And they're just handing out favors to poor folks?"

"Well, some of them are doctors," Yadriel explained. "Maritza's sister, Paola, is in medical school right now—"

"Isn't that cheating?" Julian frowned.

Yadriel scowled, feeling suddenly defensive. "Does it matter, if they're still helping people?"

Julian jutted his chin and shrugged.

"Anyway, we have to afford to live, somehow, so they get jobs where they can use their healing. And, like you said, some of them run little businesses right out of their homes and disguise it as naturopathy. That's what my mom did." Yadriel's eyes slid over to the framed photo of his mom. It was cast in shadows, but he could still make out her white teeth and big smile. "Sometimes she wouldn't even take payment, either, even though it cost her every time she healed."

"Ah, right. Bigger tasks take more magic, y'all only have so much to tap into, yada yada yada." Julian nodded, recalling their conversation from the other day.

Yadriel's stomach twisted. His mouth was dry, like his tongue was stuck to the roof of his mouth. "And if you use too much, you can die," he said, refusing to look at Julian when he said it. Yadriel could practically hear Julian's brain buzzing with a slew of questions, so he cut him off at the pass.

"And some people aren't born with much, or any," he plowed on. "Like my uncle Catriz—"

"Tall guy with the big nose, gauged ears, and man bun?" Julian asked.

Yadriel scowled. "It's not a man bun!" he snapped defensively. "Wearing your hair long and having stone plugs in your ears like that is very traditional."

Julian smirked and Yadriel rolled his eyes.

"Anyways. Even though we're from a powerful line of brujx—going back to even before the great Aztecs and Maya—his magic is so weak, he can only see and sense spirits," Yadriel explained. "He can't perform the other tasks of the brujos. They call it *dilución de la magia*, which means—"

"The dilution of magic, yeah, I know," Julian interrupted. "I told you, I speak Spanish."

"Well, my tío is an outcast like me," Yadriel went on. "I mean, Maritza *chooses* to not be a bruja, but me and my uncle weren't given that choice." He shrugged.

"He gets me, and he has my back," Yadriel said, remembering how Catriz had stood up for Yadriel earlier. How he'd tried talking sense to his dad. Even though it hadn't worked, Yadriel was deeply thankful he'd even tried. He owed his tío big time for that.

"Well, at least your family is more accepting than Flaca's," Julian said, following his own train of thought. "She's trans, but she's a 'throwaway.'"

"Throwaway?" Yadriel repeated, trying to regather his thoughts. He'd noticed—or assumed—Flaca was trans, but he didn't know what "throwaway" meant.

"Yeah, her parents kicked her out when she told them." He glowered up at the ceiling. "Throwaway. It was rough at first; she didn't have anywhere to go, so she stayed with us a lot. But now she's got some distant relatives—a cousin, I think—that she's crashing with. Most of the time, anyways."

"What about Rocky and Omar?" Yadriel asked. "If they're hiding out at the underpass because they're scared, aren't their parents worried?"

"Rocky's in a group home," Julian said, as if that explained everything.

"Not all foster homes are bad," Yadriel felt compelled to argue. One of his cousins and her husband were foster parents who had taken in a little girl. "Kids get adopted to nice families all the time—"

"Being in a group home is *not* the same as being with a foster family," Julian told him. "It's just a big house run by the state. Rocky hates it there. Too many kids, not enough beds, and some of them are real assholes." Julian heaved a deep sigh. "Whenever she needed a break, Rio let her crash at our place. Same goes for Flaca, and Luca, like I said. Doesn't even ask questions, just drags another blanket out of the closet." His expression softened. "It's a doggy-dog world out there," Julian sighed.

The corner of Yadriel's mouth twitched. "Dog-*eat*-dog."

"Whatever."

"What about Omar?"

"Omar's the best of us." He laughed. "Definitely the smartest one in the group. Good grades. Usually the one keeping the rest of us from getting into too much trouble. He's the only one who's got parents that actually *like* him," Julian said. "But they got deported."

Yadriel cringed. He thought of the brujx who had been taken away. It left a hole in their community, a pain that ached through multiple families and generations. Yadriel hated himself a little for judging Omar so quickly.

"But Omar was born here, so he didn't have to go with them. He *wanted* to, but they wouldn't let him," Julian explained. "They sacrificed everything to get to the US and make sure Omar had a better life than them, you know? It's messed up, man." He shook his head slowly. "Rio said Omar could live with us, even though we don't have much space. His parents try to call as often as they can, but . . ." Julian shrugged. "He puts on a front, acts like shit doesn't bother him, but I can tell it does. FaceTime isn't the same as having your parents *here* with you."

Yadriel knew that all too well. The way Julian said it made it clear he knew from personal experience, too.

"Do you mind if I ask what happened to your dad?" Yadriel asked.

"Got shot." The muscles in Julian's jaw clenched. "Stray bullet from a drive by. Wrong place, wrong time. He got me that necklace when I was younger." He motioned to the St. Jude medal where it rested in the dip of Yadriel's throat.

Yadriel traced his fingers over it.

"Y'know, lost cause, and all that." He grinned like it was an inside joke.

"And your mom?" Yadriel asked, dragging his thumbnail across the engraved letters.

His question chased off Julian's smile. "She and my dad met in Colombia and moved here before my brother was born. But after she had me, my mom ran off. Dad never heard from her again." Julian shifted. "My life sounds pretty boring compared to all those rumors. I think I like the sicarios-on-the-run story way better." He smirked.

"I'm sorry about your mom," Yadriel said, but Julian didn't seem too bothered about it.

Julian shrugged. "Can't miss someone you never knew, right?"

Yadriel supposed he had a point.

"Sounds like Rio really takes care of you guys."

Julian shrugged before simply saying, "We're family."

"He's got to be worried sick about you," Yadriel gently nudged.

"Yeah, well"—Julian tucked his hands under the back of his head— "we had a huge fight a few days ago, so I left. Told him I wasn't coming back." A deep crease pressed between his eyebrows. "And then I went and got myself killed, so. He's put up with enough shit because of me," he added with a shake of his head. "He was only twenty years old when my dad died. He stepped up to be my legal guardian, so I didn't get tossed into the system, but what twenty-year-old guy wants to have to take care of his kid brother? And then to take in Omar, on top of it?" Julian snorted.

"He had to take a job at the mechanic business my dad and his friend owned. Carlos lets us stay in the little apartment above the shop, and Rio works for him to afford rent and groceries and stuff. He'll probably be able to afford a *real* place without me dragging him down." Julian nudged Purrcaso's paw where it rested on the windowsill. She let out a noise of sleepy indignation.

Yadriel knew very little about Rio, but, from what he'd heard, something told him Julian was completely wrong. He doubted his brother was better off with him gone.

"What happened to your mom?" Julian ventured.

It was an obvious question. One that Yadriel was surprised Julian hadn't asked already. He must've really been holding himself back. But that didn't mean he was going to give him the details. "Car accident," he said curtly.

Julian frowned. "Why didn't someone just heal her?"

Yadriel's whole body tensed. His stomach twisted.

"Or, like, bring her back to life or something?" Julian scratched at his head.

"Brujas can only heal you if your heart's still beating," Yadriel told him. "You have to be alive. And brujos haven't been able to bring people back to life since—"

Julian sat bolt upright. "Wait, y'all can really bring people back to life? I was joking!"

"*Sssh!*" Yadriel hissed. "*Could*—we can't do it anymore. Like I told you, dilution of powers over time."

"Still!" He flopped back onto the bed, chuckling. "That's so badass."

"Yeah, well, like I said, it required a lot of power."

"So the people they brought back were, like, *definitely* zombies, right?"

Yadriel groaned. "Not the zombies again—"

"*Evilly* resurrecting someone from the dead can only lead to zombies! I know it; I read books," Julian said.

Yadriel cocked an eyebrow.

"Okay, okay, okay, but I've seen enough movies to know how this goes down!" Julian corrected through barely suppressed chuckles.

Yadriel scrubbed his hands down his face. "You're impossible!" he said, laughter jumping in his chest. He tucked his hands behind his head and stared up at the ceiling.

"I kind of made a mess of things, huh?" Yadriel said. He wasn't fishing for sympathy, just stating the obvious. Keeping secrets from his family. Putting his foot in his mouth on more than one occasion. Completely botching the conversation with Julian's friends. More sneaking, more lies. He was in over his head.

"Yeah," Julian agreed very matter-of-factly, not malicious or even teasing. "But now your mess is my mess, too." He tilted his head toward Yadriel and spoke softly. "It's bound to be easier if we're both cleaning it up, right?"

The dimples of his tired smile made Yadriel light-headed.

For the first time in a very long time, he didn't feel like a lost cause. It was nice to have someone to talk to about this stuff. He had his tío and Maritza, of course, but there were still degrees of separation between their experiences. When he came out, there was a lot of legwork and explaining to his tío and Maritza about who he was. It took time and a lot of emotional work on Yadriel's part.

But with Julian, there was no training involved because he already understood him. It was . . . easy. Yadriel hadn't known it could be that painless and simple for someone to see him as he was.

For a moment, they both lay there, quiet laughter mingling with the soft music playing from the iPhone.

Julian let out a heavy, annoyed sigh. "So, I guess I give in."

"Give in to what?"

"We can go see Rio tomorrow."

Yadriel turned to look at him. He didn't look very pleased. "Really?"

"Only to see if he knows anything, if the cops called him or whatever, and to grab one of my shirts," Julian said firmly. "And just to . . ." He trailed off. "I don't know. Just to make sure he's okay, before I leave."

Those last few words halted Yadriel's thoughts.

Before he left.

That's right. This was all so Yadriel could release Julian to the afterlife. Where he would stay, because Julian was just a normal boy. When he crossed over, that would be that. He wasn't a brujo. There would be no ofrenda to welcome him back during Día de Muertos. For Julian, death was finite. When his dad died, he didn't get to see him again. And now, Julian's friends and his brother would never see him again, either.

"All things considered," Yadriel ventured, "you're taking this whole being-dead thing pretty well."

Julian exhaled a small laugh. "I don't know, I never expected to live that long, anyways," he confessed.

Yadriel didn't know what to say. There was something so profoundly sad in how casually he said it.

"But I was thinking more like thirty, never really pictured myself older than that," he explained. "Sixteen minus a couple weeks seems a bit young." His lips tilted into a crooked smile. "The ghost part was definitely a surprise." Julian rolled onto his side, propping the side of his face in his hand. "Can I possess you?"

A surprised laugh bucked in Yadriel chest. "No. You're thinking demons."

"I mean, it's getting closer to Día de Muertos, right? You said us dead folks get stronger around then." Julian leaned over him, eyes narrowed, his face only a few inches away.

Yadriel could see the faint shadow along his jaw. There was a tiny scar on his right eyebrow.

"If I concentrate *really* hard . . ." His finger hovered above Yadriel. "Could I touch you?"

Heat flooded Yadriel's face. His chest fluttered dangerously. "I don't think so, Jules." A shaky laugh quaked his words.

Dimples cut deep into Julian's cheeks. He tipped his head to the side. "Why not?"

"Not enough brainpower."

Julian's laugh was open and unabashed. "Ssh, stop!" he ordered through his chuckles. "I'm concentrating!"

He shook out his hand before hovering it over Yadriel again. Julian's face scrunched up, lips parted.

Yadriel held his breath. His fingers knotted into the blanket under him. A thrill tickled down his spine to the tips of his toes. It was disorienting, filling his head with dangerous thoughts. He wanted to feel Julian's hands ghosting over his skin. Wondered what Julian's short hair would feel like under his fingertips, what his skin would smell like, or if his lips felt as soft as they looked.

But it was silly and stupid, because you couldn't touch dead boys, and they couldn't touch you back.

Julian lowered his hand, and for a moment, nothing happened.

"See?" Yadriel exhaled. The yearning ache devoured the hope in his chest. "You—"

But then he felt it. The shiver of the medal against his throat. The brush of an—admittedly, cold—finger across his skin.

Yadriel sucked in a gasp and clamped his hand over his neck.

Julian jerked back. "Did you feel it?" he asked, eyes wide.

"I did!"

"Yes!" Julian's smile was brilliant.

They both broke out into laughter. The fluttery, half-delirious sort that made Yadriel feel a little drunk.

"*See?*" Julian jutted his chin to a proud angle.

Yadriel rolled his eyes. "Yeah, yeah."

"I told you, I—"

But Julian never finished his sentence. For a second, he froze.

"Jules?" Yadriel started to sit up.

Julian sucked in a deep, rattling breath. He collapsed back onto the bed.

Purrcaso sprang from the window and darted out of sight.

Yadriel pushed himself up. His heart hammered in his chest. "Hey, what's happening—?"

Julian's jaw went slack, his mouth open wide. His eyes rolled back into his head, and his entire body spasmed. No, it wasn't spasming, it was shaking, *vibrating.* Julian flickered in and out of existence, like a light shorting out.

"Jules!" Yadriel's hands hovered above him, not knowing what to do or what was happening. All he could do was watch as Julian's body flashed in and out of existence.

It took him a moment to see the red stain on the chest of Julian's white shirt. It started as a dark smudge, but it slowly bloomed larger, appearing in flashes.

More quivering. Just a shadow of Julian.

Then he disappeared and didn't come back.

Yadriel heart lodged in his throat.

"Jules!"

His eyes frantically searched the bed. Yadriel fumbled, pressing his hands against the mattress as if he could feel him there, that maybe Julian was just invisible, but he was gone. There was nothing. Not even a wash of cold against his fingers.

Just as quickly as he'd vanished, Julian blinked back into existence. A gasp ripped through his throat and his eyes flew open.

Yadriel sprang back, nearly falling off the bed.

Julian sucked in breath, his hand clutching his shirt where the blood seeped. But then he started to fade.

It was like someone had cranked down his saturation and opacity.

Julian seemed duller now, his edges slightly more blurred than before. The red stain faded to nothing.

"What—what the hell happened?" Julian heaved, breathless.

Yadriel could only shake his head.

"What was that?" Panic cracked his voice.

Yadriel stared down at his hands. They trembled uncontrollably. "I—I don't know."

FOURTEEN

Y ou—you disappeared!" Yadriel stared at Julian, afraid to blink in case he vanished again. "Where did you go?!"

Julian leaped from the bed. "I—I don't know!" he stammered. He twisted left and right, patting himself down and inspecting his limbs.

"You were *bleeding.*" Panic tightened his voice, and Yadriel hated how frightened he sounded, how frightened he *felt.*

Julian pressed his hand to his chest and winced, like he could still feel it. "But why? What happened?" he demanded.

Yadriel racked his brain, trying to remember everything he knew about spirits, but it was hard to focus. He kept seeing Julian's contorted face and bleeding chest flash in his mind over and over again.

"When—when spirits have been in the world of the living for too long, when they start going maligno, sometimes they'll relive their death," Yadriel said.

"Did someone stab me?" Julian asked, his ghostly face deathly pale. "Did I get shot?"

"But you only died yesterday," Yadriel reasoned. He pushed his hands through his hair, trying to think. Some spirits turned maligno faster than others, but it had only been a day. "It shouldn't be happening this quickly."

Julian sat down heavily on the edge of the bed and winced. "Whatever it is, I don't want it to ever happen again."

"This isn't good."

Julian's worried eyes met his. "What does it mean?"

"It means," Yadriel said, "we're running out of time."

Sleep was impossible.

Yadriel lay perched on the edge of his bed, curled up on his side so he could see where Julian lay on the floor. Purrcaso curled up behind his knees. Julian's back was to him, but there was no way he could be sleeping, either, was there? Every time Yadriel started to drift off, his body would jerk him back awake. He kept seeing Julian lying there, his eyes rolling into the back of his head, the blood seeping from the wound that must've killed him.

What the hell was he supposed to do? Yadriel had only heard about spirits reliving their deaths the closer they got to turning maligno; he'd never witnessed it himself. His parents had always shielded him from that. When spirits in their cemetery went maligno, skilled brujos were dispatched to deal with it as quickly and humanely as possible.

Yadriel had hundreds of questions, but no way of finding out. Brujx history relied on oral traditions, so it wasn't like there was an encyclopedia where he could look up the answers. And he couldn't *ask* someone why a spirit would turn so quickly without them getting suspicious.

No, there was no one who he could turn to. They'd just have to get through it.

The thought of forcibly releasing Julian to the other side, like he'd threatened that first night, was unthinkable now. Julian needed to hold on a little longer.

If they could find his body, hopefully they could find Miguel and the others who had gone missing. If Yadriel could prove himself to the brujx, then they would have to let him be part of the aquelarre. Their deadline of Día de Muertos was looming. Halloween was the day after tomorrow, and at midnight, the first day of Día de Muertos would begin.

—————

When his alarm went off in the morning, Yadriel was already awake. He waited, watching as Julian sat up. "How'd you sleep?" he asked.

"I'm starting to think ghosts don't sleep," Julian replied with a wry smile. He looked tired, of course, but there was something more to it. A glazed look cast over his eyes. An intense vigilance. Julian eyed Yadriel as he crawled out of bed and dragged himself to the closet. "I guess brujos don't, either."

Yadriel grumbled unintelligibly. When he came back from taking a shower, he found Julian sitting at the foot of his bed. He wrung his hands together, digging his thumb into his palm. Worry caught in every line of his face.

"Am I going to have to talk you into letting me go to school with you again?" Julian asked with an anxious laugh.

"No," Yadriel said, toying with the St. Jude pendant around his neck. "This time I want you to come."

He was more worried about Julian disappearing and reliving his death again. By the look on his face, Yadriel was pretty certain Julian was worried about the same thing. If he couldn't stop it from happening, then he would at least make sure Julian wasn't alone when it did. Yadriel didn't want to come home and find the Julian he knew had vanished, leaving nothing but a horrifying apparition in his place.

Julian's eyebrows shot up. "Really?"

Yadriel nodded, then shrugged, as if it didn't matter to him. "You can take it or leave it," he said as he combed pomade through his hair.

"Take!" Julian jumped to his feet. The worry was gone, and that electric grin was back. "Definitely take!"

Julian waited impatiently by the door as Yadriel grabbed his stuff.

He opened his backpack to take out his portaje and stash it while they were at school, but as he grabbed hold of the hilt, he hesitated.

Again, the image of Julian convulsing and flickering haunted him. If it was a sign that Julian was slipping away, what if he lost his grip on himself while they were at school?

Yadriel looked at Julian, an uneasy feeling churning his stomach.

"Are you ready or what?" Julian huffed. He caught sight of the dagger in Yadriel's hand and raised an eyebrow. "I thought you were worried about getting caught with that thing at school?"

If Julian went maligno, Yadriel would be forced to cut his tether and release his spirit before he hurt someone.

"Better safe than sorry, right?" Yadriel said.

Julian stared at him for a second, then shrugged. "Just don't get caught, I don't wanna spend the night with you in jail," he told him.

Yadriel tucked his portaje and its sheath into the waist of his jeans and pulled on his backpack.

He listened carefully at the door and paused every couple of steps going down the stairs, but the house was silent and empty. That was odd, considering Lita was usually busy in the kitchen by now. He opened the front door, and Julian made a run for it.

"*FREEDOM!*" he whooped, bounding down the front steps.

Yadriel laughed and shook his head. Julian was in great spirits. Yadriel hesitated in the doorway and pulled his dagger out again. Did he really need it? Was it bad luck to assume the worst? Was he just welcoming something to go wrong by taking it to school? Maybe he should leave it—

Before he could make a decision, the door to the garage opened and Lita walked into the kitchen.

"I'll make some food," Lita said as she went to the stove.

Tío Catriz and his dad walked into view, each of them carrying a large box. Yadriel froze, panic cementing his feet to the floor. The voice in his head screamed at him to make a run for it, but it was like his body was short-circuiting, refusing to budge.

"Where should we put this?" his dad asked, his back to Yadriel.

Tío Catriz turned and immediately locked eyes with Yadriel over Enrique's shoulder.

Tío Catriz's face went from surprise to confusion. Before Yadriel could react, his gaze went to the portaje gripped in Yadriel's hand.

Yadriel's heart dropped to the floor.

Catriz had seen the dagger in his hand. He would recognize it as a portaje immediately.

For a split second, his tío's expression went blank as he stared at the blade, but then—

Then he smiled.

"Put them in the living room," Lita instructed, waving a hand as she put a pan on the stove.

Enrique started to turn toward the living room, where Yadriel remained rooted in the doorway, clutching his portaje.

Yadriel was doomed. His dad was going to see him with his portaje, caught red-handed.

A loud crash made everyone jump.

The box Tío Catriz was holding had toppled out of his arms, spilling prayer candles and copal incense all over the kitchen floor.

"Aye!" Lita gasped, clutching her chest.

"Careful of the glass!" Yadriel's dad warned as broken shards crunched under their shoes.

"I'll grab the broom!" Lita rushed to the garage.

"Ah, lo siento, hermano," Tío Catriz said as he and Yadriel's dad bent down to pick up the larger pieces.

"Don't worry, we have plenty more," Enrique reassured him.

Snapping out of it, Yadriel quickly slipped his portaje back into its sheath.

Tío Catriz caught his eye over his dad's shoulder and gave him a small wink.

Relief and gratitude flooded Yadriel. His tío had just saved his ass, and he didn't even seem mad that Yadriel had a portaje. He looked—well, he looked *proud*, which was a sentiment Yadriel hadn't been gifted in a very long time.

He should've known that Tío Catriz would be on his side. He wanted to tell him *everything*, but right now wasn't the time.

As they picked up the broken pieces, Yadriel slipped out the front door and ran to the gate, where Julian and Maritza waited.

"There you are," Maritza sighed, pushing herself up from where she had been leaning against the gate. She wore a black puffy jacket and tight jeans, her hair pulled back in two short French braids.

"Jesus, how are you so slow?!" Julian demanded, throwing his hands up. "I thought you were— Hey, what's with the smile?"

A huge grin plastered across Yadriel's face, his head swimming. His heart felt ready to burst, and it hammered in his chest.

"My family showed up," Yadriel blurted out. "Tío saw my portaje—"

Maritza's eyes bulged. *"What?"*

"Uh-oh," Julian said, glancing back toward the house.

"No, no, it's okay!" Yadriel rushed to add, delirious laughter bubbling through his words. "I didn't get in trouble! He even distracted Lita and my dad so I could get away without them seeing me!"

Maritza shook her head in disbelief.

Meanwhile, Julian grinned. "Awesome!"

"He was seriously chill about it?" Maritza asked, frowning. "Do you think he's going to tell your dad?"

"No, I don't think so, he wouldn't out me like that," Yadriel said. Julian beamed back at him, but Maritza was uncharacteristically worried. "Seriously, Itza," he said. "My tío gets me, he's the only one who does—"

Hurt flashed across her face.

"Aside from you, of course!" he added quickly, giving her an affectionate nudge.

"Are you going to tell him everything?" Maritza pressed, her delicately lined eyebrows tense with worry.

"I mean, yeah, probably." Yadriel shrugged. It'd be good to have an adult on his side. When it came time to reveal everything to his dad and Lita, it would be good to have his tío standing in his corner. "Obviously, not right *now*," he added. "We need to get to school and then see Rio." Yadriel started to walk down the street, gesturing for them to follow. His smile was so big, it was hurting his cheeks.

Julian bounded after him, but Maritza stood there for a moment frowning, her arms crossed over her chest.

"I guess," she finally sighed before following after them.

"See? Everything's working out!" Julian said, dimples flashing as he grinned over at Yadriel.

"It is," he agreed, heart racing. It was one more step in the right direction. One step closer to becoming a brujo. One step closer to being himself.

He was still riding the adrenaline rush when he got to his first class. He was in a great mood, and Julian was in an even better one. Yadriel didn't even mind when Julian, after immediately becoming bored in math class, got into some light mischief.

Julian waited for Ms. Costanzo to write math problems up on the whiteboard and then once people stopped paying attention, which didn't take long, he would erase a random number when Ms. Costanzo wasn't looking. Three times she had to reference her notes, a confused look on her face as she tried to figure out where the mistake was.

Julian perched on the edge of his desk and cackled. Yadriel had to stuff his fist against his mouth to keep himself from laughing out loud.

During lunch, Maritza joined them behind the bleachers. She helped Julian practice his ghost skills by flicking a triangle of paper back and forth, lining up their fingers like goal posts to aim for.

Yadriel sat back, eating a dry cheeseburger from the cafeteria. He liked watching Julian when he was focused in on something. His heavy brow got all scrunched up, eyes sharp as he caught the very tip of his tongue between his teeth. He was so animated. When he made a goal, he'd punch the air and let out an excited whoop. When he missed, he'd throw his hands up and dramatically flop onto his back in the grass. Yadriel caught Maritza eyeing him more than once. Each time, he tried to force the stupid grin off his face, but it always came right back.

By the end of the day, exhaustion was starting to win out. After two nights of very restless sleep, it was a miracle he'd made it that long. To make matters worse, the last class of the day was history, and Mr. Guerrero was the absolute worst. He spoke in a monotone completely devoid of inflection.

Slowly, Yadriel sank in his seat until his textbook was functioning as a pillow, chin propped on his folded arms. Keeping his eyes open took effort, and his hoodie was warm and soft, clearly working against him as it tried to lure him into taking a nap right on his desk.

"Hey! Wake up!"

Julian had wandered back from poking around in students' backpacks.

Yadriel let out a dismissive *rmph* in reply.

Julian dropped into a squat in front of him. He gripped the edge of the desk and rested his chin on his fingers, bringing himself to eye level with Yadriel, their noses a few inches apart. "Can we go on a walk? Let's go on a walk. Doesn't that sound nice?" he asked, a barely contained ball of energy shoved into the body of a teenager boy.

Yadriel focused on the dark eyes staring at him expectantly. He gave Julian an unamused look. He wasn't going to ditch class, especially not this close to the end of the day. He just needed to survive a little while longer.

"Just a quick one!" Julian argued, as if reading his mind. "Around the school?"

When Yadriel blinked slowly at him, Julian amended it to "Okay, okay, okay, just down the hall and back?" He drummed his fingers on the desk and bounced on the balls of his feet.

Yadriel hated to admit it, but that did sound appealing. If he could get up and move around, maybe it'd wake him up a bit. It wasn't like he'd be able to rest any time soon.

Yadriel huffed a big sigh and sat up. "Mr. Guerrero?" he asked, raising his hand. "Can I use the restroom?"

"*Yes!*" Julian was on his feet and out the door before Mr. Guerrero could hand over a hall pass.

Yadriel stretched his hands over his head, twisting his back this way and that as they walked down the empty hallway.

"Good Lord, how do you sit through that *every day*?" Julian demanded with a mystified shake of his head.

"It's not that bad, usually," Yadriel said through a yawn. "When I'm more awake, it's downright tolerable."

"I would die," Julian told him. "Like, *again*."

Yadriel chuckled.

"You're really into this school stuff, huh?" Julian asked with an amused grin.

Yadriel shrugged, rubbing his fist against his eye. "I want to get into a good college, get a good job, help support my family, be successful."

Julian cut him a cross look. "*Tch*, you don't have to be good in school to be successful," he told him, annoyed.

"No, you're right," Yadriel backpedaled, suddenly much more awake. "I just meant—"

"Carlos—the guy my dad opened his mechanic shop with?—he didn't even finish high school!" Julian went on. "He got an appendixship—"

"Apprenticeship—"

"Got a job right off the bat, learned all the tricks of the trade, made *hella* money," Julian continued, punching his fist into his palm for emphasis. "Eventually opened *his own shop* and did it all without a degree *and* zero student-loan debt." Chin tilted proudly, he gave Yadriel a challenging look.

For a second, Yadriel didn't know how to respond. He was a little caught off guard by Julian's very valid observation, and felt ashamed of himself for saying something so obviously classist.

Maritza would be ashamed of him.

"You're totally right, I apologize," Yadriel said, holding his hands up in surrender. "I just meant—"

Julian stopped. "Whoa, whoa, whoa! Wait, I missed it, what was that?" he asked, holding his hand up to his ear with feigned confusion.

"Oh my God," Yadriel groaned.

"Something about me being right?" Julian preened.

The hallway ended, and Yadriel stopped. "You're insufferable," he said, glancing around.

"Yeah, but I think you're kinda into it," Julian replied with a casual shrug.

Yadriel chose to ignore him.

There was a water fountain and restrooms on either side. Yadriel headed for the girls'.

"What are you doing?" Julian asked with a critical arch of an eyebrow.

"Using the bathroom," he said.

Julian hooked his thumb toward the door to the boys' restroom. "Uh, wrong one, dude."

Yadriel hesitated. "Uh . . . I haven't ever actually used the boys' bathroom," he confessed, face growing hot.

"What?" Julian frowned. "Why?"

Sometimes, Julian surprised Yadriel by how knowledgeable he was. Other times, not so much.

"Several reasons," Yadriel said, crossing his arms. "Including, but not limited to: people harassing me, calling me names, pushing me around, general humiliation," he listed off. Truthfully, he'd never worked up the nerve to use the boys' bathroom. In public, he always tried to find a gender-neutral stall, which was difficult. They didn't have those at school, so Yadriel just held it for as long as he could before forcing himself to use the girls', and only during class, when it was less likely he'd run into someone.

"Oh." Julian expression softened for a moment, which Yadriel hated, but then it contorted into anger, which was much less humiliating. "People are assholes."

A surprised laugh leaped in Yadriel's throat. "People *are* assholes," he agreed.

"Well, there's no one around right now," Julian pointed out. He went up to the metal door to the boys' bathroom and literally stuck his head through it, earning another laugh from Yadriel. "And nobody inside!" Julian's voice echoed from inside. He straightened and turned to Yadriel. "I mean, if you wanna see what all the fuss is about, now's your chance," he said with a grin.

Yadriel scoffed, not sure if Julian was making fun of him, but . . . his humor did make the whole thing less . . . scary. He would make himself an anxious mess, loitering outside the boys' bathroom and trying to work up the nerve to go inside, and he always ended up flaking out.

But Julian's bad jokes, easy smile, and nonchalance seemed to suck all the stress out of the situation. Or at the very least, dilute it.

"Fine," Yadriel huffed, as if he were doing Julian a favor. He headed for the bathroom, and Julian moved to follow him. "What are you doing?" Yadriel demanded.

"What?"

"You can't go in there with me!" Yadriel balked.

"It's not like I'm gonna *watch* you!"

Yadriel spluttered. "I—I have a shy bladder!"

Julian threw his head back, letting out a deep belly laugh. "Oh my God!"

"I can't go if I know you can hear me!"

"Okay, okay, okay!" Julian laughed, a big grin on his face. "I'll stand guard," he said, tapping two fingers to his temple like a salute. "Should I cover my ears? Sing a song?"

"Shut up!" With that, Yadriel stomped inside before he could change his mind.

And suddenly, he was standing in the boys' bathroom for the first time in his life. Yadriel looked around. He didn't know what he was expecting, but after all the buildup it was a little . . . lackluster. And smelly.

But he was a boy, and if this was what their bathrooms were like, then he'd get used to it.

When Yadriel walked back out, Julian was leaning against the wall, still looking far too amused.

"You're not covering your ears." Yadriel glared. "And I didn't hear you singing."

"My singing voice is too sexy," Julian said with a solemn shake of his head. "You'd fall in love with me, like, immediately."

Yadriel rolled his eyes and started back toward class.

Julian fell into step next to him. "Was it everything you'd dreamed it would be?" he asked.

"Truly magical," Yadriel drawled in response, but he was grinning, despite his best efforts. Excitement tingled up and down his arms. He'd *officially* used the men's restroom for the first time, and at *school*! Sure, there wasn't anyone else around, other than Julian, but it still felt like a huge step closer to being himself. Yadriel glanced to Julian from the corner of his eye. "Thanks."

Julian smiled. "Any time, patrón."

───────

When school was over, they met Maritza by the parking lot before heading to the cemetery.

"That was the most fun I've ever had at school, *ever*," Julian said, walking backward down the sidewalk.

"Oh, really?" Maritza asked, patting at her braids and wincing. "Did you learn a lot?"

Julian laughed. "No, but there was other stuff to keep me occupied," he said, before twisting around and heading down the street.

"Uh-huh," Maritza hummed, looking over at Yadriel with a smirk. "I'm sure there was."

Yadriel scowled, hating how hot his cheeks felt. *"Shut up,"* he hissed under his breath.

Luckily, Julian was up ahead and out of earshot, yanking leaves off bushes as he walked by.

"Hey, I'm not hating," Maritza said, at least having the decency to keep her voice down. "I mean, having a ghost boyfriend might be kinda hot." Her knowing smile was obnoxious.

He shoved her and, great, now his armpits were actually sweating. *"Itza!"*

She laughed, very pointedly looking Julian up and down from behind. "He *has* been practicing his ghost moves, maybe—"

"Oh my God, *stop*!" Yadriel said sharply, unable to take the teasing anymore. "It's not like that!" he huffed. "It *can't* be like that." His eyes trailed off to Julian, watching as he hopped up onto a short brick wall surrounding someone's house and walked along it.

Yadriel tried to stomp down the fluttery, twisty feeling, the low rush in his stomach.

"I mean, might as well enjoy it while he's around," Maritza whispered, giving him a little nudge with her elbow.

"He might not be around for much longer," Yadriel snapped. The butterflies were quickly replaced with queasy churning. "Especially not after last night."

Maritza frowned. "What happened last night?"

Keeping his voice down, Yadriel told her about Julian's unbecoming the night before. How he'd writhed in pain. The blood on his shirt. The way he'd disappeared. The memories turned the blood in his veins icy.

When he finished, Maritza's teasing smile and knowing looks were gone, replaced with one of pure alarm. "That's *so* creepy."

Yadriel shivered. "Yeah, no kidding."

"I don't think he should stay with you anymore."

It was so unexpected, Yadriel came to a halt. "Wait, *what*?"

"Maybe we should leave him somewhere during the night, like back in the old church?" she suggested, her eyes trained on Julian's back.

Yadriel frowned at her, suddenly feeling both defensive and protective of Julian. Exhaustion and frayed nerves did not help his mood. "What are you talking about?"

Maritza made a frustrated sound at the back of her throat. "What if he loses it and goes all dark spirit on you in the middle of the night?"

Yadriel shook his head. "Julian wouldn't hurt me."

"Julian wouldn't," she said. "But if he goes maligno, he's not Julian anymore."

Yadriel turned away from Maritza's knowing look. "Let's just get through today, okay?" Yadriel said. "Luca said he'd meet us right after school."

Maritza sighed but didn't argue further.

Yadriel watched as Julian dragged his fingers along a chain-link fence. He squinted in the sunlight, grinning as a cherry-red muscle car drove by, cumbia blaring from the speakers. Julian was happy in the city, Yadriel could see that. He liked the noise and the bustle and the people. It suited him. It was where he belonged. Not dead and in the afterlife, no matter how nice it was.

For the first time, it struck him how terribly unfair this all was. He hadn't really thought about what it meant, when all of this was over, after he released Julian's spirit and he was gone.

He didn't deserve death. He didn't deserve any of this. Julian had literally died protecting his friends. And Yadriel was quite certain *he* didn't deserve Julian. There was no reason for Julian to help him find

Miguel, but he did it anyway, and there was no way Yadriel could ever repay him.

He gave everything and expected nothing in return.

Yadriel's heart ached.

No, none of them deserved Julian Diaz.

FIFTEEN

otta check in with my parents and grab the dogs," Maritza said as she crossed the street to her house. "You two wait out here. They would ground me for life if they knew I was hanging out with a spirit."

Julian feigned offense.

She ran across the street and into the house. The screen door slammed shut behind her.

Yadriel collapsed against a nearby wall, letting his head fall back against cool brick as he closed his eyes. Sirens wailed in the distance. A loud drill sounded from the construction on the main road. He could hear Maritza and her family's raised voices—not yelling, just vying to be heard.

"Hey." Julian's quiet voice tickled his ear. "Don't fall asleep, you might topple over, and I can't catch you."

"Mmm," Yadriel hummed, peeking one eye open.

Julian leaned his shoulder against the wall, grinning down at him.

"It's your fault I'm this tired," Yadriel grumbled.

"Hey, hey, hey, don't use me as your escape goat."

Yadriel exhaled a tired laugh. "*Scapegoat*, Jules."

A dimple pressed into Julian's left cheek as he dragged his teeth over his bottom lip.

Yadriel's heartbeat fluttered in his throat. He forced his eyes closed, trying to push Maritza's words out of his head. *Don't do it*, he told himself. The only thing more stupid than going around his family's back, summoning spirits, and trying to solve multiple murders would be falling for a dead boy.

Especially if it was Julian Diaz.

A moment later, the sound of a screen door slamming and the jingling of collars announced Maritza's return. "We're good!" she said, Donatello dragged her forward so he could slobber over Yadriel's hand, whacking himself in the face with his tail as he wiggled with excitement. Michelangelo sat back on his haunches and burped. Maritza rolled her eyes and waved her hand in front of her nose. "Jesus, gordito."

"She didn't mean it," Yadriel said, giving Michelangelo a good scratch.

"This is for you." She tossed Yadriel a can, and he clumsily caught it. It was a sugar-free Red Bull. "Paola drinks, like, two a day."

Yadriel cracked it open.

"Oh man, I love that stuff!" Julian whined.

"You hopped up on an energy drink sounds like a literal nightmare," Maritza told him.

Yadriel took a swig and nearly choked. "Ugh!" he coughed. "It's disgusting."

"Yeah, well, it'll wake you up!" Maritza said, giving him a hard thump on the back. "So suck it up!"

When they got to the cemetery, Luca was already waiting. He rolled back and forth on his skateboard, anxiously craning his neck this way and that, as he tried to see into the cemetery without getting too close. When he spotted Yadriel and Maritza, his body relaxed and he waved at them with a smile. "Thought you guys changed your mind for a second," Luca admitted. He was wearing the same sweater again, his fingers lost in the sleeves as he fidgeted.

"Just had to make a detour," Maritza told him.

He beamed at the dogs but lurched to a stop, glancing at Maritza for permission.

"Go for it."

Luca sank to his knees. Donatello and Michelangelo viciously smothered him with wet dog kisses, sending Luca into a fit of laughter.

"The guy needs a dog," Yadriel said, smiling. The Red Bull was starting to kick in.

"The guy needs a home, first," Julian grumbled. He looked less than enthused, his posture rigid and expression surly.

It was starting to get cold out, the clouds overhead turning dark and gray. Since it was a Thursday afternoon, folks were beginning to gear up for the weekend. Garage doors stood open with people milling around inside, music blaring, red cups in hand. People cruised up and down the streets in souped-up mods and beat-down junkers.

Maritza and Luca babbled away, easily bouncing between topics while Yadriel hung back, watching Julian. The closer they got, the more Julian withdrew. By the time they made it to the correct street, he was silent and hanging back at Yadriel's side. His shoulders were hunched up to his ears, his jaw clenched tight.

"It's just up ahead!" Luca announced, kicking his skateboard into his hand as he fell into step next to Maritza.

"We'll just be in and out, really quick," Yadriel said, his nerves getting the better of him the closer they got. "We just need to see if he knows anything, and steal something that has Julian's scent on it." It was simple enough. How hard could it be?

"Anything we should know going in?" Yadriel asked.

"Uh—no." Luca shook his head. "I dunno. This is all kind of weird." He looked around. Maybe searching for Julian again. "Just try to tell the truth; Rio's really good at spotting liars," Luca told him, clearly having learned from experience.

"Awesome," Maritza grumbled.

"And he doesn't like dogs," Julian added.

Yadriel took a deep breath. "Then we're off to a great start."

The car shop was a squat warehouse with three open bay doors and a tiny office attached. The brick exterior was creamy orange, and MARTINEZ AND DIAZ MECHANIC SHOP was painted in loopy letters next to the entrance. There was a large mural of Our Lady of Guadalupe spray-painted above it. She was in her typical red dress and star-speckled blue mantle. Rays in shades of orange and yellow burst from around her. Sure enough, ST. J was written just below her feet.

Various cars were parked in a line out front, some with missing fenders or busted headlights. A shiny Cadillac was hoisted up on a lift while a man in navy coveralls tinkered underneath it. Banda music played on a scratchy radio somewhere.

Through the front window, Yadriel could see customers waiting on plastic chairs. The local news played on a small TV mounted in the corner. A woman with bright red lips and clicky high heels walked by holding a clipboard. Everything smelled like gasoline and engine grease.

Luca went right up to a man standing at a workbench, sorting tools. He was wide and tall, clad in a pair of long khaki shorts, white tube socks, and a black T-shirt.

"Carlos!" Luca called over the loud drilling of a machine.

"Luca!" Carlos smiled in greeting. One of his front teeth was gold, and there were streaks of gray in his long goatee. "Where you been, little man?" He clamped a large hand on Luca's shoulder and gave him a shake.

Luca stumbled under the weight.

"¿Hambriento? Think I got leftovers in the fridge—"

"I'm okay!" Luca cut in, beaming up at the taller man. "Um, we're actually looking for Rio."

"Oh?" Carlos looked up to where Yadriel and Maritza stood waiting. His smile faltered as soon as he caught sight of Donatello and Michelangelo. Maritza wiggled her fingers in a wave.

"That's Carlos," Julian said into Yadriel's ear.

"Got that," Yadriel said quietly, moving his lips as little as possible.

"Could we talk to him?" Luca prompted when Carlos didn't say anything.

The man's attention went back to Luca, the smile back in full force. "Yeah, yeah, 'course, little man!" He turned to the open bay doors and gave a sharp whistle. "Rio!" he called. "One of your strays is lookin' for you!"

One of the car hoods slammed shut, revealing a young man standing behind it. "Luca?" He came around and stepped into the sunlight.

There was no denying that Rio was Julian's older brother. They had the same nose and heavy brow. Rio was tall and broad. He wore navy coveralls with the top portion pulled down, the sleeves knotted around his waist. His white tank top was covered in black grease marks. His shoulders were round and the ropy muscles of his arms bunched as he wiped his hands off on a rag. On his right arm, Yadriel saw the large black-and-white tattoo of Santa Muerte Julian had mentioned before. A starry mantle framed her skeletal face.

Almost immediately, Yadriel could feel something coming from Rio. When Yadriel looked at Maritza for confirmation, she gave him a confused look, like she felt it, too. He couldn't pin down what it was. It wasn't a spirit sense, definitely something having to do with his health. Julian hadn't mentioned his brother having any illness or injury, but there was something there.

Rio had a practical haircut and a serious face. He was incredibly handsome and twice as intimidating. "What are you doing here?" Rio's copper-brown eyes flicked to Yadriel, Maritza, and then the dogs. His frown deepened as he tossed the rag to the side. "What's wrong?"

"Nothing—nothing's wrong!" Luca said quickly through nervous laughter.

Yadriel was starting to think Rio's ability to tell someone was lying was less about his own skill and more about Julian and his friends being awful at it.

"Could we go talk real quick?" Luca asked, tugging on the hem of his sweater.

Again, Rio eyed them. Sweat prickled on the back of Yadriel's neck, but he forced himself to not blink or look away. To his side, Julian glowered.

Finally, Rio nodded. "Come on." He led the way around the shop, his heavy black shoes squeaking against the oily cement. A large set of keys jangled at his hip.

They followed, but Yadriel was already starting to regret this decision. After everything he'd heard about Rio—how he cared for and looked after Julian and his friends—he'd expected him to be, well . . . different. Friendlier, at least. The guy before him didn't seem like someone who pulled a young boy out of a gang, or took in kids who didn't have anywhere else to go.

Around the side, Rio unlocked a large chain-link gate. At the back of the building, there was a storage shed and sun-bleached canopy covering a gorgeous car. It was an electric-blue Corvette Stingray, according to the logo. Yadriel didn't know much about cars, but he could tell it was old but meticulously taken care of.

Julian went right up to it, smoothing both his hands lovingly over the rounded hood. It was a strange shape, kind of like a clown shoe.

A rickety set of stairs led up to the apartment above the shop. Rio stopped at the bottom.

"Dogs stay out here," he said in a voice so firm, it was clear there was no room for negotiation.

Yadriel turned to Maritza, alarmed.

"It's fine." She nodded, waving Yadriel ahead. More quietly, she added, "You're fine."

But he certainly didn't feel fine.

He didn't want to do this on his own. Luca was there just to get them in the door, and Julian was being unusually quiet as he lingered by the car. But Yadriel sucked in a deep breath and nodded.

Maritza settled herself against the Stingray.

"Don't lean on the car," Rio said.

She leaped back.

Rio started up the stairs, and Maritza settled for walking Donatello and Michelangelo around the small yard so they could sniff at rusty car parts and old tires.

Yadriel followed him and Luca up the stairs and into the apartment. It was small. Much smaller than he'd expected.

To the right, the main room had a square table and three chairs, each of them a different style and wood. It was covered in envelopes and a set of car manuals. Against the far wall sat a flat-screen TV perched on a black-and-red tool cabinet. There was an old PlayStation and a handful of controllers, their cords twisted and knotted together. Facing it was a black leather couch. The cushions looked poufy, but the seats were cracked and the armrests were worn. There was a lumpy yellow pillow crammed into one side and a blue, scratchy-looking blanket with satin trim on the other. A floral comforter was tossed onto a green recliner in the corner, and more folded blankets sat in a precarious heap under the square window.

Straight ahead was the bedroom. Yadriel caught a glimpse of a room barely big enough to fit a mattress on the floor. Last one in, he shut the front door behind himself. There were two holes in the back at about knee height.

Luca sank into one of the chairs at the dining table, drawing one knee up to his chest. Rio turned left, into the kitchen. It was so narrow, Yadriel doubted you could open the fridge door all the way without running into the opposite counter.

Rio pulled a baking pan out of the fridge and snagged a fork from a drawer. "So, who are you?" he asked as he filled a mug up with water from the sink.

"I'm Yadriel," he said.

Rio set the pan and mug on top of some papers in front of Luca. It was chocolate cake with goopy chocolate icing. Only one small piece had been cut out from the corner. His large hand thumped Luca's chest, and Luca snatched up the fork and dove right in.

"I'm Julian's friend," Yadriel added, feeling pressured to fill the silence. While Rio wasn't looking, he gave Julian a small nod. Julian edged around the room and disappeared into the bedroom.

Rio leaned back against the counter and folded his arms over his chest, hands tucked under his large biceps. He looked down his nose at Yadriel. "No, you're not."

Julian snorted from the other room, but it lacked his usual mirth.

"I'm a newer friend," he corrected. He nearly added "from school," but he knew better than to make that mistake.

Rio's eyes narrowed ever so slightly. He said nothing and simply stood there, waiting.

"We were wondering if you'd seen Jules," Luca somehow managed through a huge mouthful of cake.

Rio let his intense gaze stay on Yadriel a moment longer before looking over to Luca. "No, I haven't. He left a few days ago."

"You haven't heard from him at all?"

"No, Luca." Frustration edged his otherwise even voice. "He left. Probably for good, this time." For a moment, his quiet stoicism slipped. Yadriel could see past it. Could spot the way his eyelids drooped, how he rubbed a spot on his neck.

Yadriel realized what he'd sensed coming from Rio when he first saw him. He wasn't sick or injured, but his fatigue was so thick, Yadriel could actually feel it.

Luca frowned. "Jules wouldn't just *leave*."

Rio glanced over at Yadriel, like he didn't want to have this conversation in front of him, but Luca was persistent.

"Really, Rio, he wouldn't!"

"He's been itching to get out of here for years," Rio told him. "We got into a fight. He said he couldn't stand living in this dump anymore. He said I—" He cut a glance at Yadriel again and stopped himself.

Yadriel didn't like the way he was talking about Julian, especially when he couldn't even defend himself. He felt himself bristling under Rio's suspicious gaze.

"C'mon." Luca tried to smile. "You know he just gets like that sometimes."

"Not this time, Luca." Rio was curt but far from yelling.

"He'd never actually take off on us!"

Yadriel wanted to agree with him, to tell Rio that Luca was right. He knew he needed to just keep his mouth shut, but it was becoming difficult to hold his tongue.

"This time he meant it. I saw it on his face." Rio sighed and scrubbed his hands over his face, leaving a smudge of grease across his forehead. Worry and exhaustion made him look far older than his twenty-two years.

"Told you."

Julian stood off to his brother's side, a gray-and-black plaid shirt balled up in his hands. He watched his brother with dark, smoldering eyes. "I just make his life more difficult. He's better off."

Yadriel clenched his jaw. He wanted to knock some sense into both Julian *and* Rio.

"The cops haven't come by at all?" Yadriel ventured, trying to steer the conversation toward something that would help them find not only Julian, but Miguel, too.

Luca's hand froze, a heaping forkful of cake inches from his mouth.

"No." Rio's forehead wrinkled. "Why would the cops come by?"

"He's missing, so *shouldn't* we go to the police?" Luca jumped in, his cheeks burning red.

Rio sighed deeply and rubbed his temple. "He's not missing, Luca, he ran away." He let out a short, bitter laugh. "He didn't even tell us he was leaving," Rio added, expression stormy.

Julian turned away from his brother, wringing the plaid shirt in his hands. His ears were turning red. The hurt was written on every tense muscle in his face, shoulders, and arms.

Anger sparked in Yadriel, and he clenched his fists, his fingernails pressing into his palms. He'd only known Julian a couple of days, but even he knew there was no way Julian would run away from his friends—his family. He wanted to yell at Rio, to tell him he was so entirely wrong.

Luca put down his fork and shook his head, sending his shaggy hair sweeping back and forth. "No, he—"

"*Luca.*" Rio's voice was firm. "He doesn't care."

Julian flinched, twisting away from Yadriel, but it was impossible to miss his pained expression, or the shine in his dark eyes.

The spark in Yadriel flared.

"If that's what you think, then you really don't know Julian at all," Yadriel said, the words flying from his mouth before he could stop himself.

All three of them turned to stare at him.

Julian blinked at Yadriel, surprised.

Rio's stare was stony and unforgiving. Luca looked between him and Yadriel anxiously.

"You think you know him better?" Rio asked. "I've never even seen you before. I've known him his whole life," he said, tapping a finger against his chest. "I kept him off the streets and raised him ever since—"

"Apparently!" Yadriel cut him off, forcing himself to stand his ground even though he was incredibly intimidated by Rio. "If you really think Julian doesn't care about you all, then yeah, I do know him better!"

Julian openly gaped.

Rio straightened. "You—"

But Yadriel refused to let him talk. He wasn't thinking about protecting his own secret, he just wanted to make Rio see how stupid he was being, how hurtful his words were. "Maybe he's got a short temper and makes stupid decisions sometimes," he went on. "But you should know that Julian wouldn't leave you all unless there was something keeping him from coming back!"

Rio eyes grew sharp with distrust. "Who are you?" he said—an order, not a request.

"What if something happened to Julian?" Luca said to Rio, his chin wobbling.

"What are you talking about?" Rio asked, but Luca turned away, refusing to look him in the eye. Instead, Rio looked at Yadriel.

He couldn't think of anything to say that wouldn't make Rio even more suspicious, or, worse, alarm him. Sensing his hesitation, Rio stood bolt upright.

"What happened?" His eyes shot between Yadriel and Luca.

"Don't."

The sharp word yanked Yadriel's attention back to Julian. He stood there, the shirt twisted around his wrists like a rope.

"Don't tell him," Julian said.

Quickly, Yadriel looked away from him. He couldn't draw Rio's attention to Julian, or he'd see the shirt hovering in midair.

"Luca," Yadriel said in warning, giving a quick shake of his head. Yadriel had promised not to out him, and he wouldn't.

Luca tucked his chin to his chest, his cheeks burning bright red.

Rio's tired expression had vanished. He was alert and protective as he stepped between Yadriel and Luca. "What do you want? And why did you drag Luca into whatever the hell this is?" Rio barked.

Yadriel's heart thudded in the pulse of his neck. "I—I—" he stammered.

"But, Rio," Luca interrupted, panic tightening his voice. "What if—"

"Luca." Rio took a deep breath and exhaled through pursed lips. He sank into a squat beside Luca so they were eye to eye. He gave Luca's shoulder a squeeze. "He *ran away.*"

Yadriel felt the cold washing off Julian in waves. Under it was a palpable ache.

Rio's voice was strange when he spoke, like he was trying to sound comforting but didn't know how. "If he doesn't want to be a part of this family anymore, then we need to let him go, okay?"

It happened in a blink of an eye. Yadriel was the only one who saw Julian bolt.

But they all heard his foot slam into the door, leaving a third hole. It flung open, clattering against the railing. As Julian stormed out, a gust of icy wind whipped in, sending papers flying.

Everyone jumped. Luca flinched. Rio was on his feet immediately.

Yadriel thought his heart was going to burst through his chest.

Rio's eyes snapped to Yadriel, wide and alarmed. He pointed at the door. "Get out."

Yadriel backed up. "I'm sorry—I—"

"NOW."

He caught a short glimpse of Luca, shielded by Rio's body. He was trembling, his eyes glued to the new hole Julian had left in the door. Yadriel ran out and down the stairs.

SIXTEEN

Yadriel raced down the stairs as fast as his feet could carry him, combat boots clomping all the way. Julian stormed off ahead, with no sign of slowing down. The chain-link gate rattled as he blew through.

"Come on." He waved at Maritza. "We gotta go."

Maritza met Yadriel at the bottom of the stairs. "What the heck happened?" she asked, her head snapping back and forth between him and Julian's retreating back. Michelangelo whined anxiously. Meanwhile, Donatello merrily chewed on something that might've been a crumpled plastic bottle. "Sounds like it didn't go well."

"It didn't," Yadriel agreed as they rounded the building.

A few heads turned when Julian cut through the busy lot, a sharp gust of wind following him.

A woman gasped and punched the arm of the man standing next to her. "Did you see that?" she asked, pointing right where Julian had passed. Undoubtedly, she'd seen the shirt in his hands floating off on its own.

The man laughed. "Those Santa Ana winds are crazy," he said, shaking his head.

Yadriel quickened his pace, filling in Maritza as they chased after Julian. His stomach twisted, sick with guilt as he remembered the looks on Luca's and Rio's faces. Yadriel wasn't sure if Luca fully believed him about Julian's being dead, let alone being a ghost. Either way, he'd definitely freaked Luca out.

He hadn't meant to upset them, but he couldn't help himself. The way Rio had been so dismissive and just so *wrong* about Julian, how was he supposed to just let him keep going? Especially when Julian was standing right there, listening to all of it and unable to defend himself. How could Rio think so little of Julian? Was that how he really felt? What he really thought? Or was he just acting out because he was hurt?

The Diaz brothers seemed to have trouble processing their emotions.

Julian stomped down the street.

"Julian!" Yadriel hissed, trying to keep up.

The shirt hung from Julian's fist, whipping around wildly. Santa Ana winds were a flimsy cover, at best. If they weren't careful, they were going to catch someone's attention. That was the last thing they needed right now.

"Wait up!"

Julian turned, disappearing behind an old church.

Yadriel, Maritza, and the dogs ran to catch up. When they found him, Julian was pacing back and forth in front of the entrance to the church like a caged animal. Rusty grates of filigree and crosses sealed off the doors and windows. An angry, frigid wind kicked up dirt and debris around him. His expression was severe and frustrated, the muscles in his jaw tight and his nostrils flared.

Maritza hung back. Donatello whined and Michelangelo shook himself out nervously. She cut Yadriel a wary look.

Her words from earlier needled into Yadriel's head.

He won't be Julian anymore.

But this wasn't Julian losing grip on himself and slipping toward turning maligno. Yadriel knew that.

"Julian—" Yadriel reached out for him, even though he knew he'd be nothing more than frost on his fingertips.

But Julian jerked away. "DON'T."

So Yadriel didn't.

Instead, he watched, cautiously. He didn't try to move closer, but he didn't retreat, either. Gently, he tried, "Hey, you—"

"I know, I know, I know!" Julian growled impatiently. "You'll flush me down the toilet!"

Maritza gave Yadriel a startled look.

A blush swept up the back of his neck and across his face. "I'm not—"

"Just *give me a second*!" Julian dropped into a squat and pressed his shirt against his face. Framed under the arch of the gated doors, the fluorescent lights spilled yellow across the steps of the church, but it didn't quite touch Julian. There was a saint painted on the cement wall above him. A faceless man in a black robe with a white rope tied around his waist. In his right hand, he held a skull. In the left, a crucifix. Colorful swirls of paint spiraled out around him.

Yadriel's chest ached, but all he could do was stand back and give Julian space as he warred with himself.

Julian's back rose as he gulped down air. Slowly, the wind settled.

He drew in a deep breath and exhaled it through pursed lips. When he stood up and faced Yadriel, his cheeks were splotchy, his edges watery. He dragged his fist across his eyes before finally letting his hands fall to his sides.

Yadriel wrapped his arms around himself. "Are you okay?"

Julian's laugh was forced. "Jesus," he sniffed, looking anywhere but at Yadriel. "Can we not talk about *feelings* right now?"

"I don't think Rio meant all that," Yadriel continued, joining Julian on the step. "He's just hurt. I mean, you could see that, right?"

Staring at the ground, Julian didn't look so sure. "I didn't mean that shit I said to him," he mumbled. His finger moved to his throat, searching for something that wasn't there. He glanced over to where his necklace hung around Yadriel's neck. "I just got so *mad*!" He shook his head, jaw clenched.

"He'll understand, he'll—"

Julian's eyes snapped to his.

"He'll *what*, Yads?" he demanded. "Forgive me? Talk it out? Welcome me back?" Julian clutched at his chest, balling up his T-shirt in his fist. "I'm *dead*."

Yadriel snapped his mouth shut. A shiver rolled through him. "We can figure something out," he offered, having no idea what. He didn't want to see Julian like this, and he didn't want Rio going the rest of his life thinking his brother had abandoned him.

Julian was already shaking his head.

"Maybe I could try talking to him again?" Yadriel offered, scratching at the prickle on the back of his neck.

"No," Julian said. The anger in his voice was quickly weighing down with exhaustion. "It's better that he just thinks I ran away," he repeated for the umpteenth time. "It's easier this way."

Maybe it was easier, but it didn't feel right. Yadriel wanted to argue, but this wasn't his family. This wasn't his choice. "I'll do what you think is best," Yadriel conceded.

Julian looked at him, eyes dark and calculating.

"Hate to interrupt..." Yadriel had nearly forgotten Maritza was still there until she stepped forward. Donatello and Michelangelo were two unmovable boulders at her sides, lying on the cement and looking thoroughly unperturbed. "But it's getting late," she said, still giving Julian a wide berth. "And my phone says it might start raining soon."

They all tipped their heads back to stare up at the sky. Heavy, dark clouds were creeping in, chasing away the afternoon sun.

"The dogs aren't really good at this whole tracking thing to begin with," Maritza pointed out. Donatello and Michelangelo stared up at her, tongues happily lolling out of their mouths. "It's already been a couple days, and if it rains..."

"Then there will be no way for them to pick up the scent," Yadriel finished.

Maritza nodded, giving Julian a nervous glance.

After the mess he'd made, Yadriel didn't expect Julian to want to continue with their plan. He didn't want to tell his brother or his friends that he'd died, so what reason did he have to help them find his body?

"Take it." Julian stepped forward and pushed his shirt into Yadriel's hands.

The material was worn soft and there was a hole in the shoulder. He got a small whiff of musky cologne and the faint sting of gasoline.

Julian brushed past them and started walking down the sidewalk.

Yadriel's heart dropped to his feet. He gripped the shirt tightly and turned to Maritza. A look of defeat crossed her face, and panic rose in Yadriel's throat. He wanted to call out and tell Julian to stop, that—

Julian glanced back at them over his shoulder. He frowned. "Don't we need to hurry?" he asked, sounding annoyed. "Come on." He jerked his chin. "The park is this way."

Yadriel stared at him.

Maritza let out a loud, relieved breath.

Julian looked between them, brow furrowed. "What?"

"I—I thought—" Yadriel stammered.

"*Jesus*, Yads," he sighed in exasperation with a grand roll of his eyes. "We've still got your cousin to find, right?"

Yadriel could only bob his head in a nod.

An amused grin tugged at the corner of Julian's lips. "So let's go," he said, waving them on. "Before the rain wipes out any chance Tweedle-dee and Tweedledum got."

Maritza gasped. "Don't you dare call them that!"

Julian chuckled.

"*You're* the dumb one," she said, starting after Julian, Donatello and Michelangelo obediently following along.

Gratitude flooded Yadriel with warmth. He wanted to stop Julian and thank him, truly and genuinely, but he could picture his reaction in his head.

Can we not talk about feelings *right now?*

Instead, he clutched the shirt tightly to his chest and chased after Maritza and Julian as they continued to bicker down the street.

Belvedere Park was made up of two parts. The north side was the community park, which had a public pool, a skate park, and sports fields. The south side had a man-made lake. The 60 freeway cut through the middle. There was a pedestrian bridge that you could take over the freeway that connected the north to the south. Julian took them to the south end, where the pedestrian bridge bottomed out at a small parking lot.

"We were coming down that ramp," Julian said, pointing to where the caged bridge ended. "Luca went up ahead, I heard him yell, saw some guy—"

"Are you sure it was a guy?" Maritza asked, scuffing the toe of her shoe against an empty beer can.

"Yes it was a guy," Julian said, annoyed. "He was taller than me, and—"

"There's plenty of women in the world over six feet—"

"Well, they were strong enough to *murder me*," Julian shot back.

"I'm sure plenty of women are smart enough to overpower you," Maritza said, casually examining her nails.

Julian spluttered, but Yadriel cut in before they got too off topic. Again.

"And that's all you remember?" Yadriel asked, turning in a slow circle.

Julian shrugged. "That's it."

The pavement was cracked and overgrown with weeds. The barrier walls were covered in graffiti and did little to block the thunder of traffic on the other side. There were some trees and large, overgrown bushes. Litter was ensnared in tufts of dead grass: straws, take-out containers, and plenty of cigarette butts.

There weren't any telltale signs of a struggle. Though, to be honest,

Yadriel didn't know what to look out for. Either way, there was nothing glaringly obvious, like blood or a murder weapon, let alone a dead body.

But that was why they had brought the dogs along. Hopefully, they could pick up on things the humans couldn't, and lead them to something useful.

"Ready to give it a shot, boys?" Yadriel asked.

The sudden attention got them both wiggling with enthusiasm.

"Fingers crossed," Maritza said, taking off their leashes.

Yadriel crouched down, holding Julian's shirt out for them to get a good sniff. Their wet noses snuffled against the material, making sounds that were more pig than dog.

Michelangelo wandered off first, probably realizing there was nothing edible hidden between the folds.

Donatello, on the other hand, didn't give up so easily.

Before Yadriel could realize what was happening, Donatello was choking on a sleeve. "No, don't *eat* it!" He yanked on the shirt, and Donatello hacked it up. "Oh, Santa Muerte," Yadriel groaned, nose wrinkling as he held it out of Donatello's reach as the dog tried to jump up on his stubby legs.

Julian ran forward. "Man, that's my favorite shirt!" he lamented.

"He didn't tear it," Yadriel said, examining the sleeve cuff covered in slobber. "It's just kinda . . . wet. Down, Donatello!"

Donatello ignored him and continued to whine, pawing pathetically at Yadriel's leg.

Julian scowled at the dog. "Some help *you* are."

"Guys!" Maritza stood next to a line of overgrown bushes that Michelangelo's entire front half had disappeared into. "I think we've got something!"

Yadriel and Julian rushed over. Leaves rustled as Michelangelo dug farther into the bush. He planted his paws and started to tug on something.

Suddenly, Yadriel realized how much he *didn't* want to see Julian's dead body. Julian stood rigid, dark eyes large and chest rising and falling with shallow, rapid breaths.

"What is it?" he asked, voice tight.

Julian was the most alive person he'd ever met. Even as a spirit, he was bright and full of constantly moving energy. A sun crammed into the body of a boy. Yadriel didn't want to see him without his light.

Maritza moved in to investigate, pushing branches out of the way as she reached into the leaves.

Yadriel held his breath.

Maritza cursed. When she stood upright, she held a white paper bag. KING TACO was written across it in red, loopy letters.

"My tacos!" Julian exclaimed with pleased surprise.

Yadriel exhaled heavily, feeling light-headed.

"Ugh, that's *rank*," Maritza said, face scrunched up as she held the bag as far away as possible in pinched fingers.

Michelangelo sat on his rump, looking very proud of himself. Donatello waddled over and tried to get at the bag of rotten tacos.

"Is that it?" Yadriel asked, stepping forward. "There's nothing else?"

Maritza pushed more branches around with her free hand, searching, but ultimately shrugged. "That's it."

Relief was quickly replaced with disappointment. He had really thought, or hoped, they'd be able to find something useful. If not a body, then at least some kind of clue to point them in the right direction. Yadriel spun in a slow circle, triple-checking that there wasn't something obvious they'd missed, but there was nothing.

"You don't remember anything else?" Yadriel asked Julian for the umpteenth time.

Julian lifted his shoulders in a shrug. "That's all I got."

No sign of Julian's body. No sign of Miguel.

"We should really head home," Maritza said, tossing the bag back into the bushes. She snagged Donatello by his collar before he could dive in after it. "I think it's going to start raining."

Yadriel knew she was right, it was getting darker by the minute, but he didn't want to go home empty-handed. He wanted to help Julian, to find Miguel. He hated the idea of just waiting around for Día de Muertos, to see if Miguel's spirit would return and tell them what had happened. And, even if he did, what if, like Julian, Miguel couldn't remember, either?

Yadriel felt the first drop on the very tip of his nose.

Julian held out his hands as it began to drizzle, and rain fell right through his palms.

SEVENTEEN

By the time Yadriel and Julian got back to the cemetery, the drizzle had turned into full on rain. Yadriel's hoodie was sopping wet, and his jeans were starting to chafe. Water had soaked into his binder, making it tight and freezing cold, sucking all the warmth from his core. His hair was a limp mess. Drops of water trailed down his scalp and the back of his neck. As they jogged across the street, his combat boots splashed in shallow puddles.

"Careful," Yadriel whispered to Julian as he slipped through the front gate as quietly as possible. "My dad's on graveyard shift tonight." The dark clouds plunged the world into night as soon as the sun went down.

Julian hadn't said much on the way back, and Yadriel hated it. Their roles seemed to reverse as Yadriel tried to fill the silence that Julian left.

"We just need a new plan," he said, trying to throw out solutions and words of encouragement that would jump-start Julian back to talking.

Julian's face was tense. Deep creases lined his forehead.

Yadriel wished he would just tell him what he was thinking. "Are you okay?" he asked Julian as they moved between graves. The slick stones reflected the streetlights, giving everything an eerie shine.

"I'm fine," was Julian's curt response, not even bothering to look in Yadriel's direction.

"You don't seem fine," Yadriel pointed out, carding his fingers through his wet hair, but it flopped right back into his eyes. "Are you still upset about your brother?"

Julian stopped suddenly and frowned out across the cemetery.

Yadriel clutched the dripping straps of his backpack. Julian had every right to be mad at him; he didn't blame him for it.

"I could try talking to my tío, see if he can help us. I mean, he saw my portaje, so he knows now," he said, rubbing the goose bumps on his arms as he shivered in the rain.

Julian gave a frustrated shake of his head and started walking toward the house again, not even listening to Yadriel's suggestions as his eyes swept back and forth across the headstones and colorful tombs.

Yadriel chased after him, desperate to get Julian to just hear him out. "I mean, I know I messed up, but I still think I can—"

Annoyed, Julian spun around. *"Yads."*

But then he froze, staring.

"What?" The word billowed in a cloud from Yadriel's lips. Electricity ran up his spine, jarring his teeth.

Julian wasn't staring at him.

He was staring past him.

Yadriel turned and found himself face-to-face with a figure. He sucked in a sharp breath. His first thought was they'd been caught—someone had seen them, had seen Julian, and now they knew he was hiding a spirit and would tell his dad.

But then he recognized the burgundy jersey. The floppy straw hat.

Relief crashed over him. "*Coño.* Holy *crap*, Tito—" He forced out a laugh. "It's just Tito."

He threw Julian a glance, but his posture was still rigid. His dark eyes wide with alarm.

"It's okay, he's—" But Yadriel cut himself off as he turned back to Tito. Something was wrong.

It hit Yadriel's senses all at once.

Tito didn't look right. He was perfectly still, his gardening shears held in his hand. His beloved Venezuela jersey was covered in dark stains. His skin was puffy and gray. The brim of his hat cast his eyes in dark shadows. Then the smell hit Yadriel's nose. It was an earthy, putrid stench.

Tito's mouth yawned open—too wide, as if his jaw had unhinged. He drew in a deep, rattling breath. His bloated fingers tightened around the handles of the shears. They made a rusty squeal.

"Yadriel!" Julian shouted.

He didn't have time to do anything more than suck in a gasp before Tito raised his arm and brought the shears down toward him. Yadriel tried to scramble away but tripped over his own feet, landing hard on his back, the wind knocked out of his lungs. He expected to feel rusty steel sink into his chest. Instead, he heard the colliding of bodies meeting with a sharp grunt.

Coughing, Yadriel rolled onto his side, trying to catch his breath, the taste of mud on his lips.

Julian was on his feet and fighting. Tito brought the shears down at him, but Julian used his arm to deflect the blow. He threw his fist into Tito's nose. There was a loud crunch and a ghoulish wail, something entirely inhuman that put Yadriel's teeth on edge. Julian sank his knee into Tito's gut with a wet thud, slamming his elbow into the back of his head when he doubled over.

The shears clattered to the ground.

Yadriel arched his back and twisted, pulling his portaje out from its sheath. He needed to sever the tie between Tito and his shears.

Ripping open his bag, Yadriel plunged his hand inside, searching for his Hydro Flask filled with chicken blood.

Julian fought hard, but this wasn't some scuffle in the school halls.

It wasn't a brawl in the street. His opponent wasn't even human anymore. The horror that used to be Tito caught Julian around his throat, fingers catching under his jaw and pulling him off his feet.

"*Julian!*" Yadriel shouted, fear shredding his voice.

Julian thrashed, hands scrabbling at Tito's arm, feet kicking wildly as he choked.

Yadriel yanked out the bottle and clumsily unscrewed the top. With shaky hands, he dumped the blood onto the blade.

"¡Muéstrame el enlace!" he said, and his dagger burst to life with glowing light.

The golden thread appeared, drawn between the garden shears on the ground and the center of Tito's chest.

Tito's head swung to Yadriel. He tossed Julian to the side with surprising strength. Julian careened through headstones and out of sight. Yadriel had no idea if a spirit could destroy another spirit, but he could hear Julian groan.

Tito lunged for him, and Yadriel was barely able to throw himself behind a sarcophagus in time. The voice in his head screamed at him to get to the shears, to cut the tie.

An inhuman screech filled the air. Tito threw himself onto the sarcophagus, nails digging at the stone in a frenzy as he tried to reach Yadriel.

Yadriel ducked out of Tito's reach, his feet slipping through slick mud as he tried to propel himself forward.

He dove for the shears, but he wasn't fast enough.

Tito was on him in a blink, knocking him off his feet and onto his back once again.

As he pinned Yadriel down, Tito's mouth opened wide. Black lips split open, revealing rotten teeth. A rattling growl flowed from the gaping hole. Something wriggled under his purple tongue.

Yadriel tried to get his dagger free, but Tito had his wrist in an iron grip. He shoved his hand against the side of Tito's face, trying to push him away, but his dead skin was slippery and squished under his fingers.

Tito's blackened teeth snapped.

Yadriel thrashed wildly, his heartbeat pounding in his ears.

A strangled shout ripped from his throat.

"¡Muéstrame el enlace!" someone bellowed.

In his peripheral, there was a flash of light, but all Yadriel could see was Tito's lumbering form on top of him. The golden thread ignited at the center of Tito's chest, shooting off to the left.

Tito raised his meaty fist over his head, ready to slam it down onto Yadriel.

He threw his arms up to shield himself, but the blow never came.

"¡Te libero a la otra vida!"

Tito's face went slack.

Yadriel could've sworn he heard a soft sigh, and, a moment later, Tito dissolved into thousands of glowing marigold petals. They fell in a gentle cascade over Yadriel, tickling his cheeks before they faded and disappeared into the mud.

Yadriel stared at the spot Tito had been, his breath sawing in and out of his lungs.

When he looked up, a man stood over him in a black rain jacket, a portaje glinting in his hand. When he pushed back his hood, it was his father's stunned face staring back at him.

"Yadriel?" He pulled him up to his feet and gripped tightly onto Yadriel's shoulders. "Are you okay?" His father's panicked eyes searched his before looking him over.

"Yeah, I'm okay." His voice quaked. Immediately, he looked for Julian, but he was nowhere in sight. "I—"

His dad pulled him to his chest and locked his arms around him tight, pressing his nose into Yadriel's hair. "Thank the saints!"

Yadriel could feel his dad's shuddering inhale. His own body trembled in his dad's embrace. Enrique withdrew, still holding on tight to his shoulders. "What on earth happened?"

Nerves and adrenaline fried Yadriel's brain as he tried to come up with something. "I—I—"

Finally, Enrique spotted the portaje clutched in Yadriel's hand. His eyes bulged, watching as the glowing blade faded back to steel.

"Santa Muerte," his dad breathed, bewildered, as he pushed his hand through his wet hair. "Where did you get that?"

Guilt and panic swarmed in Yadriel's stomach. He wanted to tell a cover story, to make up some sort of excuse, but this wasn't a situation he could just lie himself out of. "Maritza made me my own portaje . . ."

"Maritza?" Yadriel's dad shook his head, but he didn't sound surprised by that answer. "But . . . It was glowing. It glowed." He kept shaking his head, as if that would rattle his brain into connecting the pieces. "How?"

It felt like there wasn't enough room in Yadriel's chest for him to take a deep breath. His legs felt wobbly under him. He was terrified.

"I went through my quinces ritual," Yadriel told him, clutching his portaje to his chest, worried his dad would take it away. "On my own."

"On your own?" Enrique repeated, staring at the blade. "And . . . And it worked?"

Yadriel nodded.

"You received Lady Death's blessing?"

He nodded again, his face growing hot, shoulders creeping up to his ears. Would his dad ever forgive him for sneaking around behind his back? For lying? For breaking the sacred rules and traditions of the brujx?

"Yadriel . . ."

He heaved a large sigh, and Yadriel cringed, bracing for impact.

When his father spoke, his voice was small and defeated. "I am sorry."

Yadriel blinked. He was . . . sorry? Yadriel stole a look up at his dad, convinced he'd heard him wrong.

"I did not think it was possible," his dad confessed, still looking quite shocked. "I thought—" He shook his head at himself. "Whatever I thought, I was wrong."

It was Yadriel's turn to be shocked. "You were?"

He must've had a strange look on his face, because his dad exhaled a small laugh. "We have a lot to talk about," he said, scrubbing a hand over his face. "We need to speak about this as a family, with your mother."

"With Mom?" Yadriel repeated, his heart aching.

His dad nodded. His expression was filled with remorse. "You were denied your quinces for too long, and I won't let another aquelarre pass without you in it."

"Really?" Yadriel felt ready to pass out. Hope, relief, shock—the swirl of emotions was dizzying. He didn't even feel the cold or the rain anymore. "But what if the others don't agree?"

His dad gave his shoulder a firm squeeze. "Lady Death would not bind you to a dagger—your dagger," he emphasized, "if you weren't a brujo, Yadriel."

Excitement leaped in his chest, spilling words from his mouth. "Does this mean I can be part of the brujos?" he asked. "Can I help you look for Miguel? I—"

"¡Tranquilo, Yadriel!" his dad said, holding up his palms. "There will be plenty of time for learning the way of the brujos."

Yadriel wanted to jump in, to tell his dad how they'd been trying to find Miguel. To tell him about the other missing people, and about—

Yadriel held himself back. Julian. He wasn't sure if he was ready to tell his dad about Julian. As if feeling his eyes on him, Yadriel glanced to the side and saw him there, standing in the shadow of a columbaria and trying to stay out of sight. He looked unharmed—as much as a spirit could be, anyway—but his expression was unreadable, hidden in the shadows.

No, he wasn't ready to tell anyone else about Julian yet. That was a secret he wanted to keep. A part of him still didn't quite trust that his dad would even follow through. But still.

Warmth burned through Yadriel and he found himself smiling. If they were going to let him be a brujo, then he wouldn't have to release Julian at all.

"Hopefully, Miguel will return to us tomorrow night with answers," his dad continued, regaining Yadriel's attention. "For now, I need to get back to work." He straightened and pulled his hood up back over his head. "And I need you to go home and rest. Tomorrow will be a big day for all of us. When your mother returns, we will tell her—and Diego and Lita—what's happened. And then we will tell everyone else." He gave Yadriel a small smile. "Okay?"

Yadriel bobbed his head in a vigorous nod, grinning ear to ear. "Okay."

As soon as his dad was out of sight, Yadriel punched a hand into the air. "Jules, come on!" he said, waving for Julian to follow him. They ran to the house, and Yadriel threw open the door without thinking.

"Yadriel?" Lita's voice came from the kitchen.

Julian raced up the stairs while Yadriel lingered in the living room. "Yes, Lita!"

Diego poked his head out of the kitchen, saw Yadriel, and frowned. "Jesus, what happened to you?"

Yadriel barely glanced down at himself. He was soaked to the bone and covered in mud, but he didn't care.

He was going to be in the aquelarre this Día de Muertos. He was triumphant. He was powerful. He felt ready to take on the world.

He was a brujo.

"Is Tío here?" he asked.

"No," Diego said, giving him a strange look.

Yadriel was disappointed, but only a little. There would be plenty of time to tell him what happened tomorrow.

"Are you okay?" Diego pressed, stepping farther into the living room.

"Yeah, I'm fine," Yadriel beamed at his older brother, which only seemed to confuse him more. "I'm amazing!" Without further explanation, he ran up the stairs and into his bedroom, slamming the door shut behind him.

Yadriel's smile was so big, it hurt. He didn't have to release Julian to the afterlife. He could remain in the cemetery like the other spirits.

Julian could stay.

The thought made him so happy, Yadriel felt like his heart might burst in his chest.

But, when he turned, he found Julian sitting on the edge of his bed. His hands were stuffed into his pockets, his posture curved around his chest like he was in pain.

"Are you okay?" Yadriel asked, confused.

"Are *you* okay?" Julian countered, concern etched into his features.

"Yeah, I'm okay!" Yadriel laughed.

Julian didn't respond.

Yadriel wanted to grab Julian and shake him. Didn't he see how amazing this was? Why did he look so somber?

A lump under the comforter moved, and Purrcaso wiggled her way out. With a little chirrup, she hobbled over to Julian. She rubbed herself against his arm. When he scratched her chin, loud purrs vibrated through her tiny body.

Yadriel's excitement began to quickly bleed out of him. Julian must've been rattled by seeing Tito going maligno. "That was terrifying, wasn't it?" Yadriel asked, sitting next to him on the bed. Still, Julian said nothing, his attention focused on Purrcaso. He was too still, too quiet. It put Yadriel on edge.

"You saved my life," Yadriel told him. "I mean . . ." He let out a little laugh. "It was completely stupid, and reckless, and if you try something like that again, I swear, I'll—"

"Is that what I'll become?" Julian finally looked up at him. His dark eyes were empty, distant. "Is that what happens to spirits?" he repeated.

"No, not all spirits," Yadriel said quickly, wanting to say whatever he could to ease Julian's mind. "Only the ones that turn maligno." He couldn't stand the look on Julian's face.

"Día de Muertos is soon, you'll see, Tito will be all better. Like my Lito? When he died, he was so weak and tired. It was like he was only a shell of who he had been. But when he came back that first Día de Muertos? It was like he was back to his old self again," Yadriel told him. He felt like he was rambling, filling in Julian's unnatural silence. "He wasn't tired or in pain, he was downright spry." The memory made him grin.

Still, Julian said nothing.

"My point is, you'll still be you for a really long time," Yadriel told him. "I mean, there's no reason for me to release you right now! You can stay for as long as you like," he said, shy and hopeful. He felt a blush bloom in his cheeks. "And then when eventually you do cross over, you'll be able to come back every year and see me." But that wouldn't be for a very long time, Yadriel would make sure of it.

"You're forgetting something, Yads," Julian said, finally looking up at him.

"What?" Yadriel asked. Something about the look on Julian's face sent his pulse fluttering anxiously.

Julian's lips quirked into a sad smile. "I'm not a brujo."

Yadriel's heart sank. His shoulders fell. No. Julian wasn't a brujo. He didn't get to come back.

Yadriel let himself stare at Julian. He was so . . . visceral. He was so *real.* Even with his blurry edges and chilling touch, he was a force of nature. He was loud, he was stubborn, he was determined, and he was reckless. But, still, he would fade.

Yadriel remembered the other night. The thrashing and the pain on Julian's face. The blood seeping through his shirt. His gasps for breath.

If he stayed here, he'd fade until he wasn't Julian anymore, just like Tito.

And if Yadriel released him, he'd be gone forever.

"You're making me nervous," Julian said, his voice barely above a whisper, his gaze unwavering.

Yadriel tried to swallow the lump in his throat. "I'm just thinking . . ."

"Thinking what?"

"Something selfish."

For a moment, they sat there in silence. Yadriel couldn't look away, even though his heart thudded in the pulse at his neck.

Julian watched him curiously. His gaze slid down to Yadriel's mouth, his eyes half lidded.

Yadriel held his breath.

"Yads?" His name was so soft and sweet coming from Julian's lips.

"Yeah?"

But there was something about the look on Julian's face. A strange stillness as he sat there quietly, a watery reflection of the boy he'd once been.

Something Yadriel's body recognized before his head could catch up. Every muscle in his body tightened, bracing for impact.

Julian's voice was too gentle, his words too soft. "I want you to release me."

EIGHTEEN

W hat?"

"You need to release me," Julian repeated calmly. Yadriel hated it.

He forced out a laugh. "You don't mean right *now*?" There was no way he was serious.

Julian averted his gaze and toyed with Purrcaso's tail. "There's no point in waiting around."

Yadriel openly gaped at him. "You mean right now," he echoed in disbelief.

"My friends will be fine without me," Julian pointed out with a lift of his shoulders. "Rio's accepted that I ditched him and that I'm not going back."

"But you—you—" Yadriel stammered.

Julian swallowed and wet his lips. "I can feel it happening," he said, his voice low, defeated. "Like I'm losing my grip on myself." He stared down at his hands as he flexed them into fists, then loosened them again. "I don't know, maybe there's always been something in me, rotting away, and now it's finally catching up to me—"

"That's *not true*," Yadriel said sharply. He hated how tight his voice was, how strangled it sounded.

"I don't want to turn into a monster—"

"You won't! I wouldn't let that happen!" Yadriel insisted, even though it was wishful thinking at best. He had no control over when Julian might turn maligno.

Julian shook his head. "All I do is cause people trouble, including you—"

"No, you don't!" Yadriel flinched as soon as the words shot angrily from his mouth. He cut a nervous glance to the door. If he kept yelling, someone would hear him from downstairs, but he had to get Julian to change his mind. "You heard what my dad said, don't you want to stay for my aquelarre?"

Julian exhaled. "You need to release me."

Yadriel couldn't stand how calm and level-headed Julian was being. He wanted Julian to fight. He wanted him to argue, for him to get mad or *something*. This Julian was too sure, too quiet.

Julian's smile was sad and reserved. "I want to go before something bad happens, before I do something to someone I care about," he told Yadriel. He bit his bottom lip, like he was holding something back, but then he shook his head. "It's better this way. Everyone will be better off—"

"God, I am so sick of hearing you say that!" Yadriel snapped, taking a step forward. Julian looked up, surprised. "And if you think for one second that *anyone* in your life is better off without you, then you're dumber than you look, Julian Diaz."

Julian scowled, nostrils flaring, but Yadriel didn't care. At least it got that terrible, defeated look off his face.

"You would do anything for your friends, right? And they'd do anything for you, too. You take people in and you protect them, that's who you are! And your brother, too! You're both fiercely protective, which is probably why you guys fight all the time—"

"Yadriel—"

"Just a pair of idiots who don't know how to talk about your feelings so you argue instead!" he growled, throwing his hands up.

"Clean break," Julian said. "You promised—"

"I didn't promise a damn thing!" Yadriel snapped, feeling petulant.

Julian sighed and scrubbed his hand over his shaved head. "You wanted to get rid of me on day one, remember?"

Yadriel crossed his arms and glared at him. Yes, he remembered, but that didn't count anymore.

"The whole deal was you'd help make sure my friends were okay," Julian listed off on his fingers, "and I'd let you release my spirit so you could show everyone you're a brujo, right?" His hands fell to his lap. "I'm doing what you want, I will *willingly* let you release me, Yadriel. I won't put up a fight."

But Yadriel *wanted* him to put up a fight. Couldn't he see that?

"That's what you wanted, isn't it?" Julian nudged.

"Yeah," he said reluctantly. His pulse throbbed in his veins.

Irritation finally started to edge Julian's voice. "So what's different now?"

"Everything!"

A long, drawn-out silence stretched between them.

Julian stared at Yadriel, his eyes narrowed ever so slightly, like Yadriel was a puzzle he was trying to solve.

He must've really rubbed off on Yadriel, because all he wanted to do was fight back and yell until Julian realized he was being stupid.

The problem was that he *wasn't* being stupid. He'd made his point of view clear. His argument was even, dare Yadriel think it, *logical*. Warring emotions swelled in Yadriel, demanding to be felt, blinding him from any rational thought.

It was too fast. Yadriel wasn't ready. He needed more time. Desperation clawed through him as he tried to come up with another option.

But the truth was, there wasn't one.

Yadriel's throat was tight. His palms were slick with sweat. "One more day," he said, voice wavering.

Julian groaned. "We're just buying time, Yads, what's the point?"

"One more day," he insisted, firmer this time. "Tomorrow at midnight, Día de Muertos will start, and—"

"And all the ghosts get to come back, yeah, I remember," Julian grumbled.

Yadriel didn't have the time nor patience to correct him with any sort of civility. "I'll release you then. That gives us one more day."

Julian looked ready to argue. When he opened his mouth, Yadriel cut him off.

"*Tomorrow night*, okay?"

Julian's mouth snapped shut. The muscles in his jaw flexed. But eventually, he said, "Fine."

It gave Yadriel little relief. *"Fine."* He stomped over to his closet, peeled off his hoodie, and angrily threw it into his overflowing hamper. He opened his drawer and yanked out clean clothes before he shoved it closed with a snap.

Without a word, he left for the bathroom, slamming the door shut behind him.

Yadriel threw back the shower curtain and cranked on the water, twisting it to hot. When he got in, it was near scalding, but he wanted to feel the bite on his skin as he scrubbed himself clean. By the time he was certain there was no trace of that black gunk under his nails, or the smell of Tito's rotting flesh in his hair, the hot water had faded to warm. His skin was flushed and raw.

Overcome with a wave of exhaustion, Yadriel leaned his forehead against the cool tile wall and closed his eyes. The water beat against his neck and cascaded down his back. He wanted to hold on to his anger because he was scared of what would be left to feel without it, but he was too tired to stay mad.

He'd been so distracted by his own thoughts that he hadn't taken care to dry himself off properly before trying to pull on his binder. All his binders with the side clasps that were easier to get into were in the laundry, so he was stuck with a vest-style one. He managed to get it over his head, but when he tried to shrug into the tight, stretchy material, it clung mercilessly to his wet shoulders. Yadriel gave it a tug, wiggled, and squirmed, but it only seemed to get tighter. His frustration boiled over and he thrashed, practically tripping over the bath mat as he struggled. A moment later, he was stuck, only one arm through and the binder bunched and tight across his collarbone. Yadriel slumped, collapsing onto the toilet seat as he tried to catch his breath.

Why was he acting like this?

So many things had gone so right and so wrong in such a short amount of time. His dad had come around. He saw Yadriel clearly as he was. He had even agreed to let Yadriel be in the aquelarre this year. Yadriel would see his mom soon, and she would see what he had accomplished since she'd left. He would be welcomed and accepted by his community for who he was. *Finally.*

But now he would be losing Julian in the same night. Why did the pain of that impending loss hit him harder than anything else?

If they only had one day left together, Yadriel wasn't going to tell anyone about him. Not his dad, not Tío Catriz or anyone else. Julian was his secret, and he wanted to keep him all to himself for as long as he could.

Eventually, by continued forceful tugging and wiggling, he got the binder on. When Yadriel went back into his room, Julian was sprawled out on the bed. Purrcaso was curled up on his chest, her nose tucked into her tail, fast sleep.

"This is still so weird," Julian said, trailing his fingertip along Purrcaso's crooked little spine.

"I told you not to make fun of her," Yadriel said, slicking his wet hair back and out of his face.

Julian rolled his eyes, but an amused smirk still tugged at his lips. "Not what I meant."

Yadriel flopped onto the bed next to Julian and stared up at the ceiling. They lay there for a minute, with only the distant sound of traffic and Purrcaso's mighty purrs between them.

"Jules?" Yadriel finally ventured. His heartbeat like a finger tapping against his throat.

Julian hummed in response.

Yadriel stole a look over at him. His attention was on Purrcaso, his dark lashes hiding his eyes.

"Why don't you like to speak Spanish?"

Julian's hand paused, his fingers hovering above Purrcaso, who let out a displeased sound at the sudden lack of petting.

Silence stretched between them for a long moment. Yadriel thought he wasn't going to answer the question. It seemed like a strange thing to carry so much weight.

When Julian finally spoke, his words were quiet and tentative.

"My dad didn't know much English, so we pretty much only spoke Spanish at home." He didn't look at Yadriel but toyed with Purrcaso's tail. "It's not that I don't *like* speaking Spanish, I mean, it's *me*, you know? I think in it, I dream in it, but . . ." He trailed off, expression pinched as he tried to find the right words. "But it was also my dad, you know?" Julian made a frustrated sound. "I don't know how to explain it. At school we have to speak English, and my friends mostly speak in English, too, so Spanish was more like . . . It was what we used at home. It was what I used with my dad—the *only* language I spoke with him. So, when he died . . ."

Yadriel felt a pang in his chest.

Julian's shoulder pulled into a shrug. "I don't know, man. Just didn't feel right using it without him, I guess. Feels too . . ." He made a twisting gesture with his hand, frustration working his jaw.

"Intimate?" Yadriel offered.

Julian's eyes snapped to Yadriel with a look so intent, it struck him like lightning. "Yeah," he finally said. "Something like that."

Yadriel gave a small nod.

"That sounds dumb, right?" Julian asked, eyeing him like he expected Yadriel to laugh.

"No, it definitely doesn't sound dumb. It makes sense, not wanting to share something personal that means a lot to you." Yadriel hooked a finger around the chain of Julian's St. Jude pendant, letting it dangle. "Kind of like having a stranger wear this?" he guessed.

Julian stared at the silver medal. He reached out. The pendant swayed at his ghostly touch. "Yeah, kind of." Julian withdrew his hand and cleared his throat.

Yadriel didn't argue when he unceremoniously jumped topics.

"How does the whole Día de Muertos thing work, exactly?" Julian asked, glancing over at Yadriel. "All the food and altars and decorations and stuff."

Yadriel stretched and tucked his hands under his neck. "Well, to welcome our ancestors back, we make ofrendas for our family members. We use their pictures, belongings, and favorite foods. Then there's the standard stuff like mezcal, pan de muerto—"

"Sounds like a party." Julian grinned.

"It is. One *big* party," Yadriel agreed. "We decorate the cemetery with papel picado—the colorful cutouts, we string them up like banners all over the place. We use sugarcane to make arches." Yadriel gestured with his hands, drawing an arch in the air. "We cover the arches in marigolds—cempasúchitl, specifically. They're the gateways the spirits use to pass through from the land of the dead to the land of the living. The food and trinkets, the color of the marigolds and their really strong scent of apples lead the spirits back to the cemetery."

"Do they have to be buried here to come back?" Julian asked.

Yadriel shook his head. "So many of our brujx are immigrants. From Mexico, South America, the Caribbean—all over the place. There are different cemeteries like ours all over the United States. So, no, they don't have to be buried here. It'd be kind of weird to have people digging up dead bodies or lugging their ashes across the border," he pointed out. "All you need is the ofrenda."

"Is it like, *all* your ancestors ever? The cemetery is pretty big, but enough to hold hundreds of generations?" Julian gave him a dubious look, eyebrow arching.

"Just whoever we call, whoever we still remember. Some people we obviously forget. I don't know who my great-great-great-great-grandmother was or anything."

Julian hummed. "That seems sad."

Yadriel lifted his shoulders in a small shrug. "I don't think so. The way I figure it, all of their family they were close to died by now, too, right? So they get to all hang out and party in the afterlife together. There's no need for them to come back and visit."

"What's the afterlife like?" Julian was trying to sound casual, but Yadriel could hear in his voice that he was worried.

"I don't know," Yadriel answered honestly.

Julian looked disappointed.

"But it's got to be really nice. Everyone always comes back smiling and happy."

"Have you ever asked one of them?"

"No, it's kind of an . . . unspoken thing."

Another long stretch of silence.

"Is there a hell?"

When Yadriel turned his head to look over at Julian, the other boy's eyes were already staring back. He studied Julian's face in the pale light streaming in the window.

"Well, there's Xibalba—"

Julian's eyes bulged.

"But you won't end up there!" he rushed to finish. "Seriously, Lady Death makes sure of that."

"I think I would've made a good brujo," Julian told him, idly toying with Purrcaso's tail.

Yadriel grinned. "You think so?"

"Definitely." He nodded. "I'm into the whole portaje aesthetic. Yours is badass."

Yadriel chuckled. "It's more than just having a cool knife."

"I know, I know, I know." Julian waved him off. "But it's the *coolest* part." He grinned. "It's really too bad I'm not a brujo."

"A real shame," Yadriel agreed, hiding behind a tone of sarcasm.

If Julian were a brujo, they wouldn't be in this mess. Things would be simpler, easier. They wouldn't be impossible. Yadriel wouldn't have to let him go.

He wanted to stay up all night, just talking and answering Julian's questions, but even though he fought it, eventually Yadriel started to nod off. He changed out of his binder while Julian settled down on the floor with the sleeping bag again.

Bundled up under the covers, Yadriel waited until Julian rolled onto his side, facing away from him. The blue light of his old iPhone shone through his translucent form as Julian scrolled through Yadriel's music.

Yadriel turned to the window and pulled out Julian's gray-and-black plaid shirt he'd stashed under his pillow. He rubbed the soft flannel between his fingers. Yadriel closed his eyes and buried his nose in the shirt. As he drifted off to sleep, he breathed in the smell of Julian, but it was already starting to fade.

NINETEEN

I'm supposed to be in school today, and Maritza said she'd cover for me after school," Yadriel said. As long as he was present and accounted for by the time Día de Muertos rang in on the church bells, he'd be okay. "So we have all day to do whatever you want."

"Whatever I want?" Julian repeated, giving Yadriel a doubtful look.

"Whatever you want," Yadriel confirmed as he combed his hair carefully into style. He didn't remember dreaming last night, but when he woke up, there was a gaping ache in his chest and the shakiness that chased him into waking after a nightmare.

"Well, within reason," he added. "We don't have the time or funds to, like, fly to Hawaii or something."

"That's fine, I don't like pineapple, and 'fly on a plane' was never on my bucket list anyways." Julian shrugged.

"You've never been on a plane?" Yadriel didn't travel all that much, and if they visited his mom's family in Mexico, they just drove across the border. He'd only flown to Cuba a handful of times to visit his dad's extended family, but still he was surprised.

"Tch, *hell* no! Get on a big metal death bird?" Julian shook his head. "Yeah, no, hard pass."

"Well, you have some time to figure out what you want to do," Yadriel told him as he loaded up his backpack with items they would need later that night. "We have to pick up some supplies first."

"I still can't believe you're ditching school," Julian remarked as he stood up from the floor. He was already buzzing with excitement. "You seem too straitlaced for that kind of thing."

"I'm not straitlaced!" Yadriel scowled.

Julian cocked an eyebrow. "Have you ditched before?"

". . . No."

Julian smirked.

"Oh, shut up." Yadriel checked his phone again as he tucked his portaje into its sheath against his lower back. He would need it later that night, when it was time to release Julian.

But he didn't want to think about that right now. Right now, he just wanted to focus on Julian and his last day on earth.

Yadriel sent Maritza one last thank-you text. Twice she'd asked if she could go with them. Whether it was because she wanted to get out of class, or because she didn't want Yadriel going off on his own with Julian, he wasn't sure. Either way, Yadriel was letting himself be selfish.

Hoisting the especially heavily backpack onto his shoulders, Yadriel turned to Julian. "Ready?"

But he really hadn't needed to ask. Julian was all raw electricity and blazing eyes. "*God* yes." A wicked grin cut dimples into his cheeks, and Yadriel couldn't stop himself from grinning back.

"Don't draw any attention to yourself," Yadriel warned him. "We still have to get through the cemetery."

It was the morning of October 31. While most families were decorating for trick-or-treaters, or dressing their kids up for school, it was a very different scenario in the brujx cemetery.

As Yadriel quickly dashed between headstones, men and women filed in and out of the church and down the stone pathways, carrying boxes of candles, stacks of papel picado, and stalks of sugarcane. The resident spirits were also out, walking among the living and chatting excitedly. There were enough that Julian blended in with the crowds, a safe distance from Yadriel.

Lita stood on the steps of the church, calling out instructions and directing people this way and that, like a maestro. She wore one of her best dresses, a white one with short sleeves and brightly embroidered flowers along the neck and hem. A heavy beaded necklace was around her neck with a gold pendant depicting the Maya calendar. Bracelets of gold and jade clacked on her wrists.

His father stood by the gate, pointing people in the right direction as he tried to pat down his wavy hair. He wore a pair of slacks and a short-sleeved guayabera. It was bright red, which Yadriel knew was his mom's favorite color.

He was about to make a run for it when his dad stopped him. "Yadriel!" he called after, waving him over. He looked nervous, continuing to fuss with his hair.

"I'm in a hurry, Dad," Yadriel tried to deflect. "Late for school." Julian slipped out behind his dad's back, dodging between brujx and spirits alike.

"We need to put the finishing touches on the ofrenda for your mamá, so don't be late," his dad said, combing his fingers through his mustache. He smoothed down his shirt and stood up tall, sucking in his gut.

Yadriel just nodded. While he was getting used to sneaking around, he still didn't have it in himself to lie so blatantly to his dad's face. He would not be home right after school, probably wouldn't be back until very late, after—

His stomach clenched. No, he didn't want to think about that. Right now, he was only looking to make Julian happy. He wouldn't let himself think past midnight.

Luckily, his dad didn't seem at all suspicious. Enrique let out a breath, and his stomach pushed against his shirt, spilling a little over the edge of his belt.

Yadriel used his dad's distraction to his benefit. "Okay, see you tonight!" he called, giving his dad a wave as he ran out the gate and down to where Julian was waiting at the corner.

"So, where to first, patrón?" he asked, walking backward in front of Yadriel.

"The store," he said.

"For what?"

"Your favorite food. Whatever you want."

Julian's eyes lit up. "Whatever I want? But—wait." He frowned. "For me? But I thought I couldn't eat normal food?"

"You can't," Yadriel agreed, looking both ways before he crossed the street. "It's for later."

"What's later?" Julian asked, jogging after him.

"It's a secret," Yadriel told him. He expected Julian to put up a fight, or at least whine and demand answers.

Instead, Julian bit his bottom lip, a wide smile splitting his face. The tips of his ears tinged red, and satisfaction thrummed in Yadriel's chest.

They went to the local Mexican market. It was a large cement building painted yellow. As they strolled down the aisles, Yadriel dumped anything Julian pointed out into a red hand basket. Quickly, it filled up with packages of Gansitos, two glass bottles of Coke, pink coconut cookies, and some potato chips.

"TAKIS, TAKIS, TAKIS!" Julian crowed, running up to the display rack.

"Limón or fuego?" Yadriel asked, holding up the two bags.

Julian's face contorted, like he'd just tasted something bitter. "Tch, fuego, obviously." He shuddered. "I don't like stuff with too much lime."

Yadriel laughed and tossed the bag in. "You're a disgrace to your people." He bought the snacks with the cash he'd been saving over the past few weeks. When they stepped outside, there was an older man with a cart. Bags of fried dough in the shapes of pinwheels were tied around it.

"OOO, DUROS, YADRIEL!" Julian shouted so suddenly it made Yadriel jump.

"*Okay*, Jesus," he whispered under his breath. He went up to the man and asked for a bag. The vendor opened one of the bags and dumped in chamoy, a pickled fruit and chili sauce that reeked of vinegar.

"No lime, no lime, no lime!" Julian panicked when the man reached for a small green bottle.

"Sin limón, por favor," Yadriel told him. When they got a safe distance, he stopped to shove the contraband into his already stuffed backpack. "Ugh, my bag is never going to smell the same again," Yadriel said, crinkling his nose.

Julian, on the other hand, inhaled deeply, sending his eyelids fluttering. "Mmm, I'm literally drooling right now," he moaned.

"Have you decided where we're going?" Yadriel asked.

Julian tapped his fingers against his chin. "Hmmm. I've got a couple ideas, but nothing Last Day on Earth worthy." He frowned.

Yadriel's phone vibrated in his back pocket. He pulled it out and checked the screen. He was paranoid someone from the school would report him as absent to his dad and he'd be in deep trouble. He was trying to put off any impending panic until later in the afternoon, when he didn't come home from school. He felt terrible about it, but it was for a good reason. It was for Julian.

"Who's that?" Julian asked, hovering over his shoulder.

"Just a group text from Letti," he said, scrolling through the message. There was a location and lots of exclamation points. "Looks like they decided where the Halloween bonfire is going to be." Yadriel shrugged.

When he looked up, Julian was staring at him, mouth open in an excited smile. Yadriel's shoulders sank.

"Julian, *no*—"

"*Yes*, Yads!"

It was Yadriel's turn to complain. "Come on, there's got to be something else you want to do!"

Julian happily shook his head. "Nope, I wanna do this!"

"Jules—!"

"Hey! *I'm* the one dying!" he said, tapping a finger to his chest. He paused. Frowned. "Er, dying *again*—getting deader?" Julian shook his head, waving off his own confusion. "I get to choose!"

"But—!"

"Them's the rules!"

Yadriel groaned loudly and crossed his arms over his chest. "I really *don't* want to go party with a bunch of people from school." He didn't even want to be around his classmates *during* school. The idea of hanging out with a bunch of them at a party where most of them would be drunk and belligerent sounded torturous at best and dangerous at worst. Yadriel was antisocial out of self-preservation. "I'm going to stick out like an awkward, sore thumb," he added.

"Then it's a good thing it's Halloween, ain't it? We'll get you a disguise!" Julian told him, taking off down the street.

It was the day of Halloween, which meant the party-supply store was nearly cleared out. There were empty racks everywhere, and feathers and glitter littered the floor.

"How about this?" Julian said, toying with a mask made of peacock feathers.

"Yeah, *that'll* help me blend in." Yadriel glared.

Julian chuckled. "Okay, okay, okay." He flicked the corner of a sugar skull face-painting kit. "This?"

Yadriel scoffed. "*No.* I'm not supporting the mass appropriation of calaveras in Western culture—"

"Okay, then." Julian laughed, moving onto the next rack.

Yadriel made sure there was no one else down the aisle before quietly continuing his rant. "Sugar skulls are a *sacred* part of Día de Muertos, they're not a *Halloween costume* for—"

But Julian was already onto the next option. "What about this?"

"This" was a black face shield one wore pulled up over their nose. It had the lower half of a skeleton's face on it.

Yadriel hummed, uncertain. "Isn't this what bikers wear?" he asked, picking up the mask and tracing his finger over the skull's broken teeth.

Julian leaned his shoulder against the rack and gave Yadriel a look. "I don't think anyone's gonna mistake you for a Hells Angel." He smirked.

Yadriel gave him a dubious look.

"Look, it's basically a mask! It'll cover half your face, no one's gonna recognize you, *and* it matches your whole look," he added, gesturing to Yadriel's entire body.

He glanced down at his hoodie, torn black jeans, and combat boots. He squinted up at Julian. "And what's my *look*?"

Julian tipped his head side to side. "Gay goth witch?"

Yadriel grabbed a stack of jack-o'-lantern napkins and threw them at Julian's head. They went right through him and bounced off the rack harmlessly.

Outside, Yadriel tugged the mask on over his head and let it sit around his neck. "It's going to take a while to get to the beach," he said, pushing his hair back into place before pulling out his phone to look up the bus schedule.

Julian frowned. "Why?"

"We're going to have to make at least two bus transfers and some walking, depending on which beach you want to go to," he said, scrolling through the app.

"No way, we're not taking the *bus*," Julian scoffed.

"I can't afford an Uber—"

"Do you know how to drive?" Julian asked.

"Well, yeah—"

"Stick shift?"

He did *not* like the look on Julian's face. "Yes, why?" He could see Julian's mind working. That sharp grin meant nothing but trouble.

Lots of trouble.

A short time later, Yadriel was standing on the sidewalk, facing the gate behind the mechanic shop that led to Rio and Julian's apartment.

"I shouldn't be doing this. I can't believe I'm doing this." He looked over at Julian, desperate for him to say this was just a joke. "Am I really doing this? Are we really doing this?"

Julian smiled cheerily. "Don't look so worried; it'll be fun!" he said, striding up to the gate.

"Getting arrested for stealing a car is *not* my idea of fun!" Yadriel whispered, his neck whipping as he looked around for witnesses. The shop was closed on Fridays, leaving the place empty. A few cars drove by. A lady in high heels walked across the street with her two Chihuahuas. Yadriel rushed to catch up with Julian. "I can't believe you're making me do this!"

"I'm not *making* you do anything!" he rebutted. "Now hurry up, Rio is probably catching up on rest, and he is *not* a heavy sleeper." Julian walked right through the gate, leaving Yadriel on the other side.

"How am I supposed to get in there?" he hissed, throwing a furtive glance at the door at the top of the steps.

"Oh, right." Julian backtracked. He walked back through the gate and over to a small pile of cinder blocks against the wall. Eyes squinting in concentration, he reached into one of the gaps and pulled out a set of keys. Pleased with himself, he tossed them to Yadriel. "Here."

He fumbled to catch them before they hit the floor. "Your brother keeps a spare set of keys out here?" he asked. That didn't seem very safe, and Rio didn't strike him as someone who would hide keys in such a careless spot.

"What?" Julian snorted. "Hell no, he's way too paranoid! I put 'em there." He smiled proudly.

That made much more sense.

"Got tired of losing them all the time and Rio chewing me out. Putting them there obliterated the problem."

"Eliminated," Yadriel corrected, thumbing through the keys in his hand.

Julian waved him off. "Same thing. The one with the duct tape on the handle is for the gate."

Yadriel's hand trembled as he struggled to get the gate unlocked. He just needed to hurry and get the hell out of there. Figuring out what to do after tonight—with the car, the keys, and himself—would be a problem for later. When Yadriel pulled the gate open, the squealing of metal and crunch of gravel felt deafening.

Julian appeared completely unworried. He went right up to the car and smoothed his hands over the hood. "Hello, gorgeous," he sighed, leaning his cheek against the roof of the car. "1970 Corvette Stingray," Julian hummed affectionately. "Pop's pride and joy. He did all the mods himself. Took him *years* to get it just the way he wanted."

"Great, so I'm stealing a car that's priceless *and* holds deep sentimental value," Yadriel muttered. Nervous sweat pooled under his armpits. Between his unsteady hand and constantly checking the apartment door, Yadriel struggled to get ahold of the right key.

"The big one," Julian prompted, getting impatient.

The creak of the car door opening made Yadriel cringe. He climbed in and closed it as quietly as possible.

The inside of the Corvette was covered in leather, the same electric blue as the exterior. The steering wheel was huge, the seats low. A black plastic rosary hung from the rearview mirror. A prayer card of Our Lady of Guadalupe in her blue, starry mantle was tucked into the pocket where a dashboard would be in a newer vehicle. A small stack of pictures peeked out behind Our Lady of Guadalupe, but all Yadriel could see was an elbow and the corner of a building.

The car was nearly pristine. Everything smelled like warm leather. Clearly, Julian's father had taken good care of it. Judging by their apartment, Yadriel was surprised Julian and Rio had kept the Stingray in such good shape.

Julian was already sitting in the passenger seat, drumming his fingers against his knees. "Let's go, let's go, let's go!"

Yadriel stuffed his backpack down by Julian's feet. He put the key into the ignition but then hesitated. "I can't believe I'm about to do this," he said. More sweat trickled down his spine. Panic clawed up his throat. "Your brother is going to call the police, it'll turn into a car chase—"

"Car chases happen *all the time* in LA," Julian said, as if that were supposed to make him feel better. "They've got convicts and shit to be going after."

Yadriel pressed his hands against his temples. "Oh my God, my face is going to be all over the news!"

"Not if you cover it, dummy." Julian reached and tugged the skeleton mask over his nose. "There!"

But it didn't cover the death glare Yadriel shot him.

Julian laughed and shook his head. "It's like you've never stolen a car before!"

"I *have* never stolen a car before!" Yadriel snapped. His breath heated the black material covering his mouth.

"Oh." Julian paused. "I mean, it's not even technically stealing—"
"*How?*"

"Pops left the car to my brother *and* me," Julian stressed. "I've got a key and everything. I'm giving you *permission* to use it."

"I don't think that's going to stand up in court."

"Then you better drive fast, huh?" There was a flash of a grin. A reckless glint in his eye.

Julian reached over.

Yadriel sucked in a breath. "Jules!"

But it was too late. Julian gripped the key in the ignition and turned it. The engine roared to life. Reggaeton blared from the speakers.

"GO, GO, GO!" Julian shouted, laughter shaking his voice.

Yadriel shoved down the panicked voice in his head. He didn't think. He didn't turn at the sound of the apartment door banging open.

He stepped on the clutch, threw the shift into gear, and peeled out.

The smell of exhaust stung his nose. The sound of Julian's excited shout filled his ears. The beat of the bass thudded in his chest.

Yadriel drove, and he didn't look back.

TWENTY

They headed for the beach, but that meant cutting through Los Angeles first. The traffic did little to calm Yadriel's nerves. He kept checking the mirrors, convinced that any second blue-and-red lights would flash in their reflection.

Julian wasn't helping. He practically vibrated with barely contained excitement next to Yadriel, impatient and constantly shifting. He reached forward and turned the music back on, filling the car with thumping bass.

Yadriel cringed and tugged the mask back down around his neck. "Does it have to be that loud?"

"Yes, it does!" Julian shouted over the noise as he spun the dial, cycling through station after station.

Yadriel rolled his eyes and cranked down the window to get some cool air in the stuffy cab. It whipped through his hair. The buffeting wind fought with the crackling of the speakers. The air cooled Yadriel down and made it easier for him to breathe.

Julian went so fast through the stations, Yadriel had no idea how he could even tell what was playing. Sometimes he'd pause and Yadriel thought he'd finally found one he liked, but then he always ended up searching for a new song before it was over.

In between the fuzz of dead channels, there was a flash of music so quick that Yadriel barely registered it until Julian shouted, "YES!"

"Urgh, really?" Yadriel yelled over the heavy *bum ba-dum bum bum* of blaring reggaeton.

"YES, REALLY!" Julian sucked in a deep breath and sang at the top of his lungs.

Yadriel burst into laughter. "OH MY GOD!"

"SHUT UP, THIS IS MY FAVORITE SONG!" Julian yelled back, laughter shaking his words.

Objectively, Julian was a *terrible* singer, but, damn, was he committed. Shoulders rolling, Julian danced in his seat and sang like his life depended on it. The way his voice cracked had Yadriel gripping the steering wheel for dear life as deep belly laughs shook him.

Unabashed and beaming—this was his favorite version of Julian. Bright, carefree, and overflowing with infectious energy.

Alive.

Julian snagged Yadriel's eye as he looked over at him and sang-shouted, his eyebrows tipping to an earnest angle.

Yadriel ducked his head and sank down farther in his seat, his face burning bright red. This only made Julian break into more laughter, and then they were both a mess.

By the time they got through the city, the traffic had thinned out considerably. They left the skyscrapers behind, and the scenery opened up. The sky was streaked with dizzying orange and luminous pink, kissing the horizon where it met the ocean. The deep blue stretched out, sunlight sparking off the water. The lazy crash of waves joined the music. The crisp air mixed with the smell of salt water and exhaust.

Yadriel veered onto the Pacific Coast Highway where it ran along mansions and pale beaches.

"Faster!" Julian demanded, twisting in his seat to face Yadriel.

"I'm going fast enough!" Yadriel told him, the speedometer hovering at the speed limit.

"FASTER, YOU COWARD!" Julian gripped Yadriel's knee.

A chill shot up his thigh. A breath caught in his lungs. He could feel it. The pressure of Julian's fingers, the weight of his palm.

Yadriel glanced over, meeting Julian's hungry stare. There was a recklessness in his smile. Sunset burned in his eyes. Heat pooled in Yadriel's stomach. He huffed, but a grin was already pulling at the corners of his lips, betraying his crumbling resolve.

Gripping the steering wheel at precisely ten and two, Yadriel checked the mirrors. His knuckles flexed over the smooth leather, and, with a roar of the engine, Yadriel's back pressed into the seat as the Stingray charged ahead.

Julian howled with delight. He gripped the door and leaned out the open window.

Yadriel's hand shot out to grab him and felt ridiculous when his fingers went right through Julian's shoulder.

Dimples pressed into his cheeks, Julian stretched his arms out. He shouted something, but it was swallowed up by the thundering wind.

Julian was unleashed, brilliantly burning.

It gave Yadriel a head rush as they sped past crashing waves, palm trees, and beaches painted pink by the sunset. The engine thrummed through his body. His heart hammered in time.

When they finally pulled into the parking lot along the beach, the sun was nothing more than a smudge of burning red against the horizon. The party was already in full swing. A huge crowd of people gathered around the bonfire, tucked between two abandoned lifeguard towers. Music blared from a set of speakers somewhere. The crackling flames sent crooked shadows dancing toward the lapping waves.

Yadriel pulled out his phone. He had several missed calls from his dad. He scrolled through the texts before quickly clearing them out. Yadriel didn't have the stomach to read them, let alone listen to any of the voicemails, so he turned off the notifications.

"Are you *sure* you want to do this?" Yadriel groaned, stuffing his phone back into his pocket.

"Yes!" Julian said, bounding to his side.

Yadriel glared up at him. "This is my worst nightmare, Jules."

He was unbothered. "This is my last dying wish, Yads," he said with mock sincerity, tugging the mask up over Yadriel's nose.

"Come on, come on, come on!" Julian called, waving Yadriel on as he headed for the party.

Reluctantly, Yadriel followed.

For such a huge group of people, he felt surprisingly invisible, and that, for once, was a relief. When he spoke to Julian, his mouth was covered so no one could see him and think he was talking to himself. Not to mention, his voice didn't travel very far in the cacophony of music and voices.

Everyone had showed up in costume, or at least a mask. There were mermaids, devils, and detailed disguises. Some people just threw on one of those colored paper masks and called it good.

He didn't recognize anyone, and he kept reminding himself that no one recognized him, either, and no one cared. No one gave him a strange look, no one even noticed him when he accidentally bumped into them. He was just a boy in a sea of bodies.

Julian was in his element. He liked noisy places and noisy people. A stormy boy who seemed most comfortable in chaos. Everyone cheered and danced and drank. The air smelled of smoke, alcohol, and sea salt. He joined a group of people crowded around a guy in a horse mask, laughing as he gulped down a beer. Julian whooped and cheered. People moved through him, but no one seemed to notice. Either it was too cold for them to tell, or inebriation had dulled their senses. Probably a combination of both.

"Beer?" Julian asked, gesturing to large boxes of cheap beer that had been ripped open, spilling cans from their torn mouths.

"No," Yadriel said, tense with even *more* discomfort, if that were possible. There were several reasons he hated going to parties, one of them being the pressure to drink.

Julian looked around at a Styrofoam cooler and several handles of liquor stuck in the sand. "They've probably got tequila or somethin'—"

"I don't drink," Yadriel all but growled. He half expected Julian to guffaw or try to goad him into it. He braced himself, ready to argue on his own behalf.

Instead, Julian just nodded. "My bad!"

And then he was off to the next thing that caught his attention, leaving Yadriel standing there.

He watched Julian as he wandered off toward a girl in a corn costume who had elote in stacks on catering trays she was selling for a dollar. Deflated, Yadriel wondered if he'd ever stop being surprised by Julian Diaz.

He wove between people, trying to keep up as Julian coaxed him deeper into the crowd. Yadriel wanted to reach out and catch hold of his arm, to drag him closer, but he couldn't. He had to wedge himself between a pair with elaborate masks of rubber and fur, one a wolf, the other a jaguar. He nearly stumbled right through Julian.

"I keep losing you!" he shouted, and Julian had to lean down to hear him. The music blared in Yadriel's ears, but Julian was entirely unaffected.

"This is my FAVORITE song!" Julian said, his cold breath tickling Yadriel's cheek.

"I thought the one in the car was your favorite song?" Yadriel asked.

Julian only shrugged, grinning ear to ear, painfully charming.

The loud, pulsing music thumped in Yadriel's chest like a second heartbeat. He could feel it in his bones. The music was devouring, making it impossible for Yadriel to doubt or second-guess himself as he swayed to the beat. The close press of bodies normally would've made Yadriel's skin crawl. But, right now, the jostling was reassuring, like being nudged by ocean waves, lulled into an ebb and flow.

Julian's hips rolled, his head bobbed. Eyes closed and smiling, the firelight danced over his skin. Yadriel was drawn to him like a moth to a flame. To his foolhardy charm and striking features. Julian was achingly beautiful, but in the way a thunderstorm was beautiful—wild, rough, electric.

And bound to leave devastation in his wake.

A dancing couple almost separated them again, but Yadriel and Julian surged toward each other at the same time. Julian pressed close, and Yadriel shivered. A thrill shot up his spine, robbing him of breath.

There was loud singing and bursts of laughter. Push and pull. Hot breath and shuddering chills. Biting ocean breeze on sweltering skin. Julian's white teeth and dimples melted away to heavy-lidded eyes and parted lips.

Yadriel let his eyes fall shut, in a heady daze. Icy fingers fit against his hip. They ghosted over the pulse in his neck. He pressed closer still, hungry and aching. Heat rushed low in his stomach. He wanted to reach out and hold on tight.

Suddenly, bright lights flashed across Yadriel's vision. When he opened his eyes, flashlight beams cut through the crowd. The music ended. Everyone stood there in a daze, the spell broken. A confused murmur rose in the group. *"Cops!"* a voice rang out, followed by others.

Voices crackled over loudspeakers, reciting that it was illegal to have glass containers or alcohol on the beach, and that a permit was required for parties over fifty people. They sounded bored. This was likely just one of many parties to be broken up along the beach that evening.

People scattered, and someone booed, but Julian just laughed, his face lit with excitement.

But Yadriel did *not* need to be stopped by the cops when there was a stolen car a hundred yards away. "Come on!" he shouted.

They ran, stumbling over mounds of sand, laughing hard and unable to stand upright. They sprinted for the car, shoes slipping on sand-covered concrete. Yadriel threw himself into the Stingray, and she roared back to life. They took off, flying down the PCH.

Julian whooped.

Yadriel yanked his mask down and hunched over the steering wheel, laughing so hard his cheeks hurt.

Julian directed Yadriel to a lookout point. It was just a gravel turn-out on top of a seaside cliff. Yadriel pulled up to the short guardrail, beyond which the craggy cliff face cascaded down.

They got out and climbed onto the hood. The metal was still hot from the engine. It kept Yadriel warm as the crisp ocean breeze rushed in. It rustled the bowing palm trees. He could feel sand in his hair and clinging to his skin. The lights of fishing boats winked out in the sea of black. The moonlight bounced off the distant water. Waves threw themselves against the jagged rocks in lazy rhythm, crashing and roll-ing. The spray tickled Yadriel's face. His lips tasted like salt. It was almost enough to lull him to sleep.

"My dad used to drive us up here," Julian said quietly at Yadriel's side.

Yadriel tilted his head. Julian sat with his feet planted on the hood of the car. His chin was propped on his folded arms, resting on his knees. His dark eyes stared up.

"Best view of the stars," he said, squinting one eye shut as he held his palm up, lining up the sparse stars between his fingers. The orange haze of the city lights chased them off to the horizon, where the sky turned inky-black.

Yadriel watched him silently for a moment, quite liking the mental picture of Julian, his dad, and his brother up there, admiring the view. A trio of boys from East Los Angeles stargazing in Malibu.

"Who are the pictures of?" Yadriel asked, rolling onto his side and leaning his cheek against his fist.

"Pictures?"

"Yeah." Yadriel jerked his chin toward the pocket on the dashboard. "In the car."

"Oh!" Julian slid off the hood and leaned in through the open window. There was some rustling and then he was back, scooting up next to Yadriel.

"Just old pictures of us and our dad."

Yadriel sat up. They sat cross-legged, facing each other.

"That's him," Julian said, holding the picture for Yadriel to see. Yadriel had never heard him speak with such gentle warmth.

Julian's dad stood in the center of the photo. He was tall and lean with a buzzed head and some sparse facial hair. His eyes squinted as he flashed his teeth at the camera, somewhere between a laugh and a growl. He held up Julian and Rio under each arm, flexing his strength in front of what Yadriel recognized as the mechanic shop.

"He looks nice," Yadriel said, unable to keep from smiling.

"He was," Julian agreed, beaming.

"What's his name?"

"Ramon," Julian told him, his tongue rolling through the *r*.

Julian couldn't have been older than ten. He was doubled over, knees tucked and gripping his dad's arm as he was held aloft, laughing hard. It was possible Ramon was tickling him, his large hand across Julian's chest, his fingers pressed into that sensitive spot under the collarbone.

"Oh man." Yadriel laughed. "Look at your hair!" Instead of being shaved down, younger Julian's hair was a mass of unruly, tight curls.

"Photogenic as hell, right?" Julian grinned. "Rio's always been a bit camera shy."

Rio was held under his dad's other arm. He was smiling, but his lips were pressed together. He clung to his dad's shoulder, his face partially turned away from the camera and toward Ramon's chest.

Yadriel took the stack of photos and thumbed through the rest. One was of Ramon and Rio leaning over the popped hood of an old Cadillac. Ramon was pointing at something, and Rio's face was very serious, studious. Meanwhile, Julian was off to the side, scooting around on one of those wooden creepers mechanics used to get under cars.

There were some school pictures, too. Rio sat with a straight back, another tight-lipped smile, and a tie done neatly around his neck. In contrast, Julian's eyes were squinted shut and he was smiling in a way that looked like he was trying to show all his teeth at once. His tie was loose and crooked, the left side of his collar sticking up.

In another photo, they sat in a line on the curb. Julian and Rio sat between Ramon and Carlos—the man Julian had said owned the shop with his father. Ramon sat next to Rio, grinning at the camera while Rio smiled up at him. Carlos was on the other side, a finger hooked over his chin as it jutted forward, mean-mugging the camera. He leaned onto Julian, who bent under the weight of his arm, laughing as he tried to push him off.

Yadriel stared at the boy sitting next to him. A boy with a bright smile and an easy laugh. Who liked skateboarding the streets of Los Angeles and stargazing on the roof of his dad's car. Who would do anything to protect his friends. Reckless and brilliant.

The aching in Yadriel threatened to swallow him whole. Julian was still there, but Yadriel's body was already mourning the loss.

But he knew this wasn't sustainable. No one was meant to last as a spirit floating between two worlds, but especially not Julian. He was a boy made of fire who'd been turned to frost. He was meant to burn.

"This isn't how I would've pictured someone wanting to spend their last day," Yadriel said, fiddling with Julian's medal around his neck. "But it's very . . . you."

Julian cast him a narrow-eyed look. "Uh, thanks?"

"I just mean, I feel like most people would want to spend it with their families and friends." Yadriel thought about how, when someone got sick or grew old, when they neared the end of their lives, their community would come together. Friends and loved ones would stay close, keeping watch over the person. Brujas would offer them comfort and ease their pain. Everyone was there to give their support, to send them off to the afterlife surrounded by their loved ones.

"That sounds so depressing and boring." Julian frowned. "Not to mention, none of them can see or hear me. I'm already dead." He shrugged his shoulders. "Is that how you would want to spend your last day?" Julian asked. "With your dad and brother? Your Lita? Hell, the whole group of brujx?"

"God, no" was Yadriel's immediate response, surprising even himself. That sounded like a nightmare. Yadriel hated being the center of attention, even under the best of circumstances. Even his birthday felt like an ordeal. "Maybe you've got the right idea." He looked out over the cliff. Frothy waves broke up and down the beach, as far as he could see. A gust of ocean air pushed through his hair. Yadriel smiled and breathed it in. "Stealing a car and driving off into the sunset is way better."

"I'm enjoying it."

"Is there anything you regret?" Yadriel's stomach twisted. A voice in his head told him to stop asking questions. That stuff like this would only upset him. He wasn't used to death being such a finality.

But then Julian grinned. "Regret?" Giving a small shake of his head, he leaned closer. "*Tch*, no way," he said, his voice barely above a whisper, like he was telling Yadriel a secret.

"Anything you wish you'd done?"

The smile slipped. "A couple."

This was a bad idea. Too much, too close, but when Julian leaned forward Yadriel didn't want to pull away.

Yadriel's lungs felt tight, like he was holding his breath too long underwater.

A voice in his head told him to stop. That he was getting in over his head. These were treacherous waters and wading into them would only end badly. But a much more powerful force dragged him down like an undertow.

Julian squinted, the angles of his face tight in concentration. Slowly, he brought his hand up to the side of Yadriel's face, close, but not touching. His stormy eyes slid to Yadriel's, holding a question. "¿Me dejas robarte un beso?" he said softly, in the most agonizingly beautiful Colombian accent Yadriel had ever heard. It was pure and melodic, like a song.

Yadriel closed his eyes. He nodded.

Cold pressed to his cheek, sending shivers down his neck. He sucked in a breath. Julian's palm cupped his cheek. He felt each icy finger pressed to the skin below his ear, the soft sweep of Julian's thumb just below his eyelashes.

When he opened his eyes, Julian was staring back. The smoldering intensity made his skin flush.

Julian tilted his head. Cold nipped at Yadriel's nose. A soft caress ghosted over his lips, and Yadriel let himself drown in it. It was unexpectedly gentle and sweetly slow. His skin flushed, hot and wanting, and Julian's cool touch sent shivers rolling through him. Yadriel's soul ached. He leaned closer, his hands reaching out, fingers wanting to knot into Julian's jacket and pull him closer.

But they grasped at air. There was nothing to hold on to.

Buzz buzz-buzz.

A jolt yanked up Yadriel's spine and he jerked away. The shuddering of his phone's alarm shook in his back pocket. He scrambled away, arching his back to grab it. With clumsy fingers, he turned it off. *"Jesus."* He pressed his hand against his chest. His heart hammered. The sharp edge of Julian's medal cut into his palm.

Julian looked startled, his hand still hovering in the empty air.

"It's my alarm," Yadriel told him, trying to catch his breath. He had several messages from Maritza, asking where they were and when he'd be back. He stared up at Julian. His portaje poked uncomfortably into his lower back. "We need to head back or we won't get there before midnight."

Julian's hand fell to his lap. He looked out over the water again. The wind tugged at his jacket. He closed his eyes and grinned. Below, the waves crashed. The moonlight painted him in shades of blue. His edges blurred like watercolors spilling outside of their lines.

"All right, patrón." With one last deep breath, Julian slid off the hood. "Let's go."

Reluctantly, Yadriel got in the car and started driving back toward the city. Too quickly, the ocean faded from the rearview mirror.

It was too soon. Even if Julian was ready, Yadriel wasn't.

With the windows rolled up, the car was comfortably warm. They fell into an easy quiet. A slow song filtered through the speakers, tinny and slow. Julian hummed along, his fingers tapping the beat out on the armrest.

Yadriel stole glances. When the chorus started, Julian sang along, voice soft and mostly off-key. Yadriel felt himself smile. Julian's singing was terrible but endearing. People who sang in front of other people with no sense of self-consciousness were a specific and rare breed that Yadriel was decidedly not.

The singer's voice dipped low, and Julian couldn't follow, forcing the words to drown in his throat.

He chuckled, and Julian's eyes flickered to his. The corners of Julian's eyes crinkled as he smiled back.

Yadriel wanted to chase down the sunset. To not let it rise.

How long after he was gone would Yadriel be dreaming about Julian and this drive? Yadriel thought it would be worth the sleepless nights ahead.

TWENTY-ONE

Yadriel parked the Stingray a couple of streets over from the cemetery. Partly because the street was packed with cars—all the brujx families would be there to celebrate and welcome the spirits home tonight. Also to buy time until he figured out how to get it back to Rio. But that was a problem for the morning. Right now, he needed to get Julian and himself through the cemetery and back to the old church without being noticed.

"Just act natural," Yadriel murmured as they approached the gate. With Día de Muertos little more than an hour away, there was enough spirit energy filling the air that Julian could go relatively unnoticed.

The doors stood wide open as people funneled in. Brujos stood by, greeting folks as they entered, but to also keep any outsiders from wandering into a brujo celebration, thinking it was a Halloween party.

Inside the gates, it was like walking into another world of golden light and color.

"Whoa," Julian breathed in awe.

Candles lined all the paths and graves for as far as the eye could see. Towering arches adorned elaborately with marigolds stood at the heads of graves, sarcophagi, and mausoleums alike. Brightly colored banners of papel picado crisscrossed overhead. More marigolds and deep red-violet chrysanthemums lined walkways and covered dirt mounds.

Bottles of rum stuffed with peppers, meant to warm the bones of the returning spirits, leaned against tombstones. The cemetery thrummed with energy and excitement. The air felt alive and electric, like before a thunderstorm.

Ornate ofrendas filled every available space. Some altars were modest, with just a photo, candles, copal incense, and pan de muerto. Meanwhile, other folks took it as a personal challenge to outdo each other every year. Some altars stood seven steps high, piled with food and drinks. There were large, painted portraits propped on top of columbarium walls. Urns were piled with marigolds. More of the sacred flowers spilled over every possible surface. At a young girl's ofrenda, a bicycle had been covered in the bright orange flowers, her picture tucked into the spokes.

As they moved through the cemetery, gritos filled the air. The loud, trilling tongues and sharp "*Ay, ay, ay!*" cut through the air, growing louder as others in the cemetery joined in. They were meant to lead the spirits back home. As the gritos swelled, the nearby candle flames popped and flared with excitement. Golden sparks rippled through marigolds in shivering waves like a choreographed lightshow. The louder the grito, the brighter they shone.

Julian's pleased laughter made Yadriel smile as they weaved through the celebrants, spirits and brujx alike.

Everyone was dressed for the occasion. Three small girls chased one another between headstones in poufy dresses made of tulle and satin. Younger brujos came in nice slacks and pressed shirts, while the brujas went all out with billowing skirts and intricate hairstyles.

The older brujos came in sacred jewelry, passed down through the generations. Heavy plugs of jade and obsidian hung from stretched earlobes. An older woman wore a heavy jade pendant on her chest, carved to resemble a two-headed snake. An elaborate nose ornament worn by a man being guided by a young lady was made of turquoise and gold. A bell dangled from each flared side.

At the steps of the church stood Yadriel's dad with Lita at his side. They greeted brujx as they entered the church. Lita held herself like a queen, chin tilted proudly. His dad, on the other hand, looked distracted and upset. Between shaking hands and smiling, his eyes searched the crowd, deep wrinkles set into his brow.

Yadriel knew it was because of him. He hadn't messaged or called back yet, and sharp guilt urged him to pull out his phone right there and then. Instead, Yadriel tugged his hood up over his head. He could make excuses and ask for forgiveness later. Right now, he had a job to finish.

"Come on," Yadriel murmured quietly to Julian, hoisting his backpack higher up on his shoulder. It was packed tight, the zipper hardly able to close. Yadriel ducked his head to slink back into the crowd when someone caught him by the arm.

"Finally!"

Yadriel jolted, but when he whipped around, it was Maritza's angry face staring at him.

"*Jesus*, Maritza!" he hissed, pressing his hand to his hammering heart.

Maritza wore a white dress with ruffled skirts. Her fists were on her hips, where a yellow sash was tied around her waist. A marigold was tucked behind her ear amid her purple-and-pink curls. She wore her portaje around her neck, as usual. The rose-quartz rosary perfectly matched the pink in her hair. "Your dad's been looking for you and bugging *me* about it all night!" she snapped.

"*Sssh!*" Yadriel looked around, worried that someone would notice him or, worse yet, Julian, if they lingered in one place for too long.

"Did you do it yet?" Maritza searched the air around Yadriel.

Julian made a disgruntled noise and stepped up to Yadriel's side. Maritza's eyes snapped right to him.

"Good to see you, too." Julian waved.

"Not yet," Yadriel told her. "I'm taking him to the old church."

Maritza's pink lips pursed. "Yads—!"

"Just buy me some more time—"

"I've done all I can!" Maritza pressed. "We're supposed to be setting up the last of the ofrendas! Any minute he's going to freak out and send a search party looking for you!"

Frustration simmered under Yadriel's skin. He wanted more time with Julian. He didn't want to be rushed into releasing his spirit. "What if—"

"You should go."

Yadriel turned to Julian, surprised. He looked completely at ease—happy, even—which threw him off entirely. Yadriel frowned and gave a small shake of his head. "I thought I was going to release you before midnight?" he said, confused.

"Yeah, we've still got time." Julian shrugged. "I'd kind of like to check everything out, anyways." His eyes drifted around the cemetery, alight with excitement and curiosity. "Go check in with your fam," Julian told him with an encouraging nod. "I mean, this is your big night, right? You should enjoy it."

Yadriel wanted to argue. For some reason, Julian's nonchalance made him angry. "But—"

"I'll go with you," Maritza said to Julian. When Yadriel looked at her, feeling betrayed, she shrugged her shoulders. "I mean, someone needs to babysit him."

Julian scowled and hissed between his teeth. *"Tch."*

"And *I* already did *my* chores," she pointed out.

Yadriel bit down on his lower lip. It was a nice offer, but *he* wanted to go with Julian. He wanted to show him around, to point out all the details and traditions of their holiday, to enjoy and experience them with Julian, while he still had the chance.

"Yadriel!"

Yadriel spun toward the church. His dad had spotted him, a relieved smile on his face as he craned his neck to see him over the sea of brujx.

"There you are! Come!" Yadriel's heart sank as his dad waved him over. "We've been waiting for you to put the final touches on your mamá's ofrenda!"

"One sec!" Yadriel turned back to Maritza.

Julian was already backing up, his attention caught by the dance circle that was forming. "Do what you gotta do," he told Yadriel.

"Can you stash this for me in the old church?" Yadriel asked Maritza, reluctantly slipping his backpack off his shoulder.

She nodded and took it from him. "Sure."

He turned to Julian. "I'll make it quick."

"Sure, sure, sure." He was already blending into the crowd. "We've got time."

But they didn't.

Julian threw Yadriel a smile before disappearing into the crowd.

It took every bit of self-control Yadriel had left to not chase after him.

"I'll keep an eye on him," Maritza repeated with an encouraging smile. "We'll meet you at the old church. Come find us when you're done."

"Thanks for covering for me," Yadriel said to Maritza. "Seriously."

"Yeah, well." She sighed dramatically, her mood starting to warm back up. "You owe me. Like, *big* time." Maritza hoisted the backpack higher on her shoulder. "I'll go take care of this." She turned and took off after Julian.

Yadriel went to his dad.

"You had me worried," his dad told him as brujx filed by, shaking his hand.

"Yeah, sorry," Yadriel replied, sidestepping the line of people. Luckily, his dad seemed to be in a good mood. He didn't see his tío Catriz, but before he could ask where he was, Lita spotted him and gasped.

"You are not dressed!" she scolded.

Yadriel looked down at himself. The last thing he was worried about right now was his clothes. "What do you need me to do?" Yadriel asked his dad.

"I need you to get dressed!" Lita said before welcoming a family of brujx to the church.

His dad chuckled and gave a small shake of his head. "Go get changed," he said before nodding toward the church. "I set aside the calavera you made for your mamá. Take it to her ofrenda, and then you and Maritza can go enjoy the party for a while. How does that sound?"

"That sounds great," Yadriel said, not even finishing his sentence before he was off and running toward the house.

"Meet at the ofrenda by midnight!" his dad called after him. Yadriel lifted his hand in acknowledgment.

He raced through the cemetery and back to the house. Throwing open the door, he ran upstairs, taking the steps two at a time. The sooner he did what his dad asked, the sooner he could get back to Julian.

In his room, Yadriel tore off his hoodie and T-shirt and changed into an olive-green button-down. He didn't have time to obsess and worry over whether his binder flattened down his chest enough to make it fit right. Yadriel shucked off his torn black jeans for a clean, if a bit wrinkled, pair. He kept the combat boots and headed back to the church.

His heart thudded in his chest, like a clock ticking down to midnight as he dodged brujx and spirits to get back into the church. It was packed with people and long tables covered in white linens, laden with food and drinks.

During Día de Muertos, you could really see how the diverse cultures of the brujx came together in celebration. Ecuadorian colada morada— a sweet, purple corn juice made with berries—was passed around in plastic cups. Brujos from El Salvador brought honeyed pumpkin to share. The Haitian families always brought plenty of homemade beeswax candles for decorating ofrendas and tombstones. Andean t'anta wawa—fruit-filled sweet rolls in the shape of babies—had been one of Yadriel's favorites since he was little.

But he didn't have time to indulge.

There were only a couple of boxes of calaveras left sitting on one of the tables. Yadriel picked up the one filled with the skulls he'd decorated for his mom and the rest of his ancestors the other night. Carefully cradling it in his arms, Yadriel left the church and the delicious smells behind him.

Just outside the church, a large dance circle had formed. In a ring, men and women played huehuetl, large animal hide drums, and te-ponaxtle, log drums with slits. The beat shook in Yadriel's chest as he skirted around the outside of the crowd.

Clay flutes and ocarinas trilled like birds, while conch shells bel-lowed, deep and strong. The beat thrummed, and, in the center of the circle, the dancers danced. Chachayotes, adornments of shells and nuts, rattled on their wrists and ankles, shaking with each stomp. They wore traditional regalia, large and colorful headdresses made of long feathers. Women wore colorful tunics, while the men wore maxtlatl. A small girl in purple danced next to her older sister, her face serious and pinched in concentration. Sweat glistened on the dancers' skin, catching the orange glow of the candles as they danced and moved through their paces.

Yadriel wondered if Julian had seen them. He would've liked to see his face as he watched them.

His mother's grave was in the small graveyard adjacent to the church, saved for the family of the brujx leaders. His grandparents on his mother's side, as well as his Lito, were all laid to rest in the same plot. The quiet little corner of the cemetery was decorated with care and pride.

Diego's sugarcane handiwork was front and center. Tall arches and crosses stood at each grave, adorned with marigold blooms bursting with hundreds of petals. Lita's hand-cut papel picado hung in colorful banners, gently swaying in the October breeze. His father had built sturdy altars for everyone, seven steps high and covered in trinkets, pictures, and food.

One by one, he placed each calavera atop a headstone. His mother's parents had a matching set of understated worn stone. Lito's was a huge slab of jade carved with intricate Maya glyphs, befitting of a passed brujx leader.

Yadriel's mother's tombstone was made of polished white marble. Sinking down into a crouch, Yadriel placed her calavera, careful to make sure it was straight and wouldn't slip off the slick stone.

He ran his fingers along her name carved into the front in gold lettering.

CAMILA FLORES DE VÉLEZ.

Her picture smiled up at him from the ofrenda, illuminated by the soft glow of white candles.

In less than an hour, he would be able to see her again. They would be a complete family again, if just for a couple of days. She would talk to his dad, and she would see all that he had accomplished. Tomorrow night, Yadriel would be part of the aquelarre, and his whole family, and all the brujx, would see. Finally, he would be a brujo.

He should've been excited. He should've been *thrilled*. He had been fighting for this moment for years.

But there was a growing ache in the pit of his stomach. An anticipation of impending mourning was looming over him.

Tonight, he would get so much back, but he was also going to lose Julian.

He needed to get back to him, while there was still time.

The bustle of the celebrations began to fade as he ran deeper into the cemetery. The old church loomed before Yadriel. A soft glow from inside the church flickered through the dusty glass windows. As Yadriel stepped through the small gate, a strange, tingling sensation went from the soles of his feet to the top of his head.

Maritza sat on the steps, her white skirts splayed out around her.

She stood when he approached. "Is it time?" she asked as Yadriel came to a stop in front of her.

He gave her a jerky nod, unwilling to tear his eyes away from the wooden doors. Yadriel's fingers trembled, so he clenched his hands into fists and pinned his elbows tight to his sides.

For a moment, she didn't say anything, and neither did he.

Then Maritza stepped to the side. "Go on." She gave his side a soft push and said in a gentle voice, "I'll stand guard."

Yadriel forced himself to walk up the steps, breath shaky as he struggled to fill his lungs.

When he pushed the door open, his breath hitched in his throat.

Dozens of candles lined the windows and stone walls. From tea lights to thick pillar candles, they adorned sconces and sat on the floor, lining the pews.

Yadriel reached for Julian's necklace around his neck. He squeezed the St. Jude medal in his hand. It was warm in his sweaty palm. Yadriel's heavy feet carried him down the aisle, past the steadily burning flames. Tall gold stands, stocky prayer candles, and ornate candelabras crowded the main altar, creating a sea of gently swaying light.

Julian stood before them at the foot of the altar, his back to Yadriel. His chin was tilted up to where Lady Death stood in her black mantle.

Every sluggish heartbeat pulsed painfully through Yadriel veins.

Hearing his approach, Julian looked back over his shoulder. When he saw Yadriel, he turned and smiled.

Julian stood with his hands tucked into his pockets, his head tipped to the side. The flames of hundreds of candles shone through his blurry edges, like he was putting off his own light.

"I was starting to think you'd stood me up," Julian said. He squinted at Yadriel, a playful grin tugging the corners of his lips. The warm glow caught in his dimples. "Which one of us is Cinderella in this scenario?"

Yadriel's mouth was dry, making it hard to speak. "I'm the fairy god-mother," he managed to croak out. "I think that makes you the pumpkin."

Julian's melodic laughter echoed through the church and danced through the gaping hole in Yadriel's chest.

"So . . ." Julian's gaze shifted to Lady Death.

She waited for them at the altar.

When Julian looked back, that crease between his thick eyebrows was back. "What's next?"

Yadriel wanted to give Julian some kind of comfort, but he didn't know what to say. He was having a hard time reining in the flood of emotions tearing through him. His heart thudded dully in his pulse. "Give me a minute to set up."

Gingerly, he dusted the cobwebs off Lady Death's faded black mantle and plucked a couple of dead moths from the golden embroidery. He swept his fingers over the delicate feathers of her headdress, letting their colors show their true vibrance.

His backpack sat on the nearest pew. Yadriel took out Julian's favorite snacks they had bought earlier. He set the desserts, Takis, and smelly duros at Lady Death's feet, along with a pan de muerto. He could feel Julian hovering behind him as he worked. He pulled out a St. Jude prayer candle he'd snuck into his basket at the store when Julian wasn't paying attention. When he lit it, the flame trembled. A tiny bottle of mezcal and container of salt joined the snacks.

Yadriel pulled out the picture of Julian and his brother held under their father's arms. Carefully, he propped it up in the center. The marigolds he'd grabbed were a little rumpled and wilted, but he popped the flowers off their long stems and made a small ring around the make-shift altar with the petals.

Lastly, he pulled out a calavera decorated with swirls of neon green, yellow, and blue. Piped orange flowers bloomed from its eyes. *Julian* was scrawled in lopsided letters across its forehead with magenta icing.

Yadriel stood and wiped his sweaty palms off on his thighs.

Julian leaned down, his fingers brushing over the calavera, rustling the golden marigold petals. "My own ofrenda?" he asked, looking up at Yadriel.

"Didn't seem right for you to not have one, especially on Día de Muertos." He shrugged, scratching the back of his neck. "It's not much, I just thought—I don't know—"

Julian stood up. "It's perfect," he said earnestly.

Yadriel stared up at him, unable to form a coherent thought, let alone a sentence. He clutched at Julian's necklace around his neck and bit down on his bottom lip. He felt sick to his stomach. His own skin felt suffocating. That strange rushing sensation was under his feet again, throwing him off balance.

He wanted to say something important, something meaningful. He *needed* to, but he couldn't find the words, and his throat was dangerously tight.

Julian's smile fell from his lips. His pressed his palm against his chest like it ached. "You should get it over with," he said. "It's almost midnight, you don't want to be late to see your mom."

Yadriel just nodded numbly, because he didn't know what else to do. Fumbling, he pulled out his portaje and the insulated bottle he'd filled with pig blood that morning. Gripping the hilt in one hand, Yadriel dipped his finger into the cool blood before swiping it across the length of the blade.

Julian watched as Yadriel unclasped the necklace and held the chain in his fist. The St. Jude medal quivered in his shaky hand. The silver glinted in the firelight and Julian's obsidian eyes.

For a moment, Yadriel stood there, the necklace in one trembling hand, his portaje in the other.

Yadriel knew keeping Julian meant he'd be trapped between the worlds of the living and the dead, until he became a violent husk of his former self, just like Tito.

But he wanted to keep him. Selfishly, dangerously, against all reason.

"Are you ready?" Julian asked, searching Yadriel's eyes.

"No," Yadriel told him, because he wasn't.

Julian exhaled a quiet, surprised laugh that seemed to ease some of the tension from his shoulders.

The back of Yadriel's throat ached, and his eyes stung.

How could he possibly recover from falling for Julian Diaz?

A smile conjured up those perfect dimples. He stepped closer and cupped the side of Yadriel's face. His cold thumb swept across Yadriel's wet cheek. The firelight danced in Julian's glassy, dark eyes. "Do it anyways."

Yadriel drew a shaky breath. "Muéstrame el enlace," he said, his voice cracking.

The candles flared, their flames tall and erratic. The blade of Yadriel's portaje glowed bright, and the golden thread appeared, connecting the medal in Yadriel's hand to the center of Julian's chest.

Julian's eyes went to the side and his hand twitched, as if resisting the urge to reach up and touch it.

Energy charged through Yadriel's veins and danced across his skin.

Julian drew in a shuddering breath and exhaled it through pursed lips. He looked at Yadriel and gave him a small nod.

Grasping his portaje, Yadriel drew his arm back.

Everything in Yadriel screamed at him not to do it. He tightened his grip, but his hand still shook. His chin wobbled. His teeth clicked against each other and his vision blurred.

"It's okay," Julian murmured, but he was lying. He kept his eyes on Yadriel's. He didn't blink. He didn't flinch.

When Yadriel spoke, his voice broke and the ache in his chest fractured and split into a thousand sharp pieces. "Te libero a la otra vida."

He sliced his dagger through the air, bringing the blade down on the golden thread.

His arm jolted, violently jamming into the socket as golden light exploded. Yadriel squinted. The edge of the blade trembled on the line, sending off sparks where they met.

Yadriel sucked in a breath. Panic charged through him. It hadn't worked. His portaje hadn't cut the tether. Why hadn't it worked?

Yadriel's eyes shot to Julian. He looked just as surprised, his mouth open and his expression tight with confusion. Julian quickly shook his head. "It's not me, I'm—"

In the distance, the church bells began to toll, ringing in midnight and welcoming the returning spirits.

As the first chime rang, Julian's voice died in his throat and his eyes rolled back into his skull.

TWENTY-TWO

J ulian!" Yadriel pushed his portaje back into its sheath and scrambled to reach him.

Flat on his back, Julian's entire body convulsed. He flickered in and out of existence, one moment there and the next nothing more than a blurry outline. Yadriel could only see the whites of his eyes.

Julian's back arched off the stone, his face contorted in pain. The muscles in his neck bulged and strained. His fingers scrabbled against the stone floor. Terrible groans gurgled in his throat as the bells continued to chime.

"JULES!" Yadriel shouted.

Crimson bloomed on Julian's white tee, blood seeping from his chest.

He didn't know what to do, he didn't know what was happening. Frantically, he tried to press his palms to Julian's chest, to stop the flow of blood, but his hands sank right through him. Yadriel called Julian's name over and over, tried to get him to look at him, to bring him back, but nothing worked.

When the twelfth toll rang, everything stopped.

Julian's body went limp. His expression went slack. He exhaled a wet, rattling breath, and then he disappeared.

This time, he didn't come back.

"JULIAN!" Yadriel panicked, twisting left and right, searching. He half expected to find Julian's maligno spirit hiding in a corner, but the church was empty.

What the hell just happened? Where did he go?

The church doors flew open. "Yadriel!" Maritza sprinted between the pews, her skirts flying out behind her, her colorful curls wild. "What's wrong?" she asked, her cell phone clutched in her fist as she looked around. She was confused but poised to fight.

"He's gone!" Yadriel managed.

Her expression softened. "I'm so sorry—"

"No! I—I couldn't; it didn't work!" Yadriel scooped up the necklace and his portaje from where he had dropped them. His dagger was back to normal. "He suddenly collapsed and—and he was *dying*—" The terrible scene played itself over in his head.

"Yads," Maritza said gently, taking a tentative step closer. "He's already dead."

"I know that!" Frustration growled in his throat. "But he was dying and then he just *vanished*! And I *didn't* release him!" he added when Maritza started shaking her head.

"Something's wrong," she said.

"Clearly!" he snapped.

"No, not just Julian," Maritza told him impatiently. She held up her phone. The screen lit up with text messages. "Paola texted me," she said, the color draining from her face. "Miguel didn't come back."

"He didn't?" Yadriel's heart sank, confirming what he'd been so afraid of. It was officially Día de Muertos. All of the brujx spirits were in the cemetery now, returning to their families. "Then his spirit really is trapped somewhere! Why haven't we been able to find him?" Yadriel demanded. "How is there still no trace?"

"I don't know, but something else is going on here." Maritza drew herself upright with a look of determination. "I—"

Maritza stumbled, clutching her chest just as a searing pain struck Yadriel in the heart, doubling him over. Yadriel instinctively clawed at his chest, trying to rip out whatever had pierced into him, but nothing was there.

"What is that?" Maritza asked through gritted teeth.

"*Who* is that?" Yadriel said.

Maritza's voice hitched. "Did someone die?"

Yadriel shook his head, frenzied eyes searching the church. No, someone didn't die. "Someone's dying," he said through ragged breaths. The pain was intense, but had started to dull. Something tugged urgently at his ribs. Whoever it was, they were close, and they were in great danger.

"Where are they?" Maritza asked, eyes searching the wooden beams and empty pews. "Can you tell where it's coming from?"

He didn't know, but the tugging feeling was too familiar. It was just like the feeling he had when they had been drawn to the church the first time and he'd found Julian.

But how could *this* be Julian? How could he be dying when he was already dead?

They needed to find him, but how?

Yadriel grabbed his dagger and smeared some of the pig blood along the blade. "¡Muéstrame el enlace!" he called, holding up Julian's necklace.

The golden thread sparked to life. It shot through the air, past the altar of Lady Death, and through a door. "It's not going to stay lit for long," Yadriel said, already making for the door. "But we can follow it to him—"

"Wait!" Maritza caught his arm. "Should we get help?"

"He doesn't have time, Maritza! You felt it!" he said.

Maritza's eyes swept to the front doors, then back to Yadriel.

He was prepared to wrench free of her grip and make a run for it if she tried to hold him back.

Instead, she released him and stomped her foot. *"Shit!"* With a huff, she tossed back her curls and puffed out her chest. "Let's go!"

Yadriel didn't need to be told twice.

He had to throw his shoulder into the worn wood door before it groaned open, wood scraping against stone. The old sacristy was dark and dusty. Bookshelves filled with old texts lined the walls, along with an array of brujx sculptures of Aztec warriors and a slab of Maya glyphs. A golden mask of the Incan sun god was tucked safely into a glass display case. At the back of the room was a heavy desk. A toppled-over chair lay next to it.

Yadriel crossed the room, following the golden thread to where it disappeared into the floor behind the desk. In the near pitch dark, Yadriel smoothed his hand over the worn stone. As his eyes adjusted, he could just make out a square outline of green light coming from under the floor. His fingers found a hold and he yanked hard.

With effort, he lifted the trapdoor and slid it to the side. A set of earthen steps sank into the ground. The thread plunged down them.

He only hesitated for a moment. Following a mystery flight of stairs down into the bowels of an old church sounded both stupid and dangerous, but if Julian was down there, Yadriel was going after him.

"Be careful," Maritza warned as she followed him down.

The stairs coiled down into the earth. Yadriel pressed his hand against the slick stone walls as they descended to keep himself steady. He used his portaje and the golden thread to light the way, but too quickly, they began to fade.

Yadriel cursed under his breath. The bottle of pig blood was back at Lady Death's altar.

But as the warm glow faded, faint blue-and-green lights danced along the walls. They were like the lights that danced in Maritza's pool when they swam late at night during the summer. They undulated and flickered, growing brighter the deeper they went. Yadriel followed them.

The air grew damp and heavy with the smell of copal incense.

When the steps finally bottomed out, they opened up into a room.

Or, not a room, but a cave. Yadriel only got a quick glimpse—clear water, burning candles, wet stone—before he saw Julian's ghostly form slumped against a huge block of stone.

"Wait!" Maritza hissed behind him. He felt her fingers graze his back as he ran to Julian's side.

"Julian!" Yadriel dropped to the floor and reached for him, but his hands slipped right through Julian's shoulder. His edges blurred and washed out, barely there. Yadriel was frightened that, any second, he'd disappear altogether.

Julian's breaths were shallow and rapid, his face contorted in a grimace. "What happened? Where are we?" he asked, words slurred as his fingers knotted into the blood-soaked shirt that clung to his chest.

"I don't know," Yadriel confessed, tearing his eyes from Julian's face long enough to take in their surroundings. It took effort to understand what he was seeing.

It was an ancient crypt, one that'd probably been hiding under the old church for years. A steady dripping sound echoed off the cave walls. There were candles along the sides, their flames tall and crackling. Tombs were cut into the walls, housing stone sarcophagi. In the middle of the cave, four large slabs of stone were laid out in a semicircle. Light and shadows caught in the small pictorial carvings on their sides. There were shapes and faces, and several jaguar heads—the glyph of Bahlam. A body lay on each slab. Their heads were slightly elevated, and Yadriel could just make out their faces in the firelight.

A breath caught in his throat.

Julian.

Two Julians.

Julian's spirit remained at his side, barely conscious. But laid out on top of the slab he was slumped against was Julian's flesh-and-bone body. He was sickly pale, but Yadriel could see the labored rise and fall of his chest. Bright red seeped all over his white shirt.

It was Julian, and he was *alive*, but barely.

Sticking out of his chest, right above his heart, was a dagger. Yadriel recognized it straightaway. La garra del jaguar. One of the forbidden ritual daggers Lita had been looking for. It was made of oily flint that glistened in the flames. The handle was a carved jaguar head, its mouth gaping, thick fangs biting the hilt. Its eyes were round and bulging. Wisps curled from the handle of the dagger and into the air like golden smoke.

Yadriel shook his head, trying to rattle his thoughts into place, to come up with an explanation that made sense. How could Julian be alive and his spirit be lying next to him?

Julian's spirit groaned and flickered.

"Keep your eyes open!" Yadriel snapped when Julian's eyelids began to droop. He didn't know what was going on, but if they were going to get out of here, Julian—both of them—needed to stay with him.

With effort, Julian forced them back open. His dark eyes swam before finding Yadriel's face.

"Yads." Julian's voice was tight, his eyes wide and more alert. Frightened.

Next to Julian's body, three more had the matching daggers pierced into their chests. Yadriel's heart plummeted. He knew the face of the one to the left.

It was Miguel. But, unlike Julian, he wasn't moving. His body was still, his eyes closed. His skin was ashen, lifeless. The jaguar dagger piercing his heart was dark and still. No wisps floated into the air. The stone under Miguel was streaked with dark, dried-up blood.

Meanwhile, rivulets of Julian's blood ran down his own stone slab toward his feet, where it dripped into a pool of water sunk into the earthen floor. The water of the cenote was a cool, glowing blue. Dark, undulating shadows coiled in its depths. Julian's blood dripped into it, slow and steady.

"Sobrino."

Yadriel looked up.

A tall man stood facing him. A jaguar pelt, golden with black and brown spots, was draped over his bare chest. He wore the upper jaw and head of a jaguar as a crown. Its eyes had been replaced with jade orbs. The thick, yellowing fangs pressed against his eyebrows. Black and venomous green plumage spilled out behind him.

"Tío?" Yadriel said, squinting in the dark and unable to believe his own eyes.

Tío Catriz smiled. "Look at you!" his said, holding his arms out at his sides. His hands were covered in something dark and glistening. "¡Ven, ven!" He reached down for Yadriel and pulled him to his feet.

Yadriel stood there staring at him, in a daze.

His tío held the wrist of his hand that still clutched his dagger. "Your own portaje," he said in amused disbelief, chuckling as he examined the blade, twisting Yadriel's arm this way and that. "When I saw you with it yesterday, I knew what it was straightaway."

An onyx amulet in the shape of a jaguar's head hung around Tío Catriz's neck. It stared at Yadriel with glowing golden eyes.

"Tío, what are you doing down here?" Yadriel asked, his voice wavering.

"Does it work?" he asked with keen interest.

Yadriel nodded.

Tío Catriz laughed again, shaking his head. "I *knew* you could do it," he said with fierce pride. Still holding his arm in one hand, his tío cupped the side of Yadriel's neck with the other, pulling him close.

Something deep in Yadriel—a primal instinct—made him start to tremble.

Tío Catriz leaned down to look him in the eyes. "I am *so* proud of you, sobrino," he said, his smile genuine, his voice sincere. "They all doubted you." He removed his hand from Yadriel's neck and pressed it to his chest. "But I *knew* you had it in you." When Tío Catriz dropped his hand back to his side, it left a smudged handprint down his chest.

A bloody handprint.

Yadriel sucked in a gasp and wrenched himself away. "Tío, what are you doing?" His eyes flickered around the cave. To the cenote and the bodies. Miguel and Julian. The daggers and the blood.

"The dawning of a new era, Yadriel," Catriz told him, bloody palms held aloft at his sides.

Yadriel shook his head. It wasn't possible. There was no way. "I don't—"

"For too long, our bloodline has been losing its power. The brujx are a dying breed," Catriz told him with a solemn expression. "This is the only way for me to regain the powers I was born without. To take back the birthright I was denied."

"Your birthright?" he repeated.

"By using the ancient ways our ancestors long abandoned, I will become the most powerful brujo to walk the world of the living in a millennia," his tío said, flexing his fingers.

At Yadriel's side, Julian managed to get onto his knees—seemingly from sheer force of will alone.

"I don't understand," Yadriel said.

"The forbidden ritual. Human sacrifice, Yadriel," he explained patiently. "With the help of the jaguar's paw and Bahlam himself."

Yadriel's stomach plummeted. "You can't do that!"

"Tranquilo," Tío Catriz said gently. "It's okay, I have to do this for me, for *both of us*," he stressed. "The brujx cast us out. They ignored us and denied us our rights without ever giving us a chance."

Tío Catriz drew himself up. "I was the firstborn son of the brujx leader, but I was denied my right to follow in my father's footsteps." The look he gave Yadriel was one of pity. "None of them believed in you, Yadriel. Your father and the brujx have never understood you. They never even tried to. You are different than they are, so they shunned you, just like they did to me. But I have *always* believed in you," he said firmly.

"Tío, you can't do this," Yadriel tried to argue, frantic and desperate to talk sense into him.

"It is the only way," Tío Catriz said, gesturing to the four sacrificial stone slabs. "With these sacrifices, the jaguar claws have drained their spirits one by one, trapping them in the amulet," he said, touching the jaguar head around his neck. "It's a slow process, having to drain their spirits and their blood, one by one, but soon it'll be complete. Once the last drop of blood falls into the cenote, it will summon Bahlam. As my reward, the four drained spirits trapped in the amulet will give me powers our people haven't possessed for millennia."

Tío Catriz moved to the cenote where Julian's blood dripped into the roiling pool. "I had to find the sacrificial bodies, of course, but it was surprisingly easy to just pick people off the street. People with no homes or families." He sighed and shook his head. "People no one would miss."

Anger swelled in Yadriel's chest, nearly robbing him of his ability to see. "You—"

"It did pain me to use Miguel," Catriz said, stepping aside and looking back at the altar. "He stumbled upon what I was doing, saw me dragging your friend here through the back gate. He left me with no other choice."

Yadriel thought of the night they all felt Miguel die. How everyone had gone looking for him. The painful stab Yadriel had felt in his chest. How it'd brought him to his knees. He remembered how he'd felt the stir of energy coming from the old church. How Miguel had been under his feet the whole time, dying. How Julian had been right next to him.

That was why he had been drawn to the old church. He'd sensed something was wrong, he just didn't know how much.

For the first time, Tío Catriz spared Julian a glance. "I'm sorry your friend has to be the one to complete the ceremony."

Julian bared his teeth, his face contorting in anger and pain. He was more awake—more himself—and seething.

"Has he been with you all this time?" Catriz asked Yadriel with a curious lift of an eyebrow. "You did a good job hiding him."

"You can't summon Bahlam!" Yadriel all but yelled, his hands clenched into fists at his side. "If he crosses over from Xibalba, he'll—"

"I know," Catriz interrupted with a solemn nod. "When Bahlam rises, the cemetery will be filled with the spirits of the passed brujx. He will be unleashed to do what he did in ancient times. He will drag their spirits down to Xibalba and trap them there for all eternity." A cruel smile twisted his tío's mouth. It made Yadriel's blood run cold. "They will suffer, and the living brujx will be made to face the consequences of their actions. I will show them what a grave mistake they've made, and I will show them no mercy."

Yadriel wanted to vomit. He thought of his grandparents, his aunts and uncles, his mom. They were all in the cemetery, celebrating and probably worried sick about him. They had no idea what was coming. What would happen to them if Yadriel didn't do something? He would lose them. He would never see them again.

"Finally, they will see us as equals," his tío said, turning his full attention back to Yadriel. "They will never value us, or give us the chance to show them what we're capable of. We can show them how wrong they are, together." When he smiled, Yadriel barely recognized him anymore.

How was he the same man who had comforted Yadriel when he felt so alone? How was he the man who took Yadriel under his wing when even his own dad avoided him? Yadriel didn't want to believe it.

"They will never accept us, Yadriel," he said softly, reaching for him. "This is the only way to show them."

Yadriel stepped out of his reach. "No, it's not!"

His tío sighed, not angry, but tired. "Yadriel—"

"I told my dad!" He couldn't bring back Miguel, or the other two people who had lost their lives, but if he could make his tío understand, he could save everyone else from a similar fate. "He knows about my portaje, that Lady Death blessed me as a brujo, that I *am* a brujo!"

Tío Catriz froze, a look of pure shock on his face.

"He said that when my mom returns for Día de Muertos—" His stomach gave a violent churn, thinking about how she was in the cemetery waiting for him with no idea that they were all in danger. "—they'll talk to Lita and the other brujx." Yadriel swallowed hard. "He said I could be in the aquelarre."

Catriz jerked back, as if the words had struck him across the face. For a beat, he just stared at Yadriel. Disbelief turned to hurt, which quickly clouded to anger. Every smile line or bit of kindness in Tío Catriz's face hardened to stone. "I see," he said, his voice cold as ice.

"Please, Tío," Yadriel begged, his throat burning. "We can talk to them, we can work through it, but you *have to stop this*, before it's too late."

Tío Catriz's smile was forced. "I'm sorry, Yadriel," he said, detached and unconcerned. "I will take what's mine." His tío drew in a deep breath. On the stone slab, the tendrils of gold emitting from the dagger in Julian's heart snaked through the air and dove straight into Catriz's nostrils.

"Don't!" Yadriel pleaded, but his tío ignored him.

On the floor, a pained cry ripped through Julian's throat. His back arched, his body twisting in unnatural angles. Yadriel ran to kneel at his side, but there was nothing he could do. Julian's body flickered in and out of existence. Yadriel couldn't touch him. There was nothing he could do but watch as Julian writhed in pain.

When Catriz stopped inhaling, he sighed, and it was like an invisible force released Julian's spirit.

Julian collapsed in a heap, his limbs heavy and his chest rising and falling with rapid, shallow breaths. "Yads," he groaned.

"Hang on!" Yadriel ordered, though he had no idea how to stop all this.

Catriz approached the cenote. He picked up a candle and dropped it into the pool. The surface burst into electric blue-and-green flames. The ground quaked, a faint reverberation under Yadriel's knees. A low, thunderous growl filled the crypt, echoing off the walls.

"He's almost here," Catriz whispered, the acid lights dancing in his eyes. The flames curved and undulated.

Grief, betrayal, and paralyzing fear swarmed inside Yadriel. He couldn't think. He could hardly breathe through the tightness in his lungs.

At the fire, Catriz murmured the ancient words he couldn't understand. His tío withdrew a dagger and dragged the blade across his palm.

"Don't!" Yadriel shouted, but it was too late.

Catriz hissed between his teeth and squeezed his fist. The blood dropped into the water. The flames burned bright, casting glowing lights of green and blue across the walls.

Yadriel watched as a huge jaguar paw moved beneath the water. Its back rose from the cenote, a curve of iridescent black fur. Its spots shimmered in shades of venomous green and quetzal blue. The large head of a jaguar broke through the surface, revealing huge, bone-white teeth and a bloodred tongue.

Frenzied panic shot through Yadriel, a choked shout lodging in his throat. He scrambled back, placing himself between Julian and the cenote. He couldn't believe what he was seeing.

The jaguar's mouth yawned open, large enough to swallow a man whole, before it sank back into the water.

Yadriel had no plan, but if he didn't do something, he would lose *everything.* His mom and the rest of his relatives would all become trapped in Xibalba, and he would never see them again. His father,

Lita, Diego, and all the other brujx would be in grave danger. Julian, his body bleeding out on the stone table, would die and his spirit would be trapped in the amulet, just like Miguel and the others. No one would find peace. No one would be safe.

Yadriel had to keep Bahlam from rising.

TWENTY-THREE

Yadriel didn't want to hurt his tío, he just wanted to make him *stop*.

As Tío Catriz stood over the cenote, muttering as the blood dripped and the water roiled, Yadriel looked at Julian's body. The golden wisps of smoke were quickly fading as the dagger drained his body of its life.

If he was going to stop Bahlam from returning, if he was going to save his tío, then he needed to stop the ritual.

Yadriel ran to Julian's body and tried to yank the dagger out of his chest, but before he could get his hands on it, Catriz grabbed Yadriel from behind and threw him to the floor. Yadriel crashed to the ground, sharp pain exploding in his head.

"*Yads!*" Julian's spirit tried to drag itself to Yadriel's side, but could hardly move.

"It's too late to stop it," his tío said, placing himself between Yadriel and Julian.

But there was no way he was going to give up.

Yadriel threw his entire body weight at Tío Catriz, but he side-stepped him with surprising ease, hardly bothered.

Scrambling to his feet, Yadriel tried again.

This time, Catriz turned and caught him, barely even budging. His bloody hand was an iron grip, his fingers tightening painfully around Yadriel's upper arm.

Yadriel tried to pull away from him. He'd never seen such a look of anger, of barely contained violence, on his tío's face before. The amulet around his neck burned bright, pulsing with power. It was doing this to him, corrupting Catriz with the poisonous, vicious magic of Bahlam.

Yadriel hissed between his teeth, cringing as his tío gave him a rough shake.

"Don't make me hurt you, Yadriel!" his voice boomed through the cavernous crypt. His lips peeled back over his teeth. His eyes burned, their whites visible all around his dark irises.

Suddenly, the jaguar headdress was yanked from Tío Catriz's head and sent flying.

"DON'T TOUCH HIM!"

Surprise flashed across his face before his head jerked back. Tío Catriz let out an angry shout and released Yadriel.

He stumbled back to see Maritza with a fistful of Catriz's hair.

"I'LL KICK YOUR ASS MYSELF!" she shouted furiously, dragging him away from Yadriel.

A monstrous snarl twisted Catriz's face. In two swift motions, he knocked Maritza's hand away and then caught her by the throat.

Teeth bared, Maritza fought him tooth and nail, kicking wildly and clawing at his arms, swiping for his face with a frenzied look in her eyes. It wasn't clear if Tío Catriz was holding on to her or trying to keep her away.

White-hot anger exploded in Yadriel's head.

He charged for Catriz again, but his uncle tossed Maritza away and kneed Yadriel in the side. He collapsed to the ground, moaning and curling up against the splitting pain.

"Yads!" Maritza called to him. She tried to get to her feet, but her legs buckled under her.

Julian was sprawled on the ground next to her, barely even visible anymore.

Catriz sucked in a deep breath.

Julian cried out, his body seizing.

The golden tendrils of smoke flowed from the dagger as Catriz breathed them in. The amulet burned bright around his neck. He splayed his hands out over the cenote. The flames licked at his fingers as he continued to chant.

No longer clear blue, the cenote rippled thick and dark. A paw, bigger than Yadriel's chest, reached out, followed by a second. Claws, thicker and longer than human fingers, hooked over the edge of the pool, clicking against the stone.

From the dark pool, the jaguar's head emerged. Blood dripped from its fur and fangs. Its eyes were bright, smoldering orange and bulged in its skull. The jaguar's jaw hung wide open as it breathed a low, rattling growl.

Catriz's face split into a wicked, cruel smile. He let out a wailing laugh, the likes of which Yadriel had never heard. It made the hairs on his arms stand on end.

The smell of decay and rot made Yadriel's eyes burn. His heartbeat thrashed in his ears as he tried to back away. His legs felt weak. A primal voice in his head told him to run, but he refused.

Even though his body seared and throbbed with pain, he forced himself onto his feet again.

Catriz rolled his hands through the air, muttering incantations as he backed up, coaxing the jaguar to drag itself out of the cenote. One paw landed with a wet thud on the ground. Its angular shoulders emerged as it slunk forward.

Yadriel clenched his jaw and ran forward.

Catriz turned sharply and grabbed the front of Yadriel's shirt in his fist, breaking off the incantation. The jaguar slipped back into the pool, but the surface continued to bubble.

"*Don't do this*, Tío, please," Yadriel begged. His eyes stung and watered, blurring his vision as his erratic heartbeat throbbed in his temples.

Catriz held him in place and laughed. "You aren't strong enough to stop me, Yadriel." His smile bent into a sneer. He tightened his grip. The jaguar-head amulet burned bright around Catriz's neck.

Yadriel did the only thing he could think of. His hand shot out, snatching at the amulet.

Catriz jerked back, trying to get out of his reach, but Yadriel's fingers caught around the leather cord.

He tugged hard.

The cord snapped.

Catriz sucked in a breath, his eyes wide. His grip buckled, and he released Yadriel. "*No!*" he snarled. Catriz swung wildly to face the pool.

The flames began to shrink. Without the amulet, he wasn't able to keep it burning.

He spun back to face Yadriel, fury burning in his eyes as he shouted, reaching to grab the amulet back.

Yadriel planted his feet and twisted away from him, shoving his shoulder hard into Catriz's chest. The next thing Yadriel saw was Catriz stumbling and pitching backward into the cenote. Bloody water flooded over the edges.

For a moment, the blood and blue flames licked over his tío's body. Catriz locked eyes with Yadriel for a split second, anger and shock written across his face.

"*¡Tío!*" Yadriel shouted, scrambling to grab for his hand.

But before Yadriel could reach him, the jaguar reared up through the surface behind Catriz.

It sank its teeth into Catriz's shoulder, molten eyes blazing.

A scream ripped through Catriz, the whites of his eyes surrounding his dark pupils. With a lurch, the jaguar dragged him down. Catriz's howls turned to wet gurgles as he was pulled below the surface.

Dark blood and water spilled across the floor in a wave. Yadriel scrambled back as it seeped toward him. The flames sizzled out. Slowly, the pool of water began to clear.

Panting, Yadriel stared at the empty cenote. His foggy brain trying to catch up with what had just happened. The amulet pulsed in his fist.

"Yads!" Maritza's panicked shout broke him out of his stupor. She was crouched next to Julian.

"JULES!" Yadriel rushed to the spirit's side.

Julian flickered in and out. Yadriel could barely see him anymore. His eyes were closed, his dark lashes barely visible against his cheeks. He was a wash of pale gray except for the streaks of crimson over his chest. Yadriel cursed, panic rising.

"What do we do?" Maritza asked, her hand held out uselessly above Julian's form.

"I don't know. I don't know." Yadriel shook his head roughly, trying to think.

In his pocket, something vibrated. At first, he thought it was his cell phone going off, but, no—

Yadriel plunged his hand into his pocket and pulled out Julian's necklace. It shone with bright golden light. Dangling in the air, the medal shook and jolted, trembling with energy, sending off sparks of light.

"*Shit,*" Yadriel hissed.

He'd stopped the summoning ritual for Bahlam, but what about the one draining Julian of his life? Yadriel looked at the amulet.

How was he supposed to release Julian's spirit if it was trapped inside?

Yadriel scrambled to his feet and ran to the slab where Julian's body lay. His skin was gray, his lips turning blue.

The wisps continued to float through the air and into the amulet, although they were much thinner and less vibrant.

Yadriel ripped the jaguar-claw dagger out of Julian's chest and threw it to the ground. Blood trickled weakly from the wound.

He placed the amulet on the slab and wrestled with clumsy fingers to undo the clasp of the St. Jude necklace and get it back around Julian's neck. His skin felt cold to the touch as Yadriel redid the clasp.

"Yadriel!"

He turned at Maritza's shout. She stared at the ground. Julian's spirit had vanished.

But then, on the stone slab, Julian's eyes flew open. He sucked in a wet, gurgling breath, and Yadriel nearly jumped out of his skin.

"Julian!" Yadriel reached for him, cupping Julian's face in his hand. He was real, he was awake. Yadriel could feel the hard line of his jaw, the scratch of his buzzed hair against his fingers. He could feel Julian's heartbeat, rapid and weak, in his neck.

Julian's eyes rolled, unseeing, trying to find Yadriel. They weren't just black, but a deep, rich brown, the color of summer soil after it rains. Through heaving breaths, Julian's lips tried to form words, but he couldn't manage.

He was alive, but he was dying.

"Stay with me!" Yadriel told him. He turned to Maritza. "What do I do?!" he shouted.

Maritza shook her head, eyes wide. "I don't know— I—I—"

"Heal him, Maritza!" Yadriel begged. *"Please!"*

Her hand flew to her bare neck. "My portaje!" she said, feeling around her throat. "Where is it?!"

Her rosary must've fallen off during the scuffle.

"Hold on!" Maritza turned away and dropped to her knees, searching for her portaje.

Yadriel squeezed his eyes shut and pressed his forehead against Julian's. It was cold and clammy, covered in sweat. Yadriel begged. He begged for help. He begged for Lady Death to hear him. He begged her to save Julian. *"Please!"*

"Yads." A cold hand pressed to Yadriel's cheek. He opened his eyes, and Julian was staring up at him, eyes heavy-lidded but intent.

Julian's face was ashen. His lips had turned gray, save for the line of red running from the corner of his mouth. "Hey, hey, hey." Julian tried to smile, but his dimples were lost. "Todo bien," he murmured, chest heaving under Yadriel's.

"Everything is *not* okay!" Yadriel snapped.

Julian grinned. His fingers slipped through Yadriel's hair and traced his face, like he was trying to memorize every line, before he never saw them again. "Sí, lo está."

He was completely losing his mind. "You're *dying*, you idiot!" Yadriel yelled at him because he was angry and because he was terrified.

Julian's chuckle was wet. "Valió . . . la pena."

Yadriel let out a bitter laugh, gripping Julian's hand that pressed against the side of his face.

With every rasping breath Julian took, the weaker the medal around his neck glowed until it was a barely pulsing golden light. "Todo bien, todo estará bien," he repeated weakly.

Yadriel shook his shoulders roughly. "Stay awake!"

Julian reached out with his other hand and cupped Yadriel's face. He swept his thumbs gently under Yadriel's eyes, trying to wipe away the tears. "Todo bien, Yadriel." Julian drew in a rattling breath.

"You have to stay here until we can get help," Yadriel demanded. Hiccups bucked in his chest, breaking his words.

Julian nodded, but his expression was pained. His breath quickened as he tried in vain to keep his eyes open, to keep them locked onto Yadriel's. A sob caught in Julian's throat. His hands trembled. Tears spilled from the corners of his deep brown eyes.

"Stay!" Yadriel shouted at him, giving him another rough shake.

Julian tried to nod again, but his gaze unfocused, losing sight of Yadriel. His hands slid from Yadriel's face. His eyes stared, unseeing.

The St. Jude medal around his neck gave one last flicker of light before dulling to tarnished silver.

One last breath sighed past Julian's lips.

Everything that made Julian *Julian*—the mischievous light in his eyes, his dimpled smile—vanished.

Yadriel felt him leave, like his own heart had been torn from his chest.

A cry ripped through him, caving in his heart, his bones aching. Yadriel clutched Julian and openly sobbed into his neck. His body shook. His lungs burned. Every fiber of his being mourned.

He couldn't hear the voice calling him at first, lost under his primal cries.

"Yadriel!" A warm hand pressed to his back.

Yadriel turned to look, his head tucked under Julian's chin.

Maritza stood beside him, her eyes wide and frantic as they went between Julian's body, Yadriel, the blood-covered floor. She held her rosary in her fist. "Yads—"

"Help!" Yadriel begged, balling Julian's jacket into his fist. "Please! Save him!"

"Santa Muerte," Maritza hissed, quickly searching for Julian's pulse.

"Please, you have to save him, please," Yadriel sobbed uncontrollably.

Maritza's hand fell back to her side. "Yads," she said softly, placing a gentle hand on his shoulder. "I'm so sorry, Yads—"

Yadriel shoved her away. "I know—I know it goes against your beliefs—"

"It's not that, Yadriel—"

"But you have to save him! *Please*, Maritza!"

Maritza swallowed. "I can't, Yadriel." Her eyes welled. "I can't bring him back. He's gone."

Yadriel's tears trickled down Julian's neck. *"Please, please, please."* He repeated the word over and over. It echoed uselessly, hollow and empty.

Maritza squeezed Yadriel's shoulder tight.

Yadriel buried his face against Julian, letting his smell linger. The sobs slowly subsided until Yadriel was left weak and sniffling.

Then he noticed something thrumming, pressed against his side. Gingerly, Yadriel pushed himself up. The jaguar amulet lay on the stone slab. It trembled and sparked with light, wafting heat and energy.

The ritual was complete. The amulet still held the spirits of Miguel, the two others. Julian's spirit. They were trapped inside and would remain there, unable to cross over to the afterlife.

He wouldn't allow it.

He needed help. He needed Lady Death, but how could he summon a god? Yadriel's mind raced. He remembered how Tío Catriz stood at the cenote, the gateway that connected this world to Xibalba. He remembered how his tío had sliced open his own hand, had used his own blood. Only something as powerful as brujx blood could call upon a death god.

Yadriel quickly pulled out his dagger, gripping where Lady Death had been painted onto the hilt. Their portajes connected them to her.

"Yads?" Maritza said tentatively.

With a quick slice, Yadriel cut open his palm with his dagger.

"Yadriel!" Maritza shouted.

This was the only way he could think to get Lady Death's attention. He needed this favor. He squeezed his hand into a fist. Blood spilled through his fingers. "Lady Death!" he called out. "I need you!"

A bright light exploded in the crypt. Maritza stumbled back. Yadriel threw his arm up to shield his eyes.

Marigold petals showered down around him. They twisted and sparked, tickling his face as they cascaded to the floor. The sweet smell of apples filled his nose.

The light faded. Tall and glowing with a warm light, Lady Death stared down at them, her expression calm. Her skin was smooth as stone, milky white and translucent. Through it, Yadriel could see her golden skeleton.

Parts of her ghostly flesh were missing from the left side of her face. An uneven line curved around her eye and down the side of her jaw, revealing some of her golden skull, teeth, and neck.

Lady Death's hands pressed together, as if in prayer. The left one was only bone. Her white dress billowed out gently around her, like she was underwater. The hem swept along the tops of her bare feet.

Yadriel caught a glimpse of thick, black hair under her gilded lace mantle. A crown of marigolds rested upon her head, their petals gently falling around her. Bright and undulating, her right eye looked as if it had been filled with molten gold, while the other was just an empty, gleaming socket.

Yadriel openly gaped at her, barely even registering the throbbing pain in his hand.

"Mi hijo, Yadriel Vélez Flores," she said, watching him carefully. Her voice was beautiful and melodic, like a song but with the echoing weight of stone. She spoke with an accent that Yadriel couldn't place, like each syllable hit his ear with a ring from every Spanish voice he'd ever heard.

"Holy shit," Maritza breathed, open-mouthed and staring.

Lady Death's golden eyes slid to her. Her black-painted lips curled into a small smile. "Mi hija, Maritza Selena Escabas Santima."

Her eyes bulged. "Holy *shit*."

Yadriel was in shock. He couldn't believe it had worked.

Lady Death looked around the crypt. Her gaze landed on the cenote, the blood on the floor. "You stopped a terrible thing from happening here," she said, slowly shaking her head and sending more marigold petals cascading to the floor. "Without you, Bahlam would've escaped his prison."

"My tío, is he . . . ?" Yadriel trailed off.

Lady Death nodded somberly. "Bahlam has taken him to Xibalba."

Guilt ripped Yadriel in half.

"It is not your fault," she said gently. "Greed and hurt drive people to do horrible things." Lady Death turned to the bodies lying on their sacrificial slabs. "My children were taken from this world before they were meant to go."

"Can't you bring them back?" Yadriel asked, desperation leaping in his chest. Miguel. Julian. The other two whom Yadriel didn't even know.

But Lady Death was already shaking her head. "I am sorry, but I cannot bring them back," she said gently.

"*Please,*" Yadriel begged, panic clawing up his throat once again. "Please, they didn't deserve this! Like you said, they weren't meant to die! They shouldn't have lost their lives like this—just to be sacrificed for *this*!" He grabbed the jaguar amulet in his fist.

Lady Death sighed and bowed her head. "It is not my place to interfere."

Anger and betrayal boiled in Yadriel's gut. "Then why did you even come?" he spat.

"*Yadriel,*" Maritza hissed, staring at him with wide-eyed shock.

"If you can't help me, then why even bother to appear?" Yadriel raged, ignoring Maritza.

Lady Death remained impassive. "I can't undo what has been done." Yadriel seethed. "Then why—"

"But you have the power in your hands to right many wrongs." Her golden eyes drifted to his hand.

Yadriel stared down at the amulet in his fist.

"But it will come at the greatest cost, mijo," Lady Death said.

Brow furrowed, Yadriel tried to understand what that meant. The amulet continued to glow. He could feel the tingling on the back of his neck, sense the trapped spirits swarming in the amulet. The two strangers'. Miguel's. Julian's.

Tío Catriz said the power of the amulet, when fueled by the spirits of those who had been sacrificed, would help him gain the strength the brujx hadn't had flowing through their blood in millennia.

Could he use that stolen power to release their spirits? Could he set them free?

Could he bring them back?

He thought of Miguel, his gentle cousin who was a great man and a doting son. He thought of Julian's wild energy, his undying loyalty to his loved ones, and his determination to do anything to take care of them.

He thought of his mom and her kindness, how all she wanted was to heal and help others. He knew exactly what his mom would do if she were here. The same thing he was going to do.

Yadriel would let himself die, gladly, if it meant saving the four who had been so viciously and carelessly sacrificed. He refused to let them die for his uncle's selfish gains.

He would do it for them. He would do it for Julian.

When he looked up at Lady Death, she smiled.

"Yadriel," Maritza said at his side, as if just realizing what she meant. "*Yadriel*, don't do it!"

But his mind was made up.

Holding it with both hands, Yadriel pressed the amulet to his chest.

Golden light ignited his skin. He sucked in a breath as electricity surged through his veins. He felt light-headed as the power swelled. Yadriel squeezed his eyes shut.

Let them go. Let them be free. Let them live.

"YADRIEL!"

The amulet exploded in his hands, throwing him onto his back. Yadriel groaned. His head swam. He tried to sit up, but every ounce of energy quickly bled out of him. He was too tired to move, too tired to breathe.

He could feel his mind slipping. His vision blurred and darkened.

Yadriel pushed through the fog, searching for something to hold on to, for somewhere to go.

He thought about Julian. The reckless glint in his eyes as he hung out the window of the Stingray, speeding down the highway. The low tenor of his voice as they whispered in the middle of the night, sprawled out on Yadriel's bed and listening to music. The punch-drunk curl of his lips. The way he touched Yadriel's cheek. The light brush of Julian's lips. The way they made Yadriel's heart thud in his chest.

He clung to them, even though they made him weak with grief and loss. Tears rolled down his cheeks as he tried to hold on to the memory, to hold on to Julian.

Stay with me. Stay with me.

Yadriel's heartbeat slowed. His vision went dark. The sweet scent of apples tickled his nose.

He held on to the thought of Julian as tightly as he could.

Stay with me.

TWENTY-FOUR

Julian woke up with a violent jerk. He gulped down air, his heart hammering in his ribs.

What the fuck happened?!

He tried to focus and remember, pushing through the sludge in his head.

Someone was yelling, and Julian cringed as their voice rang in his ears. He wanted to tell them to shut the hell up, but all he managed was an annoyed grunt.

When he tried to sit up, his head swam. If there had been anything in his stomach, he definitely would've barfed it into his lap. Instead, he closed his eyes and took a deep breath, trying to make himself stop being dizzy through sheer force of will.

He was lying on something hard and cold. His whole body ached, like he'd eaten shit on his skateboard. There was a dull, throbbing ache in his chest. But—

Holy shit.

Julian touched his arms, his face, his chest.

He was *alive*?

He was alive!

Julian turned his heavy head, forcing his eyes open to seek out Yadriel.

He needed to tell him, he needed to show him, he needed to grab him and—

"Some goddess you are!" a familiar voice all but screamed.

Julian squinted into the dark room. "Maritza?"

Slowly, things came into focus.

He was sitting on what looked like a stone table.

It was covered in blood.

He was covered in blood.

Everything came rushing back to him. The church. The crypt. The dagger.

Julian's hand flew to where he had been stabbed. His shirt was torn open and there was a cut. It wasn't bleeding anymore, but it still hurt like a son of a—

"You're nothing but a *coward*!"

Maritza sat on the floor, shouting up at the ceiling.

Who the hell was she yelling at?

Julian pushed himself to the edge of the stone table and placed his unsteady feet on the ground. He dug his fists into his bleary eyes and looked down. Then he sucked in a gasp, recoiling.

The floor was covered in blood. Maritza knelt in it, her white dress smeared crimson. She was leaning over something, muttering to herself, her movements erratic.

"Maritza?"

She jerked her head to look at him over her shoulder. "Look" was the wrong word. It was a vicious glare. Her painted lips were peeled back, showing her teeth. Her hair was a frazzled mess. Her chest rose and fell rapidly. She seemed ready to claw his face off.

Julian leaned away from her. "*Jesus,* what—?"

"Oh, so you'll let *him* live?" Maritza shouted, looking wildly around the cave again. There wasn't time for Julian to be offended because she added, "But you'll leave Yadriel here to die?"

The words punched him in the ribs.

Finally, he saw what—who—she was kneeling in front of.

Yadriel lay on his back, limp and unmoving.

Terror ripped through him. "YADS!" Julian scrambled forward and threw himself to the ground next to him. He balled up the front of Yadriel's green shirt in his fists and shook him roughly. "WAKE UP!" he shouted.

Yadriel's head only lolled to the side. There was no warmth left in his graying skin. His lips were parted, his eyes open but only into thin slits. Julian couldn't even see the warm amber of his eyes.

Panic seized Julian by the throat. "What happened?!" he demanded. His pulse raced and his lungs burned with raspy breaths. "What did he do?!"

"He saved your dumb lives!" Maritza spat as she fumbled with a rosary.

Julian shook his head. No, no, no. *He* was the one who was supposed to die, not Yadriel! Yadriel was supposed to be *safe*.

"And she left him here to *DIE*!" She screamed the last word furiously into the cavernous crypt.

"He's dying?" Julian's hands tugged desperately at Yadriel's shirt, trying to get him to wake up. He didn't know how to do CPR; he didn't even know how to check for a pulse. When he spoke, his voice cracked. "Is he dead?!"

"Not on my watch!" Maritza shoved her hands into the puddle of blood. She grabbed her pink rosary with dripping fingers. "¡USA MIS MANOS!" she bellowed.

The rosary burst into a brilliant, blinding light. Julian flinched.

Maritza pushed Julian's hands out of the way and pressed the rosary to Yadriel's chest. "¡YO CURARE TU CUERPO!"

There was a flash like golden lightning. Julian squeezed his eyes shut, but it burned through his eyelids.

When it cleared, Maritza sat back heavily. Her smile looked drunk and delirious. "HAH!" she expelled through heavy breaths.

Julian reached for Yadriel. *"Yads?"* He cupped Yadriel's cheeks, searching his face. His color was returning. Red began to bloom in his cheeks. When Julian pressed his palms to Yadriel's chest, he felt it rise and fall in a steady rhythm.

Julian let out an incoherent cry of relief. Not dead. Yadriel was alive. He was going to be okay, he just needed to wake him up. Julian gave him another shake, trying his best to be more gentle this time, but his hands were trembling. "Wake up now, Yads!" he demanded, as if he could yell him into consciousness.

"What do you think of that?" Maritza asked, eyes unfocused as she stared overhead. A weak laugh bubbled past her lips. "And I did it *without* animal blood, bitch." With that, she slumped back into a heap.

"Maritza!" Julian yelled, anger flaring. He couldn't take care of *two* unconscious people; he could barely handle one! What the hell was he supposed to do now? What if they got trapped down there, alone? What if—

"Santa Muerte."

Julian looked up to find a man with wavy brown hair standing over him, eyes wide as he looked between Yadriel and Maritza.

The man went to Maritza and pressed two fingers to her neck.

"She's okay," he said, relief sighing through his words.

When he turned to Yadriel, Julian instinctively threw himself across him, hands braced against the bloody floor. *"Don't touch him!"* Julian snarled, baring his teeth as fear flooded through him. He didn't know who this guy was. He wouldn't let him get near Yadriel. For all he knew, he was another deranged brujo out to summon a goddamn jaguar demon to come eat people, and there was no way in hell he'd let that happen.

The man lurched back and held his hands up in submission. "It's okay," he said. "I just want to help." His eyes shifted back to Yadriel, but he didn't try moving in again.

To his left, there was movement on the stone slabs. Julian only spared them a quick glance, long enough to see two people waking up.

The others who had been sacrificed. Had Yadriel saved them all? Where was the fourth?

His eyes shot back to the man.

"It's okay," the man repeated. "He's my cousin."

Julian's lips twitched. "Cousin?" he repeated. "Miguel?"

The man blinked. "Yes," Miguel said, giving him a confused look. "How do you—?"

"HELP HIM!" Julian shouted.

Miguel jumped but leaned forward. Julian shifted back just far enough so Miguel could feel the side of Yadriel's neck. "He's breathing, he's going to be okay," he said.

Julian let out a heavy breath, so relieved he felt like he might pass out. *Thank God, thank God, thank God.*

"I'll go get help," Miguel said, getting to his feet. "Can you look after them?"

As if there were any force on earth that could tear Julian from Yadriel's side. "HURRY!" he snapped.

Miguel tore off up the stairs.

To the side, the two others—a girl and a boy, who both looked about his age, if not younger—stood back, looking at Julian like he was a wild animal.

Good. If they were scared, then they would stay away. All Julian cared about was Yadriel.

With clumsy fingers, he walked his fingers along the side of Yadriel's neck where he had seen Miguel and Maritza feel for a pulse. At first, he couldn't find it, and he thought Yadriel's heart had stopped again. But then his middle finger pressed at just the right spot and he felt the beat. Julian cursed under his breath and held his hand as still as possible. He was afraid to let go and lose it again, but he also didn't want to accidentally choke Yadriel.

Julian let out a shaky exhale and counted each and every beat of Yadriel's heart. Focusing on that and only that.

He didn't know how much time passed, but it seemed to stretch on forever. Panic wound its way through his rigid muscles. What was taking Miguel so long to get help? Why wasn't he back yet? Anger roiled in his blood. His skin crawled. Julian couldn't stand just sitting there, waiting. The only thing keeping him from running to get help himself was Yadriel.

Julian pressed his ear to Yadriel's chest, trying to hear it beat, but it was drowned out by the sound of his own ragged breaths.

It felt like hours before he heard voices and footsteps running down the stairs and into the crypt. Julian looked up as a group of people flooded the cave. Hope tried to lift his chest, but fear dragged it back down.

He recognized Yadriel's dad and abuelita. She gasped and stopped short when she saw the gory mess laid out. Yadriel's dad stared, head twisting as he took everything in.

A girl a bit older than Julian rushed to Maritza, letting out an impressive string of curses in Spanish.

When Yadriel's dad spotted his son, where he lay under Julian's protective crouch, he rushed forward, Miguel quick on his heels.

Julian tensed. "Don't!" he barked, so fiercely that Enrique tripped to a stop.

He looked between Julian and Yadriel, maybe weighing the pros and cons of getting his hand bitten off. He flicked Miguel a look. "Who—?"

"I don't know," Miguel said, watching Julian anxiously from over Enrique's shoulder. To Julian, he asked, "Is Yadriel your friend?"

The word burned. *"¡Mi querido!"* he snapped viciously.

Enrique's eyebrows shot up in surprise.

Julian blushed furiously under their stares.

Enrique knelt down and tried to move closer.

"Don't touch him!" Julian all but snarled. He tried to push them away.

"It's okay," Enrique said gently. Julian saw his hands trembling when he held his palms up in submission. "We're here to help, please." His voice was tight when he said, "He's my son."

"I *know* that!" Julian said. In an attempt to calm himself, he squeezed his eyes shut and clenched his teeth. *He knew that.* He knew they were there to help, that they were his family, but Julian was so scared and *angry.* Just because Yadriel had forgiven them didn't mean he did.

They could help, but Julian couldn't get his body to understand what his brain knew. Adrenaline coursed through him, rigid and ready to fight even though he *knew* he didn't need to.

He refused to move away from Yadriel's side, but he did shift back. As soon as he made room, Enrique and Lita leaned in.

Julian bit back the urge to knock their hands away as they touched Yadriel's cheeks, his pulse, his forehead. He was unconscious and vulnerable. Julian had to keep him safe.

"Is he okay?" Enrique asked.

"Sí," Lita said with a heavy sigh. "Just exhausted."

Enrique looked over. "Paola?"

"She'll be okay," said the girl who looked way too much like Maritza not to be her sister. She looked pissed, holding a light green rosary to Maritza's forehead. "So *stupid,*" she chided, even though Maritza clearly couldn't hear her.

"Thank Santa Muerte," Enrique said. "We need to get them out of here. The ambulances should be arriving soon."

When he and Miguel moved to pick up Yadriel, panic cut through Julian. "Be careful!" he shouted.

Enrique tried to speak gently to him. "It's okay—" But Julian wouldn't hear it. *Couldn't* hear it.

Miguel got down and jostled Yadriel as he got his arms under him. Yadriel's head lolled to the side.

"YOU'LL HURT HIM!" Julian tried to rush forward, but a pair of sturdy hands held on to his shoulders. Everything in him screamed to fight. He tried to rein in his anger but fear tore through his veins.

"You'll hurt him!" His throat ached. The sound of his heartbeat pounded in his ears.

Miguel scooped Yadriel into his arms. His head fell back, lips parted and neck exposed.

Julian's voice splintered. *"Don't hurt him!"*

"He's okay; he'll be okay," Enrique repeated, trying to calm Julian, but he was already turning to follow.

Miguel was across the cave and going up the stairs. There was more movement around him, and brujx went to help the others. Julian could only see Yadriel's dangling legs. His swath of black hair.

Julian's heart thrashed wildly in his chest, threatening to break his ribs. He didn't want them to take Yadriel away from him. What if something happened and Julian never got to see him again?

He twisted out of the grip of whoever was holding him and rushed forward. "WAIT!"

Enrique turned with a jerk, posture tense as he gave Julian a startled look.

Julian took a step back. "I need to go with him!" he insisted, fingers knotting anxiously into the hem of his shirt. Miguel disappeared with Yadriel up the stairs. Something tugged urgently at his chest, demanding he follow.

Enrique looked him down, confused and apprehensive.

Julian was covered in blood, trembling as his chest heaved with ragged breaths. Tears streamed down his cheeks, blurring his vision.

With effort, he choked back his primal instinct to charge forward, to just push past Enrique and anyone else in his way until he got back to Yadriel. "*Please* let me go with him!" Julian begged, hating the desperation in his voice.

After a moment, Enrique's expression softened. He gave a curt nod. "Okay—"

Julian tore off up the stairs after Yadriel.

They wouldn't let him ride in the ambulance no matter how hard he argued. It was too small. Enrique was the one who accompanied his son. Julian was put in his own ambulance after a lot of negotiating. He only agreed when they said he would be going to the same ER as Yadriel.

The adrenaline started to wear off on the way to the hospital. Strapped to a gurney, his body felt heavy, every muscle sore. The paramedic cut open his shirt and dressed the stab wound on his chest first, with layers of gauze and tape. He snapped at her when she pressed too hard, sending a sharp ache cutting through him.

"How long were you down there?" she asked, face screwed up in confusion. "It looks partially healed."

Julian ignored her. He wasn't no snitch.

It took the paramedic three tries to get him hooked up to an IV because he kept pulling away. Julian was too distracted worrying about Yadriel to listen to her explanation, but the stuff in the IV was cold, and he could feel it race through his veins. The tube tickled his arm with every bump of the ambulance.

As soon as they got to the hospital, Julian demanded to see Yadriel, but they wheeled him into his own room to be examined. People stood around him, poking and prodding, speaking to one another but not giving him a straight answer when he asked where Yadriel was.

"Don't worry about your friend," a nurse said with a smile. Julian growled at him. The smile quickly vanished.

One of the machines he was hooked up started to beep wildly as Julian made to stand up. If they weren't going to tell him, then he'd figure it out himself. Another icy sensation tingled through his arm and suddenly he was sunk into the bed again, conscious but impossibly groggy.

"Tranquilo," another nurse said gently, softly brushing gloved fingers over his sweaty forehead. "You assholes," he slurred. All he could do was lie there as they went to work.

Too much time had passed. He'd been lying in bed, staring blankly at the TV on the wall as it showed an onslaught of infomercials. He was ready to lose it. He couldn't stand being cooped up in this room, trapped in bed with nothing to do but obsess over whether Yadriel was all right. His body felt stiff and heavy. His stomach twisted with worry. The wait was killing him.

The only thing keeping him from storming down the hallway and demanding answers was whatever sedative they'd given him. There was a thick fog in his head, dulling his senses. Familiar voices came from the hallway and he turned to the door, chasing the sound.

A second later, the door swung open.

"Jules?"

Rio. Relief crashed through Julian. His pulse thudded in his temples as he tried to sit up.

"*Christ*, Jules," said an irritated voice. A strong hand pushed his shoulder, holding him down. Julian tried to fight it, but he was far too weak.

"Stop," the voice ordered, giving Julian a small shake that sent his head spinning.

Rio's tense face swam into focus above him. His jaw was clenched, worry sparking in his sharp eyes.

"Rio?" he croaked groggily, latching on to his brother's arm with feeble hands.

"You're hooked up to a bunch of shit. If you keep fighting, you're going to pop your stitches," Rio told him sternly. "So quit it."

Julian's head rolled to the side and he blinked hard, trying to focus. His friends stood huddled by his bed. Omar's eyes were bloodshot and he looked pissed. Rocky was pale, and there were tears freely running from Flaca's puffy eyes. Luca openly gaped like he was staring at a ghost.

"Are you guys okay?" Julian asked the first question that popped into his head.

"We're supposed to ask *you* that, dumbass," Omar growled.

"The cops said you got kidnapped by a cult," Luca piped in.

"It wasn't a cult," Rocky corrected, looking annoyed. "It was just one guy."

"They found you and three other people in a murder dungeon," Luca continued, like he hadn't heard her.

"He was about to kill all four of you," Flaca said through tears, her fingers pressed to her lips.

"But Maritza and Yadriel found you," Luca added.

Julian sucked in a breath. "Yadriel?" When he tried to sit up, he was hit was a violent ache in his chest, eliciting a groan.

"Julian," Rio warned.

"Is Yadriel okay?" he demanded, trying to push his brother's arm away.

"He's okay," Luca told him. "I asked one of his relatives. There's a whole bunch of them in the waiting room."

"Where is he?" Julian wasn't going to take anyone's word for it. The only way he'd believe Yadriel was okay was if he saw him with his own eyes. He wasn't safe until Julian could speak to him and touch him, until he knew for *certain*. "I gotta see him—" Julian tried to get up again, even though every muscle in his body screamed at him to stop.

Rio pushed him back down with ease.

Julian glowered.

"You got *stabbed*, Jules," Rio said.

"Yadriel's okay," Flaca tried to reassure him. "He's still recovering."

It did little to make him feel better, especially when Rio added stubbornly, "You're not going anywhere."

"The hell I'm not!" Julian growled, trying to get up yet again.

Luca threw himself across Julian's lap, and a scuffle ensued, if you could really call it that. It was mostly Julian cussing out Rio and his friends to let him go and them not letting him up.

TWENTY-FIVE

When Yadriel started to wake up, he tried to force his eyes open, but they slid right back shut. The strange scent of antiseptic mixed with flowers filled his nose.

"Yadriel?"

He tried again. Everything was blurry and way too bright.

"I'll get a doctor," Diego's voice said. There was squeaking of shoes on linoleum. The opening and closing of a door.

"Yadriel? Are you awake?"

With effort, Yadriel turned and saw his dad. He was a haggard mess, but he let out a heavy sigh of relief.

"Ay, Dios mío!" Lita practically wailed at his side. Yadriel flinched as she babbled incoherently, thanking every god and saint she could think of, her hand pressed to her breast.

"Jesus *Christ.*"

Yadriel's eyes swung to his left, where Maritza hovered over him.

He tried to sit up.

"Here, let me help," Maritza scolded him, carefully pulling him into a seated position.

A wave of nausea crashed over him. Yadriel groaned as bile rose in his throat. Someone pressed a cool, damp cloth to the back of his neck. "This will help," his dad told him, gently rubbing his back in circles. His bare back. Someone had taken off his binder.

"Where am I?" he asked, dragging the blanket up over his chest.

"The hospital, pendejo," Maritza snapped, huffing as she crossed her arms. She was very angry.

Yadriel rubbed his throbbing temples. "How long have I been here?"

"About seven hours," his dad said. "It's almost ten a.m."

Yadriel looked around. They all were staring at him, wide-eyed and . . . frightened?

He remembered the old church. Tío Catriz. The jaguar. "Tío," Yadriel blurted out. "He was trying to summon Bahlam— He was going to—" His thoughts crashed painfully in his head. He grimaced, trying to string them together into something that made sense.

"It's okay. Maritza told us everything," Enrique said, smoothing his large hand up and down Yadriel's arm, speaking softly.

"I'm so sorry, Dad. I'm so sorry." The apologies spilled from his lips.

Enrique blinked at him, surprised. He gave a slight shake of his head. "No, Yadriel—"

"If I had just told you everything to begin with, then—"

Yadriel's dad pulled him tight against his chest. "Yadriel," Enrique sighed into his hair. "My brave, brave son."

Yadriel wept into his dad's shoulder, hard and uncontrollable.

"That was not your fault," his dad told him, his voice soft but firm.

Yadriel's chest felt like it had split wide open. "All I did was ruin everything. Tío is gone—"

"That's not your fault," his dad stressed. "Your tío was corrupted by the desire for power. It poisoned him, turned his mind toxic." He sighed sadly. "He died at his own hand, no one else's."

Lita crossed herself and prayed under her breath.

"And we are partially to blame," his dad continued. "We were unfair to him, and *you*, Yadriel. It's too late to go back and make things right with Catriz, but I promise to do everything to make sure nothing like that happens again. You stopped him; you stopped it," his dad insisted, giving him a gentle squeeze. "Everyone's okay."

But everyone wasn't okay. Yadriel knew that. Everything in his body screamed it.

He'd watched as the jaguar dragged his tío down to Xibalba. He'd seen Miguel's lifeless body laid out on the stone.

And there was something else. A persistent tugging in his chest. Something important that was just out of reach.

There was a flicker of a memory. A spark of a smile. A flash of dimpled cheeks. Dark, piercing eyes and a cold kiss on his lips.

It all came crashing back to him.

Julian.

The memory of his lifeless body struck Yadriel in the chest like a knife. He squeezed his eyes shut. Grief welled up inside, threatening to consume him whole. He felt bile rise in the back of his throat. *"He's gone."* Yadriel choked on a sob.

"But, Yads," Maritza cut in, annoyed. "The amulet—"

Miguel. Julian. "They're *gone.*"

"No, Yadriel, escúchame." He dad squeezed his shoulders. "You saved him, Yadriel."

Yadriel's breath hitched. He blinked. "What?"

"All of them! Miguel and the others, too," Maritza added.

It didn't make sense. Yadriel pushed himself upright. "That's not p-possible," he hiccupped. He searched their faces. Hope fluttered in his heart.

"You used that amulet, and you brought them back." His dad looked just as bewildered as Yadriel felt.

He stared at his dad. His brain was still foggy. He tried to keep up, to process what that all meant. "That's not possible," Yadriel said. "No brujo can bring someone back from the dead."

"No, not any brujo could do that." His dad smiled. The kind that brimmed with pride. "But you did."

"But, that should've—"

"Killed you?" Maritza cut in. "Well, it nearly did, no thanks to *Lady*

Death!" Her glare was vicious. She crossed her arms, but Yadriel could see her hands were shaking. "As soon as you brought the others back to life, she just *vanished*, and I had to save your sorry ass!" she snapped.

Yadriel balked. "You . . . you healed me?"

Maritza wiped at her eyes and nodded impatiently.

"You saved me, even though it meant using blood?" Yadriel said, staring at her in awe.

"Yeah, well, it wasn't animal blood, and it's not like I was just going to let you just *die there*." She sniffed and lifted her chin. "I guess you lying on the floor in a pool of blood is my breaking point."

Yadriel exhaled a weak laugh. "You're amazing, Maritza."

"Don't get used to it," she said, still angry. But then she threw her arms around his neck and hugged him tight. "And you can expect a call from my lawyer," she told him, voice muffled.

Yadriel hugged her back, and for a moment they both leaned against each other, laughing and sniffling.

Yadriel dragged his hand over his runny nose. "So, the others . . ." he ventured, hoping against hope. "They're okay? All of them?"

"We called 911, and they rushed them—and you—to the hospital," his dad nodded. "You took good care of them." An amused look crossed Enrique's face, ruffling his mustache with a knowing grin. "I thought we might not even be able to get you to the hospital. That boy, Julian, guarded you and kept you safe. He was ready to fight anyone who got near you—"

Yadriel's heart leaped. "Julian?" He sat bolt upright, ignoring the churning of his stomach. "Where is he?" he demanded. "Is he here?"

Enrique nodded. "Down the hall, but you—"

Yadriel threw the blankets back and staggered to his feet.

"Yadriel!" his dad gasped.

The machines chimed as he shook off the wires taped to him and bolted for the door.

Lita, Maritza, and his dad scrambled after him.

"Yadriel!"

But he was running down the hall, his legs like Jell-O, half leaning against the wall. He passed one room, and then another. The small whiteboard outside the third room read J. DIAZ.

Yadriel shoved open the door.

Rio stood at the center of the room in his coveralls, eyes shut and pinching the bridge of his nose. Flaca, Rocky, Omar, and Luca surrounded the bed.

"This is bullshit!" a voice yelled. Omar shifted, and Yadriel saw him.

Julian was trying to push himself up off the pillows, snarling and looking surly as he glared up at his brother.

Yadriel sucked in a breath.

All eyes swung to Yadriel, but he only cared about the dark, piercing gaze.

Julian blinked. "Yads?"

There was sudden thrashing, and his friends quickly moved out of the way.

"Dammit, Jules!" Rio snapped, but Julian wasn't listening.

Yadriel didn't have time to say anything before Julian was on his feet and across the room. They collided, and Yadriel could only clutch and hold on tight as Julian slammed into him, sending them toppling into the wall. Julian's arms locked around him so tight it hurt, but Yadriel didn't care.

Julian's warm body pressed against him and a spark of discomfort momentarily flared. Yadriel didn't have his binder on and he suddenly felt exposed and bare.

But then Julian laughed. It tickled Yadriel's ear, and he could feel it rumble in Julian's chest. Yadriel squeezed his arms tighter around Julian, smothering the spark in his embrace before it could catch fire.

Julian cupped Yadriel's face in his hands. "You idiot!" he shouted, brow furrowed, but his smile was wide and dimpled. "You could've gotten yourself killed!"

Yadriel was overwhelmed by the sheer fierceness of him. Julian's spirit was nothing but a dull shadow of his real self. Alive, fiery, crushing. It was overwhelming, but Yadriel would gladly get his breath robbed by Julian's brilliant smile over and over again.

"You're so stupid!" Julian repeated. "You—!"

"Shut up—" Yadriel threw himself against Julian and wrapped his arms around his neck and kissing him fervently.

He felt Julian's smile under his lips. Felt his arms wrap around him and squeeze him tight again.

Someone let out a low whistle.

"You know we can see both your asses in those hospital gowns, right?" Maritza called.

Yadriel ignored her. He pulled back enough to look Julian in the eye. "If you ever scare me like that again," he said breathlessly, "I'll kill you myself, Julian Diaz."

Julian's grin was sharp. Bright. Blinding. "Deal," he murmured before crushing him into another kiss.

Yadriel gladly let himself drown in it.

EPILOGUE

Yadriel raced through the cemetery, pulling Julian along after him. Julian's hand was warm, his grip strong, his palm calloused. As they ran for the church, Julian easily kept up as they wove between headstones. Yadriel looked over at him. Julian flashed him a cheek-aching smile and squeezed his hand. Laughter bubbled past Yadriel's lips as he squeezed it back. He was there—he was real—and Yadriel would take any chance to grab him that he could.

The aquelarre was about to begin. It had taken a while to answer the police's lingering questions and to get discharged from the hospital. Julian had refused to leave Yadriel. Proclaimed it with such ferocity that searing heat washed over Yadriel's face.

But Rio also didn't want to let him go, which was reasonable, considering what happened last time he let his little brother out of his sight. When Rio started asking too many questions, and Julian refused to give any answers, Yadriel's dad was the one to break up the argument. He explained there was an important ceremony at the church Julian was welcome to attend. Afterward, he promised to bring Julian home himself.

Rio was suspicious—he didn't understand why Julian would be so invested in any sort of religious event taking place at a church—but he eventually caved. Yadriel suspected it had a lot to do with Luca practically nodding off on his feet, and how Omar, Flaca, and Rocky kept complaining about being hungry. Even if they didn't understand the secrecy, they were still ride-or-die for Julian.

Yadriel and Julian ran through the open gate and up the marigold-lined path to the church. Yadriel pulled Julian to a stop outside the door. Voices and laughter thrummed inside.

Poised halfway up the steps, Julian turned back to Yadriel.

Yadriel's heart fluttered in his chest. The adrenaline coursing through his veins gave him a head rush. He was nervous. He was excited. He wanted to burst through the doors of the church. His heart wanted to explode. Beyond those doors, his mom, his ancestors, and his people were waiting, waiting to welcome this year's of-age brujx.

To welcome him.

"You ready?" Julian asked, a curious look on his devastatingly handsome face.

"No," Yadriel confessed, his voice tight.

Julian grinned. "Do it anyways."

Laughter broke in Yadriel's chest, easing the tension.

He snatched the front of Julian's shirt and dragged him into a kiss. When he pulled back, Julian chased after his lips with a dazed smile.

"Later." Yadriel chuckled, pushing his face away as he ran up the rest of the steps.

"How much later?" Julian demanded, running after him. "*Later* later, or, like, drag-me-out-behind-the-church-in-five-minutes later?"

Yadriel laughed as he pushed open the doors.

"*Whoa,*" Julian breathed.

The church was full of brujx and blinding light. Unlike regular spirits of the dead, the brujx spirits who returned for Día de Muertos glowed with a golden aura. And when brujx spirits were granted their return to the land of the living, they were able to touch their loved ones.

As Yadriel wove between people, heading for the main altar, families stood together talking, laughing, and embracing. There were smiles, tears, and kisses. Parents who had lost their children, lovers separated by death, and friends long lost were brought back together in celebration.

Yadriel did his best not to jostle anyone as they made their way through the crowd, but heads began to turn, followed by astonished stares and whispers.

"It's okay," he said to Julian, pulling him along. "They just aren't used to outsiders."

"Uh, they ain't lookin' at me, Yads," Julian said, grining.

Yadriel frowned. What did he mean by that? He looked around. No, they weren't looking at Julian.

They were looking at him. Yadriel shrunk back under the sudden attention, his steps faltering. Brujx were pointing and craning their necks to get a better look at him. "But why?"

Julian rolled his eyes and let out an exasperated huff. "Aren't you the one who told me no brujx has brought anyone back from the dead in, like, a gazillion years?"

Yadriel blinked up at him.

"I think bringing four people back from the dead makes you some kind of god," Julian mused with a shrug. "Or at least a hero."

Yadriel froze. A hero? He looked around at all the smiling faces.

"Now." Julian stepped behind Yadriel and pushed him forward. "Let's go make it official," he said into his ear.

Brujx nodded their approval and clapped him on the back as he walked by. Yadriel's face burned red, but he found himself smiling. His feet and Julian's guiding hands led him deeper into the church. He passed Miguel, who stood with his mom and dad under each arm. Miguel smiled at him and gave him a small nod.

The crowd began to thin out. Yadriel caught a glimpse of his grandparents, their auras bright.

"¡Es mi nieto!" Lito announced, elbowing anyone in reach, his chest puffed up with pride.

The scent of apples tickled Yadriel's nose, and then he saw her.

His mom wore a long red dress that rustled over the ground as she stepped forward. A yellow sash was cinched around her waist. She wore her hair down, as she always did. The soft chestnut waves were adorned with marigolds. Dark lashes framed her large brown eyes. She glowed with golden light, radiating from her skin.

Yadriel held his breath.

"Mi amor." She smiled.

Yadriel stared at her, frozen where he stood. She looked exactly the same, just how he remembered her.

A small breath hitched in her throat, her fingers splayed against her chest. "Yadriel," she said, her voice like a song. She held her arms out for him.

Yadriel lurched forward into her embrace. Warmth radiated from her, easing the tension from Yadriel's shoulders as he held on tight. Her hair tickled his face. She smelled just the same, like cloves and cinnamon.

She pushed her fingers through his hair. "Mijito," she said softly, kissing the top of his head, and Yadriel melted into her. Relief and longing broke inside him. He loved her so fiercely and wanted to tell her so, over and over again, but he couldn't find his voice.

"Let me see you!" she said, taking a step back to look him up and down. "Aye, such a handsome boy, my son!" his mother declared, red lips curling.

Her eyes traveled over Yadriel's shoulder. "And this must be Julian?" she asked, lips quirking into a knowing smile.

Yadriel stepped aside and tugged on Julian's arm. He stumbled forward. "Hi, Mrs. Velez," he said, all nervous energy and bashful smile.

"Camila," she corrected warmly. She crossed one arm over her chest, tucked under her elbow as she tapped thoughtfully at her chin. "I have heard much about you. A ghost boy who came back from the dead, thanks to my Yadriel."

She squeezed Yadriel's arm, and he swelled with pride.

"I owe him big-time," Julian said with a grin.

"And don't forget it," Camila agreed with a smile and a wink. "Now, we have much to catch up on, and much to discuss!" She gave Yadriel a pointed look. "So let's make the most of our time together."

She raised a delicate eyebrow at Yadriel. "And tell me everything," Camila added in a stage whisper, nodding in Julian's direction.

Julian preened.

"Mom!" Yadriel hissed.

"But first," she went on, as if she hadn't heard him, taking a step back and waving toward the front of the church.

Yadriel's dad and Lita stood on the raised altar, just below Lady Death's alcove. Enrique and Lita were in full regalia. They wore the sacred royal headdresses that had been passed down through the brujx leaders for centuries.

Before them stood the three brujx who had turned fifteen since the last Día de Muertos. Maritza was there in her dress. She looked back over her shoulder and waved at Yadriel frantically. *Hurry up!* She mouthed.

This was it. Yadriel turned to Julian.

"Get 'em, brujo," he said, nudging him with his shoulder.

Yadriel took a deep breath and shook out his tingling fingers. He stepped forward and fell into line next to Maritza, probably a bit closer than necessary.

Maritza cleared her throat and nodded with her chin. Her rose-quartz rosary was pooled in her cupped hands. Down the line, the other brujx held out their portajes.

Yadriel quickly reached back for his dagger. It slipped through his sweaty fingers. He nearly dropped it, but he scrambled to recover without losing a finger in the process. He laid it across his upturned palms, and Maritza nodded approvingly.

His dad's chuckles made Yadriel look up.

When his dad stepped forward and held his hands aloft, the voices and laughter died down to a quiet hum. The press of the crowd behind Yadriel's back was odd and uncomfortable. He could feel everyone's focus directed his way.

Unable to help himself, Yadriel snuck a glance back over his shoulder. His mom gave him an encouraging smile while Julian flashed him a double thumbs-up, grinning ear to ear.

"It is an honor to have you all here on the last day of Día de Muertos as we welcome our children into their new positions within our community!" his dad said, looking out across the crowd. "Thank you for joining us and the incredible young adults who stand before you." He stood tall, his voice booming through the cavernous church.

Yadriel was used to seeing his dad in his checkered shirts with tousled hair and tired eyes, working in the cemetery or dozing off on the couch. But tonight, dressed in his regalia, standing tall as he smiled and spoke with authority, Enrique looked like the rightful leader of the brujx.

"Let us also take a moment to thank Lady Death for allowing *all* of us to be here together to celebrate you tonight," his dad said as a quiet murmur passed through the crowd. "We keep you in our thoughts, every day, until we can be together again on Día de Muertos."

Yadriel looked up to where Lady Death stood in her alcove, draped in white. He thought of how she had looked when she appeared before him in the cave. Both beautiful and terrifying.

"Tonight our children join a long line of brujx who have served Our Lady in healing those who suffer and guiding those who are lost," his father continued, gesturing to the four of them. Yadriel did his best to stand taller. "Tonight, we celebrate unending life. Only together is that possible.

"This is a special aquelarre for me because my son—"

Yadriel's heart leaped into his throat.

"Our son"—his dad corrected, looking to Camila for a long moment before turning his gaze to Yadriel—"Yadriel, joins me as a brujo."

My son.

A brujo.

How long had he been waiting to hear those words? Having them said aloud, to a room full of brujx, made Yadriel's legs feel weak. It was like a dream, but so much better.

"I think it's a special one for all of us, yes?" There was a murmur of agreement from the crowd. "The aquelarre celebrates *transition.* All of you are on the precipice between youth and adulthood," he said to the line of young brujx. "Between uncertainty and confidence. Our traditions should grow and change with every generation. Just because we follow the ancient ways does not mean we can't also grow. I have been shown that these past few days," Enrique said. "I failed my son, Yadriel, as both a father and a leader," he told the crowd.

Yadriel held his breath, frozen in place by his dad's sincerity and candor. There were murmurs in the crowd behind him, but Enrique continued on.

"He tried to tell me who he was, but I didn't listen, I didn't understand." He looked at Yadriel then. "But now I am listening, and I will learn to do better," he promised.

Tears prickled behind Yadriel's eyes, but he forced himself to hold it together.

"Growth isn't a deviation from what we've done before, but a natural progression to honor all those who make this community strong."

Cheers and applause ran through the crowd. Julian's enthusiastic whooping cut through every other sound. A laugh quaked in Yadriel's chest. His heart was so full, it would surely burst at any moment.

"It has been the joy of our lives to watch you grow into the incredible young people you have proven yourselves to be," Enrique said, pressing his palm to his chest as he looked down at Yadriel. His brown eyes were soft, his smile adoring.

Yadriel's chin wobbled and his eyes stung, but he smiled so big it made his cheeks hurt.

"Yadriel, you have shown great courage and strength, the likes of which no brujx has possessed in thousands of years," his dad continued. "You sacrificed yourself to save your friends, your family, and, most telling, the lives of two strangers. To do that took more than just courage and strength. Our Lady saw the greatness in you that even I couldn't. You will be a great brujo, and a great man, and we honor the sacrifice you made," Enrique said in earnest.

Yadriel didn't know how to respond. He was dumbstruck and bright red, so overwhelmed that he had to look away. Greatness? Sacrifice? He didn't know about all that. He had just been trying to do the right thing.

"We also owe Maritza our thanks," Enrique continued, shifting his focus to her. "She showed incredible strength in her own right."

Unlike Yadriel, Maritza was perfectly comfortable taking praise.

She nodded in agreement with bold confidence. The proud lift of her chin eased some of Yadriel's own nerves.

"Your healing of Yadriel was another act of great love and fortitude. Something tells me we will see great things from you both," his dad said before addressing all four of them and adding, "From *all* of you."

"He has *no* idea," Maritza whispered to Yadriel from the corner of her mouth. She threw him a wink, and Yadriel grinned back.

Knowing Maritza, he certainly hadn't heard the last of how he owed her his life, but Yadriel didn't mind. Without her, he would be dead. And while death wasn't the end, he wasn't done living yet.

When Enrique spoke again, he looked at each new brujx in turn. "You are here because you have already proven you are exactly what you were meant to be. As you become full-fledged members of our community, we will help guide you to be the eyes, ears, and hands of Our Lady Death," Enrique went on, looking at each of the four of them in turn. "We live in gratitude for the guidance and acceptance we can share with one another. We celebrate that we will move forward together as a stronger community than ever before." He held his large hands out before him, his palms facing up. "Put your faith in Lady Death, and in your community, and we cannot falter. You have each been witness to that, and shown that to us, in your progress to this day."

Yadriel took a deep breath, anticipating the next step of the aquelarre.

Enrique stepped back, making room for Lita to step forward. Parrot feathers of yellow, blue, and red splayed against Lita's head before trailing off into the long tail feathers. She wore a turquoise dress, and jewelry of jade and gold adorned her wrists. A wide necklace of hummingbird featherwork hung around her neck and shoulders, iridescent and flashing in the light. As the spiritual leader of their community, she led the final rite of passage.

When Lita spoke, she said the words in Spanish, her Cuban accent ringing. "May we live in faith; we are on the true path of our spirit. May we never fear death but remember we live on in the love we nurture in our time on earth. May we preserve life and guide life to death as Our Lady wills it. May we heal and support one another in this life and the next."

Yadriel turned to face the crowd with the other three.

"We welcome you!" Yadriel's father called out, his arms open wide, smile wrinkling the corners of his eyes.

The crowd erupted in cheers. Trilling gritos filled the air that set Yadriel's dagger exploding with golden light. Maritza laughed next to him, rosary cupped in her palms as sparks shot up into the air and rained down around them. Yadriel's mom kept having to stop her applause so she could wipe tears from her cheeks. Still, in a sea of faces, his eyes went right to Julian, and he couldn't look away. His sharp grin. His burning gaze. It sparked a fire in Yadriel's chest. It smoldered in his stomach. It flooded him with heat. Yadriel would happily let himself be consumed by Julian's fire.

Julian pinched his bottom lip, and a sharp whistle cut through the crowd before he punched his fist into the air and whooped loudly. Maritza bumped Yadriel with her shoulder, her laughter tickling his ear.

Things weren't magically fixed by an empowering speech, but it opened doors and built bridges. It carved out space for Yadriel to step forward and be who he was, as he was. There were still more obstacles to overcome and battles to fight, but Yadriel wouldn't feel alone in it anymore.

No, it wasn't the end. It was a better beginning.

ACKNOWLEDGMENTS

Writing this book was one of the best and most difficult things I've ever done, and it would've been impossible to do without my incredible support system.

The first person I need to thank is my editor, Holly West. *Cemetery Boys* started as my option book and began with a very simple concept: What would happen if you accidentally summoned a ghost and you couldn't get rid of them? When I was pitching ideas to Holly, *Cemetery Boys* was nothing more than a few sentences, a vague idea with a trans protagonist. Growing up, I never saw my own gender identity reflected in any books, and I thought it would be impossible to sell, but Yadriel's story was the one Holly was most excited about, which blew my mind. Without her, this story would've never been written. Holly understands me and my writing; working with her is like having a second, much more organized brain.

I am so incredibly thankful to have had her support and the support of the ENTIRE Swoon Squad. I owe a huge thanks to the Swoon Reads team and my fellow Swoon Squad authors. Publishing can be a scary and sometimes alienating place, but they have been my second family through and through. The incredible care package they sent me when I mustered up the courage to announce I was getting top surgery is a kindness I will never forget.

I owe Emily Settle a special thank-you. She was the one who suggested I should take my two favorite names—Yadriel and Julian—and use them for my book (#Yadrian!). A huge thanks to my publicist, Kelsey Marrujo, for wrangling me, answering my billions of questions, and making my dreams come true. I want to thank every person at Macmillan who touched *Cemetery Boys* and helped make it even better. I owe *so many thanks* to Gabe Cole Novoa and Ray Stoeve for their thoughtful feedback and guidance. My amazing friend, Francisco Echavarria, is a saint who patiently dealt with my "you up?" texts to discuss the nuances of Spanish in order to find the perfect words (*especially* for Julian).

My amazing agent, Jennifer March Soloway, was another essential part of this book becoming a reality. I reached out to her as a fellow Mills College alum for advice before she was even officially my agent. When I was telling her about the idea I had for *Cemetery Boys*, she stopped me and said, "Aiden, you know you could write about your own culture, right?" That idea BLEW MY MIND. If I thought people would never take on a book with a transgender protagonist, it didn't even cross my mind that I could make it a Latinx fantasy. Without Jennifer, *Cemetery Boys* would be incredibly different and not nearly as special and dear to me as it is now. Whenever I've gotten stressed out or overwhelmed, Jennifer has been an anchor. "You're worried, but you're well" has become my new mantra.

The ones who really had the worst end of the deal were my poor friends who had to hold me together when I was falling apart WITHOUT EVEN GETTING PAID FOR IT! Anda Stelle and Tanya Lisle helped me sort through my dumpster fire of an outline, and then Anda read my very first draft and acted as a cheerleader as I drafted, chapter by chapter. My dear Maxamaris Hoppe and Rey Noble provided emotional support and forced me to be kind with myself when I got caught in self-hate spirals. Without these folks taking care of me, I would've never made it through in one piece.

A HUGE thanks to Adriana M. Martínez Figueroa for naming my brilliant bruja Paola, and Angela Wells for naming my precious Rio.

To my incredibly talented cover artist, Mars Lauderbaugh, I owe my *entire* life! They took my boys and brought them to life so beautifully, it's like they pulled them right from my heart. Yadriel's likeness is especially precious to me. I am incredibly lucky and thankful for all the work, love, and care that Mars has put into my characters. No one else could've brought them to life so perfectly.

I want to thank my family for their love and unwavering support. My mom (De Anna), sister (Christine Sanchez) and brother-in-law (Chris Sanchez) helped me come up with the original plot for *Cemetery Boys* while we drank mezcal and ate tacos as I lay on the floor, jotting notes into my cell phone.

In the process of writing this book, I lost an incredibly dear and important person to me. My cousin, Alan Claveran, was a giving, kind, and hilarious man. Without him, the world isn't quite as bright. A part of me will always mourn losing him, but I will always treasure his stupid jokes, his relentless teasing, and his sweet laugh. See you on the other side, brother.

Something sinister
waits within the trees...

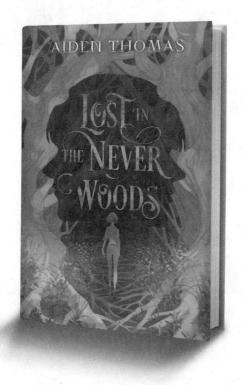

When children start to go missing in the local woods,
Wendy must face her fears and a past she can't remember
to rescue them in Aiden Thomas's next atmospheric YA novel.

DID YOU KNOW...

readers like you helped to get this book published?

Join our book-obsessed community and help us discover awesome new writing talent.

1 **Write it.**
Share your original YA manuscript.

2 **Read it.**
Discover bright new bookish talent.

3 **Share it.**
Discuss, rate, and share your faves.

4 **Love it.**
Help us publish the books you love.

Share your own manuscript or dive between the pages at **swoonreads.com** or by downloading the **Swoon Reads app.**